Praise for
The Virgin Widow

"Packed with royal intrigue and stunning reversals of fortune, *The Virgin Widow* is a thrilling romance drawn from history, beautifully told. Anne O'Brien's spirited and courageous heroine, Lady Anne Neville, a traitor's daughter and future queen of England, vividly narrates her incredible journey through treachery and heartbreak into the arms of the man she loves—the last Plantagenet king of England, Richard III."
—Sandra Worth, award-winning author of
The King's Daughter

"O'Brien pulls us by our heartstrings through the power struggles between the Houses of York and Lancaster, telling the story through the seemingly hopeless love of Anne Neville for the man who would become Richard III . . . a little-known story that you will never forget."
—Jeane Westin, author of *His Last Letter*
and *The Virgin's Daughters*

"*The Virgin Widow* is a novel so engrossing that I couldn't put it down. Anne Neville comes to full and glorious life on these pages—a courageous woman of her own time, timeless in her appeal to readers."
—Kate Emerson, author of *By Royal Decree*

"Anne O'Brien's *The Virgin Widow* takes the reader on a compelling journey through medieval history and the heart of Anne Neville, a pawn and power in Plantagenet England. The vibrant characters, especially the narrator heroine, leap off the page. O'Brien weaves love, lust, tragedy, and triumph into a rich historical tapestry to treasure."
—Karen Harper, national bestselling author of
Mistress Shakespeare and *The Queen's Governess*

THE
VIRGIN
WIDOW

ANNE O'BRIEN

NEW AMERICAN LIBRARY

New American Library
Published by New American Library, a division of
Penguin Group (USA) Inc., 375 Hudson Street,
New York, New York 10014, USA
Penguin Group (Canada), 90 Eglinton Avenue East, Suite 700, Toronto,
Ontario M4P 2Y3, Canada (a division of Pearson Penguin Canada Inc.)
Penguin Books Ltd., 80 Strand, London WC2R 0RL, England
Penguin Ireland, 25 St. Stephen's Green, Dublin 2,
Ireland (a division of Penguin Books Ltd.)
Penguin Group (Australia), 250 Camberwell Road, Camberwell, Victoria 3124,
Australia (a division of Pearson Australia Group Pty. Ltd.)
Penguin Books India Pvt. Ltd., 11 Community Center, Panchsheel Park,
New Delhi - 110 017, India
Penguin Group (NZ), 67 Apollo Drive, Rosedale, North Shore 0632,
New Zealand (a division of Pearson New Zealand Ltd.)
Penguin Books (South Africa) (Pty.) Ltd., 24 Sturdee Avenue,
Rosebank, Johannesburg 2196, South Africa

Penguin Books Ltd., Registered Offices:
80 Strand, London WC2R 0RL, England

First published by New American Library,
a division of Penguin Group (USA) Inc.

First Printing, November 2010
10 9 8 7 6 5 4 3 2 1

Copyright © Anne O'Brien, 2010
Readers Guide copyright © Penguin Group (USA) Inc., 2010
All rights reserved

 REGISTERED TRADEMARK—MARCA REGISTRADA

LIBRARY OF CONGRESS CATALOGING-IN-PUBLICATION DATA:
O'Brien, Anne, 1949–
The virgin widow/Anne O'Brien.
p. cm.
ISBN 978-0-451-23129-1
1. Anne, Queen, consort of Richard III, King of England, 1456–1485—Fiction. 2. Richard III, King of
England, 1452–1485—Fiction. 3. Great Britain—History—Edward IV, 1461–1483—Fiction. 4. Great
Britain—History—Richard III, 1483–1485—Fiction. 5. Great Britain—History—Wars of the Roses,
1455–1485—Fiction. 6. Queens—Great Britain—Fiction. I. Title.
PR6115.B7355V57   2010
823'.92—dc22   2010028773

Set in Classical Garamond
Designed by Alissa Amell

Printed in the United States of America

PUBLISHER'S NOTE
This is a work of fiction. Names, characters, places, and incidents either are the product of the author's
imagination or are used fictitiously, and any resemblance to actual persons, living or dead, business
establishments, events, or locales is entirely coincidental.
The publisher does not have any control over and does not assume any responsibility for author or
third-party Web sites or their content.

For my husband, George. In gratitude for his enduring support, and his faith in me and Anne Neville.

ACKNOWLEDGMENTS

With thanks to Jane Judd, my agent, whose belief in *The Virgin Widow* was sometimes greater than mine. To Jennifer Unter, who championed Anne's cause with great spirit. And to Ellen Edwards and all at NAL. Their enthusiasm has been beyond price.

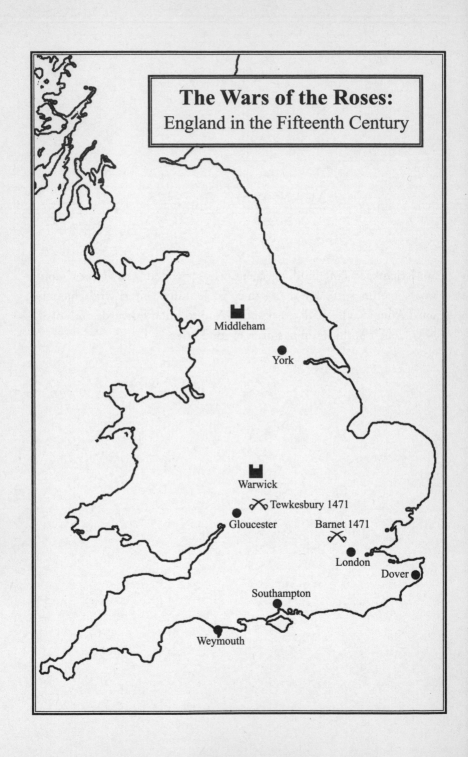

The Wars of the Roses:
England in the Fifteenth Century

Middleham

York

Warwick

Tewkesbury 1471

Gloucester

Barnet 1471

London

Dover

Southampton

Weymouth

The Nevilles and Plantagenets

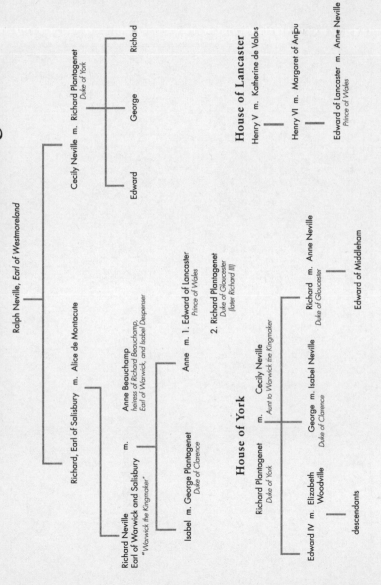

Ralph Neville, *Earl of Westmoreland*

Richard, Earl of Salisbury   m.   Alice de Montacute

Cecily Neville   m.   Richard Plantagenet
Duke of York

Edward   George   Richard

Richard Neville
Earl of Warwick and Salisbury
"Warwick the Kingmaker"

m.

Anne Beauchamp,
*heiress of Richard Beauchamp,
Earl of Warwick, and Isabel Despenser*

Isabel   m.   George Plantagenet
Duke of Clarence

Anne   m.   1.   Edward of Lancaster
Prince of Wales

2.   Richard Plantagenet
*Duke of Gloucester
(later Richard III)*

House of York

Richard Plantagenet
Duke of York

m.

Cecily Neville
Aunt to Warwick the Kingmaker

Edward IV   m.   Elizabeth
Woodville

George   m.   Isabel Neville
Duke of Clarence

Richard   m.   Anne Neville
Duke of Gloucester

descendants

Edward of Middleham

House of Lancaster

Henry V   m.   Katherine de Valois

Henry VI   m.   Margaret of Anjou

Edward of Lancaster   m.   Anne Neville
Prince of Wales

THE
VIRGIN
WIDOW

"Was ever woman in this humor wooed?"

—WILLIAM SHAKESPEARE

CHAPTER ONE

April 1469

On board ship, off the English port of Calais

Isabel whimpered. With creaks and groans the ship listed and thumped against the force of water as if it would be torn apart by the next wave, casting us into the depths. Isabel clapped her hands to her mouth, her eyes staring at the heaving wooden walls that hemmed us in, the sides of a coffin.

"Now what's wrong with you?" It was not fear of a watery death. I knew what it was, even as I prayed that it was not. The ship rolled again in the heavy swell, wallowing queasily in the dips before lifting and lurching. Sweat prickled on my forehead. Nausea clutched my belly before fear rapidly drove it out again. "Isabel." I nudged her arm sharply to get her attention. She was sitting in a high-backed chair, the only available chair in the cabin and the property of the captain, her whole body rigid, braced. Eyes tight-closed to shut out the desperate pitch and roll, she kept one hand closed clawlike on the arm. I shuffled forward on my stool. "Is it the baby?"

"Yes," she said with a gasp. Then: "No . . . no. Just a quick pain." On a deep breath her body relaxed fractionally, fingers uncurling from the carved end. "There, it's gone. Perhaps I mistook it."

And perhaps she didn't. I watched her cautiously as she eased her body in the confined space. Her face was as livid and slick as milk, drawn with near-exhaustion, her belly straining against the cloak she clutched to herself as if she were cold. It was so close and airless in that low-ceilinged cabin that I could feel the sweat work its way down my spine beneath the heavy cloth of my gown. Nine months pregnant, my sister Isabel was. And even I knew that this was no time to be at sea on a chancy expedition.

I got up to pour a mug of ale, staggering as the ship lifted and sank. "Drink this."

Isabel sniffed as if the familiar aroma of malted hops repelled her. As it had for much of her pregnancy. "I don't want it. I would rather it were wine."

But I pushed it into her hands. "It's all we have. Drink it and don't argue." I struggled against telling her that this was no time for un-grateful petulance. For two pins I would have gulped the small beer myself and let her go thirsty. "It will ease your muscles if nothing else."

"But not my bladder. The child presses heavily." Another grimace, another groan, as she sipped. "Pray God it will be born soon." Isabel never tolerated discomfort well.

"But not here!" The prospect stirred the fear in my gut again. It churned and clenched. "We should make land within the hour. We've been at sea an age. When we get to Calais, that's the time to pray for God's help."

"I don't think I can wait that long. . . ." Her complaints died on a gasp. Dropping the cup on the floor so that it rolled and returned, she hissed out a breath. Her hands clutched her mountainous belly.

"When we get to Calais . . ." Taking my stool beside her again, I tried to think of some mindless conversation. Anything to distract.

"When we get to Calais I'll never set foot on board a ship again," Isabel snapped. "No matter how much—" She bit off the words, her renewed moans rising to the approximation of a howl. "The baby . . . It must be. Where's our mother? I want her here with me. . . . Send Margery to fetch her. . . ."

"No. I'll get Margery to sit with you. *I'll* get the Countess."

Relief to escape the squalid cabin. Relief to pass the burden of this child to more experienced hands than mine. Approaching my fourteenth year as I was, I was old enough to know what would happen but too young to seek the responsibility. I think I was always a selfish child. I summoned Margery, the Countess's serving woman, to remain at Isabel's side. And fled.

I found my mother exactly where I knew she would be on the deck. Despite the cold wind and the frequent squalls, she was with my father. The Countess of Warwick, swathed from head to foot in a heavy cloak, hood shadowing her face, stood in the shelter of the high stern; my father, the Earl, was similarly wrapped. Harassed, thwarted in his planning, he clenched and opened his fist on the gunwale. The two figures stood together in close conversation, looking out toward where we would soon see land, if the clouds, thick and heavy, enveloping us all in an opaque blanket of gray-green, ever saw fit to lift. Taken up with their concerns, they kept their backs turned to me. So I listened. Eavesdropping was a skill that, as the younger daughter, I had perfected through my early years, when it was customary for our household to overlook my presence as if I were an infant or witless. I was neither. I approached with careful steps.

"What if he refuses us entry?" I heard the Countess ask.

"He will not. Lord Wenlock is as loyal a lieutenant as any man could ask."

"I wish I could be as sure as you."

"I have to hold to it," the Earl stated with more conviction in his voice than the circumstances merited, in my opinion. I knew that in recent days there were new lines of strain on his face between nose and mouth, engraved deep. Even so he placed an arm around the Countess's shoulders to enforce his certainty. "We shall be safe here in Calais. From here we can plan our return, at the head of a force strong enough to displace the King. . . ."

I was destined to hear no more as the deck heaved with increased vehemence. I stumbled, tottered to regain my balance. And they turned. My mother immediately came toward me to catch my arm, as if sensing the bad news.

"Anne. What are you doing out here? It's not safe. . . . Is it your sister?" Isabel had been in the forefront of all our minds in recent days.

"Yes. She says the baby's coming." No point in embroidering bad news.

My mother's teeth bit into her bottom lip, her fingers suddenly tight on my arm, but her words were for my father. "We should not have set off so late. I warned you of the dangers. We knew she was too near her time."

Then she was already on her way to my sister's side, dragging me with her, except that my father stopped her with a brusque movement of his hand.

"Tell her this, to ease her mind. Within the hour we'll see Calais. Sooner if this cloud lifts. And then we will get her ashore. It will not stop the process of nature but it may give her strength." He tried a smile. I knew it to be false. I could see his eyes, the fear in them. "Are not all first babies late?"

"No! They are not!" My mother shrugged off my father's attempts at reassurance. "She should never have been put through this ordeal."

A tall figure, similarly cloaked, loomed beside us from the direction of one of the rear cabins, pushing back the hood.

"What's amiss? Have we made landfall at last?"

Tall, golden haired, striking of face. George, Duke of Clarence, brother to King Edward and male heir apparent to the English throne. My sister's husband of less than a year. His eyes shone brilliantly blue; his fair skin glowed in the murk. So beautiful, and Isabel frequently crowed her victory in becoming his wife, a maiden's dream.

I loathed him.

"No. It's Isabel," I told him with barely a glance. The Countess would reprimand me for my ill manners but nothing she could say would ever reconcile me to my brother by marriage. Not that it mattered to him. He rarely deigned to notice me.

"Is she sick?"

The Countess interrupted my pert reply. "She is distressed. The child is imminent. . . ."

Clarence scowled. "A pity we had not made landfall. Will the child be safe?"

I felt my lip curl and made no attempt to disguise it, even when my mother saw and stared warningly at me. She thought my hostility was a younger sister's jealousy of Isabel's good fortune, but I knew different. Not: *Will my wife suffer?* Or: *Can we do anything to ease her distress?* Just: *Will the child be born alive?* I hated him from the depths of my heart. How Richard, my own Richard, who was now separated from me and would remain so forever as far as I could see, could be brother to this arrogant Prince I could never fathom.

The Countess swept Clarence's inopportune query aside but found time and compassion to smile at me. "Don't look so worried, Anne. She's young and healthy. She'll forget all her pain and discomfort when she holds her child in her arms."

"The child must be saved! At all costs." Clarence's face was handsome no longer.

"I shall bear your instructions in mind, Your Grace. But my first concern is for my daughter." The Countess was already striding across the deck.

With relish at the curt reprimand, I also turned my back on the Duke of Clarence and scuttled after my mother. When I arrived in the cabin, she had already taken charge. Her cloak dropped onto a stool, she had replaced Margery at Isabel's side and was dispensing advice and soothing words in a forthright manner that would brook no refusal. In our northern home in Middleham, where I had spent the years of my childhood, my mother, despite her highborn status, had a reputation for knowledge and skill in the affairs of childbirth. I feared that we would need all of it before the night was out.

*   *   *

My mother was right in one thing. With Isabel as far on as she was, we should never have put to sea when we did. Not that we had much choice in the matter, with the King and his army breathing down our traitorous necks and out for blood. A disastrous mix of ill luck, poor weather, and royal Yorkist cunning—and we were reduced to this voyage on this mean little vessel in unreliable April weather. Here we were in this hot, dark, confined space, lurching on a sulky sea, with Isabel's screams echoing off the rough walls to make me feel a need to cover my ears—except that my mother was watching—and reject any notion of motherhood for myself.

A fist hammered on the door.

"Who is it?" The Countess's attention remained fixed on Isabel's flushed face.

A disembodied voice. "My lord says to tell you, my lady: The heavy cloud has lifted and Calais is in sight. We are approaching the harbor, to disembark within the hour."

"Do you hear that, Isabel?" The Countess gripped Isabel's hand hard as Margery wiped the sweat from my sister's forehead. "You'll soon be in your own room, in the comfort of your own bed in Calais." Heartwarming words, but I did not think the Countess's expression matched them as she helped Isabel to lie down on the narrow bed.

Isabel snatched her hand away. "How can I bear this pain, no matter where I am?"

At that exact moment, bringing a deathly silence to the cabin, there came the easily recognizable crack of distant cannon fire. One! Two! And then another. Shouts erupted on deck, the rush of running feet. The ship reeled and huffed against the wind as sails were hauled in and she swung around with head-spinning speed. The drag of metal on wood rumbled as the anchor chain was dropped overboard.

We all froze; even Isabel's attention was momentarily diverted from her woes.

"Heaven preserve us!" Margery promptly fell to her knees, hands clasped on her ample bosom.

"Cannon fire!" I whispered.

"Are they firing at us?" Isabel croaked.

"No." The Countess stood, voice strong with conviction. "Get up, Margery. Of course they are not firing at us. Lord Wenlock would never refuse us entry to Calais."

But again the crash of cannon. We all tensed, expecting a broadside hit at any moment. Then Isabel groaned. Clutched the bed with talonlike fingers. Her once-flushed face was suddenly gray, her lips ashen. The groan became a scream.

Our mother approached the bed, barely turned her head toward me, but fired off her own instructions, as terse as any cannon. "Anne! Go and see what's amiss. Tell your father we need to get to land immediately."

I made it through the crash and bang of activity to my father's side. There ahead, emerged from the cloud bank, was the familiar harbor of Calais. Temptingly close. But equally we were close enough that I could see the battery of cannon ranged against us, just make out their black mouths, and a pall of smoke hanging over them in the heavy air. They had been aimed at us, to prevent our landing if not to sink us outright. Now in the lull, across the water and making heavy weather of it, came a small boat rowed by four oarsmen with one man standing in the bow. His face, expressionless with distance, was raised to us.

"Who is it?" Clarence asked the Earl.

"I don't recognize him." But I recognized my father's heavy mood of anger. "One of Wenlock's men. What in God's name is he about?"

The boat drew alongside and the visitor clambered on deck. Clothes brushed down, sword straightened, he marched across to where we stood and bowed smartly before the Earl. "A message from Lord Wenlock, my lord. To be delivered to your ears only. He would not write it."

"And you are?"

"Captain Jessop, my lord. In my lord Wenlock's confidence." His expression was blandly impossible to read.

"In his confidence, are you?" Temper snapped in the Earl's voice.

"Then tell me—why in God's name would you fire on me? I am Captain of Calais, man. Would you stop me putting in to port?"

"Too late for that, my lord." Captain Jessop might be apologetic but he gave no quarter. "Twelve hours ago we received our orders from the King. And most explicit they were too, on pain of death. With respect, my lord, we're forbidden to allow the great rebel—yourself, my lord—to land on English soil in Calais."

"And Lord Wenlock would follow the orders to the letter?" My father was frankly incredulous.

"He must, my lord. He is sympathetic to your plight but his loyalty and duty to the King must be paramount." A weighty pause. "You'll not land here."

The Earl's crack of laughter startled me. "And I thought he was a loyal friend, a trustworthy ally." I could see the Earl struggle with his emotions at this blow to all his plans. Lord Wenlock, a man who had figured in Neville campaigns without number over as many years as my life. He had been a guest in our home and I knew there had never been any question of his allegiance.

"He is both ally and friend," Captain Jessop assured him, "but I must tell you as he instructed. There are many here within the fortress who are neither loyal nor trustworthy in the face of your . . . ah, estrangement from the Yorkist cause."

"Look, man." The Earl grasped the captain's arm with a force that made the man wince. "I need to get my daughter ashore. She is with child. Her time has come."

"I regret, my lord. Lord Wenlock's advice is that Calais has become in the way of a mousetrap. You must beware that *you* are not the mouse that comes to grief here with its neck snapped. He says to sail farther along the coast and land in Normandy. If you can set up a base there, from where you can attract support, then he and most of the Calais garrison will back you in an invasion of England. But land in Calais you may not."

"Then I must be grateful for the counsel, mustn't I?" Releasing Captain Jessop's arm, the Earl clasped his hand but with little warmth and much bitterness. "Give my thanks to Wenlock. I see that I must do as he advises."

I moved quickly aside as the captain made his farewells. So we were not to be welcomed within the familiar walls of Calais. A little trip of panic fluttered in my belly, even as I tried to reassure myself that I should not worry. My father would know what to do. He would not allow us to come to harm. A sharp wail of anguish rose above the sound of shipboard action. My instincts were to hide but my sense of duty, well honed at my mother's knee, insisted otherwise. It took me back to the cabin with the bad news.

The activity in the small, dark space brought me up short. My elegant mother, a great heiress in her own right who had experienced nothing but a life of highborn privilege and luxury, had folded back the wide cuffs of her oversleeves and was engaged with Margery in pulling Isabel from the narrow bed. Ignoring Isabel's fractious complaints, she ordered affairs to her liking, dragging the pallet to the floor and pushing my sister to lie down where there was marginally more space. Margery added her strength at my mother's side with a strange mix of proud competence and sharp concern imprinting her broad face. But Margery had her own skills. She had been with my mother since well before the Countess's marriage, tending her through her difficult pregnancies, as I had heard from her frequent telling of how Margery had caught both Isabel and myself when we slid into this world. So, as she informed us, what she didn't know about such matters as bearing children, although she had none of her own, was not worth the knowing.

"Hush, child. Margery is with you. Sit there for Margery, now, and don't weep so. . . ." As if Isabel were still a small girl to be cosseted for a grazed knee.

The Countess was made of sterner stuff. Seeing me hesitate in the doorway, she pounced with impressive speed and pulled me into the cabin. "No, you don't. I shall have need of you."

"There's no room. . . ."

"Anne. Be still. Your sister needs you."

I feared that I would be the last person to soothe my pain-racked sister. Isabel merely tolerated me. We had always fought; I suspected we always would. But pity moved me at her wretched plight. "We cannot land." Adopting a martyred expression, I recounted to the Countess the gist of the conversation as I stepped over to replace Margery at Isabel's side.

"Ha! As I thought. Perhaps it's too late anyway." We staggered and clutched as a rogue wave lifted the boat from prow to stern. I covered my mouth on another surge of nausea, the clammy sweat chilling me in the hot air.

"Breathe deep, daughter. I can't deal with two of you sick. Sit with Isabel; hold her hand; talk to her."

"What about?" I looked to the Countess for guidance. Sudden fear filled this cabin. Sharp and bright, it overwhelmed me.

"Anything. Encourage her; distract her if you can. Now, Margery. Let's see if we can bring this child safely into the world."

Three hours later we had made little progress.

"We need the powers of the Blessed Virgin's Girdle here, my lady," Margery whispered as Isabel's whole body strained.

"Well, we haven't got it, and so must do what we can without!" the Countess replied more sharply than was her custom.

Sniffing, Margery resorted to the age-old remedy of a knife slipped beneath the pallet to ease the pain and cut the birth pangs, adding a dull green stone for good measure. "Jasper," she whispered. "It gives strength and fortitude to ailing women."

"Then we could surely do with such powers this day. For all of us." My mother did not stop her, but decided on a more practical approach.

"Find the kitchen, or what passes for one, wherever it may be in this vessel, Anne. Tell the cook I need grease. Animal fat. Anything to coat my hands." The Countess leaned close, speaking to me as an equal in age and knowledge, with a foreboding that she no longer made any effort to hide. "The child is taking too long. Isabel grows weaker by the minute and the child's not showing."

I raced off, returning with a pot of noxious and rancid grease—from what source I could not possibly guess.

"Don't stand gawping, Anne. If nothing else, pray!"

My mother astounded me. Stripped of all her consequence along with her veils, skirts, and underrobe tucked up, hair curling onto her neck in greasy strands, she was as rank as any common midwife, yet as awe-inspiring as the most noble lady in the land.

"Whom shall I petition?" I asked. Praying seemed to me a tedious affair when all around was fear and chaos.

"Pray to the Virgin. And Saint Margaret—chaste and childless she may have remained, accepting death as the lesser of evils, although I cannot agree with her—but during torture she experienced all the pain of being swallowed up and spit out by a dragon. An unpleasant encounter not given to many of us. Pray to her." She hesitated a moment, then held my eyes in a fierce stare. "But before you do, fetch the priest."

I did not need to ask why.

The next hours were the most horrifying of my young life. Enclosed as we all were in that cabin, it was difficult to tell when day passed into night, night into day. Candles were replaced as they guttered and food was sent in to us that we did not eat, until it was all over except for the hot reek of blood and sweat and terror. There was little else to show for it. Isabel lay as pale and drained as whey. The Countess knelt beside her, exhausted, whilst Margery fussed and fretted with pieces of soiled linen. The bones of my fingers were crushed as in a vise where Isabel had hung on in the worst of her pain. I had repeated every prayer of petition I knew, as well as a good many impromptu offerings, until my voice was hoarse, and at the end I drooped with fatigue. But all we had was a poor dead baby. The grease to slick the

Countess's hands and ease the child into the world, and the dire experience of Saint Margaret with the dragon, saved my sister but not the child—a pitiful, weak creature smeared with blood and slime that managed to utter a cry little stronger than a kitten's, then left this life almost as soon as it had entered it.

A girl. The priest, Father Gilbert, our own Neville priest who had come with us in our household, hustled in from where he had waited all this time within call, baptized her at the bedside to save her immortal soul and free her from slavery to the devil. I think we pretended that she was still alive when the water touched her forehead. It would have been too distressing to accept that her life had passed and so her soul was lost to God as well. Anne, she was called, because my mother's eye fell on me as I would have shrunk from the room at the end to find some solitary space in which to shed the tears that now would not be restrained in my weakness. Her stare fixed me to the spot, where I stood frozen as the priest touched the unresponsive face with holy water from the little vial. Isabel watched glassy eyed as her daughter was washed and wrapped and finally given into my reluctant care in my role as messenger.

"Take the babe to the Earl," the Countess instructed, touching the waxen features with fingers that were unsteady. "He will know what to do."

Such a small weight. The child lay in my arms as if she slept toilworn from the excesses of the event, the skin on her eyelids translucent. Her fingernails were perfect too, but too weak to cling to life. How could I not weep as I carried the burden onto the deck? To my father, my mother had said. Not to the Duke of Clarence.

I stood before them where they waited for me, as if I were offering a precious gift.

"Is it a boy?" Clarence asked.

"No. A girl. And she is dead. We called her Anne. She has been baptized." I knew my tone was blunt and unfeeling, but I dared use no other. Nor dared I look at him. Too many feelings crowded in, not least my hatred for this man who cared nothing for my sister other

than the inheritance that came with her name, the power of her Neville family connections that would buy him support and, as was his
ambition, the throne of England. If I had allowed it I would have sunk
down to the filthy, wave-soaked decking and howled my hurt and
disillusion like one of my father's hounds.

"Perhaps next time it will be a boy." Clarence turned away, disappointed, uninterested. He did not ask about Isabel's condition.

My father saw my distress. In a rough gesture that held his own
grief in check, he pulled me and the sad bundle close into his arms.
"Isabel?"

"She is tired and weak. I don't think she understands."

"We must thank God for your mother's skills. Without her we
might have lost Isabel too." He lifted the child from me with great
care. "Go back. Tell your mother. I will send the child's body to Calais with Captain Jessop here." I became aware that the captain had
returned and was awaiting instructions. "She is very small and barely
drew breath, but she is ours, with Neville blood in her veins. I will ask
that she be buried with all honor at the castle. Wenlock will see to it."

I nodded, too weary to do or think anything else.

"Tell her . . . tell your mother . . . I was wrong. I should never have
put to sea."

"I don't think it mattered, sir." I rubbed my eyes and cheeks on
my sleeve. "If any should take the blame it should be the Yorkists.
King Edward, who drove us on with fear of capture. King Edward is
to blame."

*And Richard, my Richard. Who has stayed loyal to his eldest
brother and is now my enemy whether I wish it or not.*

I left the bundle in the Earl's keeping, and deliberately turned
away before I could see it carried over the side.

There began for us a long and distressing voyage west along the coast
from Calais. The winds and tides did us no favors and there was an uneasy pall of death over the ship. Isabel regained her strength, enough to

sit in her chair or walk a few steps on deck, but not her spirits. Clarence did not endear himself. He remained brashly insensitive, rarely asking about her, rarely seeking her company, too concerned with the instability of his own future now that he was branded traitor to his brother. The Earl and Countess held discussions deep into the night. I knew it was about our future plans, where we would go now that Calais was barred to us. We could not return to England unless we had an army at our back—that much I understood. All my father's wealth was not sufficient to fund such an enterprise. If we returned to cast ourselves on King Edward's mercy, we would all be locked up. Without doubt heads would roll. The line between my father's brows grew deeper as his options narrowed. Not yet knowing what they were, still I realized that they were distasteful to the Earl and to the Countess. As for Clarence, he did not care, as long as there was a golden crown for him at the end.

I spent much time on deck, leaning on the side of the vessel to look back over the gray water that would separate me from all I had known, the security of my home at Middleham, my privileged life. And from Richard, who filled my thoughts even when I tried to banish him. Windblown and disheveled, damp skirts clinging to my knees, I was as silent and sullen as the weather. Until the Countess took me to task and sent me off to keep my sister company.

"Go and talk to Isabel. And if she wishes to talk to you about the child she has lost, do so. For her husband surely does not."

Her less than subtle criticism of despicable Clarence spurred me on. Without argument, I allowed Isabel to weep out her loss on my shoulder and told her that surely everything could be made right once we had found a landing. I hated my empty words, but Isabel seemed to find some solace there.

Sometimes it seemed to me that we would never reach a safe haven.

The Earl made his decision. On the first day of May, when the sun actually broke through the clouds and shone down on our wretched vessel, we reached our goal and anchored off the port of Honfleur in the mouth of the great river that flowed before us into the depths of France. Standing at the Earl's side, I watched as the land drew closer, as the sun glinted on the angled wings of the wheeling gulls. For the first time in days my spirits rose from the depths.

"The Seine," my father explained, though I already knew.

"Do we land here? Do we stay in Honfleur?" I was fairly sure of the answer. There was really only one destination possible for our party.

"No. We go on to Paris."

"Why?"

"Why, indeed, my percipient daughter. It's a question I ask myself in the dark hours." The Earl laughed softly but with an edge that grated along my nerves. "It has been an unpalatable decision to make."

So much I knew. Although I might anticipate the wealth and luxury of the French court—I had never been there, only heard of its sumptuous magnificence under the openhanded rule of King Louis XI—my father was not taking us there for the comforts of the feather beds and the culinary delight of roast peacock served on gold plate. We had all of that and more in our own home in London, Warwick Inn, where foreign ambassadors were sent to us to be impressed.

"What choice do we have but to go to the French court unless we wish to roam the seas forever?" he asked of no one, certainly not expecting an answer from me. "We are going to throw in our lot with Louis."

"Will he help us?"

"I don't know."

A brutally honest answer. But why wouldn't he? I knew my father had worked tirelessly for an alliance between King Edward and Louis. That Louis had always had a strong regard for the Earl, addressing him as *my dear cousin Warwick* despite the lack of shared blood.

"Can you not persuade him?"

My question caused the Earl to glance down at me, his preoccupation tinged with amusement. He smiled. "Yes, perhaps I can. I think he will help us, simply because it is in His French Majesty's nature to find some personal gain for himself in doing so. I can accept that. Don't we all snatch our own desires out of the miseries of others? But . . . there'll be some hard bargaining. I wager I'll not like the result." He took a deep breath, as he must, before he could tolerate his decision. I thought he might choke on the necessity of it. "Beggars can't choose where to put their allegiance." I could sense his sour disgust in the salt wind that caused both of us to shiver. Suddenly age seemed to press heavily on him. His dark hair, almost black, and so like my own, might gleam in the sun but flecks of gray told their own tale.

"Will we be made welcome?" I still wanted to know.

My father turned back to search my face with a quizzical stare. It was a strange look, full of careful calculation. "Yes, I think we will," he murmured, eyes widening as if a thought had struck home. "*You* will be made welcome, my daughter, at all events."

"I? What does King Louis know of me?"

"Nothing yet. Other than that you are my daughter. But he will not turn you from his door."

I did not know why, nor did I ask further, coward that I was on this occasion, subdued by the events of those moody past days. I was a younger daughter who had once been betrothed to Richard of Gloucester. But I had rapidly become undesirable as a bride and so was promptly unbetrothed after my father took up arms against Richard's brother, King Edward. Now I was a hopeless exile. I could not imagine why the French King would give me even a second look. But the skin on my arms prickled with an unpleasant anticipation.

Now, without words, I followed the direction of the Earl's appraisal of the French coast, where the gray waters of the vast river mouth opened up before us. The rain-spattered land was as bleak and almost as unfriendly as the shores we had just left. I tried to see it—and us, our present situation—through my father's eyes, and failed. The Earl of Warwick, powerless and well-nigh destitute, his lands confiscated, his good name trampled in the bloodstained mud of treachery.

How had it all come to this?

CHAPTER TWO

1462

Middleham Castle, North Yorkshire

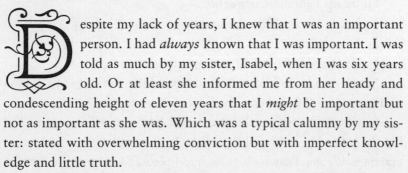espite my lack of years, I knew that I was an important person. I had *always* known that I was important. I was told as much by my sister, Isabel, when I was six years old. Or at least she informed me from her heady and condescending height of eleven years that I *might* be important but not as important as she was. Which was a typical calumny by my sister: stated with overwhelming conviction but with imperfect knowledge and little truth.

Isabel was five years older than I. Five years is a long time at that age. So with all that wealth of experience and her acknowledged position as the elder child of the powerful Earl of Warwick, she lorded it over me. She was tall for her age, with fine light hair that curled at the ends, fair skin, and light blue eyes. She looked like our mother, and our mother's father, Richard Beauchamp, or so I was led to believe, whereas I had the look of the Neville side—to my detriment, as I considered the comparison between us. I was slight and slim boned with dark hair—unfortunately straight—dark eyes, and sallow skin that did me no favors in cold winter weather. It was generally accepted that I would not have my sister's beauty when I was grown, nor would

I grow very tall. I was small for my age and wary of Isabel's sharp fingers that pinched and poked.

We had had an argument over the ownership of a linen poppet dressed in a fine court gown fashioned from scraps of old damask. It had been stitched for us by Bessie, our nurse, with embroidered eyes as black as the fire grate and a pout of berry red lips. The hair had been fashioned of wool and was black and straight beneath her linen veil. Because of her resemblance, I claimed stridently that the poppet was mine, but the squabble ended as it usually did, with Isabel snatching it from my hands and holding it out of reach.

"You're cruel, Isabel. It was given to me. It was made for me."

"It's mine. I'm older than you."

"But that does not mean that you are cleverer. Or that the poppet is yours."

"It means I am more important."

I glared, fearing that she might be right. "I don't see why it should."

Isabel tossed her head. "I am my father's heir."

"But so am I." I did not yet understand the workings of the laws of inheritance. "My father is the Earl of Warwick too."

She sneered from her height. Isabel had a very fine sneer. "But I'm the elder. My hand will be sought in marriage as soon as I am of marriageable age. I can look as high as I please for a husband. Even as high as a Prince of the Blood."

Which was true enough. She had been listening to our servants gossiping. The phrase had the smack of Margery at her most opinionated.

"It's not fair." A last resort. I pouted much like the disputed poppet.

"Of course it is. No one will want *you*. You are the youngest and will have no inheritance."

I hit her with the racquet for the shuttlecock. It was an answer to every difficulty between us. She retaliated with a sharp slap to my cheek. Our squawks echoing off the walls of the inner courtyard brought our mother on the scene, as well as our governess, Lady Masham, and Bessie. The Countess waved the women aside with a sigh of long-suffering tolerance when she saw the tears and my reddened cheek and swept us away to her parlor. There she pushed us to sit on low stools before her. I remember being suitably subdued.

The Countess knew her daughters well. She preserved a stern face against the humor of our petty willfulness as she sat in judgment.

"What is it this time? Isabel? Did you strike your sister? Did you provoke her?"

Isabel looked aside, a sly gesture, as I thought. "No, madam. I did not."

I knew it! She thought I would be similarly reticent. We had been lectured often enough on the sin of pride and she would not wish to confess to the Countess the nature of our dispute. But the hurt to my self-esteem was as strong as the physical sting of the flat of Isabel's hand and so I informed on her smartly enough. "She says that she's more important. That no one will want me for a wife." The hot tears that sprang were not of hurt but of rage.

"Nor will they!" Isabel hissed like the snake she was. "If you can't keep a still tongue . . ."

"Isabel! Enough! It does not become you." The Countess's frown silenced my sister as she leaned forward to pull me, and the stool, closer. "Both of you are important to me." She blotted at my tears with the dagged edge of her oversleeve.

I shook my head. That was not what I wanted to hear. "She says that she will get all our father's land. That I will get nothing."

"Isabel is wrong. You are *joint* heiresses. You will both inherit equally."

"Even though I am not a boy?" I knew enough to understand the preeminence of such beings in a household. There were no boys in ours apart from the young sons of noble families, the henchmen, who came to finish their education with us. And they did not count. My mother had not carried a son but only two girls.

"Well." The Countess looked doubtfully from one to the other, then back to me. "Your father's lands and the title—the *Neville* inheritance—is entailed in the male line. That means that they will pass on to the son of your uncle John and his wife, Isabella. But the lands *I* brought to this marriage with your father—they belonged to my father and my mother. Richard Beauchamp and Isabel Despenser. It is a vast inheritance—land and castles and religious houses the length and breadth of England. And it will be split equally between the two of you."

"But she is too young." Isabel sprang to her feet so that she could stare down at me with all the hostility of being thwarted. "It should all be mine."

"You are greedy, Isabel. Sit down." Our mother waited until she did so, with bad grace. "Anne will not always be so young. She will grow into a great lady, as you will. The land will be split equally. So there—you are both equally important."

"But *I* look like you." Isabel smiled winningly.

The Countess laughed, although I did not understand why. "So you do. And I think you will be very beautiful, Isabel. But Anne has the look of her father." She touched the veil on my braided hair, still neat since it was early in the day. "She will become more comely as she grows. Looks mean nothing."

I expect my answering smile was disgracefully smug. When we were dismissed, Isabel stalked off, chin raised in disdain, but I stayed and leaned close, struck by the appallingly adult consequence of this conversation.

"Mother. Will you have to be dead before we have the land?"

"Yes."

"Then I don't want it."

She smiled, hugged me. "It is a long way in the future, God willing, for both of us."

So the course of my life was to be underpinned by the Countess's inheritance, half of which would pass to me. More important, my existence was to be turned on its head by Richard Plantagenet. Richard came into my life when I was eight years old and I was not overly impressed. We were living at Middleham far in the north of the country at the time, the Earl and Countess's favorite residence of all our castles. Young boys of good birth were always living in our household, from the most eminent of families, since the Earl was the King's chief counselor. They came to learn what they would need to know for a life in the highest circles. I had little to do with them, being a girl about her lessons, whilst the arts of warfare exercised most of their time. I was still in the company of Bessie and Lady Masham, an impoverished widow from the Countess's wide-flung family employed to instruct me in the skills of chatelaine of a great household. The boys with their rough games and combative sports, an endless succession of clouts to the head, scrapes, and bruises, did not interest me. Nor did they have any time for me. Except for Francis Lovell, my father's ward, who was a permanent presence in the household and was not averse to spending time to talk to me, although he was more my sister's age. Francis was kind above and beyond the demands of chivalry, toward a nuisance of a child such as I was.

Then Richard arrived.

I first noticed him, I think, because he reminded me of myself: We both suffered similar deficiencies. Shorter rather than taller. Slightly built rather than robust. A lot of dark hair, as black as the wing of one of the ravens that nested in the crags beyond Middleham, although a lot more untidy than their sleek feathers. With the cruelty of youth I decided that because of his unimpressive stature and build he would make heavy weather of the training. What he would make of me I did not care. He was just another boy come to eat at our table and improve his manners.

My father was away, sent by the King on an embassy to the French court, so the Countess welcomed the newcomer in the main courtyard when he arrived with his escort, his body servant, and a train of baggage wagons. An imposing entourage for so young a person.

"Welcome to Middleham, Your Grace," the Countess greeted him.

He bowed with surprising deftness. Even I could see that he had been well taught in the demands of courtly behavior. Some of the lads almost fell over in the effort, flushing the color of a beetroot at so gracious a reception by so great a lady as my mother, before being taken in hand.

"My lady." His reply was low but not unconfident. "My lady mother the Duchess sends her kind regards and thanks you for your hospitality."

My mother smiled. "You are right welcome. The master of henchmen will show you where you will sleep and where to put your belongings. You will answer to him for all your training." She indicated Master Ellerby at her side. "Then my daughter Isabel will show you to my parlor, where I will receive you."

She pushed Isabel forward. The unloading began, horses led off to the stables, the escort to their quarters, our guest's possessions carried within. It all took time. Isabel had no intention of waiting until it was all complete.

"I'll come back for you," she informed the boy, shockingly ill-manneredly, and took herself off about her own concerns. But for once I lingered. Why should I do so? I had no idea except that impulse made me stay. The boy did not look particularly pleased to be with us, but then the newcomers rarely did. His face was pale and set yet composed enough. I studied him as he lifted a bundle containing two swords, a light bow, and a dagger from one of the wagons. His lips were thin, with corners tightly tucked in as if he would not say more than he had to. He had a tendency to frown. Perhaps it was his eyes that caught my imagination. They were very dark and cold. No spark of warmth lurked in their depths. Dispassionately, I decided that he looked sad.

So I followed him up the stairs into the living apartments with all the assurance of a daughter of the house. Was I not Lady Anne Neville? I got under everyone's feet in the doorway until at last Richard Plantagenet's belongings were stowed away in chests and presses and he sat on the edge of the bed in the room allotted to him for his stay at Middleham.

I took a step into the room. I looked at him. He looked at me.

"This is a very fine room," I informed him, out to impress the newcomer, but also curious. It was one of the circular tower rooms at one of the four corners of the great central keep where we, the family, lived. The stone walls curved in a pleasing fashion with the windows, long and narrow in the old style, looking out over the outer courtyard toward the chapel, so allowing more light and air than in many of the rooms. It had its own garderobe in a small turret, a desirable convenience in winter weather when it was necessary for most of the household to brave the chill of the garderobe tower. The Earl's henchmen were rarely housed so well. Even Francis Lovell, who was almost as important as I and would be a lord, was installed in a bleak little room in the northerly tower that caught a permanent blast of cold air. "I think this is one of the best rooms in the castle."

"Is it? To my mind it's cold and drafty."

I followed his quick survey of the room. Well, it didn't have the thick tapestries of the room that I shared with Isabel. Nor were the walls plastered and painted with fanciful flowers and birds, as in the Countess's own bedchamber. The floor was of polished oak boards rather than the fashionable painted tiles that had been laid in Warwick Castle. I frowned as I picked up what this boy might think was lacking. But the wooden bedstead was canopied and hung with silk drapes that must surely please, with a matching silk bedcover. The deep green shimmered as a dart of sunshine lanced across it. There was a chest and a press for garments. There was even a whole handful of wax candles in a tall iron candlestand that could not be sneered at by anyone who wished to read. . . . What more did he want?

"And where have *you* come from?" I hoped my brows rose in a semblance of the Countess at her most superior. How dared he sit in judgment on my home when his own was probably little more than a crude keep and bailey, with no improvements since its construction under William the Norman!

"Fotheringhay. My father had a new wing built with wall fire-places and lower ceilings." He cast another uncharitable eye around his accommodations.

"This castle," I stated, voice rising, "is one of the largest in the country."

"That does not make it the most comfortable. Or where I would wish to be." He looked at me as if I were an annoying wasp. "Who are you, anyway?" he asked.

"I am Lady Anne Neville," I informed him, with all the presumption of indulged youth. "Who are *you*?"

"Richard Plantagenet."

"Oh." I was no wiser, although the name Plantagenet was a royal one. "My father is the Earl of Warwick."

"I know. The Earl is my cousin, so we are cousins once removed, I suppose." He did not seem delighted at the prospect.

"Who is *your* father?" I asked.

"The Duke of York. He is dead."

I ignored the shortness of the reply, homing in on the information. Now I knew. "So your brother is King Edward." That put the newcomer into quite a different category in my mind.

"Yes."

"How old are you?" I continued my nosy catechism. "You don't look old enough to begin your training as a knight. I am more than eight."

"I am twelve years old. I am already a Knight of the Garter."

"Only because your brother is King!"

He shrugged as he bent to pat a hound that had wandered in, clearly not prepared to offer any more conversation.

"I too am very important," I observed. I had no dignity.

"You are a girl. And still a child."

Which put me entirely in my place. I turned on my heel and stomped from the room, leaving him to make his own way or wait for Isabel's tender mercies. I think it was Francis Lovell who eventually took pity on him and took him to my mother's chamber. I was not there. Lady Masham had run me to ground in her fussy manner and scolded me for absenting myself from my lessons.

I was not satisfied with my brief acquaintance.

Richard Plantagenet continued to say little but took to his studies well enough. He intrigued me. His confidence. His quiet, self-contained competence. When I could escape my own lessons, I began to haunt the exercise yard and the lists where he practiced the knightly drills. And I was right. He suffered. He did not have the stature or strength of muscle to hold his own against Francis, who was often pitted against him. Richard spent a lot of time sprawled in the dust and dirt. But he did not give in. And I had to admire his courage, his determination to scrape himself up from the floor. Quick and alert, he soon learned that he could make up in guile and speed for what he lacked in size and weight. He could ride a horse as if born in the saddle.

But still he was often on the floor with a bloody nose and dust plastered over his face. After a particularly robust session with sword and shield, Master Ellerby sent him to sit on the bench at the side of the exercise yard. Still dazed, Richard Plantagenet rubbed his face and nose on his sleeve. I crept along by the wall and sat on the bench with him. An opportunity too good to miss, to find out more whilst his guard was down. What did I want to know? Anything, really. Anything to explain this solemn youth who sat quietly at meals, who carved the roast beef with stern concentration, who watched and absorbed and said little.

"Are you content here?" I asked for want of anything more interesting to say.

He snorted, pushing his hair from his eyes. "Better when my head is not ringing from the master's gentle blows! I swear Edward did not intend me to be knocked senseless when he sent me here."

"You said you did not want to be here." The implied criticism of Middleham still rankled. "Where would you rather be that's better than here?"

"With my brother. In London. That's where I shall go when I am finished here."

"Do you miss your family?"

He thought for a moment. "Not much."

"Do you have brothers other than the King? Sisters?"

"Yes. Ten."

"Ten?" Shock made me turn to face him. "I only have Isabel. That's enough."

"But some are dead, and all are older than I. George of Clarence is the one I know best."

"You are the Duke of Gloucester." I had acquired some knowledge since our exchange of views. "Your father was attainted traitor when he fought against the Lancastrian upstart Henry, the last King."

"Yes." Richard bared his teeth. "And he died for it on the battlefield at Wakefield. And my brother Edmund with him. Margaret of Anjou, Queen Margaret, had my father's head cut from his body and put on a spike above Micklegate Bar in York. A despicable end for a brave man."

It was the longest speech I had heard him make. He still felt the hurt of it.

"Did you have to hide?"

"In a way. We—my brother Clarence and my mother—had to go into exile for our safety. We went to the Netherlands." His guard was clearly down; he was offering so much.

"Did you like it?" I could not imagine being forced to leave England in fear of my life, being forced to beg for charity from some foreign family and be unsure that I would ever be able to return. I knew I would have hated it.

"Well enough."

Now what? I sought for another topic to lure him into speech. It was difficult. "Were you called Richard after your father? I was named Anne for my mother."

"No. After *your* grandfather, Richard Neville, the Earl of Salisbury. He stood as my godfather at my baptism and so I was named Richard."

"Oh." His connection with my family was getting stronger. His nose still bled and his sleeve was well spotted with blood. I handed him a square of linen. Lady Masham would have approved, I thought.

"My thanks." He inclined his head with a courtly little gesture, then, wincing, applied the linen with careful enthusiasm.

"Where were you born?"

"Fotheringhay."

"I was born here. I like it here more than anyplace else."

"I like it too," he admitted suddenly, an admission that promptly warmed me to him. "It reminds me of Ludlow, where I spent some months when I was much younger. Before we were driven out by the Lancastrians at the point of a sword." There was the bitterness again.

"Why were you sent here? Why *here*?"

His angled look was wary, as if he were unsure of the reason for my question. I had no ulterior motive other than basic inquisitiveness.

"It was the only household of sufficient rank for my education. As King Edward's brother . . ." His shoulders straightened. "My brother and your father are very close. The Earl fought for Edward, helped him get the throne. Perhaps without the Earl he never would have done it. So where else should I have been sent but here? My brother the King has paid well for my upkeep. He sent a thousand pounds."

I nodded as if I understood. It sounded a vast sum. We sat in silence as he tried ineffectually to brush the dirt from the front of his jacket.

"Will you fight again today?"

"When I've got my breath back. Which I suppose I have, since I've done nothing but talk to you for the past minutes." He stood and flexed his muscles in back and thighs with a groan.

"Perhaps you should not?"

"Do you think I cannot?" As he looked down at where I still sat, a sudden sparkle, a glow of sheer pride, burst in the depths of those dark eyes. "I was lucky to survive my childhood, I'm told. It was a surprise to everyone, including my mother, the Duchess, who got into the habit of assuring everyone in the household every morning that I was still alive." He grinned, showing neat, even teeth. "I survived and I will be a Prince without equal. A bout with a blunt sword will not see me off to my grave."

"No." It made me smile too. I believed him.

As he would have picked up the practice sword from the bench, I found myself stretching out my hand to stop him. His eyes met mine and held, the light still there.

"I'm glad you survived."

I was astounded at what I had said, could not understand why I had said it. I leaped to my feet and ran before he could respond, or I was discovered where I should not be.

I think it was in September of that year that I had my first experience of the painful cut and thrust of political maneuvering. It was when our household moved to York for a week of celebration and festivity.

It began auspiciously enough. My father the Earl was particularly good-humored, not a common occurrence in the months after the King's marriage, which he viewed with tight-lipped displeasure. It seemed to circle around the King's choice for his new Queen, Elizabeth Woodville. She was a widow from a lowborn, avaricious family, all of them grasping and greedy for power, and so quite unsuitable. I did not understand why being a widow should make her an unacceptable wife, since her previous husband was conveniently dead. Nor was avaricious quite within my grasp. But so it was. The marriage, I learned, had been performed in "disgraceful secrecy." I wondered why a King should need to do anything in disgraceful secrecy. Could he not simply order affairs to his own liking?

"That's exactly what he's done," the Earl snarled over a platter of bread and beef. "He's followed his own desires. And at what cost to this realm? He's deliberately gone against my advice. I have to suppose

I am of no further value to him, now that he has the Woodvilles ready to bow and scrape and obey every order." Temper sat on him like a thundercloud.

Thus it was a relief when our visit to York lightened his mood. We were dressed and scrubbed and polished and instructed on our behavior, to be seemly at all times. I had a new gown because at nine years I was growing fast. We walked the short distance to the great cathedral and took our seats. Important seats in the chancel because, as Isabel whispered to me as the congregation massed behind us, we were the most important family present. The choir sang. The priests processed with candles and silver cross and incense. And there at the center of it all was Bishop George Neville, my father's youngest brother, my uncle, splendid in the rich cope and gilded miter of his office. Now to be enthroned as Archbishop of York. It was a magnificent honor for our family.

Except that a heavy frown pulled the Earl's brows into a black bar. He was not pleased. Nor his other brother, my uncle Lord John, the Earl of Northumberland. I could just see them seated together if I leaned forward. Impressive in satin and fur, they exchanged an angry, whispered conversation with each other. Their words held a sharp bite but I was not close enough to make them out.

"What is it?" I whispered to Francis Lovell on my left side. "What's wrong?"

He nodded over to our left. *Empty!* He mouthed the word silently.

I leaned forward to see. At the side of the chancel in pride of place were two magnificent thrones of carved and gilded wood, obviously placed there for some important personages. The only seats in the cathedral not occupied.

"Who?"

It was Richard, seated neat and resplendent in dark velvet on my other side, who answered with the croak of adolescent youth. "My brother the King and his wife, Elizabeth Woodville. They have not come. They were expected."

"Oh!" I saw that there was a frown on his face almost to equal my father's. "Does it matter?" I hissed sotto voce.

Richard frowned harder. "Yes. I think it does."

We were hushed with a sharp glance from the Countess as the new Archbishop took his Episcopal throne. The ceremony drew to a close and the treble voices of the choir lifted in jubilation at George Neville's investiture. Perhaps the pride on his features too was muted as he saw the proof of absent guests. His smile gained a sour edge.

Afterward we gathered on the forecourt before the west door, collecting the household together before returning to our lodging.

"We should have expected it, should we not!" The Earl made no attempt to lower his voice.

My mother placed a placatory hand on his arm. "The King himself suggested the promotion for your brother. He *chose* George personally and it is a great honor."

"But not to be present at his enthronement? God's blood! It's a deliberate provocation. An insult to our name and my position."

"There may be a reason. . . ."

"The only reason I can think of is a personal slight against me and mine. He should have been here. You can't persuade me that the King was not aware of how his absence would be read by those who wish us ill."

But who would wish us ill? I had known nothing but love and care in my nine years. The Lancastrians, of course, would have no affection for the Earl of Warwick, but they were defeated, old King Henry touched in his mind and kept fast in the Tower of London, his Queen and son in exile, whilst King Edward held my father in high regard. So who would wish to cause us harm?

"There may be other demands on his time . . ." the Countess persisted.

"Woodville demands. It's that woman's doing. She has the King wound around her manipulating fingers, as tight as any bowstring. I wager she kept him from York. Has the King no sense . . . ?"

"Hush! You'll be overheard."

"I care not."

I was increasingly aware of Richard's taut figure beside me. When

I edged close, took hold of his sleeve and pulled to attract his attention, to try to discover the reason for his stark pallor, the stormy glitter of his eyes, he snatched his arm away. The movement caught the Earl's eye, and as he glowered in Richard's direction, I thought for the briefest of moments that he would turn his anger on this youngest brother of the King. He frowned at the pair of us as if we had been discovered in some mischief, sharp words rising to his lips.

But the Earl's face softened as he moved toward us.

"Anne." He touched my shoulder, a gentle clasp. Smiled at Richard, and there was no hostility there. "Don't be concerned, boy. Whatever is between your brother and myself does not rest on your back. You need broader shoulders than yours yet to take on your brother's misdemeanors. It's not for you to worry about."

"No, sir." Richard dropped his gaze.

"Is my uncle George still Archbishop, even though the King did not come?" I asked.

"He is." My childish query made my father laugh. "We'll forget Edward and celebrate with your uncle, for his and our own promotion. It's a proud day, after all."

Yet the incident of the empty thrones had cast a cloud over the whole ceremony and again over the sumptuous feast where we continued to celebrate, when it was necessary for the chairs set for the King and Queen to be shuffled quickly away and the seating rearranged. The music and singing, the magnificent banquet, the noisy conversations of the Nevilles and their dependents neatly covered over any lack in the occasion, but it remained there, an unease, as unpleasant as a grub in the heart of an apricot. I did not understand but I remembered the harsh reaction to the name of Woodville.

I cornered Richard before he could make his escape that night. He still had a bleak expression but that had never stopped me. "Why was my father so angry?"

"You must ask him."

"You think the Earl would tell me?" I was of an age to resent being kept in the dark. "I'm asking you." Sympathy at the dark emotion in his eyes moved my inquisitive heart. "Tell me about Elizabeth Woodville."

It was as if I had touched a nerve, and his reply was without control. "My brother should never have married her. My mother hates her. I hate her too."

Without further words or any courtesy he turned his back and leaped up the stairs two at a time. He kept his distance and his silence on the matter for the rest of the visit, leaving me to consider the strains that could tear a family apart so: where ambition and personal hatreds could replace compassion and affection that were at the heart of my own experience. I would hate it too if my family were as wrenched apart as Richard's.

My childhood passed in an even seam with Richard a constant. Our paths crossed, as those in an extended family must. At prayers in our chapel. At dinner in the great hall and the supper at the end of the day. Through the rains and snows of winter, the days that beckoned us outside in summer. But nothing of note passed between us. His time was demanded by the master of henchmen, mine by Lady Masham and the Countess.

As I grew I spied on Richard less often. Perhaps I was more self-conscious of my status in the household. Neville heiresses did not skulk and spy as a child might. But I knew that he learned to wield a sword with skill. That his talent with a light bow was praiseworthy. And that he could couch a lance in the tilting yard, to hit the quintain foursquare and ride to safety, not be thwacked for carelessness between the shoulder blades or on the side of the head by the revolving bag of sand. He was spread-eagled in the dirt less often.

I applied myself to my lessons. It was the Countess's wish that her daughters learn to read and write as any cultured family would, and so we did. Mastering the skill, I read the tales of King Arthur and his knights with sighing pleasure. Sir Lancelot of the Lake and his forbidden love for Guinevere warmed my romantic heart. I wept over the doomed lovers Tristan and Isolde. The painted illustration in the precious book showed Guinevere to have long golden hair, too much like Isabel for my taste. And Lancelot was tall and broad with golden hair to his shoulders as he stood in heroic pose with sword in hand and a smile for his lady. Nothing like Richard, who would never be fair and broad, who scowled more often than he smiled. But I could dream and I did.

I recall little of all those days in detail, until the momentous day of the marriage proposal, except for the Twelfth Night celebrations. After the processions, the festive feast with the boar's head and the outrageous pranks of the Lord of Misrule, we exchanged gifts. I still have the one that Richard gave me. It has traveled with me into exile, into unnumbered dangers from imminent battle, and into captivity. I had never seen its like and would be dismayed if it were ever lost to me. Richard must have bought it from a traveling peddler when he had visited York. On its presentation I tore impatiently at the leather wrapping.

"Oh! Oh, Richard!"

I laughed at the childish whimsy of it. Not of any intrinsic value, yet it was cunningly contrived of metal, a little hollow bird that would sit in the palm of my hand, plump and charming, its beak agape like a fledgling, its feathers well marked on the tiny wings that were arched on its back. When I moved the little lever on the side, the bird's tongue waggled back and forth. When I blew across the hollow tail, it emitted a warbling whistle. I practiced, to everyone's amusement.

"Richard. Thank you." I was lost for words but I made the appropriate curtsy, lifting my new damask skirts and much-prized silken underskirt with some semblance of elegance.

He flushed, then bowed in reply with more flamboyance than I had previously seen, and kissed my fingers as if I were a great lady. His lessons in chivalry had gone on apace.

"It is my pleasure. The little bird is charming, as are you, Cousin Anne."

When he drew me to my full height and kissed my cheeks, one

and then the other, and then my lips in cousinly greeting, I felt hot and cold at the same time, my face flushed with bright color. Francis Lovell's friendly salutes never had that effect on me.

I think it was then, with the imprint of Richard's kiss on my astonished lips, that I determined, with true Neville arrogance, that I would have him as my own. No other girl would have him, I swore silently with one of the Earl's more colorful oaths. Richard, I wager, felt no such significance in his gift from me. He was more taken with the horse harness the Earl had given him, an outrageously flamboyant affair, all polished leather with enamel and gilded fittings.

And what did I give to Richard Plantagenet? What would I, a ten-year-old girl, give to a Prince who had everything, whose brother was King of England? With many doubts and some maternal advice I plied a needle. My mother said it would be good practice and Richard would be too kind to refuse my offering, however it turned out. I scowled at the implication but stitched industriously. I stitched through the autumn months when the days grew short and I had to squint in candlelight to make for him an undershirt in fine linen, to fit under a light metal-and-velvet brigandine that was a present from his brother, and his favorite garment. A mundane choice of gift from me, but I turned it into an object of fantasy by embroidering Richard's heraldic motifs on the breast in silk thread and a few leftover strands of gold. A white rose for the house of York. The Sun in Splendor that his brother had adopted for the Yorkist emblem after the Battle of Mortimer's Cross, when the miracle of the three suns appeared together in the heavens. And for Richard himself, his own device of a white boar. I was not displeased with the result. The rays of the sun were haphazard. Isabel scoffed that the boar more resembled the sheep on the hills beyond Middleham. But my mother declared it more than passable and I presented it with all the pride of my hard labors.

Richard accepted it as if it were the costliest garment from the fashion-conscious court of Burgundy. He did not remark on the less-than-even stitches as Isabel had. Nor did he laugh at my woeful depiction of the boar.

"It is exactly what I could wish for."

I blushed with pride. I know he wore it, even when much washed and frayed at cuff and neck and most of the embroidery long gone.

I might have decided that I wanted Richard Plantagenet, but I did not love him. Sometimes I hated him, and he me with equal virulence, although much of the tension between us was of my own making. As I grew I struggled with conflicting emotions that drove me to be capricious with him.

Richard and his horse had fallen heavily in a bout in the tiltyard and, mount limping, had been dispatched to the stables. I had been looking for someone to annoy, and here, on that particular morning, was the perfect target. I had no pity. He was disheveled and sweaty, one sleeve of his leather jacket ripped almost away at the shoulder seam. Favoring one shoulder with a heavy wince of pain, he hissed between his teeth as he moved and stretched about his task. There was a raw graze along one cheekbone; his hair looked as if it had not seen a comb for days. In the dusty gloom of the stall he spoke with soft words to the restive horse, running his hand down a foreleg. Beside him on a bench were the makings of a hot poultice, steaming and aromatic, and a roll of stalwart bandaging. The horse shifted uneasily. I could see the white of its eye as it whickered and jibbed when Richard touched a sore spot. With long strokes, completely absorbed in his task so that he was unaware of my presence, he began to apply the hot mess, the remedy for all equine ills, according to Master Sutton, the Earl's head groom. Richard worked smoothly, gently, despite his own discomfort. I saw that his horse's well-being came before his own ills, but I was not in the mood to admit to being impressed. I came to stand behind him.

"What are you doing?"

"As you see."

He did not turn his head, or register my presence in any other way, and the answer did not please me. It had been a bad morning and

I was in disgrace. Out of sorts since the moment I was roused from my bed, I was sullen and dull at my lessons. So I had to repeat them, and became even more uncooperative when Isabel was released to freedom. Since Lady Masham had obviously prattled to my mother about my sins, the Countess sent me to the kitchens as punishment, to help in the making of candles for the household use. It was a fit task for a child who would not mind her lessons and was rude to her governess. Some practical work would soon set me to rights.

Isabel smirked. Francis Lovell laughed and refused to commiserate, so, my fingers burned from hot tallow and my pride wounded by a further sharp reprimand from the cook for my careless dipping of the long candles, I suppose I was out for blood at the short reply from Richard Plantagenet. I did not like to be ignored. I needed to wound and hurt.

"Did you fall?"

"Go away."

I was not used to being spoken to like this, particularly not by a henchman, Duke of Gloucester, royal Prince, or not. "I will not. These are more my stables than yours! I suppose you were clumsy and caused the horse to fall."

He looked up over his shoulder at me. Squinted at me as I stood outlined by light in the doorway. Then back to the task at hand. "I suppose I was."

I had seen the pain and anxiety in his face, but I was not moved to show compassion. Why should I be the only occupant of the castle to suffer? "It will probably be crippled, poor thing. Not worth the keeping."

"It's only a bad sprain. It will heal."

"It could be broken. See how the animal does not wish to put its foot down? My father has had horses destroyed for less."

"What do you know? Go away. You're nothing but a nuisance."

"And you are a changeling!" Isabel was not the only one to listen to servants' gossip. I had a ready store of disreputable information and, to my later shame, chose this moment to display it.

For a little time, to my disappointment, Richard did not react. He finished strapping the leg, and neatly tucked in the ends of the bandage before straightening, while I waited in the taut silence. As he drew himself to his full height I had to look up. I had not realized how tall he had grown over the weeks since his fourteenth birthday. His expression was not pleasant, his cheekbones stark beneath tight skin, and his dark eyes held mine as fiercely as the talons of a hawk would hold down a rabbit before ripping it apart.

"What did you say?"

I swallowed but would not retreat even though common sense warned me that I should. Now I had all his attention, for good or ill. I stared back.

"They say that you're a changeling. That yours was an unnatural birth. That you came into this world with black hair to your shoulders, like an animal, and all your teeth already formed."

"Is that all?" Richard's reply might be innocuous but his tone was undoubtedly a seer. "What else do they say?"

I swallowed. Well, I would say it. "That you're not well formed as a man should be. That you'll never take to the field as a good soldier."

"And am I? You tell me what gossip says. What do you say?"

At the stern demand for truth rather than conjecture, I could not answer.

"Why do you not answer? What do you see, Lady Anne Neville, from your self-righteous and self-appointed position of spreader of poisonous gossip? Am I such a monstrosity?"

I kept my chin high. "No."

"Why should I be a changeling?" he demanded as if he had not heard my denial. "Because I do not bear the same physical appearance as my brother the King? The long bones and fair hair, like my brother Clarence or my sister the Lady Margaret? My dark hair is from the Neville breeding of my mother, Duchess Cecily. As for teeth I do not know, but I'm neither misbegotten nor a changeling."

So he had heard the gossip too. Of course he would. And my repeating of it as an accusation had hurt him when his emotions were most compromised by his horse's injury. I was undoubtedly in the wrong. The guilt smote heavily against my insensitive heart, a hammer blow to an anvil.

"I did not think. . . ."

"No, you did not." There was no softening, and it struck me that he would be a dangerous enemy to have against you. Usually polite beyond measure, now he did not guard his words. "You should be ashamed of yourself to so slander a guest in your household. I think your mother the Countess would beat you if she knew."

So did I.

"I did not mean—"

"Yes, you did. You would repeat what you heard, common tattle without foundation, as any kitchen wench might after a cup of ale. You're no better than any one of our Lancastrian enemies who would use whatever means to blacken our name."

He was wrong. I was not so deliberately vindictive, intent on destruction. Nor was I his enemy. Only childishly cruel with my words, demanding attention. Although perhaps there was little difference in the outcome. My attempt at silent self-justification did not make me feel any better.

"I am sorry."

"So you should be."

"Forgive me."

"Of course." Now he withdrew into himself, face impassive, eyes flat. "As I must forgive a child who does not consider the repercussions of her taunts." He turned from me, brushing me off. But I could see his tense shoulders as he began once more to stroke the horse. He had gentle hands for his injured animal even when he was furious with me. I would have given anything to take back those words. Perhaps I had lost his friendship forever over a moment's stupidity. I did not know what to do, but I could not leave it like this. Carefully I walked to his side and reached up to caress the animal's neck.

"He will be well," I assured him in a small voice. I tried hard to prevent it from catching. "I only said it to hurt you. Master Sutton's remedy is very good. My father says there's none better." I stared at his unresponsive shoulders, willing him to turn and make it easy for me, but he didn't. I took a breath. "I too had dark hair when I was born, and a lot of it."

Richard did not reply but ran his fingers through the animal's tangled mane, teasing out the knots.

"I don't think I had my teeth. My nurse says I cried and fretted when my gums were sore."

Nothing! He did not even bother to tell me to go away. Well, I would show him.

I lifted the embroidered fillet from my head and pulled off the linen veil, dropping them both carelessly on the straw. Then I unpinned my bound and braided hair without compunction, a lengthy business undertaken every morning by Bessie. Shook it out so that it lay limply against my cheeks.

"See. I too look nothing like my mother or my sister." I shook it again to loosen the tight weaving and my hair fell long and straight, past my shoulders, as dark as his.

"No, you don't." At least he was looking at me again.

"Perhaps we are both changelings."

"Perhaps." There was the slightest curve to his mouth, but still nothing that could be called a smile. "Sometimes you are the devil's own brat."

"So Margery says." I smiled tentatively. So did he.

"Does your shoulder hurt?" I asked.

"Yes. I fell on it when I rolled from my horse. But it is not deformed!"

I had the grace to drop my gaze. "I know. I only said it to hurt."

"You succeeded. I thought you were my friend." He spoke to me as a brother to a younger sister, but still it pleased me. I was rarely admitted to such intimacy.

"I am. Come with me, now. Margery has a salve that will bring out the bruise and give you some ease. She will stitch your jacket too."

"*You* should do it for your impertinence." Giving the horse a final pat, he gathered up the empty bowl and the unused bandages. "What will she say when she sees your hair?" At last a true smile creased his lean cheeks.

"She will be cross. So will Bessie." I sighed at the prospect of further punishment even as I accepted it as a price to pay to restore the closeness between us. I had learned one painful lesson: I must learn to guard my tongue. Richard might appear immune to the spurious gossip spread by adherents to Lancaster to hurt and maim, but he was not, and it would be a heartless friend who opened the wound. Richard Plantagenet had a surprising vulnerability.

I was not heartless and I would be his friend.

CHAPTER THREE

Marriage began to loom interestingly on the Neville front.

In the following year my father was absent more often than he was present. The household continued to keep its usual efficient order with the Countess at the head of affairs, but she missed him, and as I grew I sensed that something out of the way was afoot. Sometimes it was difficult for her to smile; she rarely laughed. At dinner when she sat in the place of honor I could see, when I dragged my thoughts from my own concerns, that she picked at the dishes presented to her. She was pale and I think did not sleep well.

"Where is he? Is my father at Calais?" I would ask my mother. The Earl was often called upon to be there to oversee the defense of this most important possession on the coast of Europe.

"No. The King has sent him to France again."

"Why?"

"To make an alliance between our two countries."

"Will it be good for us?"

"Yes. Your father thinks so."

"Why does he not sign with France, in the King's name? Then he could come home."

My mother's brow furrowed. "Because, my inquisitive daughter, King Edward is not in agreement. He would prefer an arrangement with Burgundy rather than France."

"Is he arranging my betrothal?" This was from Isabel. At sixteen Isabel was of an age or more to be wed, or at least promised in a betrothal. So far no arrangement had been made, a matter that was not to her liking.

"Yes. I think it is in my lord's mind." A caustic reply for so celebratory an event.

"Will it be a foreign lord? Will I have to live beyond the channel?" Isabel was relentless. For a moment, she looked doubtful at leaving home and family so far behind. Then her expression brightened again, as if marriage to a foreign Prince would please her mightily.

"I'm not certain."

"Oh. Will my father tell me when he returns?"

"He might—if his plans have progressed so far." The Countess's brief smile held a wisp of dry humor. "Don't worry, Isabel. I am sure it will be a match made in heaven."

But in spite of this amusement at Isabel's dreaming of a handsome knight, there was some issue here. My mother's expression became even more strained, a thin line of worry between her brows as she made an excuse of a word with the steward to leave the supper table. Isabel was too intent on her future glory as a bride, but I knew that the Countess was deliberately selective with her opinions. Or perhaps she herself was uncertain of the Earl's intentions.

At least she had given me some ammunition.

"I thought you would be much sought after," I needled. "No one appears to be rushing to our door to claim your hand."

"I *shall* be sought after. You're too young to know anything about it."

"You'll soon be too old. Fit only for a convent."

"I shall marry one of the greatest in the land." She was, to my delight, crosser by the minute. "Do you think the Earl of Warwick will allow his heiress to go unmarried? Or to be claimed by a man who lacks importance and authority?"

No. I did not. I thought as did Isabel that it would be of prime importance for the Earl to secure a bridegroom of standing and wealth comparable to our own. But there was an uncertainty, an unease, about the situation that I could not unravel. If at sixteen years, most heiresses were formally betrothed if not wed, why was it different for Isabel? And what if Isabel did not marry? What would happen to me as a younger daughter? Was I destined for a *convent*? A bride of Christ? I shrank from the prospect: enclosing walls, a life of strict obedience and enforced poverty. I swore that was not for me. As for any prospective bridegroom for myself, I could not picture him. At eleven years I did not care greatly, but Isabel did and was decidedly ill-tempered as the days and weeks passed with no remedy.

The Earl returned at the end of the month, but after the briefest of greetings—hardly more than a smile for Isabel and myself, a quick exchange of words with Master Ellerby—he spent the day closeted with my mother. He was wont to be an indulgent father and we were used to more of his attention, but his face bore a return to moody preoccupation and displeasure. When we were reunited before supper, after my mother's company and a cup of Bordeaux had smoothed out the lines on his face, I decided to risk his indulgence. I stood in front of him where he lounged in his favorite chair before the fireplace.

"Did you make the treaty with France, sir?" I asked.

"I see you've been following diplomatic policy." I saw an appreciative gleam in the eye he slid toward the Countess.

"Yes. It would be a good alliance for England."

"So it would, and yes, I have. King Louis will make a strong ally."

"What is he like?"

"Uncommonly ugly and remarkably devious. He spins a web to trap and hold friends and enemies alike."

I liked the picture, having an interest in powerful men—how would I not, with the Earl of Warwick as my father?—but I changed course in pursuit of information on Isabel's marriage and my own destiny. "When do you leave again, sir? Do you return to France?"

"I shall not leave." His dark eyebrows drew together. "I've had my fill of King Edward's court. And the role of royal ambassador."

"Does the King not mind?"

"No. He has other voices of counsel. The Woodvilles are knee-deep around him, by God!"

There was a harshness there. I think he was addressing the Countess more than me. This was interesting, far more so than Isabel's non-existent bridegroom. "Why is the King no longer your friend, sir?" I asked.

Slowly the Earl turned to look at me. "So you would discuss politics now, Mistress Anne."

"Yes, sir. I would."

"Anne—you step beyond what is seemly. You're too young for such weighty matters." The Countess frowned.

"I am not. I wish to know," I persisted, waited. Would the Earl refuse? Would he brush me off like a child? My heart trembled at my boldness.

The Earl gave a ghost of a laugh. "You have grown up without my noticing," he remarked, then, startling me, lifted me off my feet to sit on the lid of the coffer beside him, leaning forward, his forearms on his thighs so that our eyes were on a level. I saw the shadowy remains of temper in his face despite the Countess's soft handling and I knew that he would answer me honestly. I crossed my ankles and folded my hands demurely in my lap.

"Once, the King was my friend, that's true." He spoke softly. "I stood at his right hand, as his counselor. Do you understand?"

I nodded. "You are the Great Chamberlain of England—the most powerful man in the whole country."

The Earl laughed. "But the King is more powerful than I and now the King is finding his wings, like a young hawk. He has little more than twenty-five years under his belt. Young men find the need to test their strength."

It seemed a vast age to me, but I nodded with solemn wisdom. "But why does that mean he no longer likes you?" I asked, reducing it to the low level of a squabble between Isabel and myself.

The Earl's face became as set as a Twelfth Night mask. "Liking is not the issue, Anne. Nor the blood of family which should bind us together. The quarrel—if you will—began when the King married Elizabeth Woodville. Her family has Edward's ear now, against all good sense."

The Woodvilles again. By now I knew more of this than I had at York. Margery's gossip—deliciously forbidden—was that dark magic had been used, a spell cast to bring the King to his knees in thrall to the Woodville woman. I knew enough not to repeat the tale in this company.

"Her father, Lord Rivers, is preeminent at court as Lord Treasurer and with a new earldom," the Earl continued. "He pushes the King in the direction of Burgundy rather than France, against my advice. . . ." The words grated and I thought he no longer realized he was speaking to me. "Marriages have been arranged between the Queen's sisters and the unwed heirs of the noblest families in the land—young men to whom I myself would look for an alliance. . . ." He took a breath and smiled wryly. "But that's not important to you yet. . . ."

"So the King does not talk to you anymore," I persisted. Friendship was everything to me.

"We are still cousins," the Earl said simply, "but the King is misguided and I think I have to watch my back. The Woodvilles are no friends of ours." His face set again, and I saw his fist clench on his knee. "No one will rob the Nevilles of their wealth and power."

"Your father helped the King to take the throne, you see." The Countess intervened to draw the sting, handing the Earl another cup of wine. "We would have expected some loyalty but the King has decided to repay us by ignoring my lord's advice. The Queen is a determined woman. She will promote her family at the expense of the great magnates of the realm."

"Certainly at my expense," the Earl growled. "Does that tell you all you want to know?" He managed a smile. "There's nothing to worry you, Anne—or you, Isabel. One day King Edward will see that my counsel is good." He stroked a finger down the length of my nose, then lifted me to the floor. "Then we shall be friends again."

"Yes, sir." It all seemed very plain and I was perfectly satisfied. The King was in the wrong. The Earl would be patient and would triumph. There was no doubt in my mind and I pitied the King for his bewitchment by the Woodville woman.

"But have you got me a husband?" Isabel interrupted with a scowl in my direction for capturing the center of attention. She had been burning to ask since the Earl's horse had first set foot on the bridge over the moat, and could wait no longer.

A tightening of the muscles in his jaw made me think that this was one of the issues to displease my father. With a flicker of eyes, he appealed to the Countess. But when she nodded and the Earl smiled at Isabel, I decided I was misled.

"Yes. I think I have."

"Who? When?" Excitement vibrated from Isabel until she glowed with it, her fair skin lit from within so that her future beauty became spectacularly apparent. Even I had to admit it, though it filled me with despair that I should never rival her.

"I shall not tell you yet, Isabel," he teased. "Be patient. But it will be before you are old and gray."

So Isabel was to be wed. I picked the idea apart later in the chamber I shared with her. I would be next. How long would I have to wait? Not until I was Isabel's age, I hoped. I wanted to know *now*, even as I feared leaving Middleham. I vowed to discover all I could.

It was most frustrating. Isabel might fret, I might keep my ears stretched wide for any crumb of information, but the Earl was concerned with an outbreak of cattle thievery in the area whilst the Countess, chivvying our steward, waged war against an infestation of lice and ticks with the warmer weather. Nothing would satisfy her until the whole place and the people in it reeked of the pungent summer savory that grew in abundance in the herb garden and we itched less. Then, when I had all but abandoned my quest, the Earl summoned Richard to his private room where he invariably conducted business. The meeting was sufficiently unusual for me to take note. It proved to be a long and private conversation, and I knew it because I waited in the passage outside to grab Richard as soon as he emerged.

"What's it about?" I asked Francis Lovell, who passed from kitchen to stables, a flat bread and a slab of cheese in his hand.

"*I* don't know." He shrugged carelessly. "He'll tell us soon enough."

The door opened and Richard stepped out into the corridor. "Are you in the Earl's bad books?" I demanded before he could draw breath.

"No." Faintly bemused, he looked as if he had difficulty in collecting his thoughts, much as he had the day he had sat by me after the blow to his head. For a moment he stood immobile, hands fisted on hips, studying the ground at his feet. Then, aware of his audience of two, me demanding, Francis frankly curious: "It's nothing of importance." But we would not be brushed off.

"Is the Earl at odds again with the King? Is that it?" Francis inquired.

"When is he not these days? But the Earl is not at odds with me."

"Tell us!" I demanded.

"No. I am sworn to secrecy and *you* cannot keep secrets." He looked at me with all seriousness and I did not care for the sharp appraisal in his stare. "*You* are not old enough to keep some secrets." And, moving off with Francis, taking a bite of the flat bread, he refused to say more.

To my disgust he remained as tight as an oyster.

But that night as Bessie combed and braided my hair the thought came to me, the faintest glimmer that grew until it burned as bright as a warning beacon. Isabel's mysterious bridegroom, of course. Was he to be Richard Plantagenet? It took my breath away. I gasped, making my nurse chide me for not sitting still, thinking that my reaction was her own doing. I shook my head. Would it not be the perfect solution? A marriage made in heaven, as my mother had said. They were of an age, related by blood. He was the King's brother, important enough to be sought as a groom for a Neville bride. Isabel and Richard. Why not?

A dark and unpleasant emotion filled every portion of my heart with a pain that was all but physical. I knew jealousy when I saw it, but I had never felt anything like this. Isabel was sitting back against the pillows of our bed, braiding her own curling fall of hair. I scowled in her direction. Did she know? She had said nothing. I couldn't imagine her remaining silent on such an issue. She must have felt the force of my hostility, because she looked up and returned my frown.

"And what's wrong with you, little sister?"

"Nothing!" I hunched a shoulder. "Isabel . . . would you wish to marry Richard?"

"Richard? Don't be ridiculous. Of course not. He's not at all suitable."

I was not convinced. Richard as Isabel's husband seemed eminently suitable. I would never accept it. I did not know why, but I detested the thought. When I clutched my belly and groaned in a fit of childish drama, Bessie accused me of overeating the cherry tarts and dosed me with a bitter infusion of angelica. I did not tell her the truth. How could I when I could not yet interpret the pain that stabbed at me when I envisioned Isabel standing with her hands clasped warmly within Richard's?

"Nor would Richard want you!" It was the only response I could come up with. And I prayed that it was so.

I did not have to stoke my resentment and bad temper for longer than a day. There arrived at Middleham an imposing guest. All banners and gleaming horseflesh, more ostentatiously splendid than even the Earl when he traveled, George Plantagenet, Duke of Clarence, came to stay. Brother to Richard and Edward, his age somewhere between the two, he was unknown to me. I would never have seen the family resemblance between him and Richard, but they greeted each other with the obvious affection of a shared childhood, a shared exile as I now knew, as the younger two brothers of the family. Clarence was tall and impressively built, with waving fair hair, so fair as to shine almost gold in the morning light. His eyes were a pale blue when they darted over those who came to greet him. I heard Isabel sigh as she stood beside me to make her curtsy to this royal Prince, who was far more imposing and eye-catching than Richard. Just like Sir Lancelot, I thought on the instant I saw him.

He was received with all honor. Wined and dined, given the best bedchamber, with fine linen sheets and scented water to bathe in. He rode the estate with my father and with Richard at his side, freed from his lessons for the duration. He bowed over Isabel's hand, which drove her into a flutter of delight, more or less ignored me as a young person below his condescension, and spoke imperiously to the hench-men. Terrifyingly handsome, he reduced me in that first moment to shocked and silent admiration.

"Now, why do you suppose the insufferable Clarence has graced us with his presence?" Francis pursed his lips.

"Don't you like him?" I asked.

He slanted me a glance. "Like? Not the issue. He's arrogant and self-important. I don't trust him, for sure."

"You know nothing about him," pronounced Isabel with a depart-ing flounce. "*I* think he is magnificent!"

"But why is he here?" Francis repeated.

Discovery came quickly. After supper in one of the private par-lors rather than in the more public space of the great hall, the Earl unveiled his plans.

"I have given thought to your marriages." He addressed Isabel and myself as we applied ourselves to the platters of fruit and sweet-meats. "Isabel. It is my wish that you marry George of Clarence. And Anne . . . you will wed Richard of Gloucester when you are a little older. What could be more appropriate than Plantagenet princes for both Neville heiresses? As the most powerful subject in England, I can look as high as I choose. There is no one more suitable for either of you, in England or in Europe."

I dropped my spoon with a clatter onto the table. If I had not been so astonished, my attention tightly bound up in my own shock at the news, I would have seen Isabel blush rosily and glance through her lashes at her betrothed. He appeared unconcerned, turning his knife over and over in slender fingers. But I was so taken aback by these plans for my future, I did not know where to look. I focused on the glowing ruby set in the chain around my father's neck. Such a depth of color. I was dragged into its heart as thoughts rushed through my mind.

Richard? I would wed Richard when I was older?

Richard was looking at me. I could feel the silent stare of those unfathomable eyes. So, unable to prevent it, I stared back and would not drop my eyes even when my cheeks became hot and I was near overcome with the urge to blink. He saw what I was doing and smiled. I blinked. I felt even hotter.

"Will it be soon?" Isabel asked.

"For you, yes." Obviously warmed by his success, the Earl was in the mood to be expansive. "The matter is already in hand. We have need of a papal dispensation because you are cousins in the second degree. I foresee no problem. The Pope is open to persuasion, of a monetary kind if no other."

I did not fully grasp that part, but if my father saw no difficulty then I need not concern myself. Could he not arrange everything to his liking?

"One thing I would say." He spoke to the two Plantagenet brothers primarily, but his gaze also took in Isabel and myself. "Until it is arranged and until I have informed the King, you will not discuss this private matter beyond the walls of this room. It is a Neville family affair and should remain so until the marriage can proceed without hindrance."

So it was to be a secret. That appealed to me. But why must the King not know? Surely he would not disapprove of his brothers being united with the daughters of his chief counselor. And would his permission not be needed for so critical an alliance?

"It is equally a matter for the Plantagenets as well as Nevilles, my lord. Are you sure Edward will not object?" The Countess had sat silently beside the Earl throughout the proceedings, but now echoed my own thoughts.

"How can he?" the Earl demanded. "He has left me no choice. Not one eligible match after the Woodville inundations! Where do I find a high-ranking husband for my daughters? Does he expect me to wed them to a common citizen? A landless laborer? Unless I look abroad—and I think he will not want the Neville lands and fortune handed to a foreign Prince. No, my lady. These marriages will strengthen the English monarchy, with the Nevilles tied to the Plantagenets even more firmly than they are at present. How can he possibly object? I am Warwick. Am I not worthy of this supreme alliance?"

My mother's doubt continued to hover like a black cloud.

"It is to our good fortune," the Earl assured her, clasping her wrist in his. "Let us drink to it. And to the future stability of the realm."

"And you, my lord of Clarence?" the Countess addressed herself to Richard's gleaming brother. "What are your thoughts?"

"I can think of no better union, my lady." He bowed over his platter, smiled with evident satisfaction. "Name any man in England who would not want to take a Neville heiress as his wife. I am grateful that you find me worthy." His expression was a masterpiece of self-deprecation. I did not believe him, but he knew how to apply charm.

No one asked Richard.

As we left the room I saw my mother look across to the Earl. Distress showed on her face; she did not approve of our good fortune. But she saw me watching her and fixed her face into a bright smile, rising to her feet to walk to my side and wrap her arm around me.

"It will be a good marriage for you," she whispered against my hair. "You know Richard well. It is a good basis—friendship—for marriage."

I wasn't so sure. I wasn't sure of anything other than my relief that Richard would not wed Isabel.

The next day I climbed to the wall walk, where I found Richard propping up the battlements, looking out toward the low hills to the south, watching the distant cloud of dust where Clarence and his escort made speed toward York, as if he wished that he too were leaving. Perhaps he did, although from his expression I surmised it was not a happy thought. He did not at first react when I leaned at his side. I waited impatiently.

"Well? What do you think of the plans for our future?" Richard asked at last, continuing to rest his arms against the stone parapet as he looked sideways at me. At that moment he seemed impressively adult. He was still not tall, but taller than I, his eyes uncomfortably direct. His forthright question made me feel foolishly young and ignorant of the ways of the world in making and breaking alliances. What would this stern young man have to say to me, a barely grown girl?

"I . . ." I didn't know how to reply to him. Only that I needed to know what *he* thought. It should not have been so very important. Girls of my status were so often married to men whom they had never met. But this was Richard, who had lived under the same roof for four years, who had competed with me at archery and, I suspected, allowed me to win. Who had ridden with me when I had gone hawking for the first time. Had let me hold his goshawk on my wrist and did not laugh or mock when I first flinched from her fierce beak and beating wings. This was Richard, who had given me a little metal bird. What did he think? Would he hate to be married to me?

Seeing me, for once, speechless, he grasped the fur border of my cloak and pulled me to sit on the top step of the stair that led back down to the courtyard, out of the sharp breeze.

"Stuck for words? Remarkable!"

I kicked him on the ankle and he laughed. That was better. I felt my nerves relax in my throat. "I don't know what to say."

"Do you want to know what I think?" he asked.

"Yes."

"I don't find the idea objectionable. Do you?"

I thought. "No. Just strange."

"Marriage to a changeling, as you once so unkindly pointed out." But his smile was soft, even understanding. I blushed at the cruel memory. "It will be some years yet," he added, perhaps mistaking my pink cheeks for apprehension. "You're only eleven—too young to be a bride."

"But I think you'll leave soon." It saddened me.

"Next year. When I am of age. I hope that Edward summons me to court."

"So then I shall not see you for years."

"No. Not for a little time. But when you have grown up, when we are wed, we'll live together."

"Yes. Will you like it?" I risked a glance at him, hoping I did not see dismay.

"I expect I shall. Especially if you stop asking questions."

"I could." It suddenly mattered desperately that he should like it.

Richard put his arm around my shoulders, a warm hug. "Don't worry; I won't beat you."

"I should think not! I am a Neville." My sense of dignity returned rapidly. "And I promise I won't tease you."

A sharp voice carried up from below, aimed in our direction. I could not hear the words but knew its owner: Master Ellerby, come to discover the whereabouts of his absent pupil. Lady Masham, I suspected, would be on the lookout for me.

"I am needed," Richard said. "I've neglected my duties in the stables too long. My betrothal means nothing to the horses I must groom!" He stood and pulled me up, brushed a hand down my dust-speckled skirts. I still did not know what to say to him at this moment

of parting. Somehow our relationship had changed in that one pronouncement from my father. He was still Richard. Still an intriguing
mix of cousin and brother, of henchman and royal guest in our house.
And yet he was now so much more.

I think he saw my perplexity and demanded nothing from me as
he set off down the steps in front of me. Then he stopped so quickly
that I almost fell over his heels. He bent and picked up a tail feather
from one of the cockerels in a molt. What it was doing on the battlements I do not know—I found my thoughts incongruously taken up
with this thing of such little importance in comparison with the plans
for my future. The feather was green and black, long and shining still,
iridescent in the dim light.

"I have given you a bird. And now a feather. As a promise of
my regard." With a neat gesture he reached up and stuck it in through
the fillet that held my veil, so that it drooped ridiculously over my
brow. Then with a chivalry he never showed to me unless it was a
formal occasion in adult company, he took my cold fingers and kissed
them.

"Good day to you, Lady Anne Neville."

I can still remember, all these years after, the brush of his lips
against my skin on those cold battlements, the complex weave of my
feelings for him.

Overnight my sister, Isabel, became impossible. She summoned Margery to help her dress with an arrogant gesture of her hand as if she
were Queen Elizabeth herself. Looking down her narrow nose, she
informed Lady Masham, always a colorless lady, that the days of her
lessons were at an end. Until the Countess heard and took a hand.
The royal demeanor slipped somewhat when the Duchess apparent
was once more compelled to read the text of the day and practice her
sewing of neat seams.

Yet, when we were alone, still she was unquenchable.

"Duchess of Clarence." She spun in a circle, her silk skirts brushing against the tapestries that decorated the walls in the corridor where we walked. "A royal brother for my husband. Wife of the male heir to the throne of England. Would you have believed it? I could be Queen of England. I could almost pray God that the Woodville woman only carries girls and not the son King Edward longs for. Am I, a Neville, not more worthy to rule than she?"

"Isabel!" Her vicious condemnation of the Queen shocked me.

"What?" She tossed her head so that her veiling shimmered in the light. "No one likes her. Why should *I* wish her well?"

I could not argue against it. So I did not. "But would you wish to be Queen?"

"I would!"

There was no talking to her. She looked at me as if I were the least of her subjects, as if she might insist that I kneel before her in reverence, as the Queen did at her churching after the birth of her daughters. I escaped before it crossed her mind.

I knew which royal brother I preferred.

Well, it did not last. My good fortune was of short duration, my betrothal and Isabel's being canceled as fast as they had been implemented. Hardly had I become used to the prospect of being a Plantagenet bride than Richard was peremptorily summoned to London to present himself at court before his brother, King Edward. The brief dictate contained no indication of its purpose. Nor did Chester Herald, who delivered it, gloriously appareled in his Plantagenet tabard. He waited, impatient and dust smeared, to escort his young charge back to Westminster with no explanation. Or if he knew, he was not saying.

I existed in those following days in an uneasy agony of uncertainty. My first concern—would Richard ever return to Middleham? It was generally understood that he would take his place at court eventually when he came of age, at least a year into the future. But would Edward demand his presence early? Never had the hills around

Middleham when I rode out with Isabel and Francis seemed so empty, so lacking in color and excitement.

"When do you think he will return?" I asked Francis once again.

"Don't ask me. You keep asking me and I know no more than you."

"Will the King have heard of the proposed marriages?"

"If he hasn't he must be a fool. And a fool Edward is not! Our King has a network of spies second to none." Francis stared thoughtfully between his horse's ears. "Apart from that, what in God's name was the point in the Earl swearing Clarence to secrecy? That man has no knowledge of self-control or discretion. D'you think the Earl wanted the King to discover—to save time telling him?"

I thought about this as the sharp breeze whipped my pony's mane and my veil into a thorough tangle. "Will the King allow it, d'you suppose, or will he forbid it?" Isabel had cantered on ahead with a groom in attendance. I would never have raised the subject if she were within hearing distance. The whole household was complicit in a silent campaign to distract her from either her outrageous dreams of grandeur or her immoderate fury that the King might indeed denounce her royal union.

"He might forbid it." Francis's reply, his bland expression, were entirely diplomatic. Until I caught the twitch of the muscle in his jaw as he hid the laughter. "Don't fret, Anne. If you can't have Gloucester, you can have me after all. You can be Lady Lovell and reign over all my establishments!"

"Ha! As if I would want you!"

"About as much as I would want you, sweet-tempered Anne!"

I gave up, sighed. There was no sense or help here. I kicked the pony's plump sides and followed my sister.

Richard was not to stay at Westminster and immerse himself in the heady delights of power and politics, as I had feared. He returned to Middleham within the month, without the Earl, who, whatever his feelings on the matter, was sent to head another official embassy to the courts of Europe.

"The King! He won't allow it, will he?" I asked within minutes of Richard's escaping from my mother's presence.

"No. He won't. He said he wouldn't countenance it, by God!" Well, that was blunt enough.

Richard took my arm and pulled me along with him as he strode down the steps into the courtyard, round the buttress and into the enclosed garden between wall and keep.

"What did the King say?" I asked when Richard finally stopped and I could draw breath. I did not know what was uppermost: disappointment at my unbetrothed state or relief that life would settle back into its normal routines.

"What didn't he say!" A ghost of a smile flittered for a moment as he leaned back against a rose-drenched wall and puffed out a breath. "I have never seen Edward so angry. Not so much with us—Clarence and myself—but with the Earl, I think for his presumption. Although Edward's words were short and sharp enough when he summoned the two of us to hear his opinions." He gave a harsh laugh. "Especially when Clarence had the temerity to inform him that he thought it was as good a match as any and what was the problem with it? Enough to say—Edward has forbidden it. And informed the Pope that there must be no dispensation on pain of England's severe displeasure."

"So that's an end to it?"

"Yes. We are no longer betrothed."

I scowled my disapproval of what I could not change. "How did he find out?"

"Clarence, of course." Richard's mouth curled in disdain. "He couldn't avoid bragging, over a surfeit of ale! His good fortune in snaring a wealthy Neville heiress."

Well, Francis had read that situation accurately enough. Away to our right, from the open window up above our heads, came the sound of some commotion, then a squawk of sheer outrage from Isabel.

Richard raised his eyebrows and, as one, we withdrew farther behind the overgrown roses.

"Does Edward consider that we are not high enough for a Plantagenet match?" I whispered.

Richard shrugged, patently uncomfortable, but without reply, until I nudged him impatiently. "Anne—" He turned to look at me, our heads close together under the perfumed overhang. "It's not that Edward thinks you're not high enough. It's the direct opposite. That he would not want the Nevilles to be too close to the center of power. If Elizabeth fails to bear a son, Clarence will become King if Edward dies before him. And Isabel would be Queen, putting your father the Earl far too close to the throne. Edward doesn't want it. I understand it, I suppose. So instead of not being important enough, you are far *too* important to be taken lightly into an alliance."

I nodded sadly, even as his treating me as his equal in political understanding pleased me inordinately. How would I not appreciate the importance of his pronouncement, when politics had been discussed around me and over my head at every meal as far back as I could remember? "I understand. Strong political reasons." A favorite phrase of my mother's. Now I knew what she meant.

"Yes. Strong political reasons. The strongest. How could we expect anything other in the disposition of our lives? We are not free to choose as we wish, Anne." I smiled—bravely, I hoped—whilst Richard studied the tree before us. "I would say . . ." he added, a little gruffly, "I regret it. I would like to have wed you rather than any lady I know."

"Truly?"

He leaned close, a little reserved, and kissed my cheek.

"Truly."

Startled, I laughed. "I would have liked it too."

Which for some reason prompted Richard to kiss my lips also. Soft. A mere moth's wing of a caress that startled me more. And then he pulled back.

I watched him as he smiled at my surprise, trying to untangle my thoughts. He was mine. I wanted him as *my* friend, as *my* companion. I was still too young for much else, yet I found myself drawn into those introspective, secretive eyes. With those I swore he would bewitch any girl. Not with the golden beauty of his brother, as Isabel was always quick to point out, but with something far more enticing, far more intriguing. Yes, I wanted him, I acknowledged, as I accepted that I could never have him.

"What does my father say to all this?" It was the only possible glimmer of hope, if the Earl could persuade the King to change his mind.

"Very little and in words as curt as the King's. He's agreed with Edward that the Plantagenet-Neville alliance is off. They clasped hands over it."

So that was the end of it. My sister and I were back in the marriage market—with no possible bridegrooms on the horizon—and all the future uncertain.

CHAPTER FOUR

In the year I reached my twelfth birthday—and in my own mind became full-grown—the assured, confident direction of my life was to change forever. On the political front it was the year of "the Earl's Great Rift," as the Countess dubbed it in a moment of mordant anxiety. When my father found his plans for a French alliance irrevocably torn up and the King's feet set firmly on the path to an alliance with Burgundy, with the Woodvilles crowing over their success, he stormed from Westminster to Middleham, vowing never to set foot in Edward's presence again unless Edward made a complete volte-face. There was no hope of that. Within the week Earl Rivers, the Queen's father, was appointed Constable of England. The final blow was the betrothal of the King's sister, the Lady Margaret, to the Duke of Burgundy.

"Will your sister enjoy her marriage to the Duke?" I asked Richard, secretly horrified to imagine being sent to live so far from my home and those I loved, with a man I did not know. The Lady Margaret might never return to England.

"I don't suppose she has much to say in the matter." Richard dismissed my concerns with what I considered coldhearted indifference.

"Last year the bridegroom was to be Portuguese. Then French. I think she will not mind who it is, as long as it happens!"

I too might be destined for a foreign husband in some distant country. It was a chilling thought, as was the knowledge that we were like to be cast into political isolation. Any lingering hope in Isabel's breast for her marriage to Clarence was snuffed out, even when, in a sour spirit of compromise because he had no choice, the Earl went to Coventry to make his peace with the King. The omens for the future were not good.

At home my outlook was even less cheerful, because it was the year I fell into love after hovering precariously, unknowingly, on its brink. An entirely adult emotion that exploded through my blood, creating a fire that would burn forever and never release me.

It was all the fault of Saint George and the dragon.

In October of that year, Richard came of age. We celebrated with gifts presented to mark the occasion. Edward sent him a full suit of armor, swathed in cloth and soft leather against the rigors of travel. A Milanese confection, chased and gilded, a magnificent affair from the visored bascinet to the pointed solerets, it would encase him cap-a-pie. I imagined it would draw all eyes on a battlefield or in a tournament. My father gave him a destrier, a true warhorse of his own breeding at Sheriff Hutton, with some Arab blood in its proud head carriage and arched neck. Dark bay and fiery, it was of the weight to carry him into any battle. They would make a splendid pair.

My undoing was at the evening banquet, where it was decided that we, the younger members of the household, should enact the chivalric tale of Saint George and the dragon, our own version of a mummers' play. We'd seen it performed often enough—crude and popular in the repertoire of traveling players—so it took little preparation beyond a good memory for speeches and a delving into a box of costumes and other oddments from a decade of Twelfth Night productions. Costumes, armor, hobbyhorses, and masks—much chipped wood, scuffed gilding, and curled board, but all we needed.

Richard, of course, made a courageous Saint George. Francis

Lovell was in character as a wily dragon. Isabel would take the role of Virgin Maiden to be rescued and saved from a fate worse than death. But since I made a stand, refusing to be pushed into the background as the Virgin's serving woman, there were two of us beautiful damsels to be rescued.

There was much posturing and declaiming.

"Come to our aid, bold knight. Or we shall surely perish." Isabel wrung her hands. I fell to my knees in dramatic grief.

"Halt, sir dragon." Saint George stood foursquare before the terrifying beast. "Do you dare attack these sweet maidens?"

The dragon in mask and scaled body with a cloth tail bellowed and vowed his intent to eat us all. Clad in old gowns, once sumptuous but now musty and mildewed, that hung on our figures and trailed the floor, with diaphanous veils floating romantically from brow and shoulder, we maidens clutched our bosoms as symbols of our virtue and wailed at the sight of the dragon come to ravish us.

The dragon roared. Virgin Isabel pleaded for her life. I remained on my knees, dumbstruck.

Because I found myself unable to drag my eyes from my rescuer. In that moment Richard filled my whole horizon, his face pale with the dramatic tension of the moment, shoulders braced, all knightly courtesy and determination to overcome the brazen creature. Handsome, no—his face was too thinly austere for conventional comeliness. But striking, yes—with all the glamour of his gold armor. His voice raised in authoritative demand was suddenly, disconcertingly adult. His dark eyes blazed as he stared down the dragon; his dark hair was tousled from nervous fingers. I could not look away. Forced to take one deep breath, I found it difficult to take another. Standing, I retreated to Isabel's side. My lips parted, but I could think of none of the words I should speak, even when my sister's elbow found sharp contact with my ribs. I had fallen headlong and breathtakingly into love with Richard Plantagenet.

I did not tell Richard of my new feelings for him. Why? Because I promptly pretended that I fell out of love again within the week, when

I caught him kissing a kitchen maid. That my heroic and fascinating cousin should choose to kiss Maude, a flirtatious and extremely pretty kitchen maid, in the shadowed corner behind the dairy when I came upon him—it turned my bright daydreams to the sour lees of old ale. These kisses were not formal or passionless, mere bushes of lip against fingers or cheek. They opened my eyes to reality. Whispered words, more heated kisses, fine-boned hands that stroked and caressed. Maude giggled and tossed her head.

Fleeing to stand in the center of my room in the dim light, I ran my hands down my sides, over my chest, dismayed at the evidence of unformed waist and hips, lean flanks, the flattest of bosoms. None of the womanly curves that Maude flaunted. As for my face, I had studied it in my mother's precious mirror. The far-more-desirable Maude's fair skin and velvet brown eyes would attract. Why would he not kiss Maude, who had all the attributes I lacked? He would not kiss me with such fervor! Richard would never see me in such a light.

So my love was dead, I told myself. Killed by his perfidious preference for another. Not that he had ever led me to believe otherwise; honesty forced itself into my bitter thoughts. He held me in some affection perhaps, but I wanted more than that. I wanted those intense kisses for myself. I wept hot tears of hopelessness.

When I could weep no more, I practiced my own version of my mother's severe dignity. I forced myself to stay away from him, chin raised, head tilted, the coldest of shoulders. I stared my reproach but closed my lips when Maude served Richard with ale and a tilted chin, and he smiled that slow smile. My words were short and sharp when conversation was needed. Richard frowned, perplexed at my ill manners, but for the most part ignored my attempts to impress him with my heartbroken dignity. He asked Isabel if I was suffering from some form of ague.

It hurt. My feelings were not dead at all.

"What is it like to be in love?" I asked Isabel, driven against my better instincts to talk to someone who might know. "Is it painful?"

Isabel shrugged her disinterest. "I have no idea."

"Do you not love Clarence?"

"No!"

"But you would wed him."

"It is my greatest wish." Her smile was full of pitying condescension. "But love is irrelevant to people of our standing."

Yet I thought she lied. I thought her heart was more than a little engaged despite her terse denial. Nor did love seem irrelevant to me. It was a most painful part of my existence. How could I love him and he not love me? I hated him for it and determined to have no pleasure in life.

"I am bidden to London, madam. Immediately."

I could see the simmer of anticipation in Richard. Despite my continuing coolness toward him, it was the news I had been dreading. Relations between the King and the Earl continued to lean and totter endlessly on a knife edge. So Richard would be gone at the King's order, away from the Earl's influence, and would never return. I hugged my silent misery as the preparation and packing up of his possessions, the leavetakings, all merged together into one throbbing wound.

The Countess embraced him with real affection and a quick sadness. "We shall miss you. You have been like my own son to me."

Francis staked a claim for future friendship. "I shall demand your royal attention when I too come to London. A tankard of ale, at least, for old times' sake. Or will the Duke of Gloucester be too high for the likes of me?" Francis demanded with the sly humor of deep friendship.

Isabel wished him well in her self-important fashion.

Stony faced, ungraciously monosyllabic, I swore silently that I did not care. That his absence would make no difference to me. In reality I was frozen with dismay. I had long ago given up the pretense that I did not care, although I guarded my words and my actions around him. The days of youthful confidences had long gone. Now I might never see him again unless we visited court too, an unlikely event, given the increasingly bad blood between our families. It cast a dark shadow over that cold January day with the promise of snow on the northern hills. It was no colder than my heart.

"Will you not give me your hand in farewell, cousin?" Richard had maneuvered a moment of privacy within the swirling movement and bustle of the courtyard.

I did so, curtly. "Godspeed, Richard."

"I think you will not miss me."

"Of course I shall." I went through the demands of courtesy.

"Then adieu, Anne." He made a courtly bow with his feather-trimmed hat, as if he would mock my poor manners. "One day I shall see you at court too."

"Perhaps."

On a thought he leaned over to whisper in my ear, before I could pull away, "Perhaps we would not have suited after all. Your affection for me seems to have quite vanished, little cousin. I would want a warmer bride at my side."

"No, we should definitely not have suited," I snapped back. "For I would demand constancy and loyalty in a husband."

Richard laughed aloud at my stubbornness, eyes sparkling. I could see the excitement, the exhilaration. He wanted to be gone. After planting a kiss smartly on my cheek, he was mounted and away.

Thus it was a cold departure between us, and all my fault. I had discovered that it was in my nature to destroy what I desired most by willful contrariness. If I could not have his love, I would not tolerate the mild warmth of his friendship. Now lonely and adrift and unquestionably guilty, trailing along the battlements to the spot where he used to stand to look out toward the south, I set myself to wallow in my own self-inflicted misery. For the first time in my life the confines of Middleham hemmed me in and my desire was to escape. If we were to go to London, Richard would be there.

Calais! Not Warwick. Not London. But *Calais?*

Why were we to travel to Calais?

It was eight years since either I or Isabel had last been to Calais, so I had no memory of it. The Earl was often there, but why should he suddenly take it into his mind to transport his whole family with him? The Countess, who received the instructions from the Earl, saw no need to enlighten us.

I did not like it. There were too many secrets by half.

We journeyed south, rapidly, a strange journey, almost as if in flight from some unforeseen danger. First to Warwick Castle, not stopping there above two nights, but met there by my father. Then on to the coast at Sandwich, where we took ship. There was a tension in the party and between my parents that could almost be tasted. The uneasy crossing was also to match our mood, the seas cold and gray. Moreover, barely had we set foot on land, our household disembarked into the comfort of the great castle there with its formidable garrison, than the Earl turned on his heel and left again.

"But why are we here, madam?" Isabel asked crossly, with no attempt to disguise her disapproval of the whole venture. With betrothal in her mind, and robbed of one bridegroom, she knew equally as well as I that this military outpost was no place to achieve another.

"And where is the Earl gone?" I added.

"Returned to England, to the King's service." It was the only explanation the Countess was prepared to give in all the dreary weeks of waiting—for what I didn't know—that were to follow. I had the dismaying sensation that we had been abandoned there. But if the Earl had mended his friendship with the King, why must we be in this voluntary exile? More dark secrets as we sat in our stronghold in Calais, grasping at any crumb of news, all through that spring and early summer. We knew that the Earl spent time at Sandwich, where he was fitting out his ship the *Trinity*. The Queen gave birth to yet another girl. There were rebellions in England, in the north, against high taxation. Edward had left London to collect an army to subdue them.

"Will the Earl march with him?" I asked, with ulterior motives. "And Richard too?"

But the Countess's distracted reply troubled me even more. I had never known her so anxious as she was in those days. "Who knows the outcome. But at least the rebellions will keep Edward from concentrating too much on what we might be doing here!"

But what are we doing here?

I had given up expecting a reply. As for Richard, I gleaned comments as a mouse would seek out and store ears of corn against a hard winter. He was at the King's right hand. He was marching north with him. He was present in Edward's councils with Earl Rivers and my lord Hastings. He had become an important man at court. Did he ever think of me? The passing weeks did nothing to make me miss him less.

Finally, hopelessly, to make some contact, however ephemeral, I was driven to pen a letter that I passed to one of the couriers who frequently traveled back and forth across the channel. I addressed it boldly to the Duke of Gloucester. Writing it had taken a long time and much thought because I did not know what I wanted to say other than to beg his forgiveness for my ill temper and ask him not to forget me when all around was new and exiting for him. Eventually it was done.

> *To my cousin Richard Plantagenet,*
>
> *We are settled here in Calais. I know that you are engaged with your brother the King in putting down the rebels in the north. I pray for your health and your safety.*
>
> *Perhaps one day I shall return to London and we can meet again as friends.*
>
> *I regret the nature of our parting. It was entirely my fault. Perhaps you could find it in you to forgive me.*
>
> *Your cousin,*
> *Anne Neville*

Excruciatingly formal and not at all what I wished to say. That I missed him. I could not say that. That I loved him. I could hardly lay my sore heart at his feet. In the end, what had I said that was worth the sending? And I had no knowledge of whether it would ever reach its objective, and, of course, I received no reply. If Richard was in the north facing a hostile army of rebels, what time would he have for a foolish letter such as mine? In my lowest moments I could see him in my mind's eye, crushing it in his mailed fist with a grunt of impatience as he spurred his destrier into the thick of battle.

"I shall never see him again, Margery." I sniffed.

"Not for a little while, at least, mistress," she admitted, reading the subject of my thoughts. She opened her mouth as if she would say more. Closed it.

"What do you know that I don't?" I demanded sharply.

"Nothing, lady."

I didn't believe her, but my hopes died with the flicker of a spent candle.

At last—at last!—there were sails on the horizon, and more than one vessel. Then they were arrived and disembarking, the *Trinity* at the forefront, so that I went with the Countess and Isabel down to the quay, formally dressed and in a celebratory mood. Immediately the Earl strode across to our little knot of welcomers, his smile lighting his whole countenance.

"Is all well?" The Countess accepted his salute, hands grasping his as if she would not release them.

"Better than you could ever hope."

"And the dispensation?" I heard her murmur as she raised his fingers to her lips.

"I have it. It has all but beggared me, but it's safe." He clapped their joined hands to his breast, as if to a document, smiling down at her. Then he looked across, his eyes all for my sister. "Isabel—" He beckoned. "I bring your bridegroom at last. I think you will not be disappointed." The Earl stepped back to allow us a clear view of the man who came behind him.

The Duke of Clarence.

Isabel dimpled and curtsied, face pink with disbelieving joy. I simply stood and watched as Clarence approached, bowing with studied elegance. He lifted my sister to her feet, kissed her fingers, and expressed his pleasure in a voice as slick as close-cut velvet. "Lady Isabel. It enchants me to be here. I have lived for this day for so long."

I simply stood like a carved marble statue, denied of thought or movement. I know I did not curtsy as I ought. I could not believe it. Was this what my father had been plotting? Outright rebellion against the King by bringing Clarence to marry my sister against Edward's express orders?

Edward would never forgive us.

Edward would never support this match, and Richard, standing solidly beside his brother the King, would be divided from me forever.

I wished that trivial, ridiculous letter unsent.

I wished it even more two days later. The day after Isabel's marriage, celebrated with much pomp, the Earl and Clarence did not hunt with the rest of their guests but took themselves to a private chamber. By the end of the day there was a document, written and copied by the clerks, openly distributed for all to read, and sent to England on the first ship, to be proclaimed in London.

I read it.

It was not difficult to obtain a copy wet from the clerk's pen. It was an astonishing piece of reckless treason that finally buried even the slightest residue of hope of my being reunited with Richard. Its words were uncompromising. King Edward was guilty of poor government, willfully ignoring the Princes of the Blood—the Nevilles, of course—who would advise him well, but guilty of giving ear and patronage to evil advisers named as the Woodvilles. They must be removed for the good of the realm. If the King did not comply with the wishes of his subjects, then he should suffer the penalty of other feckless monarchs who had brought their country low. Did he not deserve the same punishment as the ill-fated Edward II and Richard II? I had learned my lessons well. They had both been done to death by foul means in distant castles. Whilst Henry VI, also included in the list, aging and mad, was a prisoner in the Tower.

All true men of England should rally to the Neville standard, to the Earl of Warwick, who would right the country's wrongs.

Well! This was what the Earl had plotted in all these weeks I had remained in ignorance in Calais. The words I held between my hands were dangerously treasonous, a direct and open challenge to Edward's authority, enough to put a price on my father's head. It would brand us all traitors.

When I showed her the letter, all Isabel could see was the glitter of the Crown that would grace her brow. "We shall not be traitors! Don't be stupid, Anne! I shall be Queen of England before the year is out, when my father has removed King Edward and made Clarence King." She closed her ears to my anxieties.

I was not so sanguine.

"Is this a declaration of war?" I demanded of the Countess when I could not bear the uncertainty longer. "Does he intend to depose Edward?"

I thought she looked as astounded as I felt at the length to which the Earl was prepared to go. "I can see no other outcome," the Countess confirmed. Her face had the sallow pallor of candle wax.

Neither could I. As daughter of a traitor, what hope was there for me now? Richard would surely hate me.

CHAPTER FIVE

sabel retched over the bowl held by the indomitably cheerful Margery. "I wish I could die," she said, gasping.

"No such thing," Margery soothed. "My lord of Clarence has performed more than well. Such a potent man beneath all that pretty gold hair." From my position at the far side of the room I smirked at her less-than-respectful observation. "An heir! And so soon!" she continued. "Let us give thanks to the blessed Virgin."

Isabel pressed a square of linen to her mouth as another spasm gripped her. I might have escaped but the Countess swept in, followed by a serving girl and a covered platter.

"We will soon put you to rights. Drink this, Isabel."

I had to admire the Countess. As if she had no thought beyond Isabel's ills, as if the Earl were not engaged in armed rebellion against the King, she took my mewling sister in hand.

Isabel gulped, swallowed desperately. "I cannot. . . ."

"Don't be stubborn." I could smell the infusion, the sharp, fresh aroma of mint steeped in boiling water that pervaded the whole room. When Isabel obeyed, the Countess nodded, satisfied. "Good! You are not ill, Isabel. Merely breeding. For which you should be grateful, within weeks of your marriage."

"I don't want this . . ." Isabel whined.

"Why not?" I could no longer keep silent as envy of my sister's Plantagenet husband once more coated me in shameful malice. "It's what you wanted, well enough, when we were at Calais! A husband and a Plantagenet heir. Now you have your wish! You have both."

I might scowl at her, but I was not truly so heartless, merely troubled and unbendingly hostile to the man who had put her in this situation and then, it seemed to me, unfeelingly abandoned her. Isabel had not set eyes on her royal husband since that brief interlude in Calais, now two months since. The bridal rejoicings had been cut short when the Earl and his fellow conspirators left immediately to return to England as an invading force, to raise men in Kent and march on London. From there the plan was to continue north to force Edward to come to terms. Meanwhile we were ensconced in Warwick Castle waiting for events to settle around us. At least Isabel's condition took our minds off other, more immediate concerns, such as the bloody penalty for treason, but Clarence could have come to see his wife.

"Where's Clarence?" she asked as she had asked so often. "Why is he not here with me?"

"He's in London, trying to reassure the Lord Mayor and Aldermen that the government of the realm won't disintegrate around their ears. He holds the reins of power there in the King's name. He'll come when he can." The Countess stroked the damp hair from Isabel's forehead. "Come and read to your sister, Anne. It will take her mind off her belly."

And I did because I felt sorry for her, left alone. As my heart was sore for my mother, who was able to do nothing but wait on events that shook the kingdom. I feared for the outcome.

We had not been short of news. There had been a battle, destroying much of the King's army, and the Woodvilles had come to grief in the aftermath. Earl Rivers and his son Sir John Woodville had been summarily executed. Impossibly weakened, Edward against all expectation had become my father's prisoner. Was not the whole world turned upside down, with the Earl, once the supreme champion of the Yorkist cause, now the arch adversary of the anointed wearer of the crown? Planning to call a parliament in York, my father took Edward north with him to Middleham under restraint. I knew that the Earl assured everyone that all his actions had the approval of the King, and that he had the King's signature on all documents with no duress, but how would we know truth from lies? I did not think Edward would make so amenable a captive.

"I wish we'd stayed in London." Isabel, revived and sitting up, interrupted my thoughts and the dolorous tale of the trials of Saint Ursula and the eleven thousand virgins.

"You would be just as sick in London as you are here," I muttered. "There are no court festivities to entertain you with Edward a prisoner."

"But think of the merchants, Anne, with their cloth and jewels and fashionable wares. Would that not be entertaining? We are in need of new gowns. You are growing by the day."

"Yes," I admitted, aware of the restrictions of my bodice. "And so will you be!"

Isabel laughed. "So I shall. Tell me that you would not wish to be there."

"I cannot. . . ." For I wished it above anything.

"And I would see Clarence. . . ."

Her face drooped again. All I could do was to hold her hand and continue to read, for I had no words of comfort. I knew the Duke of Gloucester too was in London, at liberty but impotent whilst Edward remained under my father's hand.

Yes, I too wished that we were in London.

I would have moped excessively except for an unexpected visitor to our gates. Francis Lovell arrived with a well-armed escort en route between London and Middleham. I missed his arrival; I would not miss his departure. So I sat in the stable yard on a mounting block and kicked my heels, as windblown and dust-covered as any of the

serving girls, rejoicing inwardly at seeing him again after almost a
year. I longed to talk to someone other than Isabel, someone who
would tell me what was happening outside the walls of this castle.
Someone who had been in London as well as at my father's side,
had experience of this country being torn in two again, York against
Lancaster.

I was considering the implication of that final thought when at
last he turned in through the gateway from the inner courtyard.

"Francis! Over here!"

I raised my hand, and, seeing me, he changed direction. It gave me
the chance to watch his athletic lope, to assess the changes wrought
by the intervening months. All I saw at first was the familiar gait,
the pleasing features, the deep affection in his instant grin. But then,
studying his face, I thought he looked older. Very much Lord Lovell
rather than the mischievous boy with whom I had grown up. There
was no mischief now lurking in his eyes. Indeed, I decided there was
an altogether harder edge about him, as if he had faced things that
were unpalatable and been forced to make a difficult choice. . . .

My breath caught. My heels stilled against the worn stone. My
thoughts circled around Francis's present position, his past and present loyalties. And it thudded home, a dull blow to just below my heart.
That all the ease of the past between Francis and my family could
well be destroyed. I could see the muscle tension in his shoulders, the
abrupt turn of his head to shout instructions for his escort to mount. I
could see it in new lines in his face. He was uncomfortable in this role
he was playing, in his visit to Warwick. I thought I knew exactly the
reason why. I had wanted so much to see him, talk with him, but it was
to prove a harsh lesson in reality for me, and one I would never forget.

"It's not good news." His first words as he hoisted himself on the
stone beside me. He knew I would want to know and made no attempt
to dilute the details. "There's a new outbreak of rebellion in the north,
this time in the name of old King Henry."

"Henry?" I had all but forgotten his existence, shut away in the
Tower. "Can the Earl not put the rebels down?"

"Not easily. Rumors abound that King Edward's dead, you see, since he has not been seen abroad for some weeks. So many would rather return to the old way than accept . . ." His words lurched to a halt.

"Than accept the authority of the Earl of Warwick?" I sighed.

"That's the sum of it." His mouth snapped shut like a trap. Then: "The Earl is finding it difficult to raise troops. I can tell you no more than that. Loyalty has become an issue for everyone. . . ."

I had been right in my suspicions. Dared I ask him outright? I tried a flanking action first. "Did you see Richard in London? Where are *his* loyalties?"

Francis's face became set in hard planes that I could not fail to interpret. "He's with Edward and will remain so committed. He'll not consider treason."

Treason! "Would he not even consider throwing in his lot with Clarence? With my father? For the good of the realm, if such a move will restore it to peace?"

"Never! He will not."

"And what of your loyalties, Francis?" We could fence around this for hours. I decided the more direct approach, at the cost perhaps of hurting him, was my only choice.

"As the ward of the Earl, my allegiance is to him," he replied, as if he had learned the words by rote but with his heart not in them. I could almost see his hackles rise and his eyes bored into mine. "What do you imply, lady?"

"I would never question your loyalty, Francis," I replied gently. "Forgive me. . . . But, Francis! Honest, now! You are the Earl's man—but have you never thought of going over to Richard?"

His answering smile was so faint as to be nonexistent as shadows chased across his face. "You were never one to mince words! I'm trying to compromise here, within the shades of loyalty." He sighed. "My whole life seems to be one of compromise!"

"Is it difficult? Is it possible to do so?" Would I ever be able to compromise if it were asked of me, to put my heart before my upbringing and sense of duty? I didn't know. I thought it would be an impossible decision to make.

"Difficult! Ha! I detest it! Anne . . . I hope you never have to make such choices."

How terrible this choice was for him. His inclination based on deep and lasting friendship was to stand at Richard's side. On the other side of the coin, the bonds of warmth and compassion, of family, created in our household where he had been raised, remained firm.

"I might be wary of the Earl's policies but as his ward I owe him fealty—and I have much affection for the Countess." He groaned. "My heart tells me to be Richard's man." Francis rubbed his hands hard over his face as if he could erase the conflict, but he merely left a smudge of dust on his cheek.

Now I understood for the first time the strain of being pulled apart by conflicting fidelities, when family warred with other commitments. How to choose? How to decide? I too was torn but *I* had no choice. I was a Neville, and too young to take a stand against my family. I could only mourn Richard's absence and loss. But Francis could make his own choice, and the result could be nothing but painful. No wonder he looked strained and weary.

"Is he well?" I demanded. "Richard?"

"Yes." He blinked as if drawn back from some distant and painful place. "And there! I thought you did not care what became of him!" For a little while the teasing lad had reappeared, and I was glad. I rubbed at the smear with the edge of my sleeve. "You were as cold as a January pond when he left Middleham! Enough to freeze the lot of us. And don't deny it!"

"I gave him a quizzical glance. "Well . . . I thought . . . I thought he had no . . . affection for me. . . ."

"Silly girl! If kissing kitchen wenches is all the problem . . ."

"So he did know!"

"He guessed. The kiss wasn't important."

"He kissed her more than once. I saw him!" I didn't know whether to be angry at Richard or relieved at Francis's casual rejection of the matter.

"Well, he could hardly kiss *you* in the stable yard, could he? Lady Anne Neville, Warwick's heiress? It would not have been appropriate."

"Maude was very pretty!" I pointed out.

"True." Francis grinned, much like his old self. "I kissed her myself. It doesn't mean anything."

"I wrote to him," I confessed gruffly, fishing inexpertly for information.

"I know. He told me. He got the letter."

"Oh." I thought about this, coming to no conclusion. "He didn't reply."

Francis shrugged. "Of that I know nothing. But Richard told me, if I was to see you here, to tell you this. Now . . ." He took hold of my hands and repeated the words, carefully learned. "'Thank you for the prayers. I am safe. I trust we can meet in London eventually. I have kissed no serving girls recently. There is nothing for me to forgive.' There!"

"Is that all? Say it again."

And he did, and I memorized it.

"Isn't it enough?" he added as I frowned over the words. "I had to learn it by heart!"

Conscious of a warmth within my chest that Richard should even think of me in his present circumstances, I squeezed Francis's hands in quick gratitude. "What will happen now, Francis?"

"Now I return to Middleham. I do the Earl of Warwick's bidding." His reply held firm with conviction, as if he had made a pact with himself. "The rebellion in Henry's name must be put down by one means or another." He was already on his feet.

"And then?" I stood with him, trying to brush the dust from my skirts.

"Then? Well, the Earl cannot keep Edward in prison forever."

"Would . . . would he kill him?" A terrible cold lodged in my chest to replace the warmth, as we sank deeper and deeper into waters that would surely drown us.

"No! Of course he won't do that. That's never been his plan. Don't even suggest it. There's enough rumor that the Earl might not cavil at the King's blood on his hands."

"I'm sorry. I was thoughtless." I walked at his shoulder to where the escort waited, Francis's words on loyalty and birth tumbling over one another in my mind. "All we can do is remain here until it's over. One way or another."

Francis must have seen my despair. "Don't give up hope, Anne. Perhaps it can be put right and relations mended. Despite everything, there's still a strong bond between Warwick and the King. If the wounds can be healed and Edward released, you'll return to London and will see Richard again. And, I suggest"—a wry little smile tugged at his mouth—"that you show him that you have grown up at last and bear no grudges!"

I could not smile at the heavy levity but turned my face away as I stroked a hand down the shoulder of his horse. "My father is a traitor, and therefore, by association, so am I. What matter that I have grown up? I have no hope at all."

King Edward is free! The King has escaped! He is marching to London.
The words were on the lips of every traveler, every merchant and common peddler who came past. I remember standing with the Countess in the shadow of the barbican at Warwick, listening, asking. Terrified. Dreading the next gout of news.

Warwick is dead. Warwick is captured. Warwick is in hiding.

We heard none of this, thank God, only: *Warwick is at Middleham.*

Had I thought that the world was turned on its head, with the King a prisoner at my father's hands? That was not the half of it. Within a week of Francis's visit, all had collapsed about us in a quagmire of apprehension. Our security in Warwick Castle might be transformed into an imprisonment at any moment, with Edward laying a siege at our door.

"We shall all be put to the sword. Our lives will be forfeit!" Margery knew what would happen, of course. When did she ever not? Hysteria rose in her voice like a squall at sea. "We shall all be imprisoned in a dungeon in the Tower for the rest of our lives." Margery hunched her shoulders. "We're traitors. We'll be called to account. You see if my words don't come true!"

"Don't speak like that!" the Countess snapped, her eyes on Isabel's extreme pallor. "If you cannot guard your words, then remain silent. In fact, I think you should take yourself off to the kitchens."

Margery exited with the flounce of a misunderstood loyal retainer of long standing, leaving the Countess to try to mend the harm. "All has been restored as it was, Isabel. Edward will not be driven to revenge."

Empty words, as the Countess well knew. Isabel might nod in relief, grasping at straws, but I was not convinced. Only time would tell.

We were summoned, all of us, to journey to London to meet with Edward on the sixth day of December.

"Why did you release him?" my mother asked fretfully. "Why put us in this danger?"

The Earl, returned to us, his face sharpened by frustrated ambition, admitted his failure in bald terms. "It was simple in the end. I couldn't rule without him. I could not raise an army to put down the rebellion without Edward's cooperation. And typically, Edward drove a hard bargain. No freedom, no army!"

"And shall we pay the ultimate penalty?"

I held my breath, sick to my stomach, already imagining the edge of an ax grazing my neck.

"It depends on how essential he sees the Nevilles to his government and the peace of the realm." The Earl took my mother's arm and led her toward the stairs to their private apartments. "True, the Woodvilles are fewer on the ground"—his smile as he recalled River's execution held no humor—"but with Hastings and Gloucester snug at his side, I would say we're not essential to Edward at all."

Which was in no way comforting.

We were to present ourselves—the Earl and Countess, Clarence and Isabel and even myself—before the King at a court reception at Westminster, in the magnificent Painted Chamber used to impress foreign dignitaries. I understood what awaited us, what he was about. We all did, without words being necessary among us to explore Edward's intentions. If Edward was intent on revenge, it was to be before the assembled nobility of England. Humiliation would be the order of the day.

Fear gripping hard, my heart thudding beneath my breastbone, I wished it to be over, our fate decided, whatever the outcome. Edward had deliberately set the scene to awe and impress. Oh, yes, he was the master of such display and grandeur. It was difficult not to stumble to a halt in dismay, for the whole court was assembled before us, all damask and silk, feathers and jewels. The crowd might be festive, but this gilded room with its high beams and stained windows was as heavy with authority as any place of law. Rebellion was a dangerous commodity that should be stamped out. I thought Edward would have no mercy.

Once, I had been persuaded that Edward was in the wrong and that one day he would see the light and restore the Earl to preeminence. How could he now, when the Earl had raised his sword against him? What price would we pay? Exile? Death? I glanced at the Countess for reassurance but found no help there. Her composure hid a fear as sharp as mine.

And here was Edward himself: magnificent, towering well above six feet, his supremacy vaunted in cloth of gold, a gold coronet to rival the gold of his hair, and a heavy chain on his breast catching the light. Whatever debt he owed to my father for past services to the Yorkist monarchy, now he stood in judgment and awaited our coming. He would make no concessions to the man who had ordered his arrest at the point of a sword, had kept him behind stone walls and locked doors. By the end of this night I too might have a taste of the horrors of the dungeon.

But then my heart leaped, breath caught. Suddenly the splendor of Edward, for me, paled into insignificance. For my attention was caught by the man standing at Edward's shoulder. Of course, I knew it must be, that I would see him here. Was this not one of the main reasons for my dry-mouthed anticipation? He had been at court for almost a year now, experienced enough to be at his brother's side. Taller, more substantial, his shoulders broader beneath the gleaming tunic, but that was not the change that struck me. In those few months his ability to dissemble had hardened so that his hooded eyes and firm line of mouth revealed nothing. In my dreams, dominated as they were by a glorious Saint George in gilded armor, I had remembered Richard with an aura of dark maturity. Now I saw that he had an authority that had nothing to do with his clothing or his surroundings but all to do with his direct gaze and the proud tilt of his head, the set of his shoulders. Did he see me? I thought that he did, but his eye did not linger, instead coming to rest on the Earl. I was of no account to him.

We halted within the encircling ranks of the court. I could actually hear it, the moment when the whole court held its breath. I held mine too, aware of every sensation, every little movement in the air around me. A tight band squeezed my ribs. Beside me, my mother straightened her spine. It seemed that the tension would break, shatter into sharp crystal to cut and tear. I could feel it screaming through my blood. The Nevilles would pay for their defiance.

But Edward smiled. Bright and warming, like the sun from behind a bank of storm cloud. Whereas he might have drawn his sword as a symbol of his righteous anger, he raised both hands, palms up, in openhanded acceptance. His voice might carry to every corner of that vast room but the tone was gentle, softly persuasive.

"My lord of Warwick. My brother Clarence." He stepped forward to obliterate the divide. "You are right welcome. We have missed you at court since my return here. Welcome indeed." He clasped the hands of the Earl and Clarence as if there had never been enmity between them. "You have always been my best of friends and will be again. I swear there'll be no ill will between us. . . ."

As smoothly as a length of Florentine silk against the skin, we slipped back into the stream of noble society. The rigid ranks opened, then closed around us as if nothing were amiss, taking the tone from their King, whilst Edward laid his plans before my father. So carefully constructed. So clever. So *magnanimous* in his victory. How could the Earl of Warwick do anything but accept this offer of reconciliation? Whereas Edward, cunning to the last, spoke openly of his intentions toward his *dear cousin* so that the whole court might know his desire to clip the Earl of Warwick's political wings. Alliances, dispositions of land and titles, all designed to chain the Earl to Edward's side through slippery gratitude. But what did I care? Everything in me was caught and held by that quiet figure at Edward's side who was willfully, blood-chillingly ignoring me.

"Gloucester . . ." Edward drew him forward. "I have been telling my lord of Warwick of my confidence in your abilities. . . ."

He was close enough for me to touch if I had dared. *If* I dared . . . But I had grown up since we last met, and not merely in the tally of months since that unsatisfactory encounter. I lifted my chin. I would prove my worth as a Neville daughter. I would apply my own newfound female skills. The long months at Calais and Warwick had been well spent by me.

Edward was formally introducing him, explaining. . . .

". . . I have given sovereignty in Wales to my brother of Gloucester." Edward's smile grew even more bland, if that were possible, as Clarence stiffened on an indrawn breath. "Gloucester is also Constable of England, preeminent in power, second only to myself."

I gave Richard all my attention—I could not help myself, nor could I deny my admiration for him. I could never have anticipated his new status, Constable of England, in ultimate control of the security of the realm. No wonder he had the stamp of authority, a cool dignity that kept others at a distance. He had always been solemn, but I had been able to burrow into his thoughts, beneath his skin, under his composure. I seemed to have lost that ability now, seeing only the inscrutable mask he chose to wear. Unlike the King, was he unwilling to forgive our bloody sins? Would he reject me far more forcefully than I had rejected him at Middleham? I would soon discover—although his present polite words, carefully chosen and reserved, gave me, to my irritation, no hint at all.

When politics claimed the general discussion, Richard turned, at last, to me. He bowed. I swept the floor with my skirts.

"Lady Anne."

"Your Grace."

Richard extended his hand to raise me to my feet, and I stood with smooth poise, placing my fingers, lightly, like thistledown, in his. And I remembered before everything Francis's parting advice. It might have seriously ruffled me at the time, but I would show the Constable of England that I was no longer given to petulance or foolish embarrassments. I was gracious and dignified.

"I would thank you for the message, Your Grace." I lowered my lashes, and my voice, I hoped, was demurely soft. "Francis repeated it perfectly."

"As I valued your letter," he replied, without inflection.

"I rejoice in your new office, Your Grace. At your high standing with the King."

"My brother has been more than generous."

And why are you being so obtuse? "I must apologize for the manner of our parting, sir." I smiled, just a little. Tilted my head interestedly. "I hope we can become reacquainted whilst I am at court." Now I tried a direct stare, catching those dark eyes looking at me with some unreadable intent. Curved my lips just so. Promising much but committing to nothing.

"I too hope that we shall find the opportunity, lady."

And why are you being so terrifyingly formal? Richard's brows rose infinitesimally. I was no longer sure about the straight stare, or the sharp appraisal that he made no attempt to hide. *By the Virgin, Richard! What shall I say next to spur some impulsive observation from you?*

I did not need to. The interruption to our stilted reconciliation came as shattering as a blast from one of Edward's new cannon, to spin my thoughts into a breathless whirl.

". . . so I have given it some lengthy thought, Warwick. The betrothal of your daughter Anne." My head whipped round with less than elegance. "I might reconsider a betrothal between your daughter and Gloucester. . . ."

I did not hear the Earl's expressions of gratitude nor see the ingenuous curve to Edward's mouth. I was hardly aware of any of my surroundings, except Richard, once more placed firmly at the center of my world. For a brief moment I thought he looked as startled as I. Then once more the composure was hammered back in place.

"It will give me the greatest of pleasure." He inclined his head in a little acknowledgment. Which he might well say if invited to sample a bowl of thick pottage on a winter's day! What was he thinking? I had no idea.

"Well?" whispered Isabel when she could.

"I don't know. He was as bereft of words as I. At least he did not spurn me as the daughter of the enemy."

"No . . ." Isabel sounded entirely unconvinced. "But that might be because Edward demanded his acquiescence. How can you know his true feelings? How can you ever know?"

"Do you see what he's doing?" the Earl demanded. "Every man at court must see what he's about—and probably rejoice in it. The mighty being brought low!" Behind the closed doors of Warwick Inn, he exploded in fury, face white, eyes burning. All the pent-up emotion of that long evening erupted to bring me back to earth from the bright cloud on which I had floated since the astonishing proposal.

"He's isolating us," Clarence snarled, much as he had snarled since he had bowed himself out of his brother's presence. "Handing out gifts and preferment to every grasping family who will lick his boots and promise fealty. But not to me! Not to his own brother! Gloucester made Constable of England over me . . ."

Despite her own misgivings, the Countess tried for peace in her household. "*I* see what Edward has *not* done. If not for his mercy, we might have been settling into the dubious hospitality of the Tower. With an ax hanging over our necks."

"So we are forgiven!" acknowledged the Earl. "How generous of him!"

"You are as powerful as you have ever been," the Countess countered. "Edward has not robbed you of any of your power or your lands."

"He's walling us in on all sides with families who would glory in our downfall. Stone upon stone he's building, until our Neville heads will not show above the parapet. The Percys in the north. Gloucester and the Herberts in Wales. The Staffords in the Midlands. Even my brother of Northumberland is rewarded above me. Now Northumberland no longer but Marquis Montague!" My father almost spat the words. "A Marquis, forsooth! To take precedence over me! Preferment to all but the Earl of Warwick. All we have, as you so aptly remarked, is our necks."

"For which we should be grateful. And Richard promised for Anne. Is that not what you wanted? Both our daughters to tie the knot with Plantagenet tight?"

The Earl shook his head. "I see the mailed fist within the velvet gauntlet. I'm not persuaded of Edward's good faith, however fair his manner. I think he would lull us, rob us of potential allies, and then grasp the first opportunity for revenge."

But I could find no fault. I could see nothing but pleasure. Richard was to be mine at last, with the blessing of the King. I knew it was only because I was useful to tie the Nevilles to the crown, to soothe my father's thwarted ambitions. I could accept that because a political marriage had always been my destiny, just as for my mother. But nothing could quench my spirits, that little bubble of satisfaction. I wanted this marriage, and I wanted more than a political alliance with Richard of Gloucester.

I had come to the decision as he had assured me of his *great pleasure*. That was not enough. I wanted his heart as well as his hand. It was not enough that he should wed me because his brother ordered him to do so. If I loved him, I would have his reciprocation. I set out to woo Richard Plantagenet, whether he liked it or not.

I applied myself to a campaign of *pursue and retreat* in those weeks at court with commendable vigor. I knew I must be patient—difficult, but necessary—to attract him, catch his wayward regard, and then withdraw into a chilly distance. Entice him from his chivalric manners and see if I could entrap him. I determined to coax or shock or lure him, whichever would best work, from this newly acquired and impeccably polished self-possession.

Surely it could not be so difficult?

But perhaps it could. Perhaps I had a battle on my hands. I understood his conflicting emotions, and was not without compassion, but I had not liked what I had heard. A seed of dismay had effectively been sown when I heard the stark condemnation fall from Richard's lips.

"Do you not, then, wish to wed me?" I had asked, eyes decorously downcast. How weary I was of being decorous.

"I must, lady, if it is the King's wish." He wasn't *unfriendly*, I decided, so much as *disciplined*.

"I thought you wanted our union. Before." I resisted glaring at him. Instead I allowed myself to glance at his face through my lashes. Unfortunately there was no relenting in his stern mouth.

"That was before I realized I was part of Warwick's plot to overthrow my brother. Marriage to you would secure my loyalties to the

Nevilles. *Then* I was too young to realize it. Now I do." The dark eyes settled on mine, bright with indignation. "I do not like to be used."

"Who does? It's no better for me." Soft voiced, a hint of gentle suffering.

"I disagree. It would always have been your fate to marry where the Earl decided."

He had trapped me. As helpless as a coney in a snare. No good would come of arguing that point, as he well knew. "Well—if you choose to keep me at arm's length, Richard, and not to make the best of a marriage between us . . ." Crossly, I gave up on patience and soft words and went for the direct attack.

"Have I said that I will not?" Good, a hint of temper there. "All I said was that I dislike being manipulated."

"I know what you said! I find you most *ungracious*—and will seek better company."

And I did.

But now Richard's sense of ill usage must not be allowed to stand in my way. I would overcome it. And if I failed . . . But I would not. I was a Neville. So I flirted, when I could, with Francis, who saw my intent and complied with a boisterous goodwill that I fear fooled no one. Otherwise I kept Isabel's company, to the detriment of our tempers and sisterly relationship. Never had a chaperoned lady stuck more closely to her chaperone when the object of her desire came close. Never had a chaperoned lady been so bored. . . .

But Richard appeared to be weakening.

"Will you join me in the hunt, Lady Anne?"

"I am gratified." I curtsied. "But I will ride slowly with Isabel. In her condition she needs my company." It almost killed me to refuse, committing myself to a sedate perambulation at the rear of the field, when I could have galloped at his side.

Did I see Richard laugh as he rode off to join the King?

We worked through the whole gamut of Twelfth Night celebrations, maneuvering aside and around each other as if we were engaged in the steps of a round dance. Were we an object of amusement for those who watched? Unaware of anyone else, I neither knew nor cared. Richard remained as perfectly well mannered as any lady could desire, but so impregnably distant that it infuriated me. As I walked along the ill-lit corridor between Isabel's and the Earl's accommodations, Isabel having kept me at her wretched side to bemoan her increasing girth, I was finally forced to accept the inevitability of a cold political match between us.

"Well, lady. You took your time. I've been here a good hour. And damned cold it is too."

I lurched to a halt, heart leaping. A figure stepped out. "Who is it?"

"Who do you think would be waiting to waylay you?"

I smiled in the shadows, my declining spirits stirred instantly into life. Two could play at that game! "Francis! Is it really you?"

"Vixen! Francis has no intention of meeting with you in dark corners!"

I heard the laughter in his voice and saw that I had been marvelously outwitted. So caught up was I in my plan that I had not realized. I was not the hunter, never had been, but the hunted. Richard had more patience than I. More skill. But what now? Allow him his victory? Give in gracefully or retreat behind a fortified pride and disdain . . . ?

"What do you want?" I managed a fair imitation of a frown.

"You've been trying hard to avoid me of late. And successfully."

"I have not."

"Then you'll not resist my capturing you."

"I shall." I would not give in to such cunning wiles, but my response made no impression. The Constable of England, I realized, had a campaign from which he would not be distracted.

"You are my betrothed, Lady Anne." His teeth glinted in the flicker of light from a distant cresset. "I have every right to speak with you."

"Not without a chaperone, you don't! Margery should be with us."

"But as she isn't . . ." His hands clasped lightly on my shoulders to draw me close. The kiss, which startled me, was a soft experiment of lips against lips.

"That was a kiss a brother might bestow on his sister!" I gasped.

"You don't have a brother."

"So?"

"So how would you know?" His hands tightened. "What about this?"

His retaliation was to be expected, I supposed. I had not expected the heat, the urgency of it, nor the response that flashed along my skin. Mouth crushed beneath his, I had no breath to make a smart answer.

"You'll be my wife, Anne Neville, because it is Edward's wish," Richard breathed in my ear. "But will you be my love, because *I* would have it so?"

"I might." I hid my face against his shoulder, holding fast to my delight. "But only if you would be mine."

"A bargain, is it? Yet how can I love someone who plots and torments?"

I did not listen to his words, only felt the strength of his arms, the warmth of his breath against my cheek. My heart, already shivering on the edge, fell at his feet.

"You can love me because it was always intended to be so," I offered, speaking the truth as I saw it. "Because you have known me forever, good and bad. Because you own my heart."

"Then I must take a care of it, mustn't I?"

"Will you?

"Always."

"In spite of everything? The treachery and secrecy? I am still Warwick's daughter."

"In spite of everything, daughter of Warwick, I love you. I think I always have. Ever since you informed me how relieved you were that I hadn't died at birth."

My laughter echoed his softly in the drafty corridor. Typical of

Richard to say so little and mean so much, leaving me truly ensnared. I allowed him to kiss me again. Then again, perhaps I didn't *allow* it, but he kissed me anyway. My lips smiled beneath the pressure as desire skipped shiveringly over my skin. All my secret plotting had been hopelessly futile and unnecessary. Richard had wanted me; I had possession of his heart all the time.

It was a magical time, when I was scarce able to catch my breath from one day's end to the next, my blood running hot with excitement, a naive passion that robbed me of sleep and appetite. I could not wait to rise from my bed at the beginning of each day to meet with him again. What did it matter that Margery shadowed me? The stolen kisses were sweeter for their snatched infrequency. If those around me smiled with condescension upon my blissful state, I was unaware. Richard filled my heart, all my vision.

It had to end, with responsibilities on all sides to direct us into our disparate lives. From my earliest years I had learned that a man of authority had demands on his time, so that I could not expect to remain close at Richard's side forever. So I returned to Warwick with my mother and Isabel. The Earl remained at court with Edward. Clarence journeyed between London and Richmond in the north whilst Isabel grew big and indolent. Richard was in Wales to oversee the rebel castles he had occupied, to take soundings of any further rebellion.

"I don't want this," I had declared as we parted in London, clutching at the breast of his velvet tunic with both hands, regardless of the crushed fabric. "How shall I live for a whole day without you, much less weeks—even months?" I widened my eyes in parody of distress, luring him to say what I wanted to hear. "How do I know you'll regret my absence? I swear you'll enjoy the campaign and have no thought for me." I was learning the trick of pushing my sometimes taciturn lover into statements of a nonpolitical nature, although not always with much finesse.

The corners of Richard's mouth twitched as if he read my intent. "I will think of you at least once a day."

"Is that all?"

"Is that not enough?" He gave in. "You have all my devotion. Feel my heart beat for you." And he flattened my palms beneath his, against his chest, so that I could feel the steady throb. "When I return we will marry."

In a final gesture Richard stroked his knuckles down over my cheek. "Gentle Anne! Still I love you!" His soft mockery touched my heart. I caught his wrist, turning my face to press my lips there. When I smiled into his eyes, all I could see was his love for me imprinted on my reflection as it smiled back at me.

"And you have all my love. God keep you safe."

I was content. It was as if the last year, with its upheavals and deceits, had never happened. We basked in the full light of royal forgiveness and generosity.

Richard was mine.

CHAPTER SIX

I was given no presentiment of looming disaster. The storm came without warning to break over our heads.

"What's amiss?" I asked the Countess as I joined her at the head of the outer staircase from the old keep at Warwick. "What's happened? Surely we're not at war again?" We looked down on the suddenly chaotic scene below to where the Earl's master at arms had just ridden through the gates with a force of armed retainers, outfitted, to my eye, for battle. Neville pennons flew from the tips of a half dozen lances.

"I don't know." She ran down the steps with me hard on her heels.

As soon as she opened the letter delivered to her hand by the Earl's courier, I saw the recoil. Her eyes held the glassy blindness of panic as she lifted them from the words to survey the soldiers who filled our courtyard. The news was surely bad. In my innocence I thought it could mean only one thing, and a cold hand tightened around my throat.

"No," I whispered. "Not that!"

"What?" Face so pale, eyes wide, even her lips white, the Countess had difficulty in answering me. It must be the Earl! Only so critical a disaster could rob her of her self-possession.

"Is he hurt?" I moved to stand closer at her side, fearful that she would sink to the floor, but although she looked through me as if I did not exist, her hand closed viselike around my wrist.

"What?" She gasped as she took my meaning. "No . . . no. Your father is well. But . . . I knew he was disturbed, angry. . . . I knew the bitterness that drove him, that he feared Edward's soft words as a mere sop to cover his true motive. But I had no idea that Warwick would consider this! That he would refuse to let matters lie quiet and wounds to heal. By the Virgin! Why has he done this?"

"But *what*?"

My mother's fingers tightened further until I winced with pain, and she released me with a brusque apology, her mind clearly distracted.

"Rebellion against Edward. Again." She forced the words through stiff lips. "He's instigated an uprising in Lincolnshire, to draw Edward north into a trap, where the Earl can defeat him in battle. Our master at arms is here to muster troops for my lord's use."

"Will he take Edward prisoner again?" I found it difficult to follow the reasoning. The King's imprisonment had failed last time, with humiliating results. Why risk another appalling failure? Why risk Edward's goodwill a second time?

"No." The Countess crushed the document in her fist as we watched the deployment of the men at arms. "Clarence is with Warwick. The plan is to depose Edward and make Clarence King. Clarence . . . ! And Isabel then will be Queen. Ha! As if I care about that! All very well if my lord can carry it off. But if he cannot . . . If we fail, Edward will not forgive us this time. There'll be no mercy for us at his hands."

I could not think of that. In a moment of pure selfishness all I could see was that we had been cast in the role of traitor again. Rebels. Enemies of the King, destroyers of the peace of the realm. Objects of Edward's hatred and vengeance. For the first time I think I questioned the wisdom of my father's actions. Yet surely I could rest on his just decisions. I could not start apportioning blame.

Truth struck like a viper.

Oh, Richard. My dearest love. Where does that leave us now?

"What do we do?" I asked helplessly, the answer to my question stark and brutal in my mind.

"We wait. What else can we do?"

One decision was made for us. At Clarence's insistence, delivered shortly and verbally by the courier, we packed Isabel into a traveling litter and sent her with a strong escort out of harm's way. She would journey slowly to Exeter, where she would lodge in the sanctuary of the Bishop's palace, under God's protection and far from the dangers of warfare. Far from Edward, who might take it into his mind to take her and hold her and her unborn child as security for Clarence's good behavior. Margery traveled with her for her comfort. My mother was reluctant but saw the sense of it. We watched my sister's entourage disappear into the winter landscape.

"I should not allow her to travel without me at this time," the Countess murmured, her anxieties showing in her hands clutching white-fingered on the coping stones. "She's not strong. It would be better for her to remain here. If anything amiss occurs on the road . . ."

I shuffled wordlessly at her side. Clarence's high-handed orders had not endeared him to me. Far better for Isabel to remain safely behind the walls of Warwick Castle. Then the Countess braced her shoulders and regarded me with a steady stare.

"So! Do we lay up for a siege, daughter, or do we gather our possessions for instant flight?"

"It's Richard! Richard's here."

I raced from the battlement walk with no consideration for anything except that against all the odds he had come. "Richard has come. And Francis with him." I slid to a halt, ridiculously wishing I wore my new damask in rich cerulean with gold-embroidered bodice rather than my present hard-wearing woolen gown. Delight that I would see him again flooded through me. But I saw my mother's fixed expression and the heat chilled; the fire died. How would either Richard or I face this redeployment of loyalties? Richard and I were on opposite sides, delineated by spilled blood and black treason. And as I had feared, Francis might be Warwick's foster son but was now riding in Richard of Gloucester's train. I could not imagine how we should receive them. Nor what Richard could possibly say to me to give me hope, no matter how becoming my dress.

"It had to happen," was the Countess's only observation. "Youth cleaves to youth. They were always good friends."

We welcomed them—in a fashion—in the open spaces of the courtyard, but the greeting was edged with frost.

"I cannot stay, my lady." Richard dismounted, flung his reins to his squire, and approached and made a chillingly formal bow, addressing the Countess but with his eyes seeking me out. "It's not fitting that I should be here with rebellion afoot and the Earl's allegiance a matter of censure. I regret this. The rift is not of my making." There was a brittleness about his movements, as if he wished himself anywhere but within the walls of one of Warwick's castles.

Francis too was ill at ease as he saluted my mother's fingers. There was no warm embrace between them on this occasion. "I had to follow the dictates of honor, lady."

"I understand." The Countess managed a thin smile. "If I have instilled honor into you, Francis, I must be satisfied, must I not? We must deal with circumstances as we find them."

"I am here to have conversation with Anne," Richard intervened with less than patience. "If you will permit it . . ."

"It is not seemly," my mother replied coldly, to my dismay. Would she refuse? Deliberately, she would not meet my ferocious stare.

"Anne was my betrothed," Richard said. I noted the tense with a sickening lurch of my belly. "It is *seemly* that I take my leave of her. I would ask your indulgence, lady. Just this once. Is it too much to ask that I make my final farewells in person?"

Just this once. How empty a phrase it seemed. *Final farewells?* How cruel, how devastating. How could I survive if he were forced to simply mount up and ride away? Silently I prayed that the Countess would reconsider, whilst, dark eyes intense and unyielding, every inch the Duke of Gloucester, Richard would not retreat but challenged my mother to refuse outright, which would have burdened her with unheard-of discourtesy. The hesitation lengthened as she considered. She was going to refuse—I knew it; I could sense it as her lips parted. . . .

"If it please you, madam." I would beg for this as I had never begged before. "As Richard says, it will be for the last time. I doubt we shall see each other again. I need . . . I need to . . ." My voice almost broke on the words. I had no argument to lay before her.

But the Countess, undoubtedly knowing the pain of separation for herself, nodded once, as if the concession were dragged from her. "Very well. Go to the chapel, Gloucester, and take your farewell. God will watch over you and judge the sincerity in your heart. Anne, remember that you are my daughter and conduct yourself accordingly. You will remain there no longer than a half hour." She turned on her heel.

It was a cold and austere place, built into the oldest part of the castle, with heavy pillars creating deep, dank shadows even in the height of summer. No sun shone on that winter day to warm the colored glass to give it a welcoming beauty. As cold and as heavy as my heart, the atmosphere in the chapel was a fitting reflection of our emotions. Francis remained outside, seated with his back against the wall to allow us a brief privacy. With the door closed against the world, I watched as Richard tossed cloak, hat, and gloves onto a wooden bench but kept his sword buckled firm. This would not take long. He had come out of courtesy, out of love, but his allegiance to the King would determine all his future actions. Nor could I blame him. Did I not love him for his loyalty, his rigid sense of honor? I could hardly now condemn him for it, simply because it undermined my own happiness.

We had so little time, so few minutes. Already they were flying away. I vowed to remain calm, with at least some of the Countess's dignity.

Richard remained rigidly at arm's length, as if distance would make the parting easier. "I had to come. I couldn't leave you without explaining—without telling you that I'm summoned to raise a force and join with the King, without . . ." His words died. He lifted one shoulder awkwardly and I saw the habitual little pull of the muscle beside his mouth when his emotions were compromised.

"Without making your farewell," I added for him. "I understand. There's no future for us, is there?" I laughed—or was it a sob?—an unnatural, harsh sound in the still air. "Of course there is not. There can never be a future for us." An assertion now, not a question.

"No. Warwick and Clarence have again chosen to put themselves outside the law. Edward has withdrawn his consent for our marriage. There can be no easy coming to terms between Warwick and the King this time."

"Is it very bad?"

"As bad as it gets." His eyes were flat, his face bleak and strained, pale in the winter gloom. "Warwick's promised to bring troops to meet with Edward at Leicester, to help him crush the rebels. Edward suspects a trap, that Warwick is in truth bringing up reinforcements *for* the rebels. So Warwick plans to catch my brother unawares, Warwick on one hand, the rebels on the other, crushing Edward between them." Richard raised his fist, fingers clenched tight. "As neat as cracking a hazelnut."

I frowned at the picture he painted. "Will it happen? We don't know who will win, do we?"

"There'll be a battle before the week's out. Edward will push for it, to bring the affair to its head. Hence my haste." Richard paused as if unsure whether to continue, hands now curled hard around sword belt, studying the altar with its dull gleam of candles and silver crucifix. Deciding at last to speak his thoughts, however unpalatable to me. And I valued his honesty. "I think Edward will not lose this battle.

He's a gifted tactician and has the measure of your father. If Warwick and Clarence stand against him and Edward wins, he'll take brutal revenge against them both."

I breathed slowly, painfully, against the truths I had known since the courier's visit. "And we will once again be foresworn traitors with a price on our heads."

"Yes."

"And you could not wed a traitor," I ventured, knowing the answer. Richard did not reply.

"Oh, Richard!" I whispered, a lump like a rock in my throat.

Richard abandoned his carefully preserved stance. He strode forward and I found my hands grasped to pull me close, face buried against the metaled strips of his brigandine. I breathed in the familiar scent and heat of him, but as his breath stirred my hair, his voice was terrifyingly severe. "It hurts now, I know. But you are young, Anne. It will fade as time passes. You'll find another husband. As Warwick's daughter, you'll always have value." An icy finger inched its way down my spine, a ghostly foretaste of what would come, but Richard continued, his fingers painful around mine. "I swear you'll marry and raise a handful of argumentative children. You will be content."

I looked up at him in horror—or was it anger?—that he should so precipitately arrange another marriage for me. I was incapable of seeing my future other than as a black void.

"I will not," I hissed. "I do not seek *contentment.* Can you cast me off, in so cursory a manner, as if I mean nothing to you?" So much for my vow of dignity. My fear of losing him was so sharp and real it drove me to extremes. "So I will find another husband. Of course I will. Am I not a Neville? But will I find another love? You say that the pain will fade. I don't believe you. Are you saying that it will fade for you?"

"No." He sighed on an exhalation.

"Then why should it for me? Tell me this, Richard: Did you ever love me? Do you love me still?"

"How can you doubt me?" His eyes, stark with dismay, glinted in the dim light but he would not turn away from the accusation in my face. "Anne . . . what choice have we with my brother and your father facing each other across a battlefield?"

"I know!" My anger segued into despair, my biting words of blame into a stifled sob. "And my father planning to lift the crown from Edward's head. The worst of treachery."

"God damn Warwick to the fires of hell!"

"But he's my father. He demands my duty and my affection."

"So he might, but he has effectively destroyed any happiness we might have had together." My hands flat against his chest felt the anger, so far held in check, build to fill his whole frame, until the thunderous beat of his heart matched mine. "Never doubt my love, Anne," he murmured. "It is yours and will be for all time. This wounds me as much as it hurts you. And it destroys me that I can do nothing to comfort you."

"Richard! It's time. . . ."

He raised his head at Francis's voice beyond the door. We could not linger. I could sense the urgency in him, even as his hands gentled to tenderness. Was there nothing more I could do or say?

"Will you take this?" I tugged off a little ring, a plain gold circle set with a ruby, even though it was far too small for a man's hand. I pushed it, not without some difficulty as it caught on his knuckle, onto his little finger. "Will you wear it?"

"Yes. I will."

A last kiss. One final embrace. A desperate bruising of my lips as Richard claimed me as his for that last time. No joy, no sweet promise. Just a cruel ending. Until he framed my face in his hands.

"I must go." He kissed my damp cheeks, the soft hollow of my temple, my eyelids. "I think it was your eyes I fell in love with. So dark, yet so full of light when you looked at me. I fell the whole way into them and now I think I cannot escape. Yet I must. . . . God keep you, my love. God keep you safe."

I could not bear it. So he would be honorable and self-sacrificing, would he? He would set me free. I did not want this; I did not want to be sacrificed.

"Richard . . ."

But I did not know what more to say when there was nothing to be said. I released him as if his flesh burned my fingers, and clutching at pride I drew myself up to my full height. After all, he was a Prince of the Blood, whilst I was a mere subject, and a disloyal one at that. I sank to the stone paving in formal obeisance.

Catching up his cloak and hat from the bench, Richard would have gone, left me. Preempting him, I pounced and snatched up his embroidered leather gauntlets. He held out his hands for them.

I shook my head, turning the soft kid leather over and over in my grasp. There was the white boar, Richard's heraldic badge, shimmering in its satin stitching on the cuff, stiff and powerful with gilt tusks, yet so impotent in its rigid embroidery. The creature blurred when tears welled.

He laughed softly, a joyless sound. "So you would steal my gloves?"

"Yes." I hid them behind my back.

"They're too big for you."

"I know."

He knew why I wanted them. Richard always understood me. "Then keep them, if it brings you comfort."

I saw pity in Richard's eyes. And despised it. I flattened the gauntlets against my breast but my mind shrieked, *This is not enough. How can this be all I have of you for the rest of my life? A pair of gloves the only solace for a lifetime of regret.*

"Adieu, Your Grace." I would not weep again in his presence.

"Farewell, my lady. My love."

I closed my eyes to shut out the reality of his leaving me. And Richard was gone, so that all I could do was sink to my knees on the altar step, where I stayed until I heard the bustle of departure die away. Then I ran quickly up to the battlements again to watch, and remained there until I could no longer see his figure for the tears that turned my sight to blindness. If he looked back, I did not see him. If he raised his arm in farewell, I was not aware. Only one thought echoed and reechoed in my head: If I was indeed fated to live out my life in exile, I would never see him again. It seemed to me that there was a strange emptiness in my chest where my heart had been, a vast wilderness that nothing would ever fill. I pushed my hands into the gloves, hoping to absorb the warmth of his hands there, but the fur linings were already cold. Sobs shook me until I could barely stand.

In her wisdom the Countess allowed me to indulge my misery alone on the windy stretch of the battlement walk, until I was sufficiently chilled and wretched and trailed down to where she waited for me.

"He has gone." I sniffed, hoping my veil would hide the worst of the ravages, as I stuffed the gloves into the bodice of my gown.

"I know."

She placed a hand against my cheek. One look at my face and she swept me off to the kitchens, sat me down at the rough table, and poured me a cup of wine whilst the cook placed before me a bowl of broth. I sat in mutinous refusal to be comforted. Ignoring the surprised glances of the kitchen servants and the damage to her skirts, my mother pulled up a stool at my side, grasped my shoulders, and forced me to look at her.

"Drink the wine, Anne. And eat."

"I don't want—"

"Yes, he has gone. You must accept it. You'll not feel any better for the food, but you need strength and determination now, as you have never done before."

Nothing could have persuaded me more of the hopelessness of my love. "He has left me. . . ." I could hear the misery rising again in my voice.

"Yes, he has." There was no sympathy, only an implacable will. "Richard has no choice to make, Anne. Loyalty demands that he follow the King."

"I need him," I stated simply.

"No, you don't. You must learn to live without him and you

will. But now *I* need you. You will not let this loss press you into the ground. Do you understand me?"

"Yes." I scrubbed at my face with my sleeve.

The Countess stood but halted to look down at me. "If our lives are to be forfeit for my lord's actions, I need to rely on you. I cannot have you malingering over Richard." Her eyes bored into mine. "So eat!"

The Countess's demands of duty and pride stiffened my courage. Although it was an effort not to choke on the pottage, I ate, and after waiting for a moment to see that I would obey, the Countess went about her own affairs. But as she left, and as I mopped up the final dregs of the broth, she leaned close in passing and kissed my hair. She understood. She knew about heartbreak and separation and loss.

"He has not left you through any lack of love. I saw it in him when he came from the chapel. He is as wounded as you."

It was some sort of balm to my heart, but not much.

In the end we fled for our lives.

We gathered together what we would need, as well as bags of gold coin and the Neville jewels. Only God would know if we would ever return to our home here, and it might be that we would need all the wealth we could carry. Then we sat tight with our banners fluttering bravely on the towers, but the wagons packed and defeat in our hearts as we fretted with short tempers and wakeful nights. I did not even have Isabel to sharpen my tongue against.

"We march south," Warwick ordered when he finally arrived with a surly and glowering Clarence. No time for greetings. "Can you be ready within the hour? Edward is on the hunt for us. We are defeated. We sail for Calais." He looked beyond weary.

"Is Edward not disposed to show mercy?" the Countess asked.

"No." There was no attempt to soften the words. "I rejected Edward's demand that I face him, you see. He has an army of such size that I'm not strong enough to challenge him. Edward denounces us as traitors and will deal with us as such if we fall into his hands. If you raise arms against the King a second time and fail . . ." Now he looked directly at my mother. "It must be Calais for all of us. Who knows when we will return to England again?"

So there were no more words or minutes to waste. How could I ask about Richard's whereabouts, whether he had survived the battle, when faced with this disaster? We were gone within the day, the start of a long and tragic journey that would lead us to the unexpected rejection in the sullen seas off Calais. To a difficult birth and a dead child and a bitter acceptance of our new lives as traitors to the English crown.

CHAPTER SEVEN

Life must go on and we must find refuge. So here we sat in a lively sea, waiting for the tide off the French port of Honfleur, nothing less than fugitives dependent on the goodwill or greedy self-interest of King Louis of France, with my anxious query snatched up by the wind.

"Will we be made welcome?"

And the Earl's unfathomable reply. "*You*, my daughter, will be made welcome at all events."

I did not understand. What *was* clear, even to me, was that all would hang on whatever deal the Earl could make with King Louis, on whether King Louis was even willing to come to an agreement with a landless and attainted lord.

"Louis will receive us at Amboise," the Earl announced. "But there will be a price to pay."

A price. I considered it, turning it over in my mind. What would the price be? And who would pay it? On reflection it seemed an obvious answer. The first sacrifice to be made would be my father's pride.

* * *

"Welcome, my inestimable cousin of Warwick. And His Grace of Clarence too, of course. It pleases me to see you here. Come, my lord Earl, and introduce your family to me. Then you will eat at my table. . . ."

I had expected the royal fortress of Amboise to be magnificent, in the way of Warwick Castle, with spacious new wings, low ceilinged and large windowed, to add a range of comfortable family apartments to the original defensive towers and keep. Throughout all the years of his service to the Yorkist cause, my father had pushed King Edward into joining forces with France, to create the most powerful alliance in Europe. If that was so, then Louis must live in considerable grandeur and wealth.

So Amboise was a shock. Magnificent, yes, in an overpowering way, like Middleham. A formidable fortress, true. But little beyond that, reminding me of the dominant bulk of the Tower of London, a place where I would never care to live. The round towers of Amboise, the high walls, the deep moat, were all vast and forbidding, without softness. Was this to be my future home? I prayed it would not.

We were shown to a suite of small, sparsely furnished rooms in one of the towers, hardly more accommodating than our little border fortress of Penrith, our meager luggage unloaded and brought after us. We were a particularly joyless party: Isabel still pale and fretful, still mourning the loss of her child and unresponsive toward any who tried to comfort her. Clarence, all his ambitions to take the crown for himself having died a death unless my father could work some miracle, prowled in a fury of ill temper. The Earl, thin lipped and caustic, waited for the royal summons. Amidst all, the Countess worked to preserve a calm facade.

Almost before we had time to draw breath and consider the state of our travel-worn appearance, a dignified official in severe black fetched us to be presented to His Majesty. I regretted the salt-stained hem of my gown, the dusty folds and grimy veil. My mother, beating at her skirts with the flat of her hand, groaned when she noticed the matted state of one of her sleeves that had trailed in some noxious substance. But then I saw the muscles of her jaw grow taut. Were not our blood and lineage enough to take us into the royal presence? I could not quite follow her example. We might have had all the confidence in the world, all the high blood of an old family, but we were still beggars, homeless, dependent on the magnanimity of this man who summoned us to attend him in the rigid formality of the chamber of state.

"Welcome, my inestimable cousin of Warwick. . . ." The man's voice, of a clear, light timbre, carried effortlessly down the length of the room.

"Is that the King of France?" I whispered to my mother, aghast as the same man stepped down from the dais beside the lofty fireplace and advanced to greet the Earl. My only knowledge of kingship was the impressive stature and love of display that belonged to King Edward. Did not all kings look like Edward and conduct themselves with such majesty? "Can that be King Louis?" I repeated below my breath, stunned at my first sight of him.

"Hush." The Countess's lips twitched.

I had heard him described as the Spider. Well, he was ugly enough, with a large nose, long and hooked, that dominated his face and took the eye so that it was difficult to look elsewhere. His own eyes were downturned at the corners and heavy lidded, effectively disguising what they might show of his thoughts. At this moment he was smiling benignly at my father, but I was soon to see that in repose his mouth also turned down, as if in perpetual disfavor of the world. For certain, he was neither handsome nor impressive. His robe was plain and undecorated, his stature of little more than middle height, with no breadth of shoulder to take the eye. His hair was hidden under a close felt hat, as any merchant in London might wear. No hint of superior majesty here, with only one servant to attend him.

Yet my future was to be dictated by this man.

"My lord Warwick. So many months since we last met. So much ill fortune for you to suffer." His condolences were gentle, reassuring us of his kindness. The King waved us toward the warmth of the fire.

"I trust your accommodation is to your liking. I will provide anything I can to add to your ease at this unfortunate time."

And this too took my interest—his closeness to the Earl. He had addressed him as *cousin*. This powerful man was receiving us at his court with such generosity, as if we were his equal in status and influence, rather than the truth of it. The Earl completed the introductions. We curtsied to the floor. When we rose I found Louis's sharp hazel eyes trained on me. Uncomfortable with the fierce scrutiny, I looked down at his extremely large feet.

"Ah . . ." He walked slowly forward to stand in front of me. "Look up, my dear. Lady Anne . . . Your unmarried daughter, you say, Warwick?"

"She is as yet unmarried."

"But of an age to be wed."

Obedient to the order, I looked up. For a moment behind the smiling facade, Louis looked like a cat contemplating a meal of a particularly tasty mouse under its claws. His self-satisfaction shone clear as his smile widened.

"Lady Anne. A charming young woman."

I swallowed nervously.

"You are not married, but is there a betrothal?" he asked me. "Is there some young lord in England who hopes to wed you?"

Richard. I will not think of Richard. If I do I will weep for the loss of him.

"No, Your Majesty, there is no betrothal."

"Good. Then we will have to see what we can do."

I could make nothing of this beyond the possibility of a son of a noble French family as my future husband. It held only a mild interest for me. Far more critical to my mind was what exactly this remarkably ugly but all-powerful man would demand in return for his slippery hand of friendship toward my father. We did not have to wait long to discover. With warm geniality we were invited to sit with him at his banquet as if the Earl were indeed the favored cousin Louis dubbed

him. Louis began to play his hand immediately, with a magnificent
cunning that even I could read.

"Sit by me, my lord of Warwick. Take a goblet of wine. And your
Countess and fair daughters. Be seated and at ease." He signaled to
the servants to pour wine and serve the first course. Only then did
he sketch a brief gesture toward Clarence, indicating a chair farther
along the board, as if he were not the brother of the King of England.
"And you too, Your Grace. You'll have an interest in our debates."
Louis settled himself in the solid, plainly fashioned chair at the head
of the table and rubbed the palms of his thin hands together. "We
have much to discuss, much to decide. Where better to have a meeting
of minds than over a dish of roast meats?"

In this manner, over a course of frumenty with venison and a side
dish of Vyaund de Cyprys, he opened the delicate negotiation with my
father as if they were alone and intimate in a private chamber, driving his own policies forward to the exclusion of all else. I watched his
manner of achieving his own way, astonished that a man who had so
little presence could dictate the proceedings so effectively, controlling
the negotiations with all the skill of a master swordsman wielding a
needle-sharp rapier in a duel.

"Tell me, cousin." Louis drove straight to the heart with that same
rapier. "How do you see the immediate future for yourself and your
family? What are your plans?"

The key question. A brutal question, forcing my father to face the
reality of his precariously balanced position from the outset. The Earl
considered the wine in his cup, then answered with a direct stare and
astonishing openness. "The immediate future? Uncertain. Edward is
well on his way to restoring his grip on England. So my preference
is to return to England soon, before he can tighten his hold further.
There are enough who will support the Neville banner if I can make
an impression of strength."

"But how do you see your chances of success, my lord?" Louis
inquired, picking at a stuffed *poussin*.

I listened, trying to interpret the meanings behind the innocuous exchange of words. So did the Countess, I noticed, who sat to my right, across from the French King, her concentration more on the two men than on the subtle mix of sugar and spices in the Vyaund. Was it truly possible that we could go home soon and oust Edward yet again? Before my father could consider his reply, Clarence leaped in with hot words.

"We have every chance of success, sire! When we return, my presence in England will attract all who are dissatisfied with Edward."

I might have turned to marvel at Clarence's rude interruption, but Louis barely gave the Duke a passing glance. Louis kept his eyes fixed on my father's face.

"Well, my lord Warwick?" he repeated. "What chance of success?"

"Not good, sire."

"So you look to me for help." Louis smiled, leaning back in complacent ease that was shared by no one else in the room.

"Yes, sire, I do," the Earl admitted. "I can't see my way to defeating Edward on the battlefield with only my own resources." Despite all his efforts to make a dispassionate assessment, I could feel the blow to his pride as he was forced to admit his failure to bring Edward to heel. Begging for help from a position of weakness was not something my father had ever had to do. I imagined it roiled like poison in his gut.

"So you would want—what? A fleet. Finance. Troops. You want me to back your invasion." Louis compressed his downturned mouth, giving himself an even more jaundiced air. "It's risky, my lord. Such a full-scale attack would not come cheap. I might lose all my considerable investment in such a chancy project. And you could end up dead or in prison."

"No!" The Earl leaned forward to press his point, pushing aside his platter, arms folded on the table. "There'll be no talk of failure here, sire. I will be successful. Times have changed since the beginning of his reign. Edward is popular no longer. His wife is hated; the country groans under higher and higher taxation. If I can put myself forward as a viable force to Edward, the English lords will give me their allegiance. Any investment in men or gold that you make will not be at risk."

He was so confident! I looked through my lashes at my mother. She sat immobile but her fingers linked in her lap were white-knuckled. She too had given up on the *poussin*. Beyond her, Clarence kept silent, his angry eyes darting between the two protagonists.

"So!" Louis indicated for the table to be cleared of the debris of the meal, waiting as the servants went about their tasks placing sweet jellies, silver bowls of sweetmeats, and sugared nuts before us, intricate delicacies that caught my eye despite the imminence of a violent storm. "Let us say, then, that you overthrow King Edward. That you depose him. What then?" Louis's stare was astonishingly innocent. "Do you seek the crown yourself, Cousin Warwick?"

"No," the Earl replied. "I have no designs on the throne, nor ever had."

"Yet you might claim that you are a Prince of the Royal Blood. And that you have, without doubt, the power and the aptitude for the position."

"No. I will not claim it, sire. It has never been—nor will it be—accepted as a legitimate claim."

My spoon hovered, then came to a halt between the dish and my lips. My father had a claim in his own right? I had not known this. A close family connection was one thing, but a claim in his own right? Although the Earl had quickly rejected any such pretensions, my interest was truly deflected from the Crustade Ryal with its spiced egg filling.

Louis appeared satisfied. "Who, then, will you make King in Edward's stead?" The French King knew the answer. I could see it in the tilt of his head, the glint in his eye. But if he knew, why ask the question? Illumination came blindingly as I brought to mind the deliberate lack of acknowledgment of Clarence here at Amboise. Louis did not want Clarence as King of England and so would maneuver the Earl to disown him.

He wants my father to make a denial. He wants my father to reject

Clarence! But if not Clarence, who will the French Spider support, and force my father to support, in return for French troops?

"Who will be King of England, my dear cousin of Warwick?"

Clarence's patience broke under the slow but sly probing. Again he forced himself into the debate. "Warwick will give the crown to me, of course. *I* am the legitimate heir of the House of York, Your Majesty. *I* shall take the crown. This has been understood between my lord Warwick and myself since I wed the Lady Isabel. Who else has the right to rule but myself?"

"I think you have not that right, Your Grace," Louis observed, barely attempting to cover his displeasure. In the little silence that followed this impassioned declaration, we all looked to Louis, who turned his head and allowed his sardonic eye to rest on Clarence's heated countenance. The coldness in that appraisal chilled me. It was my father who took up the strands of the negotiation.

"True—it was originally in my mind to make Clarence King."

"No." Louis played a new card from his hand. "I am not in favor of this, Warwick," he stated simply, unequivocally, as if the furious subject of his disfavor were not present. "My agents tell me Clarence would not be acceptable in England. He does not have a strong base of support."

"I would refute such claims," Clarence leaped in. "I have every right to rule. It's well-known that Edward is a bastard, the illegitimate product of some base union between my mother, the Duchess of York, and a common archer. He should never have claimed the crown in the first place. . . ."

I watched him in growing disgust as he continued to heap disgrace on his brother. Even Isabel gave her attention to the uneaten sweetmeats on her plate in embarrassment. How despicable he was to blacken his mother's name so. *It's well-known that . . .* Only because the rumors had been spread by Clarence's poisonous tongue. Did anyone truly believe the Duchess of York capable of consorting with a mere archer in her husband's employ? I doubted it. But Clarence had no compunction about using it as a political weapon to sully Edward's golden reputation. My pity for Isabel swelled, that she should be married to a man so unprincipled.

"I would be prepared to swear that it is so!" Clarence ended his diatribe.

Louis looked again at Clarence, lingering on his vividly handsome features as if he would dissect the character behind the impressive appearance. The tension around the table tightened a notch. "I am not persuaded." Louis addressed Clarence directly. I suspect he had not liked what he saw.

Clarence slammed his cup to the table. "I will not be so cast aside. . . . I am my brother's heir!"

"Your brother's heir is a three-year-old child—a girl. Your legitimacy, Your Grace, as the future ruler of England, does not have sufficient credibility." Louis swung back to the Earl, his decision made. "I will not put my money or fleet, or an army, at your disposal, my lord Warwick, if the object of my generosity is to be His Grace of Clarence."

My father's expression remained completely impassive. I had expected to see some flicker of anger, of resentment, at least of frustration. There was nothing but bland interest. Again it made me think. Had he expected this rejection of Clarence, this destruction of his plans? What was it that he had said at Honfleur? *There is a price to pay.* Perhaps *this* was the price. The end of Clarence's ambitions was the final reckoning. And I knew beyond doubt that it had come as no surprise to my father. The Earl had been prepared for this outcome from the moment he had begun bargaining with Louis.

"Then I would ask, Your Majesty," the Earl continued, as if following a carefully prescribed set of steps in a dance, "if Clarence is not to replace Edward, whom do you suggest?"

Louis's smile widened. "I think it would be wise for you, my dear cousin, to speak with Margaret of Anjou."

Clarence's chair was thrust aside, toppling backward to smash against the floor as he lurched to his feet, his hands gripping the edge of the table regardless of the stiffening in the watchful figures of the royal bodyguard, hands on weapons. His face bone white, his eyes blazed as his features were twisted into a snarl of rage. He leaned to tower over my father's seated figure.

"No. No, I say. You'll not rid me of my birthright. I married your daughter. You vowed to support me."

"Yes. I did." The Earl was unmoved.

"Have we not collaborated together for this moment, when I will take what is rightfully mine?"

"His Majesty has the truth of it. Too many will question your right. The climate in England has changed," admitted the Earl softly.

"By God, it has changed beyond recognition if you would consider a union with the French whore!"

The Earl did not even hesitate. "I will consider it if I must."

"You've betrayed me, Warwick!"

"No. I have not yet made my decision."

"Have you not, by God?" Clarence's harsh, humorless laugh echoed off the walls. "You've effectively disinherited me. You've betrayed me for a purse of French gold. God damn you!" He thrust himself away from the table. "Isabel! Come with me." And he strode from the room with Isabel, who threw an apologetic look over her shoulder, pattering in his wake.

The shock at the outburst remained in the room. It was to be expected, yet it still left an uneasy taste on the tongue. Clarence might be uncontrolled but his words could not be denied. My father had abandoned him for a purse of French gold. The Earl would argue that he had no choice, but I felt the shame of it. And my father in alliance with Margaret of Anjou? It was an unthinkable situation. My mother placed her spoon down with careful deliberation and folded her hands in her lap. I think she was as awestruck as I.

Louis was singularly unruffled. "So," he continued, as if nothing had happened to disturb the tenor of the pleasant gathering, "Margaret of Anjou must figure in your planning."

The Earl's brows became a black bar of resistance. "God's blood!"

But you knew, didn't you! This is no surprise. You knew this would be the outcome and you know you must! I could see it in the Earl's carefully governed features.

Margaret of Anjou was a name as familiar to me as my own, for she was our sworn and bitter enemy. Wife to Henry of Lancaster, once King Henry VI, Margaret sat in exile at Louis's court, petitioning any who might listen to her strident pleas for gold and troops to take her back to England. Since the Earl had been instrumental in her husband's defeat and her own exile, she hated the Nevilles with a venom matched only by the detestation that my father felt for her. Unlikely bedfellows, all in all. What would it take for him to enter into an alliance with that woman, the French whore? I could not imagine it.

"Think of the advantages, my dear cousin." Louis at his most urbane. "It is by far the swiftest route to your return to power in England. The best pawn you can have in this evenly matched game between yourself and King Edward is Margaret's son, Edward of Lancaster. He is now seventeen years; his blood is true, his claim genuine as son of Henry VI. Since you need a suitable candidate for the throne, this is the best you can get. He is personable and I wager can be groomed to bear himself as the future King. Also"—Louis's hooded eyes gleamed—"the boy will do as his mother instructs him. Margaret keeps her son on a tight rein. He should be easy enough for you to handle."

"That woman has been my sworn enemy since the day I was old enough to first attend court." I saw my father's fingers tighten around the stem of his cup. "I will never negotiate with her."

Undeterred, Louis chuckled. "And she sees you in exactly the same uncomplimentary light. She blames *you* for her husband's downfall. But you are a man of many talents, Warwick, and of great charm. You can rewrite the relationship between you."

"I could . . . but I don't desire it."

"Listen, my lord." Now Louis stretched out his hand and fastened his fingers around my father's wrist, as if to shackle him to the idea. He painted an attractive picture in low, urgent tones. "Bury your past differences. Speak with Margaret; join forces with her. Return to England under the banner of Lancaster, overthrow King Edward, and rescue Henry from the Tower. Make him King again. He can't live forever. Once he is dead, then Edward of Lancaster will be King, with you at his side as his most trusted counselor, restored to your lands and position of power. A far better prospect for you than Clarence's dubious loyalties."

Still the Earl resisted. "Margaret of Anjou will be at his side, not me."

It was the obvious weakness in the whole plan. Louis acknowledged it with a twist of his lips but continued to push the point, like a huntsman pursuing the hare even when it had gone to ground. "Margaret will not be short of gratitude if you win the crown for her son."

"Perhaps. I still don't like it."

I watched as a little muscle quivered at the corner of the French King's mouth. Louis's patience had a finite quality. He withdrew his hand from my father's wrist and raised it palm upward as if to make a final offer. "Think of it from this angle. I will give you all you require for an invasion. But only on one condition: that your invasion is in the name of Lancaster and with Margaret as your ally. Without that, I am not open to an agreement between us, however sympathetic I might be to your plight." The hooded eyes gleamed. "Do you desire to remain in exile, impotent and dependent on my charity for the rest of your life, my lord Warwick?"

Their eyes locked and held but there was really no more room for maneuver.

"You give me no choice, sire."

"No, I don't, do I? But this should soften the blow. Margaret needs a man of military skill to lead an invasion for her. That man, I suggest, is *you*, my lord. So, as you see, a dual dependence here." Louis's smile was not without appreciative malice. "She has no choice either, however much your name might be an anathema to her. Do you not agree? With myself and Lancaster at your side, you cannot fail but to be victorious."

"Then I must accept, sire."

They joined in a firm handclasp of mutual respect.

"I will arrange a meeting. She'll be reluctant but she can be brought to see sense." Louis paused, and when I looked from my father to the French King to see what had taken his notice, I discovered that he was appraising me. His eyes were keen and considering, not a casual glance but a long, speculative look taking in every detail of my face and demeanor. I thought there was some humor there, but not much. I quickly looked away, my cheeks heating under his assessment.

"Think about this, my lord of Warwick," Louis remarked. "You have a major card that you can play in this alliance with the Lady of Anjou, if you have the skill to do so in the diplomatic game. I think you will understand me."

"Yes, sire. I think I do," the Earl replied slowly as if he would read through Louis's wily words.

A major card?

The content of the negotiations swirled in my head to form a series of uneasy patterns. I caught the look on the Earl's face, a deep complacency quickly hidden, but I had not been mistaken. This was what he had wanted all along: a Lancastrian alliance to ensure his restoration to power, to guarantee the return of our estates and property. The day of Clarence's usefulness had passed. If it had become necessary to abandon York and step in tune with Lancaster, then so be it. A victory indeed. Louis might plot and scheme, but I thought he had met his match in my father.

I took to my bed, too concerned with Isabel and her thwarted husband to sleep. What was it my mother had said before we retired? "Clarence's pride will be hurt beyond bearing."

To which the Earl had replied, "Better his hurt pride in France than that he become involved in an unplanned, failed attack on England, resulting in an ax on his pretty neck! I am not concerned. I shall keep him at my side."

But would it be so simple? Perhaps it would. Clarence could no longer pretend to have any place in Louis's plans, yet unless brother Edward was willing to forgive him, an unlikely prospect in the circumstances, the Earl was his only friend, which gave Clarence no choice but to stay and swallow his pride.

Poor Isabel. What manner of marriage was she now committed to, Clarence stoked with a fury of resentment? I found it in me to feel sorry for my sister.

And then when I finally closed my eyes, it was only to see again Louis's speculative stare turned on me, making my flesh creep. Tossing until the bedcovers were impossibly awry, I was relieved when my mother came into the room, carrying a night candle, hair tidily braided, nightshift covered by a heavy bed robe.

"You look tired, love." She plumped the bolster, smoothed the coverlet with casual efficiency. "Can you not sleep?"

"My brain races with all I heard." I sat up, grateful for the intrusion and seeing the possibility for some enlightenment. "Edward of Lancaster. Have I ever met him? I don't remember."

"Well, I think you might, before his father, Henry, was deposed. You would have been—what? Three years old. I doubt you'll remember."

"No. I have no recollection. What is he like? As lacking as Henry?"

"Just a young lad, mad for horses and battle when I last saw him."

I was not sufficiently concerned. I turned my mind to a matter of far greater interest. "When Louis asked my father if he would claim the throne, my father agreed that he has a claim. Is that true? And why will he never act on it?"

"The legality of it is not strong." The Countess made herself more comfortable. "It's no secret. Your father's grandmother, who died long before your own birth, was a lady called Joan Beaufort. Her father was John of Gaunt, one of the sons of Edward III. John married three times, and his third wife was Katherine Swynford. She had been his mistress for well over twenty years, all through his previous marriages."

"A scandal?" I was intrigued.

The Countess smiled. "It *was* a scandal. She was a widow, and governess to the daughters of John's first marriage. Most unsuitable, but their love proved indestructible, despite the condemnation of their unholy union, and so John wed her. He'd had four children by her outside the blessing of marriage, and one of them was Joan. These children were called Beaufort after a lordship John had once held in France. Hence all your Beaufort relatives."

True. There were any number of Beaufort uncles and aunts I could claim.

"The children were all illegitimate," continued the Countess. "But after John of Gaunt wed Katherine they were all legitimized."

"So my father *could* make a claim to the throne." My interest was piqued.

"Not so," the Countess explained. *"Excepta dignitate regali."*

My Latin was good enough to take the meaning. Legitimate but barred from ever making a claim on the crown. It opened my eyes to a thing or two. So I had royal blood in my veins.

"My father is very proud," I observed.

"Which Neville is not? But yes. And it hurt his pride beyond bearing when Edward turned to the Woodvilles."

"Enough to make him a traitor." It helped me to understand.

"Yes."

"So I shall never be Queen of England." With a clear image in my head I sat up and allowed mischief to take a hand, turning my head with marvelous condescension, stroking my hand down my hair as I had seen the Woodville Queen arrange her veil. "Don't you think I could wear the crown as well as Elizabeth Woodville?" A foolish flippancy that hardly deserved a serious answer. Yet the Countess chose to make one.

"Yes. You could. Your birth is certainly better!" It seemed for a moment that a shadow crossed my mother's face. Then she chuckled at my disrespectful mimicry and I decided it was just a trick of the light.

CHAPTER EIGHT

The Angevin woman will never agree to put her trust in the Earl. I know she won't." There was an edged satisfaction here as Isabel stitched immaculately at the furred cuff of her new gown. "She'll refuse to have anything to do with this invasion, and Louis will be forced to support my father with Clarence as King. Besides," she added in her misplaced loyalty, "it's only right that it should be so."

"Isabel!" How difficult it was to keep patience with this blinkered obstinacy. Even I could see what was and was not possible. "Of course she'll give way if she's serious about returning to England. She won't get there without Louis. Or without the Earl."

"What do you know!" The corners of Isabel's mouth dragged down.

"I know that Louis will not give her what she wants unless she takes on the Earl. *You* know it too! And what's more, you must stop calling her 'the Angevin woman'! If we are to be true Lancastrians, we must address her as Queen Margaret."

"I won't."

"You must." She was beyond my bearing. "Can't you see—"

"But then there'll be no hope for Clarence. And I can do nothing to help him." It came out as a wail of despair, with a splash of tears onto the sable fur.

"Perhaps not. But weeping will not help. And it's not your fault, Isabel."

"But disappointment makes him so ill-tempered. And I lost the child. . . ."

Which explained her fraught mood. I cursed with silent venom the vain, self-indulgent man Clarence was. Isabel was destined for a life of complaint and dissatisfaction and sour criticism at his hands. His failures would always be the fault of anyone but himself. So I sat with her, hugged her. Little lines of strain and disappointment had appeared around her mouth in recent weeks. She leaned her head on my shoulder for a time, as if she enjoyed the comfort, but then shrugged me off in a quick return to her previous sulk.

"I can't believe that Clarence will never be King. I will *not* believe it."

I sighed. *I can!* I said nothing, simply squeezed her hand. Even I could see that Clarence, with his claims and demands, had become an embarrassment. I stirred myself to entertain her, involving her in a game of cards as I buried my own misery, delivered thoughtlessly that morning by a Neville courier.

"Tell me of His Grace of Gloucester. Have you news of him?"

The courier had brought a warning to the Earl from his brother Montague: *Don't even consider an invasion of England at this time.* Edward, suspecting that we might take up the Lancastrian cause, was raising a vast army and fitting out a fleet to prevent our return. The Queen was carrying a child again, Edward ordering Masses, that he might at last have a son. No mention was made of Richard. There was no reason why there should be, but I had followed the messenger as he departed, caught him in one of the antechambers, plucked at his sleeve, and demanded to know.

He looked down at me, opened his mouth to brush me off but obviously saw my status. "What would you wish to know, lady?"

Everything! "Where is he? What is he doing? Is he in the King's good grace?"

He indulged me. "The Duke is constantly at Edward's side, lady, with the King's entire confidence. His authority grows daily as his experience grows."

All well and good, but I wanted more. "Is he in good health?"

"As far as I'm aware. He travels the length and breadth of the country often enough without ill effect, so he must be." Impatient now, he made for the door. "King Edward plans to reward him for his loyalty."

"Good. That's good."

"It's the highest reward."

"Is it a new office?" I felt my heart swell with pride for him.

"No, lady. The King is negotiating a marriage for him."

"Oh!" Everything stilled around me. A hand clenched around my belly. I repeated the words silently in my head: *The King is negotiating a marriage for him.*

"A major coup, so they say," the courier continued as he pulled on his gloves, unaware of the ice that had frozen my blood. "With the daughter of Duke Charles of Burgundy. The lady is heiress in her own right. She will be Duchess of Burgundy on her father's death."

"Mary of Burgundy." I heard my voice confirm the name, yet it did not seem to be mine. "She is of my age, I think."

"Yes, lady. And a beauty by reputation. Such a marriage is much desired by the King and by the Duke of Gloucester also. It's promoted by the King's own sister, who is the lady's stepmother. Now, your pardon, lady. I must go."

I was left to stand alone in the empty room as I considered the news. Mary of Burgundy for Richard. Encouraged by Richard's own sister Margaret, who had married Duke Charles. Of course she would see the advantage of such a marriage. When Mary became Duchess in the fullness of time, Richard would become Duke of that wealthy and powerful little duchy. And she was beautiful, so rumor said. Fair and auburn haired, with neat features and an inborn elegance. What a catch for Richard. Jealousy swam strong and bitter through every inch of my body until it choked me so that I could barely swallow. If I could not have him, what right had she? I might have been brought up to understand that people of our rank had no choice in whom they wed, but at that moment I was as blind to reality as Isabel was to Clarence's future. Richard was mine. He was not free to wed another.

Then the opening and closing of a distant door woke me to my present situation, an uncomfortable guest of the French King with no home, no wealth, no status. My separation from Richard was permanent. Any fool must know it and accept it. Of course he would wed a lady of consequence and power, a lady of reputable beauty. *Besides*, the devil whispered in my ear, taking advantage of my distress, *how fickle is a man's heart. Richard is free to give his heart where he wills, since it cannot be yours.*

Dismay overwhelmed me.

"What is it?" Isabel asked, laying down her cards, seeing the desolation in my face that I had failed to hide.

"Nothing!" Then: "Richard! He is to marry."

"What did you expect? You knew he must."

Of course I did. It did not make the pain any less. Later, in a moment of abject weakness, I contemplated writing to him as I once had when I was a child and lonely. By what means I would have the letter delivered, I had no idea, but I set to with pen and parchment and a heart of stone.

My dearest Richard,

I am here at Amboise. My father negotiates to betray York and lead a Lancastrian invasion to England in the name of Margaret of Anjou. You will probably meet with him on the battlefield. I cannot bear the thought. I hear that you are to wed Mary of Burgundy.

My heart is broken.
Anne Neville

I could think of nothing more to write, either that he would want to know or that I could express. Any words of love were dried up, or perhaps drowned in my wretched misery. I could have spoken them, if he had appeared at that moment in the doorway and I could have stepped into his arms. But to write them? When I knew that his promises and loyalty, his kisses and the intimacy of his body would be given to another? I think that at that moment, as jealousy once again poisoned my thoughts, I hated him. I wept helplessly over that letter, blurring the words until they were illegible before smearing them even further with an impatient hand. What use mourning the past that was dead and buried? So I burned the sorry letter in the hearth. I watched the edges curl and collapse into ash, exactly as my dreams of finding Richard again withered and died, then shook myself from my wretchedness. To wallow in misery would bring me no advantage. I dried the useless tears and drove myself to seek out Isabel, to suggest that we request horses from His Majesty's stables and explore the countryside along the river Loire. It did nothing to restore my spirits. Isabel's surly agreement exactly matched my mood, and my attempts not to think of Richard Plantagenet failed hopelessly.

"Your Majesty!" His long-suffering impatience superbly disguised, Louis addressed the small woman who sat in formal state on the dais, her ladies-in-waiting flanking her as if she were in fact still Queen of England. "I would present to you the Countess of Warwick. Also her younger daughter, Lady Anne Neville." He extended his arm in an expansive gesture, beckoning us forward.

The initial stage of the contest of will between King Louis on our behalf and Queen Margaret—see what a loyal Lancastrian I was becoming—was played out at the château of Angers without our presence. I heard of the vitriolic exchanges thirdhand. She was shocked, horrified, and furious in equal measure. And speechless. A miracle worthy of Thomas of Canterbury. When she had recovered sufficiently to find suitable words, she stamped herself into a furious tirade of argument against "that thrice-damned Neville, this worm of Satan." Yet however much Queen Margaret might detest him, worse than a poisoned chalice, still she had lived up to her reputation of being as changeable as a weathercock in a gale. We had been summoned to Angers.

I was rigid with fear.

We approached and curtsied, kneeling, since Louis had advised us that such a show of deference might be no bad thing in the circumstances. But only the Countess and myself. The Queen still held all the court cards in the pack, as far as I could see. At the last she had refused to see my father. Or Clarence and Isabel. But she had graciously consented to allow the presentation of myself and my mother. It was a burden on our shoulders to make a good impression and persuade her to change her mind again and allow the Earl to approach.

The heat of July pressed down upon us, on the heavy velvet of our new gowns. Beneath my veil I could feel perspiration prickle uncomfortably along my hairline. In the silence that followed Louis's words, we remained on our knees, our gazes on the floor. The seconds passed as I studied the pattern in the tiles. How long would she keep us like this? And what would she say when she had humiliated us to her satisfaction? What would she find to say that would give this meeting any value?

Consign them to a dungeon. Confiscate their possessions. Lock them away as my husband, Henry, is incarcerated and robbed of his rightful inheritance.

"You may stand."

Her voice was low, carefully neutral, pleasant on the ear. She spoke English with a smooth fluency, having made a deliberate effort to learn it on the occasion of her marriage, but her accent lingered despite her years in England. Perhaps, I decided, knowing the lady's reputation for stubborn self-will, she had never tried to modify it.

"I do remember you, of course, my lady of Warwick, but not your daughter."

I risked a glance. Cold. Frigidly hostile, she stared down at us.

Margaret of Anjou was no friend to us, nor ever would be. Standing at last, I could remedy my curiosity about this woman whom I had been taught to regard as the enemy, evil incarnate, the French whore—any number of such appellations to be found within Yorkist circles. I suppose I expected some old hag, harsh featured, face riven with deep lines, much like the witches and imps of ill intent in folktales. I could not have been more wrong. Seated on a gilded throne, her small jeweled hands curled around the carved arms, was a formidably handsome woman.

Her air of intelligent vitality, of enormous energy, impressed most. Small in stature, she might be dwarfed by the magnificent chair with its swagged canopy, but there was no repressing her unbending authority. At present it was all directed in a gaze of pure hatred toward the two of us. Her hair was covered by a swath of turbaned damask, but I knew that she would be fair. Her skin was soft, light, with a dusting of freckles across the bridge of her straight nose. Her lips were small and firm, as was her chin, now raised against us in contempt. And her eyes, sharp and brightly hazel in hue, betrayed nothing of her thoughts other than sharp detestation of this whole episode. I had seen such an expression before on the face of our steward at Middleham, Master Hampton, when our storerooms had been overrun one autumn with a plague of rats. In a vicious campaign he had set loose the dogs to catch and kill with a fierce shake and a bite to the neck. This was Margaret, appraising the wife and daughter of her enemy, resenting every moment that she must consort with vermin such as us. And, under Louis's watchful eye, she could not dispatch us as easily as Master Hampton had the rats.

"What have you to say to me?"

The Countess, reluctant but resigned, had been well briefed. She folded her hands at her waist and spoke with an impressive display of deep sincerity. "I would advise you of my lord Warwick's sincere intent toward you and your son, Your Majesty."

"You would, of course." Margaret turned her flat gaze from my mother and stared at me with no lessening in her disfavor. "And you. What have you to say, as daughter to the arch traitor? Your father robbed my son of his inheritance. Now you know what it is to be stripped of your lands and your birthright. *Mon Dieu!* It gives me great satisfaction to know it. What do *you* have to say about your noble father's honor?" Her teeth showed in a quick, feral smile. "Does such a thing exist?"

I was speechless, overcome with nerves. I had not expected this. I had not expected her to address even a single word to me, much less ask my opinion. I did not even understand why she should ask to see me. "Your Majesty . . ." I swallowed the nerves. "My father has seen the error of his ways. He would unite with the cause of Lancaster. He would restore King Henry to the throne."

I watched as the small mouth twisted. "Well taught indeed."

"I hear what my father says," I replied, keeping my wits to defend the Earl. "I have never known him willingly to break his word or to act without honor."

"He married your sister to Clarence without Edward's consent, did he not?" she snapped back immediately. "Is that honor? Is that not a betrayal of trust?"

"It is true. He did arrange the marriage." My mind sought for something—anything—to explain away that obvious show of rebellion. "Perhaps it was a betrayal because King Edward spoke heatedly against it. But His Grace of Clarence was old enough to give his own consent and did not need his brother's permission." I repeated the opinions I had heard. "A papal dispensation was sought. My sister too was of an age to give her consent." It was the best I could do.

Margaret did not deign to reply, waving aside my explanation with an imperious hand. Relief washed through me.

"And how old are you?" she asked suddenly. Again a surprise that jolted me into sharp awareness.

"Fourteen years, Your Majesty."

"Hmm." She looked me over, from head to foot, as if I were so far below her that she would crush me, like a black beetle, beneath her gilded leather shoe. We waited as the tension built until it seemed that the whole space beneath the arched roof was full, packed tight from arch to arch with Margaret's animosity. It had a weight of its own that lay on us even more heavily than the breathless heat. Then Margaret's eyes shifted once more to the Countess.

"Your husband has vilified my good name. He has smeared the parentage of my son. He had the temerity to suggest that the Prince is the offspring of adultery. How do I forgive that?"

What use in denying what was universally known? "The Earl regrets it, Your Majesty. He was wrong to do so. He would ask your pardon for any hurt he has caused you and the Prince, your son. My lord the Earl asks nothing more than to be restored to your good favor, and be allowed to serve you, as a sign of his sincere repentance."

How smoothly the Earl of Warwick's abject contrition was offered. I could feel my mother's disgust in her rigid shoulders, the little quiver of her gossamer veiling on its golden wires, that she should have to make the gesture, but nothing showed in the calm voice or in the respectfully bent head.

Margaret would have none of it.

"A pardon? Service to the cause of Lancaster? Only because he cannot return to England any other way. Repentance, by God!" All the cold, banked anger flared into hot-blooded fury. "Liars! All of you! You will say what suits. You may call it pragmatism. I call it hypocrisy." She stood so suddenly as to cause her ladies to step back in wave of consternation. "I recommend that you resign yourself to exile in some foreign court, as I have been so condemned. To throw yourself on the charity of the few who might listen to your distress." Lifting her skirts with one hand, she gestured to her gown. "Poverty is hard to bear for those who have known only luxury."

Rich enough, the bright green of summer beech leaves, her gown was furred and beribboned, but I had not noticed until this moment that the nap was worn on the front panel, at hem and sleeve; nor was it in the style of present fashion. Her rings were her only jewels, forcing me to consider that she had probably pawned the rest to raise a loan.

"I know what it is to beg and hoard the meager wealth I have," she confirmed. "To sell and pawn what is mine like some common merchant. How will proud Warwick face such humiliation? I know what it is like. I would wish it to be three times as heavy on his black soul as it has been on mine. Don't look to me for aid, my lady of Warwick. I will never accept the Earl of Warwick as an ally." She all but spat the last words, then turned from us to bow her head curtly to Louis, who had sat silently through the whole proceedings. "Your Majesty. I have done what you wished of me. I have met with this traitorous family. I have nothing more to say to them. I shall now retire to my rooms."

What abject failure of our mission. Proud and vindictive, Margaret swept from our presence. All we could report back to the Earl was that she was not willing to give an inch.

At least the accommodations at Angers were an improvement on Amboise.

Angers had a library. It helped to make my life bearable as a place of refuge where it was possible, if only for a few hours, to forget. It did not rival King Edward's collection of fine books and manuscripts at Westminster, but as the summer settled into a period of unseasonal rain, it offered me the stories of Boccaccio and histories, books of fine paintings of plants and flowers, a hearty relief from Lady Masham's works of piety and morality.

We had settled into the royal castle at Angers. Well used to travel as we were, this was not the same, with no comfort of familiarity, no ease of well-remembered rooms. Nor did we have our possessions around us, our servants other than our most personal attendants. Everything was strange. All I owned was packed into one small wooden chest. Dresses and shifts, a winter cloak lined with fur, the necessary accessories for me to appear decently in public. A metal bird and a pair of embroidered gauntlets. How vulnerable we were. I had no experience of this bone-chilling insecurity, but learned it tenfold in those days when Neville failure and defeat faced us at every turn. Queen Margaret swept through the corridors and audience chambers of Angers, her childhood home before her marriage, with the confi-

dence of ownership, meeting us without even the barest acknowledgment of our existence, haughty in her knowledge that hers would be
the deciding voice in any negotiations.

Not that there were any after her rejection of our suit.

We had been there more than a week when another heavy shower
drove Isabel and myself from the formal terraces to the refuge of the
library. Running from the deluge, shaking the rain from our gowns,
we entered with laughter and flushed cheeks, a momentary return of
youthful spirits not much in evidence in recent days.

We were not the first to seek its refuge.

A young man, resplendent in vivid silks and velvet, their deep
blue enhancing the russet lights in his hair, stood before the fireplace,
where a fire had been lit against the chill morning. Soft voiced, he
was engaged in issuing orders in rapid French to a servant. Yet not a
servant of Angers, for we immediately recognized him. Thomas, the
Earl's youngest squire, an angular and unpolished lad who had been
waylaid by the unknown gentleman and commandeered into service.

"Bring me wine. And then build up the fire. It's cold in here." The
courtier turned his head in our direction, hearing the opening and
closing of the door, the clamor of our voices when we first entered. He
immediately bowed to us with a graceful flourish. "Then serve these
two ladies who look in need of refreshment."

He was young, perhaps the age of Isabel. His welcome should
have put us at our ease, his face being open, pleasant, a little smile
on his lips, yet I found myself immediately, uncomfortably aware of
our less-than-tidy appearance, the damp hem of my gown, beside
this exquisitely groomed courtier. Before I could stop, I found myself
smoothing the folds of my veil and twitching my sleeves into place.
I could feel my face heat with annoyance under his cool appraisal.
Meanwhile Thomas went about his work, slow at first to comply. He
could speak French, as I knew, as any well-educated youth from a
good family would, but the young man's accent and drawled delivery
perhaps made the words difficult to grasp.

"Come, boy. Wine, I said. King Louis's servants are usually more efficient." Decorative, imperious, smiling still, the courtier pointed to the chased silver flagon and stemmed goblets set out on the cupboard.

Thomas, flushed, poured and carried the cup as he had been meticulously taught, presenting it to the young man with an inclination of his head, as he would to the Earl. The young man took the cup.

"My thanks. But you must learn not to keep me waiting, you understand. You are very young, I suppose, and not used to the ways of this court." He leaned forward, lowering his voice intimately. "You should show me more respect when offering me wine."

He struck Thomas a blow to the shoulder with the flat of his hand, as a friend might in a companionable gesture of good humor, but the impression stayed with me that there was more weight in it than friendship. Enough to make Thomas, slight at only twelve years, stagger a little as he kept his balance. Enough to make me march forward with sharp words, except that Isabel took tight hold of my skirts. Thomas kept his composure and brought the silver tray with two goblets for Isabel and myself. I could see his fingers grasping the curved rim, white as bone, as he determined to do the job well. Although I smiled reassuringly and murmured my thanks, Thomas blinked with anxiety.

"Now build up the fire."

The clear order made Thomas scurry to manhandle the large logs on the hearth, aware that every movement was closely watched, carrying out his task with credit despite a clumsy nervousness. Then he straightened to await more orders.

"Do you require any further service, my lord?"

"You should kneel before me." It was gently said, simply a smooth reminder.

Thomas promptly did so. Head tilted, the young man surveyed him for a long moment. "Good. That is all."

Thomas leaped to his feet and departed, with more speed than elegance, and only a quick bow and glance in our direction, and that of pure shame. A ripple of unease touched me. I had never seen the Earl or the Countess strike even a servant in our household, much less a squire from a gentle family, as this courtier had done. Yet he had smiled, showing no evidence of temper or anger. I decided I had been mistaken. Thomas had been caught unawares, unbalanced, whilst the courtier's words, his whole demeanor, had been pleasant enough.

Isabel and I were still standing just inside the door. The young man set down the goblet and approached. Once more he bowed, a gleam of white teeth. He was all courtesy and well-bred good manners. As I felt the warmth of his charm the little throb in my throat picked up its beat.

"Make use of the library, *mesdames*. It should now be warm enough to your comfort." He spread his arms, engulfing us in a cloud of cloyingly sweet perfume yet with an underlying, more pungent aroma within it, as he indicated that we should move toward the fire. His eyes touched on mine, then passed on to Isabel. The smile deepened. "You must forgive me if I leave you. I have a pressing engagement. . . ."

He walked out, leaving the door open as he strode along the corridor.

I was forced to admit the attraction. Any woman would. And yet why had he not acknowledged us? I knew, from the glint in his eye, that he had recognized who we were. As he must have known who Thomas was, that he was not a mere servant. The Neville bear and ragged staff had been clear on his livery for anyone to see; it was not an unknown heraldic motif. I frowned at the courtier's departing back, at the arrogant swing of his cloak and the stylish peacock feathers in his cap. He should at least have shown us some respectful recognition, whatever the disagreements between our two families.

Isabel and I looked at each other. "And that, I presume, is the man whom we would wish to put on the throne of England," she stated.

"Yes. He's very handsome." I spoke the first words to come into my head.

"I can't deny it." Isabel scowled as if she would like to. "But do you think he would be a better candidate than Clarence?"

In all honesty I did not know. My cheeks heated again at the memory of his close, knowing scrutiny. We knew who he was without any introduction. The rich auburn hair and fair skin, the mix of green and brown in his eyes, all the exact coloring of his mother. Even without the gleaming display of ostrich feathers in gold on his breast, we knew who he was.

Edward of Lancaster.

I spent the day—the following few days—thinking over that first meeting. I did not see him again—although I admit I looked for him in the vast rooms and rain-drenched gardens—but the impression remained strong with me. Physically beautiful, tall and athletic, well proportioned in leg and arm, the Prince would steal the eye, whether at a banquet or when engaged in the lists or in the disciplines of a tourney. I could imagine him—and did so in my many moments of idleness—riding forward, all elegant grace and honed skill, armor gleaming, horse burnished but well controlled under his hand, to claim a lady's scarf to wear on his sleeve. I imagined myself in the role of presenting him with my favor, tucking it intimately beneath the plates of his shoulder guard, and his carrying it to victory, to the jealousy of every other lady present, as the sun touched with red-gold his hair that curled and waved with silken extravagance when he finally removed his helm to receive the victor's reward from my hands.

It was an engrossing image that filled my thoughts.

I sighed as the days passed without any recurrence of our meeting. Edward of Lancaster was handsome, astonishingly so, yet in no degree feminine. Any delicacy was offset by a stubborn chin and a masterful nose, whilst his eyes were fierce and challenging. I remembered that his fingers around the cup, as jeweled as his mother's, had been long and slender. As for his presence . . . If his mother claimed little money to spend on her own appearance, it was not so with her son. Was all she had, all she could raise in loans, to be spent on him, to portray him as the Prince of Wales, England's heir? The heavy collar set with fine sapphires that had graced his chest, the matching ring-brooch in his cap to secure the peacock feathers, would have outfitted a ship to take him across the channel.

Then, because I was not given to dishonesty, guilt struck. How could I allow my inner eye to be ambushed by this unknown young man, simply on the strength of a brilliant smile? And I found myself drawing a mental comparison with Richard of Gloucester, placing the two side by side so that I could see them both in my mind. I did not like the result. At first Richard receded in that comparison. Less impressive all around in form and figure, his coloring less brilliant, Richard faded alarmingly beside the glowing Prince Edward. Nor did Richard's austere features win him any merit beside the handsome heir of Lancaster.

Was I as fickle a lover as I had accused Richard of being? The thought did not please me, but how easy it was to be blinded by Margaret's son. If when he smiled his eyes had remained cool and thoughtful, what did that matter? If he had pretended ignorance of our state, was that important? Perhaps it was a product of living out his adult life in exile, on charity, his future uncertain, that made him circumspect. And to live under the dominion of Margaret of Anjou, as the sole object of her interest, into whom she poured every drop of her ambition—would that not have an effect on the man, making him careful and quick to hide his thoughts?

And yet he had struck Thomas. Richard, my Richard, would never act like that. I blinked against a quick rush of tears that took me unawares. I must not let myself dwell on the past. Everything had changed. Mary of Burgundy's Richard would always act with respect and consideration. In my mind I could see him as I had on that last occasion at Warwick, intense and driven, his eyes dark and full of secrets. Did he pin my image next to that of the lovely Mary of Burgundy? If he did, I would be found wanting. The tears spilled over and I made no attempt to stop them.

Two melancholy thoughts troubled my sleep. Richard could never be mine. And Edward of Lancaster, however attractive he might be, was nothing to me. I was not even sure that I liked him very much, although I could not have explained why.

*   *   *

Relief swept through our apartments, a soothing breath of wind in the June heat. When we had all but given up hope, Margaret of Anjou agreed to meet with the Earl. If she would but agree to the alliance, we could be on board ship, sailing for England again by the end of the year. But with what I thought might be habitual spite, the Queen kept us waiting interminably through the hours, until the late evening of the day. Weary but determined to wring from the occasion as much advantage as we could, we were ushered into her presence once more, again with Louis present to smooth our difficult path.

The Countess and I led the way, curtsied as we had before. Unsmiling, again enthroned, Margaret gave a curt inclination of her head, the slightest lift of her hand from her lap. We rose, stepped back. So far, so good. Next came Isabel and Clarence. Margaret barely looked at them as they showed their respect, but impatiently waved them to stand beyond her line of sight. Because there, before her, the object of her undying hatred, was the Earl. He stood at Louis's side, richly but somberly clad in black velvet and richly draped cap, jewels glinting in the final rays of the sun.

"Do you think it wise . . . ?" my mother had asked on seeing his magnificence.

The Earl had been uncompromising. "I will beg for forgiveness because I must, but not as a pauper or a commoner. My family is as good as hers."

"She's the daughter of a royal family," the Countess chided, although I could see without much hope of success. "King René, her father, is—"

"King René is naught but a penniless client of Louis's."

My mother conceded defeat. "Just don't let her see that you think she is inferior!"

I held my breath. So, I think, did my mother. Louis halted. My father continued to approach. He bowed low. Then he knelt before the Queen, straight backed, head bent to await the verdict. Silently I exhaled. This was the moment of decision for all of us. As we waited, an interruption that caused Louis to frown, a rapid footstep sounded from behind me as a newcomer entered the chamber, and onto the dais stepped the young man of the library. As impressively clad as before, he knelt before his mother in quick reverence before standing to take his position at her side. One hand resting on his sword hilt, the other gripping the carved back of the throne, he cast an all-encompassing glance over the scene. Then as Margaret sat immobile, Prince Edward leaned, one glittering hand on the arm of the throne, to whisper in her ear. White-faced, Margaret said not one word, neither to her son nor to my father.

It seemed that the silence would smother us all. It was Louis, of course, who broke it. "Your Majesty. As you agreed, my dear cousin the Earl of Warwick is here, at his own request, to beg your forgiveness and offer his services to you to restore your power in England."

Still Margaret took her time to consider. And then: "Warwick! I never thought to see you kneel before me. It is my inclination to damn your soul to the fires of hell for eternity."

"I put myself at your mercy, Your Majesty."

Unblinking, she stared at his bent head. "You are the source of all my ills. How should you expect mercy?"

"I stood against you," the Earl admitted. "I saw you as my enemy, an enemy who would destroy me and those who were my friends. I had not deserved such animosity and so I struck back. I admit my mistakes. All I ask is that I can show my good faith by putting right the wrongs I have done."

"And what is best for the future? What is best in the eyes of the Earl of Warwick? How will you right the wrongs?" the Prince intervened before his mother could answer. There was no anger in his question, rather a calm understanding of our dilemma. He took one step forward as if to encourage the Earl. "What would you ask of Her Majesty, as well as her mercy?"

"An alliance, my lord Prince," the Earl replied without hesitation. "Lancaster and Neville. That I might lead an invasion in your name. I swear on the blood of Christ that I will be as much Edward of York's foe in future as I have been his friend. And as much *your* friend as I have been your foe." All spoken with my father's eyes never lifting beyond the hem of the Queen's gown. Margaret pursed her lips.

"I must consider." Which she did. Time crawled, endlessly. "You would rescue my lord Henry and place the crown on his head once more?"

"I would, Your Majesty. I swear it."

Then a longer silence, her needlelike scrutiny flitting from the Earl to Louis, then back to the Earl, while she kept my father on his knees. Spine erect, muscles braced, he maintained his position without any sign of physical discomfort. Or of the humiliation to the very depths of his soul. How could he ever serve this woman who could reduce him to this role of beggar? How could he put himself—and his family—so completely into her hands?

"How do I know that I can trust you?" she demanded at last.

And Louis was there at the Earl's side to make the reply. "I will personally guarantee the Earl's fidelity, the sincerity of his words. He will not betray you."

"Then I have decided." Her eyes held the Earl's, dagger bright. "There are conditions, of course. You will publicly withdraw your slanderous remarks about my son's birth and my own honor. You must take an oath before God to serve me loyally."

"I will, Your Majesty."

"Then . . ." With a faint frown she looked up at her son, as if groping for an assurance of the rightness of her decision, and he responded with a smile of such sweetness that it took my breath. He leaned again to place his hand on her wrist, the lightest pressure of fingers on the soft fur of the cuff. And for the briefest of moments I saw Margaret's face as it softened in maternal love. Could Margaret with her fierce and driven ambitions and hostilities be capable of such a tender emotion? It seemed that she could.

Her face hardening again, as stony as the towers of Angers, she made her response. "My lord of Warwick. My son and I are in agreement. I will agree to pardon you. I will agree to enter into an alliance with you."

It was done. The agreement was made as at last—*at last*—the Earl was allowed to rise from his knees. I felt the relief flutter under my rib cage and begin to grow until I had to struggle against the desire to laugh aloud at the new horizon that had come into view. No longer homeless exiles. My father would return to England with an army and, with France behind him with all its wealth and power, and Edward of Lancaster as a figurehead to draw the nobility to his banner, he would surely defeat Edward of York. Then we could all go home to Warwick or to Middleham and life would be as it had always been. All the security and comfort that I had taken for granted would be mine again. . . .

My thoughts came to a dramatic halt, as if in collision with the very stone wall that hemmed us in. If Edward of York was defeated, what would be his fate, and that of Richard? If they survived the ensuing battle, it would be to escape into exile. And if in exile, powerless and without hope of restoration, would Richard's betrothal to Mary of Burgundy be rejected? I knew the answer to that, right enough. The Burgundian marriage would be abandoned—but neither would my father consider him as a candidate for me. Relief turned sour. There was no chance for me, for our reconciliation, whichever way it fell out.

My thoughts had wandered, leaving me deaf to those who spoke around me, my eyes focused on the brilliant gems on the Queen's right hand. Then I blinked back to my surroundings, my senses alert.

What was that? I looked around me.

Something had happened to spike the tension again. Margaret was angry, red-faced with emotion. Prince Edward governed his features. Isabel was staring directly, furiously, at me. Beside me the Countess inhaled sharply. Whatever it was, I appeared to have become the center of attention. What had I missed? I looked helplessly toward the Countess, whose return gaze slid along the edge of pity. The Earl caught my eye, stern and unsmiling.

What had I done?

"How dare you suggest so outrageous a step!" Margaret demanded, surging to her feet.

"An excellent suggestion," Louis disagreed. And there he was beside me, actually taking one of my hands in his. What had he said? And what was it to me? All I could think was that his hand was uncomfortably hot. My inclination was to snatch mine away but I could not, so I stood and endured his sweat-slicked palm sliding over my fingers as he repeated the suggestion that had created such passions.

"Your Majesty. I know that the Earl of Warwick is more than willing to offer his daughter's hand in marriage to your son. You should grasp it with both hands. It is an inestimable offer."

"For whom? I see nothing of value in it!"

The words circled my head, moths around a dangerous flame, whilst I tried to pluck them from the air and make sense of them. The Earl offering his daughter . . . ? But *I* was his daughter. And to wed Edward of Lancaster, who would one day be crowned King of England?

By the Virgin! How stupid I must be, how blindly slow to see the new direction here. What my feelings were, I had no idea. I could barely grasp the words, much less their implication. It was not real. Surely I must at any moment awake from a dream—a nightmare—to find it all a mummers' charade. Heart lurching sickeningly, I turned my head to see what the Prince might think. I couldn't tell. Those hazel eyes were quite still, fixed on me, deep in some consideration that I could not read. Then he smiled. Gave a little bow as if it would be the greatest pleasure in the world for him to take me as his wife.

I will be Anne of Lancaster, Queen of England.

"No! I will *never* consider it." Margaret destroyed that thought.

And I breathed out slowly against the constriction in my chest, part fear, part excitement. Of course she would never agree. What could Louis have been thinking? Since it had taken a miracle for Margaret to come to speaking terms with my father, she would hardly consent to a closer alliance with the prospect of her future grandchildren, the future rulers of England, carrying the Neville blood in their veins. There was nothing for me to worry about. Astonishingly, my first thought, and it came to me as a heartfelt relief, was that I would never have to face Margaret of Anjou as her daughter-in-law.

But another revelation crept in to supersede the first. What if the original proposal had not come from Louis? What if my father had broached it? His oblique observation on board the ship off Honfleur, meaning nothing to me then, now came back to me. *You, my daughter, will be made welcome at all events.* Had he had this marriage alliance in mind all along?

Surrounded as I was by a major battle of wills, I began that day to learn a lesson in political maneuvering. Louis might have the nose for duplicity, but when power was at stake, the Earl could be as self-interested as the French King. Perhaps neither could be trusted.

There will be a price to be paid.

Another of the Earl's now apparently portentous statements that I in my ignorance had misinterpreted. I had presumed the price would be paid by my father's dignity. Or even by Clarence's ambitions. Now I saw I had been wrong on both counts. *I* was the one to pay the price. And it had been in the Earl's mind from the moment we had left the shores of England.

Margaret blazed with fury, her small figure almost shaking with the emotion, hands balled into fists at her sides, as if she would strike out at anyone who came close enough to risk her wrath. Certainly she was beyond considering her choice of words as she vented her anger on the King of France.

"Is this to be what I must do in return for French gold?" she demanded of Louis. "I have made the alliance you wanted with this man. Is that not enough? Do I have to take the daughter as well? Do I have to bind the royal blood of my son to a commoner and a traitor?"

Louis was unperturbed. Taking Margaret's arm in a hold that could not be resisted, he led her aside to a window embrasure, where he bent his head and proceeded to drop words of heavy persuasion into her ear. If my mind had not been centered on the enormity of the suggestion, I could guess the content of the advice. The marriage would tie Warwick into the scheme, his loyalty ensured for all time. He would never act against the chance of his daughter becoming Queen. Louis's soft tones, the faintly hissing syllables, continued on and on, drifting across to us. Margaret listened but with no alteration to her set features. Sometimes she replied shortly, with sharp hand gestures, while her son watched her across the distance of the room, with a fine groove between his brows. As for the rest of us, we stood like statues. Eventually Louis straightened, speaking so that we all must hear.

"Yours is the final decision, Your Majesty. But you must weigh the costs to your invasion plans if you reject her."

"I know the costs far too well, Your Majesty." The reply was snapped back.

Margaret returned to the dais as if unwilling to give my father the advantage of height, lifting the weight of her skirts to face him. The interlude had at least given her the time to harness her temper.

"I am told that I must give you an answer. This is my answer. Did you think I would leap at your offer, Monsieur de Warwick? I find it beyond belief that you would offer your daughter as my son's bride when you once deliberately challenged the legitimacy of the Prince's birth. Such hypocrisy is not to be borne. I will not agree."

"Consider the strength of our joint attack on England, Your Majesty," the Earl urged, trying to repair the damage. "Consider what your son and I can achieve together for Lancaster."

"My audience with you, Monsieur de Warwick, is at an end."

I was rejected. So much hatred expressed in such controlled sentences.

It was late when we returned to our accommodations. The end of a long day with strange doors opening and closing. I made my curtsy to the Earl and Countess, too tired to think any more. I saw the same exhaustion etched into every face. Clarence followed Isabel, halting briefly by the door to look back to the Earl, face drawn with self-pity after the momentous decisions.

"It was all for nothing, wasn't it? I betrayed my brother, broke my oath given before God to be loyal to my King. And for what? What have I achieved? Nothing."

There was no reply anyone could make in denial.

I had all but stretched out my hand to the latch on the door when, without warning, it was flung back to thud against the wall. Dramatic to the last, Margaret of Anjou stood on the threshold, the Prince a step behind her. She strode into the room to come to an abrupt stop close before the Earl, eyes feverishly searching his face.

"I have been persuaded. Very well, Monsieur de Warwick. I will agree. My son will wed the girl."

"Your Majesty! I am honored! You have all my gratitude." Showing no surprise at this complete volte-face, the Earl bowed, hand on heart.

Margaret continued, driven by some strange emotion. "Don't thank me. It is against all my better judgment, but I am led to believe that I must."

"Our alliance will restore Lancaster."

"That is my one hope. I pray for it every minute of every day. But one thing I will not allow." Her features hardened further. "I will not allow my son to accompany you on the initial invasion."

I saw my father stiffen. "Surely that is our strongest weapon, Your Majesty—to show Prince Edward of Lancaster to the nobility of England and give them a figurehead for their allegiance."

"I will not allow it. The Prince will travel to England with me, once the invasion is begun and victory is secure. Once Edward of York's hold on power is destroyed. Then the Prince will take his place at the head of the troops, in his father's name. That is my final word on it."

She extended her hand, stiffly gracious with magnificent condescension, to allow my father to salute her fingers. If she felt any distaste over the contact, she mastered it admirably. As did my father in accepting the Prince's absence. Removing her hand from my father's hold, Margaret held it out to me.

"Come here."

I obeyed. Stood before her.

"I do not choose you as wife for my son, but I must accept that the enemy of my enemy must become my friend." Her lip curled as if she would accept no such thing. "Let us hope you can learn to bear yourself as a Princess. My son has been raised from the cradle to know that he is Prince of Wales. Edward!" Imperiously she called to him. "Come and meet your bride. She is become the key to the door that is England, the route to your throne, so it seems." She regarded me with an uncomfortable intensity that lacked even a vestige of tolerance. "Here is your bride, Edward." She joined our two hands with hers, enclosing mine within her son's and her own, small and soft yet strongly binding, making us both the prisoner of her will.

I tried not to pull away, not to squirm in discomfort at what I read in Margaret's face—that I was not more attractive, that I was a despicable Neville. Whatever she thought of me, the deal was made. I was now the betrothed of the Prince of Wales.

"My lady Anne." Margaret had released us and Edward brought my thoughts back to him with the firm pressure of his fingers. "Allow me to say how fortunate I am, to win so charming a lady as my bride." He lifted my hand and kissed my fingers with cool lips, his eyes never leaving mine. More green than brown in the candlelight, they were bright, his smile warm and reassuring. He did not hate me. It made the leaden lump of anxiety beneath my heart ease a little. "I think Lady Anne will make me the perfect Princess," he remarked.

"We shall see." Margaret's stare raked me from head to foot. I shivered inwardly. "I would speak with you tomorrow. Come to my chambers in the afternoon. We must become acquainted."

It was not a thought to encourage a night of restful sleep.

CHAPTER NINE

I presented myself at the apartments of the Queen, Margery beside me in self-important attendance, at the insistence of my mother. "You'll need some Neville support in that rabid den of Lancastrians. If I do not accompany you, Margery must."

I wondered what my father would say if he knew that his Countess was so little won over to our new political allegiance. I suspected that my mother's heart would remain Yorkist to the end. As for my own, I was not entirely sure, but I valued Margery's solid presence at my side. Dry mouthed, belly queasy, I braced my shoulders as Margery knocked on the outer door, her lips suitably downturned in disapproval.

"This is not the marriage I would have chosen for you, my lady," she hissed once again in my ear.

"Nor I." My nerves leaped like a pot of eels. "But the Prince is kind and handsome. . . ."

Margery frowned at my easily won admiration. "Handsome? Maybe he is. And a damned Lancastrian, son to the Angevin vixen!"

"Hush." I scowled at Margery's viciousness. At least my mother had the tact to keep such thoughts to herself.

The door was opened.

The lady-in-waiting—Lady Beatrice, as I was to discover, tall and angular, with sharp features and as forbidding as her mistress— ignored Margery and looked through me as if I did not exist as she opened the door wider. "Her Majesty is waiting," she stated, waving us forward, leaving us to find our own way.

So I had been found wanting by at least one member of the Queen's household. How dared she overlook me in that manner! I lifted my chin and strode forward through one reception chamber after an- other, beneath the anonymous painted gaze of past kings and ancient dignitaries, toward the partially open door, my mind on decorous outward show despite the rebellion in my heart. Under my mother's instructions, I had dressed carefully, a plain veil with a simple fillet, without ostentation or exuberance. The Queen could not take issue with my modesty. But what would be her mood today? I raised my chin another inch, my mother's advice in mind.

"Be respectful, mind your words. But be honest. And never forget that you are a Neville." Then she had added, caustically for her, "She should be glad to get such a bride for her son—an untried, pretty youth who has no kingdom and no hope of getting one unless your father takes a hand in the game."

So my heels stuck the stone paving with authority as I marched forward, only to come to a halt in the partially obscured doorway upon my hearing voices within. My presence went unobserved, which was indicative enough of the force of the exchange of views coming from within—the venom in one of the voices, at least.

"It is my wish, madam, to accompany my lord of Warwick to En- gland immediately. And I will do it, with or without your permission!"

"You will not. I forbid it."

Prince Edward prowled to the window, moving out of my line of sight, and back again to take up a determined stance before the Queen, who sat where the light from the window could fall on the needlework on her lap. "In my father's absence *I* should lead the troops into battle."

"My son!" The Queen folded her hands neatly on top of the linen as I saw her struggle for patience. With her son, she had a care. "You have no experience in the field."

"I have the heart for it!" Although I could not see the imprint of temper on the Prince's face, I could hear it in his reply. "What I lack in experience I will make up for in dedication. I am trained in all matters of warfare. It's more than time I saw battle and put my skills to good use. Richard of Gloucester is little more than a year older than I and *he* is Constable of England."

"I know. And so you shall." Margaret leaned forward and would have touched his arm, but he pulled sharply away. "Have I not brought you up to fight for your inheritance? But not until victory is in our sights."

"So why not let me go? Why do I have to wait? I am no child to be wrapped up and cosseted, kept here in silks and velvets whilst others take on my duties to my kingdom." I could almost see the passion begin to heat beneath his skin, his features tight with a fierce intensity. Again he could not remain still but marched the length of the room, flinging his arms from his sides as if he would engage in immediate combat with his enemies. "Spawn of York! I would tear them limb from limb. How I managed to keep my hands from Clarence's throat when he approached you . . . ! I would punish him and his brothers for their misdeeds until English soil is red with Yorkist blood. I'll have them executed on the battlefield for daring to lay hands on my father. Every last one of them—dead, despoiled, their bodies cast aside in the mud for Lancaster to trample."

He flung back to stand once more before the Queen. "Do you remember when you had the head of their father and brother—York and Rutland—as well as Warwick's own father, spiked on the gate of York for all to mock and wonder at? So I would impale the quartered bodies of the rest of that thrice-damned family on the gates and bridges of London. King Edward, as he styles himself. Clarence. Gloucester.

Edward's misbegotten children with the Woodville woman. What a victory that would be!" His voice fell to a plea. "Let me go, I beg you. My father would place me at the head of his troops without question. Why will not you?"

I sensed Margery slide a glance in my direction but refused to meet her eyes. I knew what she was thinking; her thoughts mirrored my own. Unease slithered beneath my skin at such a show of uncontrolled temper, even as I understood the reasons for the Prince's rage. The insecurity of life in exile, the constant wearying anxiety over what the next day would bring, had taught me much. Yet such vindictiveness shocked me.

Queen Margaret remained unperturbed and adamant. "Edward, it must not be. You must become a cunning politician as well as a good soldier. If I allow you to cross to England in the first line of invasion, what would happen to our cause if Warwick betrayed us? What if he handed you over to Edward of York as a symbol of his goodwill toward his old master, as a hostage in exchange for York's forgiveness? What a bargaining counter you would be. I don't trust Monsieur de Warwick and neither should you. As for that creature of York who holds your crown, he would clap you in the Tower beside your father whilst Warwick returns to power at his side. Do you think I would risk that? Until the Yorkists are overthrown, I will not. I don't trust our Neville ally."

"Nor do I," the Prince shot back. "But I still say it would be a grave mistake to allow Warwick to go back alone and consolidate his own power. Men who oppose York will flock to *his* banner. They should flock to *mine*."

Now the Queen gripped her son's arm, resisting strongly when he would have stepped back, and she pulled him to his knees beside her chair. Although she lowered her voice it was still perfectly audible in the quiet room. "You are all I have, in whom to put my hopes. When York is deposed and your father released to wear the crown again, only then shall we return. And I will be at your side to rejoice at our victory."

"But none of the glory will be mine. It will all be Warwick's, and I shall be bound to him by chains of obligation," the Prince spat with petulant temper. "As for this damned marriage . . ."

Every muscle in my body tensed.

"Quietly, my son," Margaret murmured. "Nothing is yet certain."

"Once the Bishop has pronounced the blessing of Holy Mother Church over our union, I shall be committed to this girl whether Warwick succeeds or not."

"Not so. Do you think I have not thought of that? I have a plan. . . ."

This time Margery and I definitely exchanged looks. Margery's thick brows rose, her lips parted as if to speak. My hand closed on her fingers like a trap.

"What are you planning?" the Prince demanded. "Tell me!"

How similar they were, mother and son, in the little cameo before the sun-washed window. Hawk's eyes, fierce and bright. Neat, even features now lit with inner convictions, even brighter than the intrusive sun, now that success was at last within their grasp.

"Not yet. It is too soon," murmured Margaret. "You must learn patience."

And I saw the Queen smile at her son. I watched as she lifted a hand to brush her fingers through his hair. For good or ill, there was a bond here. All the Queen's hopes were placed on the shoulders of this young man, and he was content to have it so. And I knew, with terrible foreboding, that any woman who became a part of that relationship would not find it easy to dislodge Queen Margaret's dominance from her son's life. Mine would be an uncomfortable marriage. I shivered at the prospect of being caught up in this three-cornered union.

Margaret drew the Prince closer, smiling down into his face. What mother would not love so beautiful a son when she had lost all else?

Unaware, I must have moved. I saw Margaret's hand grip Prince Edward's wrist tightly as her head turned toward the door, her fierce stare latching onto mine. So did his. I waited, breath held, to see how they would receive this unwanted intrusion. Lively emotion still burned in the Prince's eyes.

His reaction was immediate, supremely comforting, amazingly gratifying.

"Lady Anne." Rising quickly, gracefully, without embarrassment, he swung across the width of the floor to fling back the door, to bow, to take my hands in a light clasp, and to kiss my cheeks, causing me to flush vividly. His smile was warm, hospitable, as if he could envisage nothing better than to spend some time in my company. As his hands continued to hold mine, I could feel the heat of them warming my blood and my face.

"Forgive me," he said. His head tilted, lips smiling. "I didn't know you had come. I've been taking up your time with madam, the Queen." The familiar perfume from the library, the sweet overtones of frankincense, teased at my senses, until as before the base notes of something entirely unpleasant made my nose wrinkle.

I curtsied tentatively. "I would not interrupt, my lord." And as his smile widened, encouraging me to respond, I found myself smiling in reply.

"A good thing you did interrupt," he remarked, drawing me forward into the room. "As my lady mother will tell you, sometimes I am too bloodthirsty for my own good. Being inactive does not suit me and I wish beyond anything to have my feet planted on English soil. Impatience sometimes draws me into words that I might wish unsaid when in a cooler mood." He laughed, a low, attractive sound. "Her Majesty tells me it is the extreme emotion of youth and I will benefit from a few more years under my belt. Forgive me, lady, if I seemed too callous for your ears."

The Prince's candid self-deprecation was totally unexpected. It presented an instant appeal, magnified by his attractive features, now serious with his need for forgiveness. "Sometimes the pain of exile becomes hard to bear, and then I'm carried away with the emotion of it all," he explained. His smile vanished; a flicker of emotion that could have been grief crossed his face. And, knowing it to be true, my own experience of exile being far from joyous, my heart softened toward him.

"Of course. I understand your need to return, my lord."

"As we shall. Together. You look in good spirits today, Lady Anne. Perhaps I dare hope that the prospect of our marriage has given you such a bloom of happiness. And the deep rose of your gown becomes you. A most becoming fashion."

I flushed a deeper color than the velvet at his compliment. "Thank you, my lord. Your flattering words enhance my happiness."

He leaned over to whisper in my ear, a charmingly winsome gesture. "You must call me Edward, as we are near betrothed. And now I'll leave you. Perhaps we can meet in the garden and walk there when the evening is cooler."

I curtsied again, wishing he would not leave, drawn by his serious and gentle treatment of me. It would surely smooth my audience with Queen Margaret.

But he left me to bear that burden on my own.

"Come forward!"

I obeyed. Experienced now in the ways of Margaret's court, and with a mind to propriety, I knelt before her, hands folded, eyes downcast. In truth my knees trembled as my blood beat heavily, loudly in my own ears.

"At least your manners are pretty enough," she remarked.

At least! Outwardly composed, inwardly terrified, I kept my silence.

"Sit beside me." She picked up the piece of intricate knotwork that she had earlier abandoned and applied herself, glancing at me every now and then. Her fingers were small and skilled, deft in their movements. The work seemed to take all her concentration. "Do you embroider?" she asked.

"Yes, Your Majesty."

"You read and write, of course."

"I do, Your Majesty."

"I know that you understand my own language."

I made no reply, deeming it unnecessary.

"Can you sing? Dance?"

"Yes. I can hold a tune. I can play the lute to better effect." It pleased me that my voice remained firm under the catechism.

"And I suppose you are skilled in the management of a household," she observed. "To oversee accounts, the efficiency of the servants, and such matters."

"My mother has ensured that I am well taught, Your Majesty."

She made a few thoughtful stitches, her face expressionless, but antagonism seemed to flow from her to engulf me, wave after wave. Her calm stitchery was a mere facade.

"Are you a woman yet, able to take on the full responsibilities of a wife?"

"Yes, Your Majesty." I knew her reference. My courses had already begun.

"Hmm." Her glance was sharp. "You were betrothed to Richard of Gloucester, before your father's change of heart."

Now where would this conversation lead? "I was, Your Majesty. The Duke of Gloucester was educated at my father's home at Middleham. I have known him since I was a child."

"Is there any remaining attachment there, between the two of you?"

Why would this interest her? The match between us had been long abandoned. All I knew was that I must deny any *attachment*. In this delicate game of diplomacy I must tread with care. "No, Your Majesty. There is none."

"Excellent! I want no distractions." She stabbed at the fine linen with her needle. "It will be your duty to bear a son. The whole inheritance of Lancaster rests solely on my son the Prince's shoulders. It needs strengthening. He needs sons to his name. Your mother's inability to carry a son does not fill me with optimism."

"I understand, Your Majesty. I will do what I can."

Her flat stare took in my face, my gown, my tightly clasped hands.

"Now that you are to wed my son, I think it would be best for you to become part of my household. To learn the requirements of a Princess and future Queen."

The appalling prospect of life within this woman's governance was a weight in my belly, but I knew I could not refuse. What I wanted to ask was: *What is your plan to loosen the commitment between the Prince and myself? I have a plan. . . .* Instead: "I hope the marriage pleases you, Your Majesty," I responded as calmly as I could, as a good daughter would say.

"Louis tells me I need Warwick; hence I need you." She aimed a lethal glance at me. "And I do not wish you to walk unchaperoned with my son in the gardens. Do you understand?"

"Yes, Your Majesty."

"You will refuse, if he asks you. Now you may go."

And that was the end of it, leaving me to wonder why she had so desired this conversation. What had she learned from it, if anything? All she had discovered was my education and my past relationship with Richard, neither of which could have been a surprise to her. Perhaps she had simply wished to see me and make her own judgment.

Margery lifted her skirts as we climbed the worn stairs to our own rooms. "She's as cold as an icy ditch in February. And twice as bitter."

"I know."

"Be on your guard, lady."

"I will."

The Queen had no liking for me at all. But at least I did not think that the Prince hated me with every breath he took.

"Here comes Her Royal Majesty, returned to our midst. Do we curtsy? Do we kneel at her feet?" Isabel looked around as I entered the door but did not stir from her chair. The virulence in every word hurt my heart. Her eyes flared with self-pity whilst her hunched shoulder was a calculated insult. Since my marriage had been broached she had built an impregnable wall around herself. It seemed higher than ever this morning. "Are we to be informed when this magnificent union is to take place?" she asked, her brows raised in a semblance of polite inquiry that hid a bellyful of disappointment.

I ignored her. I lacked the energy to deal with her.

"Well?" the Countess inquired, a pale smile in recognition of my refusal to be drawn. "I see you survived the ordeal."

I sank inelegantly onto a stool at her side, clasping my arms around my knees, studying the toes of my shoes so that I did not have to meet my mother's eyes. I had no intention of allowing her to read the conflict in my mind.

"She hates me. She doesn't trust my father. She doesn't trust any of us," I stated baldly. "She didn't say so in so many words, but she didn't need to. It was written in every bone in her body. She gave the impression that she had to force herself to stay in the same room. I don't know why she sent for me in the first place." I scowled at the soft leather, noticing the scuffs from hard wear and rubbing at them with my fingers.

"You amaze me!" Isabel announced. "Anyone would expect her to worship the ground you walk on, if you—or the Earl—can magic a crown out of disaster for her dear son!"

I turned my back on her, pressing my lips together. Once I would have let my fears tumble from my lips. Now I simply locked them deep inside.

The Prince expressed a desire to execute his enemies, to impale their body parts, but assured me of his pleasure in marrying me. He smiled and urged me to call him Edward. He said he would like to spill the blood of every Yorkist. His lips were warm on my cheeks when he kissed me in welcome, but he does not want me—he called it a damned marriage. . . .

I shrugged. I did not want to think of it. "The Queen says I must become part of her household," I said instead. "She intends that I should come under her guidance so that I will be worthy of her son."

The Countess grimaced with a short laugh. "It will be for only a short time. When you are wed and returned to England, then you will have your own household. You'll be free of her."

"What will it mean for me?" I asked as the vast changes in my life suddenly seemed to gallop toward me with a breathtaking speed.

"Why, all the rank and wealth of a Princess of the Blood will be yours, with land throughout England from Cornwall to Chester. You'll choose your own attendants and ladies-in-waiting, your own officials to oversee your affairs." The Countess kept her tone light, with a brief, warning glance in Isabel's direction. My sister sniffed audibly. "You will enjoy extensive apartments in numerous royal palaces and castles up and down the length of the country. When you travel it will be in comfort, with servants to answer your every need. The most luxurious fabrics, the most valuable jewels will be yours to command. You can set the fashion, if that is your choice. And you will be at the center of every court ceremonial. I shall have to request an audience with you, my own daughter, when I wish to see you."

She paused for a moment, then continued quietly:

"You will be shown every respect and honor. Particularly when you have carried a Lancastrian heir, a son, for the kingdom. That, more than anything, will give you more power than you could imagine and allow you to shake off the Queen's control."

Her words ran through my mind, jostling in an uneasy counterpoint to the suspicion that she was working too hard at this to embroider an attractive scene. It gave no recognition to the bloodshed, the battles that must surely be fought before the Prince could be restored to his inheritance. Nor to my isolation within the Queen's household, where at best I would be tolerated, at worst loathed. Nevertheless I realized the truth of it, of her final observations, where they touched on my mother's own private sorrow.

"You must pray that you quicken soon," she added in a low voice.

And because our conversation had opened the Countess to such a query, I asked her, "How long were you married before Isabel was born?"

"Seventeen years." The little smile that came and went was not a happy reminiscence.

"Forgive me. I did not mean to make you sad."

"You haven't. Your father and I did not live together for all that time. We were betrothed when we were very young, too young to set up our own household. And then it was God's will to deny us a child for many years. Finally He gave us two much-valued daughters who will bring honor and glory to the Neville name. What more could we ask?"

But no son on whom to pin all your hopes. As Queen Margaret would with the Prince. I felt my mother's unspoken grief as I offered up a silent prayer that I would bear a son, and soon.

Isabel sat silently, stony faced throughout. Until, unable to bear it further, carefully folding her work and placing it on the table as if it took her entire concentration, she stood and walked from the room without a word. My mother sighed. We watched the rigid spine and unforgiving carriage of her head as my sister closed the door behind her with ferocious control.

"Perhaps I should not have brought up the subject of heirs and children," I said.

"It's not that. It's Clarence."

"What's he done?"

"It's more a matter of what he has not done!" The Countess stood to pour two cups of ale, passing one to me with a thoughtful expression. "He's gone from Angers. Early this morning without warning. And he refused to take Isabel with him. He could not stomach the negotiations in which he has no part and which will finally strip away his birthright—as he sees it. He's gone into Normandy, to one of the ports, he says. Isabel feels abandoned."

"He would return to England?" I asked, unable to think why he would.

She returned to her chair, sipped the ale. "Not alone, he wouldn't. He dare not; he dare not risk King Edward's wrath. Whether he will eventually accompany the Earl at the head of an army, or will try to contact his brother and cobble together some sort of peace between them, I know not. I doubt Edward would even consider a rapprochement. This is the second time that Clarence has betrayed his brother. If I were in Edward's shoes . . ." Her forehead wrinkled as she considered it. "Well, I don't know what I would do."

Nor I. Once, the King had welcomed Clarence and my father back to court with soft words and promises of restored power, but now if either of them fell into Edward's hands, I feared it would be a bloody end.

"Meanwhile Isabel is forced by circumstance to remain here," the Countess continued, "to watch your triumph. We must be sympathetic to her."

"I want to slap her!"

The Countess pursed her lips. "Isabel always wanted the gold and ermine for herself, did she not?"

"Will I be wed soon, do you suppose?" The overriding anxiety of my own future returned triplefold.

On my words the door opened. We looked up, expecting the return of Isabel and another sour blast of her temper. But it was the Earl who entered in time to hear my unhopeful question.

"Not anytime soon!" He was dressed for a royal audience, another in the endless round of negotiation and compromise, but the lyre marks between nose and mouth were heavily accentuated.

"Surely she has not already reneged!" my mother demanded. "Anne has only just returned from her august presence."

"Oh, no. It's not Margaret's doing this time. I suppose I should have thought of it but I didn't." He smiled at me but bleakly from the stance he had taken before the empty fire grate. "Anne and Prince Edward are related. Cousins in the fourth degree, both great-grandchildren of John of Gaunt. A papal dispensation must be applied for." He groaned, stirring the remains of a half-burned log with the toe of his boot. "My coffers are beginning to rattle as the gold disappears."

"It could take months!"

"I know. At this rate, if we ever get the Angevin woman to a be-trothal it will be a holy miracle."

The Countess sighed with desperate patience. "Then we must pray for one."

From this day I will be acknowledged as the Lady Anne, Princess of Wales.

I stood and shivered in a robe of blue silk embroidered in gold thread with the Prince's heraldic feathers on the bodice, before the high altar in Angers Cathedral. I was to be betrothed before God. My role was assigned to me—all I had to do was to obey. My only show of resistance, if that was what it was, was to state, "I refuse to be be-trothed in a borrowed gown!"

My refusal was ignored. Clad in the blue silk overlaid with a cloak of velvet and ermine, both borrowed for the occasion from Queen Margaret herself, I took my place with Prince Edward at my side, arrow straight, much taller than I, so that I had to look up to catch the sheen of victory on his face. I shivered. Betrothal before God to Edward of Lancaster would alter that path of my life irrevocably, pav-ing it in gold. It would be the first ascending step to Anne Neville's becoming Queen of England.

It made no sense to me. It must be some other girl standing here in these hastily altered robes that still folded heavily around my feet, some other young woman making these vows. Margaret scowled throughout the ceremony. I sensed it even when my back was turned to her, having lived in daily expectation of her canceling the whole pro-ceedings, unsure of which side of the coin—reluctant acceptance or willful rejection—I would most prefer. Yet the urgency of an invasion had driven her to this moment and I must accept the consequences.

Prince Edward knelt, and I likewise. The bishop joined my hand to the Prince's. It was all unreal. This was not me. How could it be me?

Confident, Edward spoke the words of the vow in a clear voice, legally binding himself to me in a tie as unbreakable as that of the formal marriage ceremony. When he felt the shivers run through me yet again, he turned his head with a smile of such understanding and concern that my breath caught on the words I must utter.

Don't worry so. You will be my wife. Our future together will be assured. What can now prevent our return as King and Queen of England?

It was as if the words of assurance flowed from him to me through our joined clasp, so that I too made my vow in as steady a voice as I could manage. For a brief, heart-stopping moment, I saw Richard's familiar dark features superimposed on my betrothed's face. I blinked, running my tongue over suddenly dry lips. Then it was Edward again, his rich hair gleaming, his handsome face alight with the glory of the achievement.

It had all taken less time to make me a Princess than it took me to break my fast at the start of a day.

CHAPTER TEN

The Earl faced Queen Margaret in her audience chamber. Standing discreetly with her ladies, a careful expression much practiced of late stamped on my face, I could read the impatience in him. He was past the moment of urging her with soft words and encouragements. It made me wonder what he would have to say. If it stirred the Queen to anger, I would feel the repercussions.

"I can wait no longer, madam, marriage or no marriage. The time for invasion is *now*. Edward of York faces a rebellion in the north, in Yorkshire, and has taken an army there to suppress it. What better time to launch an attack from the south? If we are to dislodge him from the throne with the least possible bloodshed, now is the time. I can be in London before the end of next month, God willing."

The Earl had proved more than accurate in his prediction. There was no marriage anywhere close on the horizon. The Pope was proving resistant to French and Neville gold. As the summer had crept on, July into August, frustrated at the delay, the Earl had already moved his operations to the coast, where he was gathering troops and transport, leaving the rest of us in Angers. Now as autumn loomed he was back in Angers, in no way pleased, to lay his plan before Margaret.

She looked skeptical. Her fingers tapped against the arm of her chair. "Too soon, Monsieur de Warwick. We are insufficiently prepared to take on the Yorkist forces. We know that the usurping Plantagenet is skilled in battle."

The Earl swept away the cautious words with a controlled gesture. "I am prepared, madam. London is the key to controlling England. Once in London, I can rescue His Majesty King Henry from the Tower. When he is restored to his crown and his kingdom, all true Lancastrians will rally to his banner. The Yorkist support will melt away. Then all will be in place for your return to your husband's side."

"Yes!" At his mother's side, Prince Edward hissed his delight, his face illuminated at the glittering prospect. "You must indeed go, my lord."

The Earl bowed. "Meanwhile, madam"—he gave his attention back to the Queen—"I must leave my daughter and the matter of her marriage in your care." His glance flickered momentarily to where I stood.

"Of course, Monsieur de Warwick." Margaret was smooth as day-old whey. "I anticipate the event with as much joy as do you. And I agree. Nothing should be allowed to stand between you and success in England."

She smiled thinly and allowed the Earl to salute her fingers.

I was permitted to leave my post beside the Queen to take my own leave of the Earl with my mother and sister. Heavy emotion met me at the door of the private room, even though the Earl and Countess had said privately all they needed to say to each other. How many times had the Earl ridden off to war, leaving my mother behind? But it never became easier for the women of the household whose lot it was to wait and worry and imagine the worst. The Countess was well versed in controlling her fears but she found it difficult to smile.

"Will you get word to us?" Still she clasped the Earl's hands in hers, reluctant to let him go.

"When I can. You must be strong and have faith. Have we not overcome all obstacles in the past?" The Earl took her into her arms and held her close. She sighed with her face hidden against his shoulder.

The sense of loss forced me to fight against a sudden threat of tears.

"I know. But I shall worry."

The only surprise for me was that Clarence was there, returned to Angers with the Earl and in some good humor, probably with the promise of action at last. He was full of energy and quick laughter, and beamed at Isabel. I found the change of mood astonishing. All the confident ambition, the arrogant assurance of the past seemed to have been restored.

"We shall be in control before winter sets in." His eyes glittered at the prospect. "With Louis's forces behind us, my brother is doomed. Soon we'll be together at Westminster, Isabel; I swear it."

I could not understand his enthusiasm. There would be no ultimate glory in the outcome for him, so why would he choose to fight under Edward of Lancaster's banner? He had got little or nothing out of the deals brokered by the Earl. Except for some insignificant recognition that if Lancaster failed, if I bore the Prince no heir, then the crown would in some distant time revert to the children of Clarence and Isabel. A worthless, ephemeral sop to keep Clarence loyal, in my opinion, yet it seemed enough to transform him into this gleeful anticipation. Or was it? I watched him as he reassured Isabel. Something momentous, beyond the mere invasion, had occurred to change his manner. I tried to crush my dislike of him. At least Isabel, under his attentions, was stirred from her lethargy.

"God keep you." The Earl pressed his lips to my mother's forehead. "I'll send for you when it is safe."

"And I will come."

For me it was the first of such leave-takings that I remembered. When my father had fought at Edward's side at Towton, I had been only

five or six, with little understanding. Now this uneasy parting seemed
to have no reality to it. It felt no different from the numerous times the
Earl had ridden from Middleham to London on royal business, but the
tiny, ugly thought squirmed its way into my mind that this was war.
This could be the last time I would ever see him. The Earl's own father
had died on a battlefield. . . . I pushed the thought away, furious with
my weakness. It would not be. Was our victory not inevitable?

"Be a good daughter," he urged, drawing me close. "Don't allow
the Queen to depress your spirits. You will make a magnificent Princess, and one day Queen of England."

My cheeks grew hot at the unexpected compliment. "I will. When
we meet again in London, I shall be married and Prince Edward will
be restored." I firmed my shoulders and lifted my head. I would make
him proud of me. That would be the memory he would have of me as
he faced Edward of York in battle.

The Earl walked toward the door, catching Clarence's attention
to join him.

"Don't let the Queen slide out of this marriage." His final advice
to the Countess.

"Surely she will not. The betrothal is sanctified before God."

The Earl turned back for one moment, his face grim. "Do you
think? When would anything be allowed to stand in Margaret's way?
If she can find a means to get the throne for her son without a Neville
commitment, she will surely do it. Even at this late hour."

"What did Clarence tell you to put you into such a good mood?" At
the end I had seen Isabel in a close communication with Clarence, and
not merely a hasty farewell. She had touched his hand, a nervous, fluttering gesture, her face lifted to his as if she hung on his every word.
Something of importance, to stir my suspicions again, as I appraised
the strong color in Isabel's face and the glow to her eyes. It was almost
conspiratorial. "What did he tell you?" I pursued as I saw a mulish
expression tighten her features.

She made to turn away, hesitated. "I cannot say."

"Why not?" Moving swiftly to prevent her escape, I stared her down. Her lips might be pressed close to fold in a secret, but she was bursting to tell someone. It might as well be me. She looked at me, clearly deciding whether to confide in me as her sister, or spurn me as her hated rival for the crown. She glanced toward the Countess, who had followed the Earl to the door.

"If I tell you, you must promise not to tell anyone."

So I was her sister for the occasion. "I might."

"You must swear it." Her hand crushed my fingers, increasing my suspicions.

"I swear it, then. But quickly. I must return soon. The Queen has a sharp tongue, and when displeased she can lash out. . . ."

Isabel was not interested in my plight. "My lord has had a letter from Edward," she whispered, her face alight.

"A letter? From *Edward*? Asking what?" The suspicion grew to terrible proportions, to fill my chest, to grip my throat.

"Edward asks him to change sides," Isabel confirmed. "To abandon the Earl and the Lancastrian claims and return to the English court, with promises of forgiveness and restitution."

Hard shock robbed me of words as my mind tripped over the implications.

"Have you nothing to say?" Isabel demanded.

"Does he trust Edward's offer?"

"He is his brother. They share the same blood," she replied simply.

"And will he do it?" I was aghast. "Will he betray the Earl?"

Now Isabel's glance turned sly. "He has thought of it."

"Isabel!"

"Hush! Don't fuss, Anne. Don't draw attention. He has decided not to do so. He still thinks . . . he thinks he would do better at the Earl's side than at Edward's."

But seeing the way in which she clearly dissembled, I wondered exactly what it was that Clarence still thought. The horror of it left me cold. My father hemmed in by untrustworthy allies. King Louis was his own man, selfish to the last. Queen Margaret would always put her own interests and those of her son first. And now Clarence, considering a leap from Lancaster back to York . . .

"I warrant he's not told the Earl of this nasty little plot!" I flashed back. The thought of the Earl engaged in battle, unaware that his son by marriage planned to go over to the enemy—how terrifying a prospect . . .

"No. Of course not! And neither will you!"

"But if Clarence is thinking about betrayal, the Earl should know. . . ."

"He is not! Have I not told you? He will not betray the Earl. But see, Anne. We cannot lose. If the Earl succeeds, then we return to power under Lancaster's banner. But if our present situation fails— well, Edward will welcome Clarence back to his side. Edward has promised."

How ridiculously simplistic! And the thought stayed with me that Isabel, selfish Isabel who could contemplate this treachery with such an ingenuous lack of principle, would not be past persuading her husband to do just that, to hop to Edward's side, since there was nothing to be gained for Clarence in the Lancastrian camp. Could she not see that to do so could put the Earl's life in danger? Was she so self-interested to place her husband's ambitions before her own father's safety?

"I don't like this, Isabel. . . ."

She turned on her heel, disgusted, I presumed, that I should question Clarence's basic honesty. He had none, as far as I could judge, but Isabel would be deaf to any words of mine. It left me torn apart by indecision. Should I tell the Countess? What could she do? It would achieve nothing other than to give her another source of anxiety. The invasion was under way, for good or ill. And if Clarence was still firmly attached to my father's side . . . But I despaired at the thought that the Earl might put his trust in a man who would change sides as readily as he would change horses in the thick of an energetic hunt. And my own sister could see no reason to blame him for it. I could do nothing, I decided finally, but hope that the Earl would never fully trust Clarence and would have his every movement watched. And if the Earl defeated Edward, then all my fears over Clarence's betrayal would come to naught.

But if this invasion went awry through Clarence's treachery . . . where would it leave me?

"We were in great danger. There were soldiers fighting all around us, dead and dying. There was blood on my clothes. We had to escape from the Yorkists or we too would be put to death."

I walked in the garden with the Prince. Now that we were betrothed I was allowed to do so, but never without a chaperone in close attendance. Not Margery, of course, because I was allowed no English attendant of my own. One of Margaret's own women, Lady Beatrice, who also shared my room, walked close to overhear every word before reporting back to her mistress. Not that the Queen needed to worry about any treacherous comment I might make to her beloved son. Did she fear that I would try to undermine her control over him? She need lose no sleep over that. The conversation between us was all one-sided. Prince Edward thrived on reliving every detail of his flight as a hunted fugitive from England.

"We'd been defeated, our forces scattered, our fortresses seized. So we fled for our lives. We had rough ponies and set off with guides, riding only by night. I remember there was a servant who led my pony when I wanted to ride it myself. I was quite old enough, but my mother said I must tolerate the hand on my rein. . . ." He stopped to draw breath, narrowing his eyes at a stand of hollyhocks, as if he could still see the detail of his youthful adventure. Could still feel the anger at being thwarted.

"It must have been very frightening for you, my lord." It was difficult to know what to say. He did not need my participation other than as a silent companion to listen and—I suspected—to be impressed.

"Yes. But I was brave," he continued without even a glance in my direction as we continued to stroll along the path beside the outer wall. "My mother said I was the bravest son she could ever have wished for. Was I not royal? Was I not born to be brave and strong?"

"I'm sure you were, my lord."

"One night, when we had been traveling for I know not how long, we were caught, captured by a band of outlaws—thieves and murderers, every one of them. They wanted to take our possessions and kill us. They threatened to kill me and forced my mother to hand over her jewels. . . ."

He detoured up the steps that would take us to the battlement walk, with its views over the soft green countryside, not waiting to see if I followed. I did, his words carrying down to me in his excitement. "A furious argument broke out amongst them, a rough, uncouth lot, over who would have her rings. They came to blows. My mother was so courageous, you would not believe it. She saw the chance, grabbed hold of my arm, and ran. We ran and ran until we could not breathe and then we hid in the forest. When a traveler passed by—another rough brigand, by the look of him—I shook off my mother's hand and faced him. 'I am Edward, the Prince of Wales,' I said. 'One day I'll be King. I demand that you take us to safety.' So the brigand took us up onto his horse. We escaped and got away to Scotland, where the Queen welcomed us to her court."

This was my experience of the Prince, who was charming, enthusiastic, full of attractive energy. His words spilled out without reticence, unlike Richard, where it had taken persistent effort to get him to talk about his family and his childhood. The Prince was always ready to tell me about his early memories. And I listened avidly, because his rambling tales opened a window onto both the Prince and Queen Margaret, on the bond between them. He so obviously admired her, to the exclusion of any other influence. I had fast come to the conclusion that there *was* no other influence in his life.

My thoughts drifted as they would as the Prince launched into yet another tale of bravery and daring on his part, and melancholy settled heavily in me. I might owe my present loyalties to the Prince at my side, but Richard of Gloucester insisted on creeping into the periphery of my consciousness. What was Richard doing?

What could you possibly wish to know that would bring you any comfort?

The voice in my head drowned out the Prince as it lectured me for my foolishness. What would he be doing but service to King Edward?

He is Constable of England with the security of the realm on his shoulders. He is Lord High Admiral and chief justice of the Welsh Marches. He has replaced your father as chief steward and chamberlain of South Wales. He will be sitting in judgment in the courts, raising troops, riding at Edward's side to put down the rising in Yorkshire. He will be betrothed by now to Mary of Burgundy. And he has no thoughts for you!

As the Prince rambled into yet another memory, I imagined Richard on the battlefield, determined to preserve the crown for his brother with every skill learned and nurtured at Middleham. The Prince at my side was so immature, so self-obsessed in comparison, but then, I reasoned, trying for fairness, the Prince had never been given the opportunity to show his mettle. Perhaps when he became King he too would wield power with impressive authority.

"If madam the Queen could risk so much, and all for me, then so must I risk everything to get the throne back for her."

The Prince's words caught my wandering concentration and I forced Richard to fade once more, so I could make an appropriate reply. "Your father will be King, of course," I reminded him gently.

"My father is not fit to rule. He is a witless idiot, old before his time. With luck he will not survive much longer." The sharp retort caught me up. Had Margaret encouraged him to think in this manner? "My father will be put away somewhere in safety, where he can mumble and pray and believe that he still rules the land, but *I* shall rule as soon as I am of an age. My mother says that it will be so."

And then he returned—again—to his former preoccupations.

"When I sailed from Scotland we were dressed in rags as if we were peasants. You would not believe . . ."

I sighed silently. He stood looking out over the wall toward a distant and invisible England. I stood beside him with my back to the warm stones, only half listening. He never asked about me, never encouraged me to talk of my past, my memories. He had no desire to listen to me, never considered my feelings on being exiled and homeless. I thought that perhaps he had no other to talk to. I felt sorry for him.

"How old were you when you left England?" I asked into a little pause, attempting, as any woman might, to turn the direction into a more personal recollection.

"Ten years."

"Did we ever meet?"

He lifted his shoulders in obvious disinterest and began to retrace his steps back along the walk. "I have no idea. I doubt I would have noticed you if we had, a baby and of no interest to me." He saw no need to flirt a little or flatter me. His indifference hurt. He had no interest in anyone but himself, but I would ask anyway.

"Will you allow my father to advise you when you are King?"

The reply, both content and clipped tone, left me cold. "I doubt it. It was all Warwick's fault that my father was deposed and I was dispossessed in the first place. I owe him nothing."

"Even if he defeats Edward of York and hands you the crown again?"

"I shall be grateful, of course. But I shall choose my own counselors. I doubt Monsieur de Warwick will figure amongst them." The Prince came to an abrupt halt and his eyes snapped to my face as if he were suddenly aware of who I was. A smile lit his face, banishing the heavy frown. "But enough of that. You are my betrothed, Lady Anne. I have a gift for you." He raised his hand to signal to a servant who stood discreetly at the entrance to the garden.

"A gift?"

The servant approached and at a gesture from the Prince sank to his knees to offer me a little gilded cage. Inside, to my delight, a pair of finches, colorful little birds with jewel-like feathers, hopped from side to side, silent and nervous.

"There, you see?" The Prince ran his finger along the bars of the cage, agitating the creatures more. "I do think of you. And when these birds sing to you each morning, *you* will think of *me*."

"They are lovely. Thank you. . . ."

I took the cage, lifting it to examine the little birds. We had no such pets at Middleham, only the hunting dogs and the feral cats that ran wild in the stables. These were so pretty, sleek and black eyed, and the Prince had the power to surprise me. He had thought of me, was kind enough to give me a gift of beauty. Perhaps he was not as lacking in affection toward me as I had thought.

Back in my room I placed the cage in the window, where the sun was warm, encouraging the little birds to settle on their perch, fluff their feathers, and twitter. The intricate struts that enclosed them, finely wrought with leaves and flowers, gleamed softly. I was still kneeling beside them, marveling at their exotic plumage, when Lady Beatrice came to find me to attend the Queen.

"So he gave you a gift." She stared down her long nose.

"Yes. Are they not beautiful?"

"Unquestionably. And do you think the Queen knows?"

Which made me glance up quizzically. Why would it matter that the Queen knew or not? If the Prince chose to give his betrothed a pair of singing birds, why should she be concerned? But Beatrice shook her head, her mouth quirked sardonically.

"What do you choose not to tell me?" I demanded.

She shook her head. "You'll know yourself one day. Now come with me. The Queen does not like to be kept waiting."

And she turned her back on me. I had no authority here, even less than as a child at Middleham. At least a Neville daughter could command some respect. Here I was as caged as the finches behind their bars of gold.

My life in Margaret's household could not be called pleasant. What did I need to learn about the demands of court life that I had not already absorbed from my mother's formidable teaching? A Neville household could compare with any. Besides, I knew that this had never been Margaret's intent. Quite simply, she wanted me close. To bend my will so that I would become a meek and biddable daughter-in-law. But also to show me how little she thought of me and this marriage that had been forced on her. Never cruel, she used cunning little slights and subtle jibes. There was always that edged undercurrent of mockery of all that I did. I was to be put and kept firmly in my place.

"The Lady Anne will show us how to embroider this panel of the altarpiece. Let us see how well she sets the stitches. . . . The Lady Anne will entertain us. But perhaps we will not ask her to sing, after all. . . . Perhaps the Lady Anne will read to us? Ah—no. I think not. Her accent is not pleasant enough for ease of listening. . . ."

And so it went on, and I could not pretend not to see the sly smiles, hear the soft laughs that dripped malice. When loneliness crept up on me, as it sometimes did, in the depths of the night, I would struggle not to shed tears into my pillow. I would never give Margaret the satisfaction, the knowledge through her efficient spies, that she had caused me any grief. For I was given all the proof I needed that my actions were watched, my words reported back.

"I forbid you to encourage the Prince, my son, to appoint your father, the Earl, as his adviser." The Queen rounded on me.

"But I did not—"

"It is reported to me that you broached the topic." So much for our intimate stroll in the gardens! "You will not do so again. Do you understand?"

"Yes, madam."

"If I hear of anything else to displease me, I shall curtail your walks with the Prince."

I stitched and prayed, played the lute, and waited upon the Queen, keeping my thoughts and resentments to myself. It was a narrow, austere lifestyle of waiting. Always waiting for the day when I might be wed to the Prince and free of his mother.

*   *   *

The Earl sailed to England with an impressive fleet of sixty ships. The news was good. Queen Margaret's eyes gleamed, although she expressed no overt approval. The Yorkist upstart had sent out his own fleet to foil their landing, but storms scattered it and the Earl put in at Plymouth without hindrance. Clarence was ostensibly still at his side. His flirting with treachery had indeed come to naught.

At Angers, the Prince fretted at being left behind. In his mother's presence he hid his frustration beneath a mild and smiling exterior. The perfect courtier, he dined and danced and waited upon her every whim with true filial duty. Occasionally he smiled at me. Away from her side he threw himself into bouts of furious energy and sheer bad temper. When we heard that the Earl was marching to London, men flocking to his banner, the Prince took himself hunting with hounds and hawks through the autumn woodland beside the Loire.

"My lady!" On his return he rode up to me immediately, where I stood with a little knot of Margaret's ladies taking the air. He maneuvered his horse, pressing forward toward me, leaning down over its withers to address me, cap in hand. "The hunt was splendid, the game excellent. What a run we had!" His flushed face was vivid, his eyes bright with the extreme exercise. This was the first time he had sought me out in days.

"You look as if you enjoyed it, my lord." I smiled up at him.

"It was beyond anything. See what we have brought? A fine buck. It almost escaped the hounds, but I would have pursued it to the gates of hell itself." He looked back over his shoulder to the bloodied body of the many-tined deer, slung across the horse of one of the huntsmen. "We shall dine well. And I shall ensure that you, Lady Anne, shall have the best cuts of the animal on your plate. As my betrothed, my Princess, do you not deserve the best?"

"I shall be honored, my lord." I curtsied graciously as he rode off, my facade nailed firmly in place. It had need to be. I should have been gratified at his singling me out, impressed by his skills, but how could I? The Prince's horse, pushed close against me, a magnificent roan stallion, high blooded and fine spirited, lathered with mud and sweat, its once glossy coat stained and streaked with the demands of the hunt, had stirred my compassion. Its eyes had rolled white in fear as the Prince had gripped the rein with iron strength, sawing at its mouth as the animal jumped and sidled. There was foam and blood there. Its sides too were liberally coated with blood where the Prince had used his spurs, not carelessly but with deliberate intent. Then I saw him dismount and cast the reins to his groom with not one thought for the health and well-being of the horse.

"Take the horse and see to it. A clumsy animal but served me well enough." He struck out at the stallion with his whip.

Richard would not have done that. Richard's concern over the injury to his horse, his fear that it would not recover as he applied the poultice, leaped into my mind. The Prince gave no heed even when the horse continued to toss its head, the wildness in its eye, I would have said, caused by pain. The Prince ignored it.

"Is he always so inconsiderate of his animals?" The words were uttered before I could think of the wisdom of them.

"He enjoys riding, my lady," Lady Beatrice replied. "The stallion must obey. The Prince breaks their fierceness if they are not obedient. Her Majesty encourages him to be a masterful rider."

I should not have spoken. Doubtless my tactlessness would be reported to the Queen. Resenting the reprimand, I glowered when I saw the Prince strike out at the groom for his slowness, reminding me of Thomas in the library, and my attempts to vindicate the Prince when I didn't know him.

Did Margaret know of his uncontrolled manner? She gave no indication when the court assembled for dinner, and I suspected that she would forgive all but the worst of sins. Even then she would find an excuse. On this occasion the Queen said nothing other than to compliment her son on his success with the hounds. The best cuts of the venison were, of course, presented to Margaret with Prince Edward's compliments, not to me.

"You will be the man your father never was," the Queen murmured as he bowed low before her, the venison steaming and fragrant on the table. "You will wear the crown of England with more authority than your father ever wielded."

"I will. I swear it."

And Margaret took her son's face between her small hands and kissed him on the cheeks, and on the lips. It seemed to me far more intimate than a kiss of fealty.

The weeks staggered past. No word of my impending marriage, no news of the Earl's progress. The Prince hunted more frequently. The Queen's temper grew sharper. The finches trilled and twittered every morning, to my pleasure, but did nothing to lighten the brooding atmosphere.

Until, perforce, we heard.

"Your Majesty!" A messenger, one of my father's own men bearing the Neville livery. Travel stained and gray with exhaustion, he flung himself at the knees of the Queen. She could barely wait, but stood to loom over the man, intimidating for all her small stature. "Excellent news at last!" he said between gasps. "My lord of Warwick holds England. London is his. Edward of York is defeated."

The Queen's eyes blazed. "Is he alive?"

"He is. He is alive still, but has escaped into exile, to Burgundy."

"And my lord King Henry?"

"Released from the Tower, Your Majesty. In my lord of Warwick's care."

Margaret clasped her hands together, tight knuckled rather than in prayer. "God be praised! This is good news."

"I am to tell you—England is open for Lancaster's return, lady. There is nothing to prevent it. My lord of Warwick urges you to travel as soon as the winds permit. As does His Majesty King Louis. It will be arranged that you are met and escorted with all honor to Westminster."

At last a small smile touched the waxy chill of her face. But then, when I would have expected her to show some reaction, Margaret sat, suddenly still and thoughtful.

"When do we leave, madam?" Prince Edward demanded. He could hardly contain himself with the need to move the whole royal household to the coast immediately.

"Not yet, I think." Margaret stood again, smoothed her skirts, and beckoned for her ladies to follow as she walked to the door. "I shall pray on it. How do I know that England is safe for us even now? That there will be no rebellion in York's absent name? It is too soon, my son."

"But, madam—"

I did not stay to listen. I could imagine the direction of the argument. Instead I hung back and waylaid the messenger before he reached the door.

"Is the Earl in good health?"

"Yes, my lady." *Thank God!*

"Have you spoken with the Countess yet?"

"No, my lady."

"Do so. She'll wish to know without delay." And then I asked what I needed to know in my heart. The one unknown fact that had spoiled all my pride in the Earl's achievement. "And Edward of York's brother. Where is His Grace of Gloucester?" I dared to ask: "Is he too alive?"

"Yes, my lady. He is fled with his brother."

I exhaled with relief and let him go.

I would think of this when I was alone.

Louis flung an impressively sealed document onto the table before the Queen, then stood glaring at it, as if daring it to vanish before his eyes.

"There it is!" he growled. "The dispensation. His Holiness would try the patience of a saint." Louis fixed Margaret with his habitual sardonic expression, challenging her to produce yet another reason for refusal. "Now at last we can celebrate this marriage before God and man, and be done with it."

It was almost the end of the year. The Queen acquiesced—she dared do nothing else in the face of Louis's determination—and I became Lady Anne, Princess of Wales, within the week. In Amboise once again, in the austere grandeur of the royal chapel, I became wife to Edward of Lancaster.

It was the strangest of events. Neither the father of bride nor groom could be present. The family of the bride, given the preeminence of the Nevilles in English politics, was poorly represented. There was no need for me to search for familiar faces in the congregation that gathered at such short notice. There were none—only the Countess of Warwick and the Duchess of Clarence, my mother and sister, to witness my elevation to the dignity of Princess. The groom, on the other hand, was supported by his mother, Queen Margaret of England, and a whole array of relatives from the royal family of Anjou. Even the Queen's own father, King René, had emerged from his solitary retreat in one of his châteaux along the Loire. It made for an august crowd on this cold winter's morning, furred and bejeweled, as bright as a flock of iridescent starlings in the pale sun. Louis wanted it to be well witnessed that the alliance between Queen Margaret and the Earl of Warwick was sanctified through their children.

I presumed his suspicions were as sharp as mine.

I have a plan. . . . As Louis had flung down his gauntlet before the Queen, I had remembered those words, uttered to the Prince in confidence. A plan to escape this undesirable union. It was now surely an irrelevance, whatever the plan had been. England was all but in her grasp, and here I stood before the altar. She could not renege now.

The rich overlayering of cloth, heavy with gold thread and satin embroidery, pressed down on my shoulders, but I saw no omen there. The slide of it against my skin was sensuously luxurious, a symbol of my new status. Softly warm, the fur nestled against my neck and wrists. And so I had the ermine that Isabel had so coveted. My hair was loose on my neck and shoulders, as befitted a maiden, the whole lightly covered by a simple transparent veil. Simple it might be, but the fillet that held it closed was of glittering, engraved gold.

My betrothed was finer than I. Nothing short of magnificent. The burnished auburn of his hair might strike a discordant note with the black and red of his heraldic ostrich feathers, but every inch of him proclaimed royalty. Queen Margaret had left nothing to chance. The cloth of gold of his close-fitting tunic announced to all that here was a royal Prince merely waiting to come into his own. If the cloth were not sufficiently eye-catching, the jewels were. The gold chain, the rings, the ring-brooch that anchored the swathes of velvet in his hat, rivaled the splendor of the stained windows when the winter sun cast its blessing on us. The future should have beckoned as bright as the sapphire pendant that glittered on his breast as he turned to me to make his commitment before God. And tomorrow my own Neville coat of arms, the bear and the ragged staff, would be matched with those ostrich feathers of Lancaster.

Then it was over. The Prince's hand was hot on mine, gripping hard as if he wielded the hilt of a sword in battle. The heavy ruby ring he had pushed onto my finger dug painfully into my flesh as he squeezed even harder in triumph, as he turned me to face the congregation. I was the Princess of Wales. And when we traveled to Paris to celebrate Christmas there, at King Louis's insistence, I would be presented to the French court as the future Queen of England. It was beyond my comprehension—but so it was.

The Prince inclined his head to me, a formal gesture of acknowledgment that brought color racing to my cheeks.

Can I love this man who is now my husband? Can I respect him? Will I find friendship with him?

The questions crowded in and I could find no answer enough to comfort me. I could not love him, but perhaps we could build some bond between us. How elegant and courteous he was, all gentle good humor and polished manners for the occasion. How bright the pleasure in his face when he smiled at me. Gone was the sharp temper and intolerance and I was reassured. Now that the tide was swimming in his favor, what need for anything but gratification? When the Prince was King there would be no need for petty frustrations and bitterness.

He proceeded to smile benignly on all who wished us well, pressing his lips to my fingers and telling me that I was the fairest lady in the whole of France. It might not be true, but I loved the gesture.

Making our way formally through the assembled ranks, the drag of my cloak hampering me as the assembled courtiers sank to their knees, I glanced across to where the Countess stood. Her head was bent, her eyes cast down. I did not know what she thought of my miraculous elevation. I had no difficulty reading the hostility in my sister's fierce stare. The distance between us drove a renewed stab of loneliness into my heart. All that I had taken for granted through my life—the closeness, the easy affection—was at an end. Nor would it be replaced by Queen Margaret, who would stand in the role as my mother. Pray God the Prince would care for me so that I was not totally bereft. He would not love me, but friendship could be enough.

"Hurry!" Lady Beatrice advised. "I wager the Prince will not be willing to wait long before putting his prowess to the test!"

The door closed behind us, shutting out the usual round of coarse and ribald jokes that men enjoyed at the expense of the lack of experience and ability of the bride and groom. I had heard it all before at other feasts, at other marriages. But not when I was the one whose virginity was causing such interest.

A bedchamber had been prepared for the bridal night with a sumptuousness that would have overpowered me if my mind had been fit to register it with more than a passing glance. The vast bed was made up with the finest linen, the bed hangings swooping and billowing from their carved restraints and embroidered with gold-stitched French fleur-de-lis. A fire burned cheerfully in the hearth. And if thirst and hunger assailed us through the long night, there was a flagon of hippocras and a platter of nuts and fruit and sweetmeats. My throat dry, I could not imagine having appetite for either.

"He was ever keen to demonstrate his manhood." Margaret's ladies were as bawdy as the men. "Yesterday the tiltyard, today a softer opponent . . ."

I swallowed against what I could not deny was a dart of fear as I was stripped of my finery, twisted and turned as if I were a doll, the velvet and ermine, even my linen shift, laid aside and my hair bushed into a gleaming curtain over my naked shoulders. So at length I sat dwarfed by the huge bed, unable to relax against the feather pillows, the linen clutched to my chin to hide my lack of womanly curves, with an empty expanse beside me for the Prince. Dried flowers and herbs had been scattered beneath me to promote fertility and a successful joining, although the brittle sprigs of lavender and rosemary seemed to have no property but to irritate my skin. The Grand Vicar of Bayeux who had performed the bridal ceremony stood in pompous readiness to sprinkle us, the fortunate couple, with holy water and sacred words.

All I needed now was the bridegroom.

I tried to imagine the coming hours. I did not fear him, I decided. And I knew what to expect. The Countess had been sufficiently explicit.

"Do you suppose he's drinking himself into a state of courage?" Lady Beatrice was incorrigible.

I hoped not. One of us would need sharp wits this night. I prayed fervently that the Prince was not as ignorant or as unskilled as I. The observations became more malicious as boredom threatened and the ladies began to yawn behind their elegant hands. "What's keeping him? Has he found more accomplished entertainment for the night? Some court whore to complete his tuition?" Then: "Perhaps he's waiting on the Queen. Maybe she'll insist on accompanying him and remaining for the event." And finally, sotto voce: "She supervises every other breath he takes! And much else!"

I knew their intent. To embarrass, to unnerve by reminding me of my lack of experience. Even to reduce me to a bout of terrified hysterics. They had never been my friends, and my new status would not change that—but I would not be cowed by them.

"The Prince needs no court whore to guide him," I remarked with an ingenuous smile. "*I* shall ensure the Prince has good practice tonight."

"Remember, though, that you must rise early tomorrow for the journey. Do you think Edward will be *up* betimes?"

With a knowing smile I intercepted the glance. "Definitely he will! I intend to keep him up all night."

"And you a virgin! Do you have the appetite for it?"

"*I* do. I hope the Prince is hungry."

The resulting laughter was no longer at my expense. I was now wife to Prince Edward, and this would be the first time for me to be quite alone with him, with myself as the sole object of his notice. *Holy Virgin!* I prayed again that we would find some measure of communication.

A roar of coarse mirth from the other side of the door blasted our ears. The halt of many feet. The clatter of metal on stone as someone dropped a drinking vessel, followed by a string of curses. Then with a cursory knock against the panels to unnecessarily advertise their presence, the door was thrown open.

Prince Edward had arrived, attired in a chamber robe of magnificent hue. Smiling, his face as striking as the crimson and gold, full of wine and good humor. Yet not, I thought, too overcome, unlike Clarence, who was all but carried to Isabel's bed on the occasion of their marriage. From somewhere in the depths of his selfish heart, the Prince, my husband, found the sensitivity to slam the door back in the prurient faces. For a moment silence fell in the room, as soft as a fall of snow. The sounds of merriment receded as the Prince's wedding party returned drunkenly to the scene of the feast and I experienced some measure of relief. At least I would be spared an unpleasant dose of male coarseness. Margaret's ladies would, I hoped, be more circumspect in the presence of my mother and the bishop.

Edward approached with leisurely steps. My fingers curled into the bed linen, even as I tried to prevent myself from clutching the material to my flat chest. Edward seemed totally unaware of my rioting nerves. His gaze as it traveled over my face, over as much of my figure as he could make out beneath the covers, was just a little hazy but not beyond what might be expected. He halted at the side of the bed, bowed deeply, then captured my hand, lifting it lightly to his lips.

"My sweet, delicious bride. How lovely you are. You're not afraid of me, are you?"

Margaret's ladies smirked and whispered behind sly hands. The bishop beamed. The Countess merely hid her anxiety behind a rigid composure.

"No, my lord," I managed on a croak and a gasp as a wave of the Prince's favorite perfume washed over me. I swore he had drenched himself in it, the cloying sweetness of the frankincense but with the underlying tone even stronger than usual. *What is it?* I resisted the urge to sneeze. *Civet! More cat than civet!* It revolted my senses.

"I shall make you my own, my sweet love, with all care and gentleness."

How thoughtful of my nervousness. I should have been seduced by his soft voice and gentle fingers, the featherlike touch of his lips. Surely this could not be an unpleasant experience at the Prince's considerate hands? But the constriction around my chest tightened even further. I did not trust him.

Releasing my fingers, he walked carefully around the bed to his own side, casting away the furred and embroidered night robe to reveal his neatly muscled body. His chest almost hairless, he looked no more than a young boy, yet paused to draw the appreciative looks of the assembled room. I tried not to let my gaze linger on the soft arrowing of red-gold hair on his belly, at his manhood that was impressively erect despite the wine and the very public show, but with hands on hips the Prince invited admiration from all present. So I looked until, satisfied, the Prince flung back the counterpane, hoisted himself up onto the high mattress, and settled himself comfortably next to me, beckoning to the Grand Vicar to complete the ceremony whilst I swallowed against the suffocating perfume and fear in equal measure. The cleric promptly raised the vial of holy water and began to shake drops onto the bed, onto Edward and myself, walking around us so that not an inch might go unblessed. In a sudden feverish wave, I felt an urge to laugh that we might actually be drenched before he was quite satisfied.

The priest raised his hand in a final blessing. The words rolled over us, heavy and sonorous, as he pronounced the hopes of the whole Lancastrian cause.

"God bless you, my lord Prince. And your fair wife. May you prove loyal to each other and endlessly fruitful for the House of Lancaster. May the glorious heir of Lancaster be created from your loins this night, my lord Prince. As God wills it. Amen."

With a reassuring smile, the Countess leaned close. "God bless you, daughter," she whispered in my ear, echoing the cleric. "Hold tight to your courage."

Courage! Easy to say! I quaked inwardly, fingers like claws in the bed linen as the disloyal thought came to me that I did not want the Prince to touch me. Repugnance filled me as, now that the moment had come, I imagined his hands on my body, stroking, exploring. . . . I closed my eyes against the image—as I deliberately closed my mind against any image of Richard that threatened. *He* had no place in this cold marriage bed. For better or worse I was the Prince's wife and must accept my duties.

The door opened without even an attempted knock as polite warning. The announcement was as shattering as a thunderclap.

"This will go no further."

Queen Margaret stepped across the threshhold, still in her festive velvet and ermine. Still crowned with gold, yet as pale as her son was flushed. She stalked to the bed, close beside her son. It seemed to me that her whole body throbbed with furious, barely controlled energy.

"Out!" she ordered, barely glancing at the women, her eyes only for the Prince. "Get out!"

The women scuttled for the door, tripping over their hems in their flight, but my mother stood firm. I thanked God for it.

"Your Majesty!" The Grand Vicar drew himself up to his impressive height. "What can you imply?"

"I *imply* that this marriage will go no further." The Queen barely glanced at him. Her eyes were fixed on her son's face. "I have no intention of being ambiguous, Your Grace. There will be no consummation."

"There must be a misunderstanding, Your Majesty," gabbled the priest. "There is no cause to forbid this union of these young people. All is correct by my hand and in the sight of God. It is most acceptably done!"

"For you, perhaps. But all is not acceptable to me!"

I sat openmouthed. So, momentarily, did the Prince, as if he could not believe the exchange of words. I looked toward the Countess, seeking an answer. Surely this was not what she had expected. Had it been decided that because of my lack of years this completion of the marriage bond should be postponed? Had the Queen, in arbitrary judgment, suddenly at this eleventh hour decided that I was too young to permit the physical union? I had not thought so. I would not be the youngest bride to accept her husband's demands in bed. I would not be the youngest royal wife to carry a child.

"Madam! In God's name . . . !" At last the Prince reacted, leaping from the bed and shrugging his arms into the bed robe, as if to face this crisis naked would put him at a disadvantage. I remained where I was, unable even to think what I should do next. Inconsequentially I was aware that my husband's show of awe-inspiring masculinity was a thing of the past. I forced myself to sit without moving and allow the scene to play out. Edward quickly had the furred garment belted tight.

"I demand to know, madam—"

"I do not have to explain myself. You are my son and you will obey me."

The Grand Vicar intervened, planting his feet like an oak. "I would advise you, Your Majesty, that you have no right to dictate to the Prince in this matter. He is of age and so can determine his own behavior toward his wife." His hand clenched around his pectoral cross as if to invoke the power of the Almighty.

My mother merely stood, speechless, frozen. I watched as panic played across her features.

By this time the Prince had found his confidence but lost any ability to remain cool. "By the rood, madam! I demand an explanation. This woman is my wife before God and the law, and I should bed her."

"Your wife she may be, but this marriage will not be consummated."

"Why not? In God's name, why not?" Gone was all filial respect. The Prince shouted his disbelief.

"I forbid it."

"*You* forbid it! *I* am Prince of Wales. My father's heir, heir to England's crown. *You* have no right to forbid it."

"I can and I will."

Edward took a step toward her. A dangerous step. He lifted his arm, the flat of his hand raised. We held our breath as it appeared for one horrifying moment as if he would actually strike the Queen. The volatile temper, the unbridled violence I had suspected in the Prince were about to be displayed.

"My lord. Your Majesty. Let us not be carried away with hot humors." The Grand Vicar cleared his throat to draw attention, stepping forward nervously. When Edward's arm fell to his side, he continued in low tones, "On what grounds do you take this step, Your Majesty?"

The Queen did not even look at him, or at me. I was as nothing in her plans. She continued to hold her son's blazing gaze. "It is not required that I give an explanation."

"Tell me!" The bark of anger that echoed from the walls startled us all, the Prince's beautiful features obliterated in a furious scowl. "Explain to me!"

I simply sat in the great bed and held my breath for the outcome. The trial of strength between mother and son. I saw the jewels glint on the Queen's breast as she inhaled slowly. Her glance flickered to my mother, then to me, and finally back to the Prince. When she spoke I knew that this had always been her plan, and that we were all tied securely into it with no way out. "There is no reason why you— all of you—should not know," she explained with terrible reasoning.

"If there is a way out of this marriage for me, any way at all, I will take it. If I can have it annulled I will do so. Monsieur de Warwick will be a creature of mine. I will never be one of his."

"You want room to annul the marriage," the Countess murmured, aghast. "So if my lord of Warwick fails, my daughter will be cast aside from an incomplete, unconsummated marriage. You will put an end to this marriage before it has even begun, and with such humiliation for my daughter. It is cruel!"

"I will not be dictated to in this manner . . ." the Prince broke in, but the Queen waved him aside as she focused on the accusation.

"Cruel, *Madame de Warwick*?" Margaret was on firm ground now, victorious ground. She oozed confidence, even allowing herself a smile. "Not cruelty but a matter of political necessity. I will do whatever needs to be done to restore to my family what is theirs by right of inheritance. You of all women should know of such things. You have been raised all your life surrounded by political intrigue. You were married for the sake of land and titles. Where is the cruelty in that? It is what we do. Why should you be so surprised?" Now there was a lick of disdain, sharp as a whip. "I will not tie my son to a marriage that will bring him no advantage."

"My husband has risked his life for you and the Prince."

"We still do not know that Warwick will be successful."

"The Yorkists are in flight! My father is crowned King again," howled the Prince. "What more do you want?"

"I want all Yorkists run to ground and dispatched. I want no hostile forces on English soil. Even now, Warwick can still fail. What if the Yorkist upstart should return from exile with a Burgundian army at his back to restore him to the throne?" It seemed that my bridal chamber had suddenly become a chamber of war as Margaret hammered home the fears that drove her. "Could Warwick stand before such a force? I doubt it." She looked again at me, an expression of pure distaste. "If he fails, what use will it be to me for you to be tied to the Neville girl? Only an embarrassing burden on us if Warwick can offer us nothing. In that eventuality I want you free to take another bride who can bring us power and military force. I will not be moved on this." The Queen faced the Prince. "You, my son, will now obey me by returning to your own rooms."

To give him credit, he still stood his ground before her. "I refuse to do it. She is my wife. I demand to stay here."

"You'll not defy me, Edward. I have not brought you up to defy me. If you try, I will have you taken by guards and locked in your chamber. And I shall continue to keep you there until you bow to my wishes."

"You would not dare!"

Unmoved by her son's challenge, the Queen merely surveyed him dispassionately, her lips curved in a thin smile. "I would. You know I would."

I feared the Prince would explode with passion. He might be taller, broader than her slight figure, but the Queen's obduracy filled the room. All the determination that had carried her through defeat and exile, humiliation and penury, was distilled into sheer force of will as she stared down her son. Would he retreat before Margaret's overwhelming resolution? I was not at all sure. At that moment, if he had worn a sword, I swear that he would have drawn it. The thought spurred me into action. I abandoned the linen and my own acute embarrassment and leaped from the bed. It was so few steps to fling myself to my knees at Margaret's feet, my hair my only covering.

"Your Majesty." I felt the shame of my shivering flesh as I knelt with head bent. What I hoped to achieve I had no clear idea; I simply knew that I must speak out and fight for recognition of my own position in the marriage. "We are legally bound, Your Majesty," I urged. "The Prince is my husband. I beg you—"

"In name only. Get up." She would not listen. "You will remain a virgin until my son is acknowledged before Parliament as heir at Westminster."

And when would that be? To remain a virgin bride at this woman's whim, to be an object of prurient curiosity and speculation—how could I bear it? Panic began to beat hard, like a military drum, against my temple. I struggled to marshal my thoughts, to snatch at any argument. Despite her brusque order, I remained on my knees and raised my eyes to hers.

"If I remain virgin, Your Majesty, your son will have no heir."

Margaret tilted her head as if considering this. Then she stepped to stand in front of me, raising a hand to touch my head with surprisingly gentle fingers. Would she listen to me?

"Would England not welcome the Prince's return, Your Majesty," I asked, "if he had a son to follow him?"

I held my breath.

The caress tightened into a painful grip on my hair. A sneer disfigured Margaret's face as she bent toward me.

"A true Neville, I see. Brought up in the tradition of political debate. Monsieur de Warwick would be proud of his daughter's facility with weasel words. But you'll not sway me, however clever your reasoning. This marriage will not be consummated. An heir of Lancaster with Neville blood in his veins? Never!" She released me with a contemptuous flick of her hand. "Now get up."

"I'll not obey you! You can't force me."

The harsh challenge startled everyone as the violence that I had seen building inside the Prince, hot and deadly, erupted to scald all of us. Pushing to my feet, I stepped out of his destructive path as he swept the cups and flagon from the nightstand, spilling the contents in a bloodlike pool across the floor. "I will not be refused. I will not be ordered to my rooms as if I were a child." He kicked out at the bed hangings, tearing some of the fragile cloth, making the dust motes dance. He hurled a jewel-encrusted candleholder to crack against the wall. Then, in some irrational redirection of anger, he turned his ire on me.

"I should have known that marriage to you would bring nothing but disaster. It would bring me no satisfaction, but dishonor and insult. That I, a man, not a boy to be ordered and lectured, should be barred from your bed . . . I wish I had never set eyes on you. You have shamed me. I wish I had refused the marriage in the first place!"

"But, my lord, your condemnation is unjust." Could he not see that the fault was not mine? I faced him, my eyes a challenge, my hair falling thick and straight over my shoulders. Naked I might be, but I would neither cower nor retreat before him. The only dishonor between us, the only shame, was from his unfounded words of accusation against me.

"Enough! I'll not speak with you!" Fury flared into leaping flames. Before I or anyone could react, Edward thrust out a hand to grasp a fistful of my hair and dragged me against him so that I had to brace myself with hands against his chest. He ignored my cry of protest, of pain—of shock at the physical assault—and took my mouth in a kiss as vicious as it was startling. A hard press of lips, a scrape of teeth, my hair wound tight against my scalp. It was cruel, taking my breath, forcing my lips to part against my teeth. When he had had enough of me, he pushed me away, my lips bruised, torn so that I tasted blood.

"My son!" Margaret intervened, laying her hands on his shoulders, looking up into his face, her own softening. "Enough. Calm yourself. This is not the manner in which a Prince should conduct himself."

"You have made a mockery of my marriage, madam!"

"No, I have saved you." Margaret's voice was soothing. She reached up and kissed him full on the mouth. "We will work this out together. Later, when you are restored, I will come to your room and explain. Do you understand me? Now you must go."

"I want—"

"No, Edward." Another kiss, gentle, tender. "You will be calm. I will come to you."

The Prince, without another word, clutched his robe around him and strode from the room with one final thunderous stare, as if he hated me.

The priest spluttered. The Countess looked appalled. Margaret watched with hooded eyes. I merely stood, my wrist pressed against the blood on my lip.

"Since you are both still here, I have a use for you," she declared, making her own way to the door in the wake of her tempestuous son. "You will bear witness that this marriage is not complete. You, Anne Neville"—she looked at me in passing disinterest—"will be acknowledged as Princess, with all honor and respect as my son's wife, but you will sleep alone. With Lady Beatrice in attendance to ensure that it is so. The door at night will be locked and I will keep the key."

"It is not right . . ." the Countess retaliated, her voice unsteady in dismay.

Margaret did not even turn her head to look at her. "It is my will."

"My daughter should not be made a victim in this. . . ."

"Your daughter will do as I instruct her."

Then Margaret was gone—leaving the bitter dregs of my sham marriage to swamp the room.

My mind could barely grasp the horror of it.

Through the vicious heat of it all, followed by frozen shock as my room emptied of all the main players except for myself and my appointed jailer, this cataclysm seemed nothing more than the weird development of some nightmarish dream. Or a malice-driven plot from a childhood tale, into which I had by some magical means fallen. But then I heard the key turn in the lock, and knew that the Queen, single-minded, inflexible in her fury, would turn that key every night until she was convinced beyond her multitude of doubts that my father had fulfilled all his promises. Until she was certain that I could not be jettisoned as so much worthless dross.

Even then I thought she would find an excuse.

The Countess was powerless; that much was clear. As was I, my new rank notwithstanding. We would all dance to Margaret's cunning tune. Never had I felt so alone, sobs gathering ominously in my throat. My mother had been able to do no more than kiss my cheek as a brief comfort before abandoning me to my imprisonment with the words, "Be brave, my dear daughter."

How could I be brave?

What would the Earl think of this Lancastrian treachery when the news reached him? In my shame I did not care.

It was not the bridal night I had expected. I sat on the edge of that vast expanse of empty bed, clad again in my chamber robe, conscious of the richness and luxury only at a distance. Those fine linen sheets, fit for a Princess, would not be witness to the end of my virginity. Not now, not ever. Nor any succession of sheets, fine or coarse, as we began our journey to Paris on the next morning. I continued to sit in disbelief. What now? Should I simply tuck myself under the coverlet and go to sleep, to wait until whatever the morrow might bring? Held by a strange lethargy, I could not bring myself to do it. It was as if Margaret had drained my will and my senses when she had condemned me to this pretense of a marriage and ordered her son from the room.

Lady Beatrice, resentful, glowered from where she stood on guard beside the door. I choked back my feelings, part sob, part dark, sharp-edged amusement, as I imagined the scene. Did the Queen truly expect Edward to defy her, to return and break down the door? To insist on his physical satisfaction in the face of his mother's denial? I knew that he would not. Despite our short acquaintance, I knew the Prince better than that. After his loss of face he would take himself to his rooms to prowl and sulk. Or to engage in some ferocious passage of arms where he cared little for the injuries sustained by himself or his unfortunate opponent. Or to hunt until his horse foundered and his ill temper was swept away by the heat of blood and the kill. Then he would return full of boundless enthusiasm, disturbing in its extremity, to ignore what he could not change. He would pretend that his authority had never been questioned.

I frowned down at my bare feet that did not quite reach the floor from the high bed. They were cold. As was I. My lip ached, raw and tender. Shivering, I turned my thoughts to more practical matters. Moping with lingering sighs would achieve nothing; nor would sitting here until I succumbed to a chill or a desperate lowering of spirits. I could vent my anger—for that was what moved me most—on the one person at hand. I spoke to Lady Beatrice with more sharpness than might have been tactful toward one of the Queen's ladies.

"You have no choice but to remain here, Lady Beatrice. It is not my wish but neither is it my fault, and I will not suffer your ill grace. I think we should both prefer it if you occupied the pallet in the dressing room." I waved toward the door to the small room adjacent to my own, set aside for a serving woman. The consummation might be forbidden, but until an annulment I was a Princess and I would insist on the respect due to me. "I trust you will hear if the Prince seeks to force entry in the dead of night. I give you permission to enter to drag us apart and summon the Queen!"

How I enjoyed her stiff resentment as she obeyed. She might have to stay within call, but I would not have her sour face beside me all night. I hoped the dressing room was cold and damp.

The hours stretched endlessly before me and sleep was far away. What would a rejected bride do, alone without comfort, without consoling hands and words? Looking back, I know that this discarded wife grew up quickly. I had not known what unhappiness could be, but I discovered it that night, alone and without hope. I did not know the depths of it that could tear at the soul, until then. Straight backed I sat against the pillows amidst all that borrowed luxury, and cared nothing for it. What value the magnificent bed, the ermine of my cloak, the gold of Lancaster's ring on my finger compared with this dishonor? I would not weep; I would not give in to useless emotion. No one would know of my grief, my fury at being so publicly discarded. No one would smirk and gloat at my expense. As for the capricious and volatile Prince . . . it took all my will not to detest him to the depths of my soul.

I have never, from that day, been able to tolerate frankincense or civet.

I was awakened with a start to voices outside the door. At some point near dawn I had crawled under the covers, falling into a heavy and unrefreshing oblivion, now disturbed by a clash of wills, low but rising in volume. Footsteps died away into the distance, only to return. More words of a briefer, more curt nature. The key turned and my mother entered, warmly dressed for travel despite the bare traces of gray light, followed by Margery. The Countess strode into the center of the room. Pale faced she might be, with smudges of sleeplessness beneath her eyes, but her expression was set, and the proud resolve of her Despenser ancestors hung about her. This morning she was not the supplicant for the Queen's favors but every inch the Countess of Warwick.

"You may go." A clipped order as Lady Beatrice emerged from the dressing room. "You may tell the Queen her wishes have been fulfilled. The Princess is a virgin yet. Her Majesty must make whatever arrangements she wishes on the journey." She waited until the outraged lady had gone. "Well, that was an unforeseen outcome, was it not?" Her manner did not change. She flung back the drapes herself and motioned Margery to place a tray of food and ale on the table and then stir the fire. "The Queen has a talent for drama, without doubt. She continues to amaze me. I doubt you slept well."

"No." Suddenly I had to struggle against a fit of helpless tears. During the long hours, my determination to bear myself as if nothing were amiss had weakened. All I wanted was to hide from the world. "I feel ashamed. And now I must face Margaret's sneering court."

If I had hoped for sympathy, there was none to be had. The Countess regarded me bleakly. "Yes, you must. And there must be nothing in your appearance or your bearing to cause disparaging comment. I will not have the world seeing you as—how did she put it?—an embarrassing burden. You are at this moment the most valuable asset Margaret has, with all your connections. She needs Warwick whether she will admit it or no. Get up, Anne."

"I suppose I must." I didn't move.

"After last night's debacle, we are at war here just as much as the Earl is in England. Our weapons are different, as is the enemy, but this is a battle we shall not lose. Listen to me, daughter. We leave Amboise within two hours. You must be ready."

"For what? To hear the Prince tell me he hates me and wishes he had never set eyes on me?"

"Don't put on that woeful face for me—or for anyone else here."

"How shall I face the court? The gossip, the smiles and whispers? Everyone will know what Margaret did and why." Where had my stubborn courage of the previous night gone? I was horrified to hear the whine in my voice. Yet I climbed out of bed to wash my face in the scented water poured by Margery.

"Of course they will. And the Queen will treat us as filth beneath her feet. But you are not responsible, Anne. You are the victim here of the Queen's treachery. You will put on a brave face."

"But—"

"If I have to beat it into you, you will be a proud Neville to the end! And no daughter of mine will hide in her bed when there are trials to be faced!"

She would not beat me. That was never my mother's way. I smiled wanly at the prospect and she nodded. "Think of your aunt Cecily when your spirits fail. She would never bend before any man—or woman."

Cecily Neville, Richard's mother, a beauty in her youth who had taken the eye of the Duke of York, had a name for formidable bravery and astonishing arrogance. Proud Cis, the commoners dubbed her, and not from affection, but her courage was legendary, even when she had faced a rampaging mob in the town of Ludlow, where she had stood in the marketplace, unprotected, with her youngest children around her and defied the rabble to harm her. Nor had they. Yes, I too would look the world in the face and defy those who hated me. I would be like her.

"So I hold up my head." I allowed Margery to begin lacing my gown.

"You do. You are the Princess of Wales. You will ignore those vulgar enough to make comment. You will *not* apologize for Margaret's doing. And certainly not to the Prince. You have both been sacrificed to her whim and ambition."

True. I forced my shoulders to straighten beneath the green patterned damask. "The Prince . . ." I glanced across at my mother. "I don't know what he will say this morning. . . ."

"Edward has already gone to the practice yard, even though we leave so soon." The Countess's lips twitched maliciously. "They say he has a sore head, so perhaps he'll not feel like conversation. Besides, it does not matter what he says, today, tomorrow, or next week. You will eat well, sleep well, conduct yourself as if this is of no matter to you, and all will be resolved between you when you both reach London. Do you understand?"

I understood. There was much that I understood now. What a child I was when I sulked at Isabel's side as she was delivered of that ill-fated child. Since then I had been dropped into a tangle of political intrigue deadlier than any I could have imagined. I was a pawn in a game where the outcome was uncertain, used by both Neville and Lancaster. I did not like it, but even my youthful eyes saw the value of the Countess's advice. I would follow it with impeccable grace. No one would suspect my inner fury; my conduct would be exemplary. And my heart was full of admiration for the Countess, who, unlike me, had clearly spent the night hours in plots and plans to preserve our Neville dignity.

"When we reach England and the Earl drops the crown into the Prince's lap—for King Henry is surely not fit to wear it—then how we shall crow as the Queen has to retreat," she continued. "Then she will be forced to allow her son to claim you as his wife in body as well as in words." She took my shoulders, looked me over. "No. That gown is too dark, too somber. Margery—she must wear the red. See to it. It is more becoming to her complexion and is a royal color. We will make a blazing statement of power as we travel."

So Margery unlaced and relaced with resignation. The Countess's lecture continued until I stood in the glory of the crimson gown and overgown with its black patterning and sable cuffs. The intricate gossamer veils fluttered decorously on their gold wiring. At last I was ready. Whatever anxieties were in my heart would remain locked there. At least I looked like a Princess. "Am I very pale?" I asked, with some concern.

"Yes. No surprise at that! And your lip is bruised, but we can remedy that too." The Countess touched my cheek in a quick brush of comfort, the first softening she had shown since she entered the room, and from her wide sleeves she produced two small vials. "What nature does not provide, artifice can remedy. We'll paint a joyous color into your cheeks and lips!"

So it was done.

There was never a prouder, more satisfied wife in all of England or France than I when I took my place in the traveling litter beside Queen Margaret. And if the Queen saw fit to ignore me, I did not allow it to prevent me from smiling and waving to those who stopped to watch us pass. I had my finches beside me on the cushioned seat. It pleased me that the Queen disapproved—a curl of the lip—but I refused to acknowledge it. And if the Prince was as ill-tempered as a goshawk in full molt before he spurred his horse off into the distance so that I saw no more of him that day, what did that matter? I was Princess of Wales. Much could happen to hinder Queen Margaret from ridding herself of a daughter-in-law she did not want. I had my own plans.

Christmas in Paris? What better time and opportunity to lure my new husband to *my* side, away from his dominating mother. I swore I could do it as my little birds settled in their strange surroundings and began to sing. I would seduce his affections. I would *not* be cast aside if I had anything to say in the matter. As a wave of homesickness swept through me, I made the decision that, if nothing else, I would persuade the Prince to return to England with or without the Queen's permission. And I would go with him. I would no longer be able to live at Warwick or at Middleham, but it would please me to be home at last.

Settled in Paris, lodged in the dank and somber apartments of the Cité Palace on the island in the Seine, at King Louis's command I was feted and exhibited to the French court in my new status. Prince Edward followed his own pleasures, his path rarely crossing mine, which did not suit my purposes at all. I quickly discovered his habits and rose early to break my fast with him, braving the icy temperature in one of the stone-floored parlors that looked out over a drab garden in the grip of winter.

"My lord." I curtsied, waving aside the constant shadow of Lady Beatrice.

"Anne." Edward's face actually brightened at the sight of me. "Have you come to watch me in the tiltyard?"

"I came to keep you company, as a wife should when she is kept from her husband's side." I sat on the stool he pulled forward for me, arranging my skirts gracefully. "It is not my desire that we should be estranged in this way." I smiled as sweetly and innocently as I could. "My lord—do you like me even a little? Do you trust me at all?"

The gold-russet brows pulled together. "Well, you're a Neville, of course. And madam the Queen says I must not spend time with you." He looked at me in some puzzlement, as if he had never in his life had to consider his feelings for another. But then, why should he? The Queen had made him answerable to none but herself.

I pressed on. "I am your wife; of course you can trust me. And I needed to speak with you privately, before we are unable to be alone together." I put my hand on his where he grasped a knife to attack a fat capon and leaned forward confidentially. "We should not be here in Paris, Edward. We should be in England. Before Edward of York can return. The Duke of Burgundy is promising to aid him." I saw no point in subtlety. With the Prince it was far better to get to the point. "You are the Prince. You should not be wasting time in games and frivolities here. You have such an important role waiting for you at Westminster. Everyone anticipates your arrival. Don't disappoint them, I beg of you."

"Madam the Queen says it is not yet safe. And I am about to be engaged in a joust." In wayward mood, he shook off my clasp as he carved a slice of the white meat. I hid a sigh. A challenge to a joust with lances took precedence. Nor did he need my companionship other than as an admiring audience. He did not even see the need to consider my own provision of food or ale. The Prince began to eat with fierce concentration, gulping down the small beer.

"My father says it is the perfect moment," I murmured, continuing to lean close as if sharing an intimate secret. "Do you not wish to be at his side? Do you not wish to take your place at the head of your own army if Edward of York steps onto English soil and challenges your right again? We can be in England before the end of the month." I replaced my hand on his arm, tightening my grip, to hold the knife steady with its burden of capon. "How magnificent you will be beneath the banner of Lancaster as you ride into battle. Can't you feel the glory of it?"

His eyes locked on mine, his imagination caught. "By God, I can!" he stated through a mouthful of bread and meat. "I agree, my dearest Anne. I will think of it after the joust. But first I must defeat this arrogant French lord who thinks he can best me. I'll teach him, by God!"

Brushing crumbs from his doublet, he emptied the cup and seized his gauntlets from beside his plate. Any hope I had collapsed as he rose and strode out without a backward glance. I poured my own ale, disconsolate at the empty table. I had done all I could, but there was no guarantee that the Prince would even remember this conversation.

My words did not go unheeded. Edward did give my suggestion a passing thought. Unfortunately it all came to naught, except that the Queen locked me in my room with only myself for company for two whole days.

"You have been speaking to my son about England. You will not do so. The decision is not yours to make. How dare you inveigle my son into going against my wishes? How dare you turn him against me? He is my son and I will not have you usurping my power over him. By what right—" Margaret's lips closed like a trap, her face flushed with temper.

An impression, soft as goose down, brushed my mind. It seemed to me a very female jealousy, of a woman who would keep her hold over a man. Then it was gone.

"Your position at my court is not beyond my power to dictate,

Mistress Neville!" Margaret continued after a moment. Her scorn scalded me. "You will learn that at your peril."

"I am Princess of Wales," I challenged her, marveling at my temerity.

"Perhaps you are, madam. But for how long?"

I could not mistake the threat, held like Damocles' sword over my head.

In all those long days in Paris, if I learned anything it was that I must take care. And with the Prince too, who leaped from lover to adversary within a handful of minutes. When the mood took him, he was not beyond curling his arm around my waist, kissing me in full public view. Yet just as frequently the Prince snapped and snarled, enraged when the weather closed in and he could not stir from the palace. I was left standing in one of the audience chambers, alone, as he brushed off my attempts to engage him in a game of chess.

"I won't play. I should be in England!"

"Then why not go? Tell the Queen that you intend to sail with or without her blessing. Louis will support you with men and ships." I felt like slapping him as I might a tiresome younger brother.

He stared at me through narrowed eyes, as if he suspected some evil behind my suggestion. "My mother says your father is still not to be trusted."

"What will make the difference?" I snapped back. "What will convince her that all's well? Henry has the crown. What more can the Earl do?" *I doubt anything would stir her to action, not even if he brought Edward of York's head on a platter to lay at her feet, like John the Baptist's head to Herod!* I bit back the words before I could damn myself.

"The Earl must come himself, to France, to escort her back," the Prince stated. "With a fleet and an army of loyal English soldiers, as is her due."

"Why should he do that?" I tried to hide my amazement but could see the tightening of Edward's muscles at my raised brows, the descent of the thundercloud. "Could he not meet her on the coast, at Dover, and just escort her to London?"

"No. He must come *here* for her!"

As Edward's scowl deepened, I retreated into soft words, my hand on his arm. "Edward . . . perhaps it will be so. But until then—come and play chess with me."

"No. I won't. I don't want that." He turned on me, thrusting my hand away as if I were his worst enemy. "I think my mother the Queen sees the truth of it. I cannot trust any of you. If Monsieur de Warwick betrays us, watch your step, Mistress Neville."

"My father will never betray you," I retaliated. "And I am no longer Anne Neville. I am your wife!"

"So you are. But destitute and friendless. What value are you to me?"

"I don't fear you." I held his eyes with mine.

"You should. You'll not speak to me like that!" His eyes blazed with sudden ungovernable temper, his sudden grasp hard around my wrist, as fast as a snake. "I'll not have it."

He flung my hand away. I let him walk away from me, aware of a building anxiety. What would life be like for me with this man? Wearying in the extreme, I decided, as I tried to predict his moods, his selfish demands. I could never trust him, even if I encouraged him to trust me. The lack of control in the Prince, I acknowledged, often frightened me.

When I eventually returned to my bedchamber it was flooded with sunshine—but I was met with silence. It brought me to a halt in the doorway, focused my attention. Where was the trill and chatter of my finches to greet me, the rays warm on their feathers? And I saw that the door to the cage was open—had they been released by some mischance?

I knew. Oh, I knew!

Of course they had not flown—that would have been too easy and would have given me only a passing regret. I knew what I would find.

I approached, anticipation slowing my steps, until there was nothing I could do but look into the cage. There they lay, tumbled at the bottom, their coloring no longer bright, their eyes clouded. No ordinary death this. Their necks were twisted at impossible angles, their feathers ruffled, their claws curling impotently. Such a simple manner in which to take revenge. To make me pay for my confrontation with the Prince.

This was Edward's work. I knew it.

I learned a hard lesson that day. Edward was not a younger brother to be cajoled or slapped. Inaction was driving him to vitriolic spite against any who questioned him or stood in his way. Margaret had spoiled and indulged him, his desires never checked or curbed as a young horse broken to the bit and saddle, but this mindless killing of my finches went far beyond that. I stroked the ruined feathers, my teeth buried in my bottom lip as I admitted how dangerous the Prince had become.

I did not weep. I could not. My emotions seemed to be frozen. When I lifted the cage down and handed it to Beatrice to dispose of the bodies, I met her gaze in silent defiance. She knew as well as I, but we did not speak of it. I mourned the birds in my heart, saying nothing to the Prince about my distress. I thought he might enjoy it.

And Edward? He made no reference to them at all—except for a bright smile in my direction across the width of a room when he saw me next. The glitter in his eye was full of malicious triumph.

Yes, I did fear him after all. That fear began to live with me day and night.

CHAPTER ELEVEN

We shall leave," the Queen, finally at the birth of the New Year, announced to those of us gathered in her audience chamber. "We shall go to the coast. To be ready for the signal when it comes."

And what signal would that be, Your Majesty? The blaze of a comet through the heavens to herald our return? I hid my jaundiced doubts behind a semblance of pleasure. But the rejoicing was premature. We did not sail from France until the second week of April. By which time all had turned sour, rancid as old cheese. Edward of York had returned to England, landing in the north, at Ravenspur, with fifty thousand crowns from the Duke of Burgundy in his pockets. Englishmen were not slow to rally to his banner.

"We should have gone in January. Why did we wait?" Edward, swooping between feverish elation and the darkest despondency, tossed back yet another cup of wine, his complexion unflatteringly mottled from the excess alcohol. "Why would you not listen to me? We could have been entrenched in London before the Yorkist bastard ever set sail."

"I do listen. Endlessly!" the Queen snapped, on the defensive. "So be it! We sail within the week."

"At last, by God!"

"I always act in your best interests, Edward. Do you doubt me? Come here."

There was an unexpected softening in the pair of them. When I thought to see Edward stride intemperately from the room, instead he sank to his knees before the Queen, raising the hem of her robe to his lips. He looked up and their eyes met, their so-similar fair faces relaxing into smiles. The Queen reached forward to let her knuckles trail gently down her son's cheek, while the Prince turned his head to brush his lips over her inner wrist. A caress as tender as a lover might employ . . .

My awareness snapped back to the past.

As Richard had once caressed me. As I had responded to him, back in the days of our early love at Westminster.

That awareness lurched sickeningly back to the present.

I made not one movement as I saw the moment before me between Queen Margaret and the Prince unfold and hang in the air, but horror must have chased through my eyes. What had I seen here? I dared meet no one's eyes in that overheated room. Or was it merely hot against my forehead from the pent-up emotion in that small space? My ribs felt clammy as a flush prickled over my skin.

"Edward. My son, my King. Of course we shall sail for England. . . ."

The Queen lifted his hand and pressed her lips in the center of his palm.

The words, the gestures, struck me as powerfully as the punch of a fist against my belly, bringing with them a wave of nausea as I remembered the moments in the past when the closeness of mother and son could not be ignored. They crowded into my mind, image after image, mocking my previous ignorance. How could I not have seen? The close dependence of one on the other. The intimacy of the kisses that might be interpreted as more than those of respect, of affection. The barbed whispers of the Queen's ladies on my wedding night. Margaret's jealousy of any woman who would replace her in her son's life. I swallowed hard against the bile that rose up in my throat. How effectively she had put a stop to the physical consummation of my marriage.

Eyes wide, breath a mere shallow flutter, I watched as Edward stood and the Queen rose to her feet to press her hand on his forearm, leaning against him a little. Intimate, possessive. The love of a mother for her son? So I had thought, but not this. Not this! Knowledge crawled beneath my skin.

So this was the reason she would allow no other woman in Edward's life. Unnatural, shameful. Condemned by the teachings of the Church and the mores of society as an abomination. To my mind there was little room for doubt.

"When I am King of England, I will restore the crown to your head with my own hands, madam." Edward bent his head to brush his mouth over her cheek.

I pressed a kerchief to my lips.

The Queen snapped her gaze to me. "What's wrong with you, girl?"

"Forgive me, Majesty. The heat . . ."

Already dismissing me, she waved me away. She was taken up with her beloved son, who leaned to whisper in her ear.

I fled. Did I for the first time sense pitying looks from the Queen's ladies? Or did they sneer, enjoying my discomfiture, the destruction of my innocence? I fled to the nearest garderobe and retched with dry heaves until my belly was sore.

She had intervened to keep us apart. She had forbidden me to walk alone with the Prince or discuss matters of high politics. I knew that she would remain a presence in my marriage until the day she—or I—died.

I retched again until I was weak and spent. Wiping the perspiration from my brow, I pulled myself to sit upright against the wall in that noisome closet and forced myself to consider. Margaret had created a monster. Would she still be able to control him when he was King of England? I thought not.

I was certain *I* would not have the power to do so.

I dared not tell the Countess. What would I say to her when I had no proof, only suspicion? Was it an innocent affection that I had misread? I did not think so. I must deal with this myself. Since there was nothing that I could either do or say to change my relationship with the Queen and the Prince, I must tread a rigid line. From that moment of blighting revelation I vowed to keep a still tongue, to cultivate patience and self-control. I must be careful. Always watchful. Never provocative. Fiercely protective of my own frailty in this unhappy ménage.

We would sail within the week, Margaret had ordered. The spring storms had other ideas. For seventeen wearying days we were trapped in Dieppe by contrary winds. When we finally put to sea the heavy swell attacked the balance and the stomach. It was a vicious journey, with little joy to expect in our homecoming. All in all it was enough to cast the whole party of us into the black pit of gloom along with the Prince.

But that, for me, in those days at Dieppe, was not the worst of it. Queen Margaret's revulsion with me, her undesirable daughter-in-law, plummeted to new depths, while the Prince decided that he despised his wife worse than the pox.

It was all Isabel's fault. Or Clarence's. Or perhaps it was mine, if I were of a mind to be honest. Wherever the culpability lay, it was set in motion by something as innocuous as a letter. And one that was not even written to me.

I cannot forgive Isabel. On our arrival at Dieppe, she had shaken herself out of her lassitude and miseries as fast as a snake shedding its skin on a hot day. The Queen might stall and quibble, but my sister became amazingly single-minded now that home was almost within sight. It was as if the power of the gray waves, stormy and thundering against the harbor wall, had scoured her of all her self-pity and whipped her into action.

"I can't wait," she stated with unusual force, a return to the old Isabel, with sharp words and snapping eyes. "I can't tolerate this indecision while we hang on the Queen's reluctance. I will sail to England as soon as a ship can be commandeered, in the first lull between storms."

The Countess tried a dousing of common sense. "Isabel, you will not. We should cross together. This is no time for us to act independently." Then, clearly uncomfortable, she added, "Nor do we know what will meet us in the way of enemy forces when we do arrive."

"There's no guarantee we shall ever stir from here," Isabel retorted, as petulant as ever. "It's four months since Clarence and I were parted. I wish to go. I wish to go home. And I will."

"Where is Clarence? Can you safely meet up with him?" I asked, amazed at her intransigence after months of weak tears and bad temper.

Isabel lifted her shoulders, choosing not to address the *where.* "Anything is better than staying here."

"Such as falling into the hands of Yorkist troops?" I asked, my mistrust deepening at her evasion. "You seem remarkably sanguine at the prospect."

"I need to be with Clarence."

With a warning glance in my direction the Countess demanded, "Why do you need to be with him specifically, Isabel?"

Hands deep in a box of folded clothing—an ideal way to hide any nervousness, in my opinion—Isabel replied casually enough, "What other reason than that I am his wife?" She continued to fold and smooth with innocent concentration. I noted her cool, fair beauty, marveling at her ability to retain her composure when I feared what was in her mind. I found the words springing to my lips before I could stop them.

"What is Clarence doing, Isabel?" Nor would I be put off when my sister glared at me over her shoulder. "Something reprehensible, I warrant."

"Has something happened that I know nothing of?" the Countess demanded, looking from one to the other.

"That's it!" I knew immediately as my thoughts flew back to Angers, homing in on one little scene, as accurate as a falcon swooping on a fat pigeon. When Isabel had denied her husband's treachery. "Clarence has decided to change sides, hasn't he? In spite of all his vows of loyalty and trust . . . In spite of all *your* assurances, Isabel, that he would not consider betrayal! Clarence plans to betray the Earl and fall in with his brother. Perhaps he has already done so! Is that why falling into Yorkist hands gives you no fears?" I made no attempt to hide my disgust.

Isabel's composure showed signs of slipping. "Yes . . . no. I don't know what he will do. But I won't remain buried in this place!"

"Isabel! What is this?" In two long strides the Countess was with her, a fistful of Isabel's velvet sleeve in her hand. "Why would he change sides? Edward will never forgive—"

"He will! He's promised. He'll welcome Clarence back."

"Tell me, Isabel." I saw the cloth crease and crush as my mother's fist tightened. "What do you know? Do you not see how fatally dangerous this could be for the Earl? For your *father*! And you would say nothing of it to me?"

Isabel's pretty mouth settled into a familiar sulk.

"I think you are making this up. I think you have no idea," the Countess stated with a shake of Isabel's arm, no doubt hoping that it was so. "Why do you do it? Simply to be interesting and attract attention? For shame! How dare you make such pronouncements, tell such lies, when you know the Earl's safety is my first concern." But I saw a flash of knowledge in Isabel's eyes before she turned her face away. She did know. She knew exactly what her treacherous husband intended.

"He's been in touch with you again, hasn't he?" I accused. "Edward of York has been in touch with you."

Isabel looked at me, then nodded as if she had decided that between the three of us, honesty was the only course left to her. "Yes, he has. When he was still in exile in Burgundy. Edward has offered Clarence forgiveness if he will reconsider."

"I can't believe that a daughter of mine has been engaged in nefarious negotiations that could bring death and dishonor to her own family." I had never seen the Countess so bitingly angry. "Nor can I believe that Edward has any intention of welcoming his brother back to the fold. He will use him, manipulate him, but forgive him? Clarence would be a fool to put his trust in Edward. And so would you!"

"But it's true," Isabel shot back. "I have proof. Look." From the bodice of her overgown she drew two sheets of well-worn parchment. "Read them if you must. They are quite authentic and Clarence did not doubt their content."

With sharp movements expressive of her dismay, the Countess opened the first and read it rapidly. From Edward of York, it was short and to the point as I read it over her shoulder. If Clarence would agree to forsake Lancaster and Warwick, Edward would forgive him. If Clarence would make his retained forces available for his brother's use, then Edward would cancel the attainder and restore to him his land and former positions at Westminster and in the King's government. Comprehensive and enticing, I admitted, wiping away the sins of the past. A tempting offer to an ambitious man who had gambled on the wrong side and lost all.

"Isabel . . . this could be disastrous." My mother failed to control her mounting horror.

Isabel snatched the letter back and hid it within the folds of her gown. "It is good sense."

"What's the other?" I asked.

The Countess opened it. There was no superscription, a mere few lines, and I did not need to read the signature as I took the letter from her. It was in Richard's familiar angular fist. How forceful it was, with its strong lines up and down; how persuasive, even though it made no additions to Edward's request. I scanned the short sentences, almost able to hear his voice speaking them to his brother, unambiguous, without ornamentation. There was nothing to be gained at Lancaster's side. Come back, where he belonged by blood and inclination, and throw in his lot with York. All past disloyalties would be forgiven. There was a warmth there, a brotherly concern.

I look forward to the day when we stand together again under the banners of Plantagenet and York.

In that foolish moment, neither the words nor the sentiments mattered to me, only the fact that Richard had written them. That his hand had created this letter; his fingers, agile and capable, had wielded the pen as ably as they could wield a sword. Unobserved as my mother took issue with Isabel once more, I pressed the parchment between my palms as if I could absorb some essence of him into my blood.

"So what did he say?" the Countess demanded. "What reply did Clarence make to these treacherous offers?"

"He said . . ." Isabel bit her lips before the Countess's wrath but gave no quarter. "He said he would join Edward when the opportunity presented itself. Which is now, when he is back in England. Can you not see? I must be there with him."

"And what will you tell him—this so noble husband of yours who cannot keep his sworn word?" The bitter irony of my mother's question burned.

"I will remind him of his debt to the Earl." Isabel stood her ground, although I thought she had difficulty in holding the Countess's eye. "I will remind him of his loyalties to me, and to the Earl. *I* am no traitor."

"As if he would listen! I still say you should not go."

"I am determined."

And short of locking her in her room, there was nothing we could do but allow it. Isabel was her own mistress. She would make her own choices. There was a break in the weather that Margaret would not take but that Isabel would, a cold, bleak leave-taking, and Margery was sent with her.

"Keep safe." It was all I could find to say.

"Until we meet again in England."

Isabel, defiant to the last, did not touch on the fact that we might be on opposite sides. That we might be enemies. And yet in my heart I wished I were going with her. Returning to England would be like sailing for a safe harbor compared with negotiating the dangerous shoals and rocks of the French court.

"Do you believe her?" I asked the Countess. "Can we trust her to plead our cause in Clarence's ear?"

"No." The Countess's face was stark with dread as the ship's crew began to set sail to maneuver from the harbor. "I fear for the Earl."

We watched until the ship dwindled into the distance and the cold wind drove us indoors, until Isabel had sailed for England and for whose camp we knew not. She had taken back Edward's letter, carrying it with her. But in the heightened tension of the exchange, she forgot the one written by Richard. It had slipped her notice that I had kept it, sliding it into my sleeve. If she had missed it I would have returned it, claiming a chance misplacement. But she did not, so it remained with me. How thoughtlessly I did it. How stupidly, foolishly naive I was. Was I not aware that the room in which I slept, my possessions, were searched regularly by Lady Beatrice on behalf of the Queen?

I was aware, and still I kept the letter. Blinded by the dull, aching knowledge that my life would never cross the path of Richard of Gloucester, that the memories would fade but not the pain of that lost love, I stole Richard's letter and I read it over and over. Not for its content, obviously, but for the warm concern for his brother. For the memories it brought me. I needed a memory of his affection, his declared love, in a household where I was shown nothing but suspicion and hatred. The letter was not addressed to me, nor did it concern me directly, yet I kept it and comforted myself with the sight of something that came from him. It brought him close. I traced the words and remembered. I had so little of him, I would keep it. I had no pride.

I left Richard's letter tucked away beneath my shifts in the clothespress.

How absurdly indiscreet. I did not at first notice its disappearance. Until it brought the Angevin wrath down on my head.

I was summoned.

The Queen sat in her room, much as she always did, with documents spread before her, letters from those in England who would entice her back with fair words, but I could sense the lurking danger, the frisson as soon as I walked in. As thick as smoke, it all but choked me, warning me to keep my wits about me. The ladies-in-waiting who turned their eager, expectant faces in my direction made no attempt to hide their anticipation. The Prince stood at her right hand. His expression told me all—the familiar temper, barely held in check, when affairs did not play to his liking. He would stand in judgment on me. I could expect no mercy here.

"Well, my lady Anne." Margaret's voice was seductively pleasant. "What have you to say for yourself?"

"Have I done aught to displease you, Majesty?" I tried to calm my breathing, but the nerves in my belly leaped like frogs in a pond.

"Displease? What a trite word!" Now the bite, the lash of loathing. "I have to struggle hard not to despise you. You should be on your knees, begging for mercy."

"What have I done, Majesty?" I braced myself. When she pointed to the floor before her, I knelt.

"I know not what you have done. Maybe nothing as yet." Her lips curled in a bitter parody of a smile. "This was found." Richard's letter was lifted from the table, waved gently to and fro. "You have nothing to say? You must recognize it. And from Richard of Gloucester, I see. It was found secreted in your clothespress. Was it sent to you?"

"No, Majesty. It was not." Without a superscription, only the content and signature would prove incriminating. Yet I knew they would be enough. A request that the reader should abandon Lancaster and put his future into the hands of Edward of York. A splendidly treasonable note that would weigh against me.

"So, if it was not sent to you, why do *you* have it?"

Because I love him and have nothing of him but his hand on this letter, even though it is not addressed to me. I have been separated from him for more than a year and the pain is as strong as ever. I am trapped in a loveless marriage where I am neither wife nor true bride. I am surrounded by those who hate me. Richard is the one constant in my life. I have it because it brings him close and soothes my sore heart. Because I love him . . .

I remained on my knees, lips clamped shut, my spine straight as I stared ahead. If she read my posture as defiance, then so be it. Better than to dissolve on the floor at her feet in pathetic grief that she would surely read as guilt.

"You do not answer," the Prince snapped. "Have you indeed given your allegiance to the Yorkist bastard?"

What should I say? *It was not me!* Should I denounce Isabel and Clarence as the recipients? I did not need to. Margaret was nothing if not politically astute. She raised a hand to silence her son, rising to her feet so that she towered over me, her skirts swishing, brushing against my shoulder with regal insolence as she stalked around me, to return to look down at me again. When she spoke it was the Prince she addressed.

"It would not be sent to your wife, of course. How should it have been? Of what importance is she, other than as your wife? She has no influence on events. But her sister, who decided without warning to leave our court. And her husband, the Duke of Clarence. Yes, that is it. A warm letter from a loving brother to entice Clarence to change sides and throw in his lot with York." She swung around to point an imperious finger at me. "Was there a letter also from Edward? Did they both use their wiles to entice Clarence?"

I shook my head but must have flushed.

The Queen laughed sharply, a crack of ill humor. "I see that there was. I won't ask how they got here. Or how many weeks this letter has been in your possession. There are spies under every stone, behind every wall hanging, looking for any opportunity to spread their poison. And would it surprise you to learn that this heartrending plea for support, for a change of loyalties, was successful?" She swung away from me to seize another document from the table, returning to thrust it under my nose. "Your treacherous brother by marriage has proved weak indeed. And I expect with your sister at his side, spurring him on. Does it surprise you?" She angled her chin as my gaze fell before her accusations. "No. I can see that it does not."

So Clarence had done it. Had Isabel concurred with his choice or had she tried to keep him loyal to the Earl? I could only guess that she had willingly taken her husband's part. There was no need for me to deny my knowledge. I knew it was written on my face.

"It was the most touching of reconciliations, dear Anne." The Prince advanced and offered a hand to raise me to my feet. I could not refuse, even though his courteous gesture, his endearment, did not fool me for a minute. Fury raced across his attractive features, while his smooth tone was as deceptive as the Queen's. "Carefully staged near Warwick. Both armies in battle array as if they would fight to the death, only half a mile between them with banners displayed. The damned Yorkist bastard advanced, and so did Clarence as the heralds blew their triumphal blasts." The Prince's teeth glinted in a wolfish smile. "Clarence knelt. Edward promised him restoration of all his estates. A remarkable display of brotherly love between traitors as they both returned to York's camp, arm in bloody arm. To share a cup of wine and plot the downfall of Lancaster. God's wounds! One as damnably deceitful and backstabbing as the other. But no surprise at their reconciliation, is there, madam wife?—with letters passing between them."

I remained silent.

"Twelve thousand men Clarence took with him to York's side, when he had sworn his service to *me*." The Prince continued to hammer at me, leaning close. "*Twelve thousand* who would have fought for *us* and are now lost to us."

The Queen's eyes turned on me once more, hard with accusation. "But why do *you* have this? Why is it in *your* hands?"

And I cursed my careless, reckless decision to keep the letter with no excuse other than my loneliness—and that was no excuse worth mentioning.

"It is clear. It is from Gloucester. Is that not explanation enough?"

The Prince's lips curved unpleasantly. He might have little thought of my value, but if my allegiance were compromised he would seize and hold fast. "You were once betrothed to him. Did you offer to be an intermediary, to ensure the letters reached your sister?"

The Queen nodded slowly as she considered. "Of course you would. You are as false as all the Nevilles. What a deplorable bargain I made when I agreed to take you as my daughter. Deceit and double-dealing bred in you from the cradle. Not only would you and your family swing to York at the least provocation, but *you* would look fondly on Richard of Gloucester. I wager you still hold him in some affection, despite your marriage."

"That is not so!" Spurred into denial at last. I could not admit my feelings. Dared not.

"And I should believe you? When did you last communicate with Gloucester?"

"Never. I have no contact with him, none since our betrothal was ended and I left England, almost a year ago." Fear at what awaited me at the hands of the Queen fired my resolve to deny her accusations. "There is nothing between us. I have never been anything but loyal to my lord Prince, my husband."

"Perhaps she is not even a virgin," Edward observed slyly.

Shame engulfed me, and also a fury to match Edward's, that I should be forced to answer such an accusation in so public a manner. It fanned the flames of resistance within me even higher, and I looked directly at my husband. My reply burst from me. "I am a virgin. As I was when we wed, so I am still, and through no choice of mine." It delighted me to see the high color flagged on his cheeks at the implication. "I am true to my marriage vows. I am true to you, my husband, even though you have not bedded me. You will not accuse me of disloyalty or infidelity in this manner!"

"True in body, then." A sneer marred his lips as he tried to recover his ground. "But not in thought. You are not fit to be my wife."

"You have no cause to distrust me. I have never given you cause."

"Enough!" the Queen ordered. "Go to your room. You will be

watched closely. Soon we shall be in England. You should pray to God
that Monsieur de Warwick delivers what he has promised. Or I shall
break this charade of a marriage without compunction."

I would have gone, anything to escape from the staring eyes, the
faces bright with a fascination that would feed court gossip for weeks
to come. But Edward barred my way, shaking off his mother's restraining hand.

"I thought you hoped for my success. How deceived I have been.
Here is the truth of your treachery."

His hands might have loosened from fists, but he lashed out at me
all the same. I did not see the blow but his aim was good, without control. With the flat of his hand he struck my cheek, a shockingly sharp
slap of a sound in the room. I had never been struck before. Certainly
not a blow delivered with such intent and power. I felt the silence that
followed it as much as I felt the pain along my cheekbone, in my jaw.
For a moment my sight was dimmed as I staggered to keep my balance,
as the pain ricocheted through my head. But I did not fall. I would not.
Blinking against the pain and the pure shock, I called on all my strength,
my self-possession, raising my head, holding his furious regard.

"I have done nothing to merit such treatment from you, my lord."
I was astonished at my calm words, when my face throbbed, stiff and
already swollen from the blow. "You do me an injustice. I swear my
innocence before all present here, if that is what you require. I have
had no communication with the Duke of Gloucester since the Earl my
father took up arms against York and offered his allegiance to Lancaster." I managed a curtsy, albeit with a dangerous wobble. "I do not
deserve such treatment from your hand."

I curtsied to the Prince and the Queen with magnificent dignity,
then turned and left the room. I could hear the whispers break out as
soon as I had passed through the door.

Until it faded I covered the bruise with a layer of heavy white powder.
It was in my mind to reveal to all the act of violence against me by my

husband, but I could not. I would not be the subject of more speculation—or even worse, pity. For I was not locked into my room as I had feared but forced to continue with my duties. To serve the Queen with all eyes on me. It was in a sense a permanent imprisonment, since I was never alone. Lady Beatrice shared my bed, as far toward the edge as she could withdraw. Worst of all, I was forbidden my mother's company. And Margery, who might have given me some solace, had gone with Isabel. The Prince did not come near me.

So I was thrown back on my own devices to keep my spirits high and my self-control strong. In those difficult days I discovered within myself a remarkable fortitude. I kept a cold dignity wrapped around me. I conversed when required, stitched and read for the Queen with a formidable composure. I never wept. Even at night, when, by her shallow breathing, I deemed Beatrice to be asleep, I stared dry-eyed into the darkness. I would never show weakness in this hostile place, even though for the first time I truly acknowledged how greatly I feared the Prince, not merely the humiliation but the physical dominance. In my rampant imagination, brought on by loneliness, I flinched from the thought that one day he might deal with me as he had dispatched my finches.

It was from Beatrice that I was given the only crumb of comfort. As I sought to disguise the bruise she came to stand behind me, picking up the little pot of powder from the chest. "I admire your courage." She handed me the pot. "Not everyone can withstand the weight of the Queen's anger. Can I suggest you apply a little more along the cheekbone? It will disguise it almost beyond comment."

"You took the letter to Margaret!" I turned on her, all my pain surfacing.

"I did, and with no remorse. If I had not and it was found by another, I too would have been punished. It doesn't do to disobey the Queen. It's a lesson you should take to heart." She lifted her shoulders. "Let me help you."

She applied the powder with skillful fingers, then left me without another word. It was little enough but I was grateful for it.

As for Richard, I forbade myself the freedom to think of him. But my dreams betrayed me—I could not determine their content—and so I saw him there. They were muddled and disturbing, full of blood and death and violence, cloudy and formless for the most part, giving me no rest. Once, a scene came crystal-clear so that I recalled it when I awoke. I saw him stand beside the Prince in some vast, shadowed building. A dagger lay between them on the floor. Hands reached for the dagger and I cried out helplessly in warning, but who picked it up I could not see. Nor could I tell the outcome. Then the dagger vanished and the worn paving was obliterated in a spreading pool of blood.

I awoke to a throbbing head and another day of storms and high winds.

Richard's letter, of course, was lost to me forever. Margaret had torn it to pieces and cast it into the fire.

England. At last the soft outlines of the coast came into clear view, drawing closer with every minute.

"What will you do, my lord, when we land?"

I could see a seawall backed by the crowded dwellings of fishermen, the larger ones of merchants, the turrets and battlements of a defensive fortress. Weymouth, far to the west, was where the Queen hoped to recruit troops. Maybe there was a hostile Yorkist army awaiting us, out of sight, but all I could think was that it would be a relief to set foot on dry land that did not dip and sway.

I could not predict the Prince's mood. We had not exchanged any words since the explosion of temper over the letter, a difficult thing to achieve in the close confines of the ship. For the most part I was pleased to keep out of his way, having anxieties of my own, but was it not in my interest to test the waters for even the basest level of reconciliation? I would have to live with the man, forsooth. I decided that this was a better time than many to venture the olive branch—however false a twig—as he leaned, braced against the ship's rail, straining to see what would await us. He was alone and, although he had seen me, he had not immediately walked away when I had come on the deck. I carried a goblet of wine as a placatory gesture, a gesture of necessity even as my heart recoiled from any mending of fences between us.

Besides, I wanted to glean some information.

"What will you do? Will you march immediately?" I asked, looking ahead as he did, clasping the goblet in my hands.

He did not turn his head but answered readily enough. "When the troops are gathered. Then I will march on London."

We did not know what awaited us, other than that Edward of York was once more a force to be reckoned with. The matter appeared to take the Prince's full concentration. Today he was calm, thoughtful, not driven by wild enthusiasms and ill-conceived plans. Nor was any lingering enmity toward me evident. I tried to forget the slap of his hand against my cheek. I could never forgive him or justify it as a moment of extreme emotion, but were we not tied together? Necessity might drive me to act against my nature.

"Do you think there will be a battle?" I knew there would—all common sense pointed in that direction—but I would encourage him to talk rationally about his plans.

"A battle? Yes. Of course there will." He grinned, a sudden and charming revelation. The sullen boy had gone, replaced by the handsome knight as he closed his hand over mine where it rested on the wood. "What an omen this will prove to be, Anne. We land at Easter. A sign of God's blessing, I'm certain. Tomorrow on Easter Day we will observe High Mass to give thanks for His endeavors to bring us to this place. Then on to London and at last—once and for all—see the end to York. There will be no more resurrections of Yorkist power, I promise you."

"What then?"

"What do you mean?" He dragged his gaze from the spot where our ship would put in to port within the half hour, to glance down at me. "I shall expect to meet up with Warwick and his forces, of course. The Earl will stand beside me on the steps of Whitehall."

"I know." How to put it? "When you have taken London—what then? What of your father? Will he wear the crown again?"

Prince Edward's face darkened as he looked off, over my shoulder in the direction of London, as if he could see across the miles to where his father was once again in Yorkist hands and consigned to a room in the Tower of London.

"I think not." He frowned. "His treatment of the Woodville woman when the Yorkist bastard fled and abandoned her suggests that my father has lost all ability to determine friend from foe. To assign a midwife to her, and pay a London butcher to supply her and her household with half a beef and two muttons a week, is beyond my comprehension. Much better to send her and her newly born bastard of a son—and all the foul daughters—to the scaffold. That's what I should have done." As ever his violent thirst for blood brought me up short. "I shall be regent and I shall wield the power in his stead if need be. And then, when the time comes, I shall be King. And you, my wife, will be at my side as my Queen."

So for now I was restored to a state of grace, until some other matter reminded him of my questionable allegiance. I remained wary, and stood motionless beside him as the sails were lowered, until he turned as if aware of me once more.

"You are very quiet."

I glanced at him, weighing my response, finding none that I cared to make to him.

"Do you fear for your mother? Ships often go astray and founder, with all lives lost," he observed, callously indifferent, watching for my reaction. Edward had a well-honed nose for distress in others.

And I gasped at his careless cruelty. For it was true. The fear, almost paralyzing when I allowed it, did prey on my mind. We had sailed on sister ships, but strong winds had driven us apart and we had lost sight of the one carrying the Countess. In my heart I prayed, as I had every night, every morning, that the vessel had not foundered.

"They might have put in to a different port," I ventured, and crushed my fear beneath my silk-damask bodice.

"Perhaps." But Edward had again turned his attention elsewhere. "Look!" He gestured with his arm at the bustle on the quay, at the seagulls that swooped and dived with wild cries, at the muddle of horses and men that awaited us under the proud banners and pennons of Lancaster. "This is mine. My realm, my people, and I have not seen it for seven years. How the sun bathes it in light."

Indeed it did. Cool, pale spring sunshine flooded it. A good omen, as he had said. I refused to allow the blood-smeared images of my dreams to creep in and spoil this return. It should be a moment for rejoicing.

"I will pray for your success, my lord. Perhaps we should drink to it." I offered him the still-untouched wine.

"What an exceptional wife you will be." Heavy with irony, the Prince took the cup with a feral baring of teeth—a baseless fraud of a smile—and lifted it to his lips. Then he halted, the silver rim almost touching his mouth. He frowned, lowered it, peering into it. "No. I won't."

"Why not, my lord?" I did not at first read his reaction.

"You might poison me."

I was stunned. "Do you think I would?" This incredible volatile switch of mood. I should be used to it by now. And what a depth of distrust.

"You might." Lifting his arm, he tossed the cup far overboard into the water. We both watched the ruby contents fan out into a wide arc of droplets with the force of his arm, until they spattered onto the surface of the waves. "Who knows what you might do, if Gloucester asked it of you. Not worth the risk, is it, madam Princess?"

So my presumed crime still occupied the Prince's thoughts. How dared he accuse me of so foul a deed? I felt anger begin to bubble through my blood.

"I would never threaten your life!"

"No? But then, I'll not give you the chance, madam!"

Before I could vent my fury at his capricious accusation, the Prince marched off to oversee the disembarkation. He left me with thoughts that churned and jostled, none of them happy ones. We had returned and with that would come battle. Battles brought death. My father had been abandoned by Clarence, and Richard would be somewhere in the enemy ranks. My mother's whereabouts were unknown. The Prince was beyond my managing. Whatever the future held, today I would set my foot on English soil. So would Prince Edward, the hope of Lancaster—and then there would be no more waiting.

CHAPTER TWELVE

entered the abbey church by the south door from the clois-
tered walk, Beatrice beside me, hoping to slip in without
notice.

We were settled into Cerne Abbey. It would not be for
long, God willing, as the Queen informed my lord abbot. She had
experienced the brutal thorns of the Lancaster rose. Now with her son
at her side she would anticipate its glorious blossoming. The years of
suffering were over.

My heart was not in the rejoicing. How could it be when there
was still no news of the Countess? I forced myself to cling to the belief that her ship had put in to a different port and even now she was
traveling to meet up with us. I could not eat. Could not sleep. So I felt
unnaturally weak and light-headed as I entered the abbey to join the
Queen for Holy Mass on that Easter Monday morning.

Mass had already begun. If I could kneel in the cool dimness, in
God's presence, would I not find some reassurance? I saw the Queen
and the Prince kneeling far ahead in the chancel, the abbot about to
raise the Host before the altar. Stepping forward into the center of the
nave I watched the ceremony unfold. It was distant, almost unreal,

as the light from the great east window was sufficient to glint and sparkle on the silver and gold of the precious vessels, on the abbot's ceremonial cope. I felt my heartbeat slow and a calm spread through me. When the abbot's voice, sure and true, began the Latin cadences I felt an inner surge of hope. It was all timeless, all familiar. In that moment I believed entirely that my mother was safe and would join us at Cerne. All would be well. Surely all would be well.

With a lifting of spirits I would have walked forward to pray with fervor.

From behind me, a shaft of sunlight, as sharp as an arrow, angled across the floor to trap me in its brilliance as the great west door was opened a little way. Three men not of our household entered in haste, to stride past me with barely a look, brushing me with their muddied garments, marching the length of the nave to stand before the Queen, who had risen to her feet on their approach. The whole focus in the abbey suddenly changed. Even the abbot fell silent, turned his head. The messengers fell to their knees before the Queen. I saw the conversation ebb and flow. It lasted no more than a minute yet seemed to stretch out forever.

Then feverish activity. The figures shifted and re-formed into a different pattern, a ripple like wind over water. The messengers fell back, their task complete. The plainsong halted as if God had struck the singers dumb, and the monks abandoned the choir stalls in disarray. A hum of tension rose, muttered words, whispers. In the center of it all stood the Queen and the Prince together, now moving from chancel to nave, toward me. The Queen's voice rang out, sharp with emotion.

I was drawn forward by some terrible foreboding. Margaret looked at me, eyes wide and strangely blank. Cold dread deepened in my belly.

"You will want to know." Her voice rang out as clear as the abbey bell.

"My mother?" It was my first thought, my first fear. The ship had foundered and she was lost to me. "No, not that," I whispered. "Tell me that she is safe."

Margaret gave a sharp inhalation of breath. "Of what interest is the fate of Warwick's wife to me? This is far worse . . . a disaster beyond all imagining. A terrible reversal."

"What could be worse? I don't—"

"All our planning is in disarray. . . ."

"Just tell her, madam!" Striding up with furious steps, the Prince was beside me, and took hold of my forearm, fingers hard, and shook me. Startled, I gasped with the sudden bite of pain. "The Yorkists have defeated us in battle. Warwick is dead."

No! No!

My lips framed the word but no sound came. I shook my head as if the action would deny the Prince's brutality. "No!" This time I forced it from my lips.

"Yes. At . . ." He swung around impatiently to the messenger. "God's wounds! Where was it? Where was it that all my hopes soaked with Warwick's blood into the ground?"

"Barnet, my lord."

It was as if I heard the words but could make no sense of them as they rattled and echoed within my skull. The Earl dead? My father? But he had such skills in battle. He could not have lost his life in some obscure battle, and not without my being aware of such a loss. And surely, with all their shared past stretching back over a decade, with the bloodshed, the loss of family and the glory, surely Edward of York would not seek the death of my father. The pain of the Prince's fingers around my arm was nothing compared to my outrageous loss. It stole my breath. It throbbed in my head.

"No. You must be wrong." I looked from one to the other, my eyes feverishly seeking a different truth from the Queen or the messenger.

"Warwick is dead." It was an unequivocal confirmation from the Queen. "This man saw it."

The messenger bowed. "It is true, lady."

"He will tell you in what ignoble manner the Earl died!" Margaret spat.

"The battle was over, lady, lost." The messenger spoke carefully, measuring his words. "The Yorkists held the day. The Earl tried to take horse and escape."

"Coward!" hissed the Prince. "To run from battle when there was still a chance. Damn Warwick! Foul traitor! How could he have allowed the Yorkists to take the advantage? All is lost. Is it not true that he abandoned his men? That he would have fled to Calais, abandoning our cause?"

"So it is said, my lord."

"He should have negotiated, come to some terms to save his army. Now they are all lost to us, those who escaped routed and leaderless. Warwick was not worthy of my trust. . . ."

I could no longer listen to the Prince's ranting. "There can be no doubt? The Earl, my father, is dead?" The voice was not mine, the lips that spoke them not my lips. I felt as if my whole body were suspended in some strange weightlessness so that I could not feel or think or make sense of what pressed in on me.

"No, lady. King Edward made sure there would be no doubts. The Earl's body was stripped naked of his armor . . . and taken to London. So he might be displayed in a public place." The messenger must have seen the blood drain even more from my face and he continued rapidly, to tell the news as quickly as he might. But nothing could lance the pain of the telling. "He was placed so that all might see and know that the Earl did not survive."

The Prince drew his sword in a glittering rush, light spilling along its blade.

"My lord!" the abbot exclaimed.

But the Prince was deaf to him as he advanced up the chancel, almost pushing the abbot from his path. Reaching the altar he knelt there, laid his sword there, and placed both hands on the festive altar cloth. Flinging back his head, he almost shouted the words so that all in the vast building would hear.

"I swear, on Christ's risen body, that I will hunt down this scum of York who would still deny me my rights. I will not rest until the crown is mine. God will seal the blade of my sword with His power, so that

I may spill the Yorkist blood and take my revenge in His name." His voice grew harsh with fury. "I call down Almighty God's vengeance on those who bear the name of Neville. For Warwick has surely damaged my cause beyond repair!"

Leaving the glimmering blade on the altar, the Prince stalked back toward us, his face vivid with purpose. As true a dramatic piece of mummer's work as ever I saw. To draw attention, to put himself at the center of the scene. To gild himself in his mother's eyes. And in that moment I despised him. I hated him with every beat of the blood through my body and I would never forgive him. To make that conceitedly grand gesture on the dead body of the Earl, with never a thought of me, of my loss. When it was necessary for him to walk past me, he did so as if I did not exist. As perhaps I no longer did for him. I was nothing but the encumbrance his mother had branded me. I had been taken as his bride for a purpose, a purpose that no longer existed. The Earl was dead and his use—and mine—at an end.

"Edward! My son! Control your anger. . . ." The Queen thrust out her arm to stop him as he strode past her, but he was beyond that. She could not restrain him.

"No!" the Prince shouted, his voice echoing in the vast space. "My cause is ruined. And you have tied me to this . . ."—he pointed an accusing finger—"to this whore!"

A monster I had called him when he had killed my finches. I did not then know the half of it. Today I had seen the beast in him. I watched the Prince in my distress, seeing my future life spread out before me, all degradation and slights to bring me low. Should I fear even for my life? Lack of sleep, lack of food, and now this impossible tragedy had their effect. Darkness clouded my sight and I could not breathe, yet the cloying scent of the incense was intolerably sweet. The fluttering of an imprisoned pigeon became loud in my ears as the Queen's stark face and the Prince's twisted features wavered and swam. I tried to lift my hand, to take hold of some firm support, but there was nothing. . . . An engulfing cold touched my limbs and I fell to the floor.

*   *   *

When conscious thought returned I was lying on my own bed. I lay still, absorbing the silence, until what had occurred in the abbey church hit home like a mailed fist. I knew not who had brought me there, but it did not matter. Opening my eyes, I saw that Beatrice was with me, seated by the window. I could not tolerate her presence, spy as she was for the Queen. I turned my face to the wall so that she would not see my distress.

Warwick is dead.

My father. Gifted with skill and talent, outrageously proficient in battle and in diplomacy, and yet he lay dead and cold somewhere in London, his body defiled for all to see. His name was known and acknowledged throughout the land, by some with hatred, by some with admiration, but by all with respect. He had wielded a sword, held power, had negotiated terms and settlements since coming of age well before his twentieth year. How could such a charmed life be snuffed out with no cataclysmic reaction? I tried to bring his face and figure to mind as I had seen him last when he left to prepare for this futile invasion, damned from the start by Margaret's procrastination and lack of trust. Now all was lost and Warwick's body lay in an open coffin to be mocked by those who would.

I could not accept it. Would not! He could not have been a coward to flee the field, to abandon his men to their fate, whatever the Prince claimed. Yet the messenger had confirmed the accusation. And how could Edward—King Edward—have allowed his death? Had he truly forgotten all he owed to his friend and cousin? Had my father's betrayal wiped out all affection?

My mind detoured into even less pleasant waters. If King Edward was in the mood for revenge, had he allowed the Earl's body to be desecrated? And where was it now? For all I knew it had been dismembered, the significant parts hacked and spiked on gates and bridges in London as warnings to those who would disobey. I turned my face and groaned into my pillow. I could not think of it.

"Some wine, lady."

Beatrice had risen quietly and come to my side with a cup. I did not even bother to respond.

"It is God's will," she murmured. "We must accept such pain."

"No, it is not." I would never accept it.

For there was the other dreadful image luring me. What of my mother? If she was alive, did she know? Had she had some premonition that the farewell at Angers was to be their last? I did not know how she would survive this devastating news. Husband dead, one daughter firmly anchored to Lancaster, the other dragged willy-nilly into the train of York by a self-serving husband. How would she survive such isolation?

An insistent throbbing of my forearm caught my attention at last, and I looked down, surprised to see the bruising. I brushed my hand over the tender skin and winced. And remembered. The Prince's anger had again destroyed all his control toward me and I knew that my mother was not the only one to face a lonely and uncertain future. I pulled my sleeve over the cruel prints to hide the evidence but I could not hide my fears. Despair walled me in and I wept, deep sobs that shook me, regardless of Beatrice's presence. I did not care that she knew of my grief. I did not care.

At last I must have slept.

Ten days we remained at Cerne as the army beyond the abbey's protective walls grew. The days were endless now, in a cold and subtly hostile environment from which there was no escape for me. The Prince was gone for much of the time, recruiting, interviewing, building the army that would take him to London. His energies were enormous and all-consuming. He left at dawn, not returning until after dusk, snatching a mouthful of bread and meat as and when he could. This was what he had waited for all his life, to reclaim his inheritance. Now, his ambition almost within his grasp, he would stop at nothing to achieve it.

Left to my own devices, I met and spoke with everyone who came to the great door. Every traveler who sought sanctuary, every messenger who arrived to report to the Queen. Every sick and desperate beggar who limped or hobbled to enjoy the monk's charity. Anyone who might have news of the Countess. I was a ghost, haunting the entrance and the walls that gave me a clear view of the road.

Lady Beatrice was the only one to approach me during my long watches. "Come away, my lady. This will do you no good." She would have pulled me back into one of the parlors.

"I cannot."

How wretched I was, swept by dark terrors and a shattering loneliness. My world, the world I had known since I was a child, lay before me in pieces. The Earl was dead, Isabel and Clarence tied to Edward of York's sleeve. And now my mother lost to me, perhaps dead also. Our castles and possessions in England were long gone. I was a penniless, landless petitioner, my Neville blood a curse, my future dependent on the charity of a woman who hated me and a husband at whose hands I increasingly feared violent recriminations.

Black despair swamped me. I think it was there in the confines of Cerne Abbey, when my eyes were finally opened, that maturity hit me hard with the entirely adult acceptance that my father was not the hero, as I had always seen him. Do not all mortals have feet of clay? Where could I put the blame for the loss of all I loved and treasured? I knew the answer. My father, the Earl.

It hurt so much. My heart wept, but in those bleak days I could not.

What had made him so blind? What had driven him to risk all by challenging Edward of York? I knew that as well. Ambition. Overweening, driving ambition. When had the Nevilles not been ambitious? The Earl could not tolerate the rising Woodville star that threatened to eclipse his own shining glory as the King's chief counselor. I accepted now that the King had kept the hand of friendship open to my father, but the Earl had turned his shoulder. He would not share the royal patronage with his rivals. And so he had fought for reinstatement of Neville fortunes, whatever the cost, even if it meant bending the knee to the detested Angevin Queen.

As I watched for travelers on the road, I remembered the Earl's simple explanation at Middleham that had convinced me King Edward was in the wrong. Now I turned the coin to see the reverse. I knew to what extremes ambition could drive a man. Did I not see it every day in the Prince, in the tempestuous energies that convinced him he could not lose?

Hollow with loneliness, I saw only the inevitability of our downfall from the moment Isabel had wed Clarence against Edward's wishes, and I could place it nowhere but at the Earl's feet. Sometimes in the dark, sleepless hours bitterness choked me. He had destroyed us. He had used me to bind an impossible alliance. Would a loving father do that? In those hours I acknowledged that Edward Plantagenet was King and the Earl had no right to challenge him. For having raised his sword against the anointed King at Barnet, perhaps he deserved death. The father I had adored had brought us all low.

Then Neville pride took hold of me. My father had placed that crown on Edward Plantagenet's head. Did the Earl then not deserve King Edward's loyalty? Were the Nevilles to be tossed aside at the whim of Edward and his Woodville Queen? By God, they were not! I too was a Neville, in flesh and blood and bone. I would not be swept aside but would fight for the recognition due to me.

But who would stand for me?

I swear my heart was broken and I lived in a bottomless well of agony. There was no way out for me.

Until a traveling troop of jugglers and acrobats, making the most of the lull in hostilities, came to me.

"She's safe enough," their leader in scruffy but colorful motley announced when I was fetched to the gate.

"Safe?" The word formed a little center of warmth in my icy soul. "Safe!"

"The Countess landed at Southampton, lady." The traveling player thrust out his chest as if he performed before an audience. "She was traveling west, to join you, when she heard the news. Of Barnet. She took refuge in Beaulieu Abbey and says that she'll not leave her sanctuary, having no faith in any man."

"Ha!" Did I not know exactly how she felt? "Did she speak of the Earl?"

"No, lady. She did not."

"How did she seem? Was she well?" I wanted more, much more.

The man wrinkled his forehead. "The Countess was herself, lady. But her eyes spoke of grief. I think she suffered. She fears that King Edward will take her prisoner and have his revenge on her."

I sought to find words to thank the traveler and fled. In the abbey I fell to my knees before the altar to give thanks for her safety. But there was no lessening of my sense of loss and desolation.

"Why are you not here with me, to give me advice?"

I railed against fate. I wanted to rant and weep, to tear the costly silk of my gown, to rend my veil and loose my hair with frenzied fingers. I wanted to call down curses on those who slew my father, or take some outrageous action to honor the depths of my despair. Why must I behave well, when my heart was broken? Instead, I crouched on the floor and buried my face in my hands, for my future loomed with a terrible certainty, beating relentlessly in my brain.

If Margaret had her way, I would be Princess no longer, my un-consummated marriage annulled as quietly and rapidly as possible as she cast around for a more suitable candidate for her son. She need compromise no longer with the detested Neville alliance. I imagined the glee with which she would rid herself of me. How long would it take her to realize that Warwick's death was not a tragedy after all?

Not long, I acknowledged. She no longer asked me to read to her or entertain her. I had become an outcast. My isolation grew as each day passed.

We left Cerne Abbey. Rather than the progress of a mighty force, sure of its success, the Prince's army bore keener comparison with a frantic and ill-managed, ill-matched hunt. We were the courageous stag, doomed despite the magnificence of its crown of antlers. Edward of York followed us, tracked us, spied on us through every moment of our advancement. Even I could sense the inevitable outcome. Eventually he would hunt us down, tear us to pieces without compunction, with all the fierce efficiency of a pack of hounds. I could almost hear the eager baying of the dogs, as if they were already gathering their strength to pounce. The prickle of cold fear touched my arms, my neck. My dreams of blood and death returned to haunt me, looming close, terrifying in their detail as they grew stronger with every hunted step we took.

The days became one long burden of unseasonable heat, of thirst and filth and exhaustion. Of nameless towns that either welcomed us or spurned our approach. We took to horseback, riding before the army to avoid the dust and turmoil of the passage of so many men. The saddles chafed and rubbed sore patches that wept and bled, but there could be no respite. Would we be forced to fight on some windswept heath? Would I meet my death in some wood as my father had done, surrounded and cut down?

Yet through it all I felt the presence of ghosts at my shoulder, astonishingly comforting, as if in truth flesh and blood. The Earl's courage, grimly present in death. The Countess's warmth and love even in her living grief. In the darkest of days, when I would have slid from my saddle to weep in the dust from the sheer punishing demands of the march, they stiffened my spine and I rode on without complaint. I was the perfect lady-in-waiting, answering the Queen's every truculent need. With gritted teeth and pain-racked muscles I gave her no cause for reproach.

And if I felt the presence of Richard too somewhere in the approaching army—a more tangible presence, for I knew that Edward of York had given him the glory of leading the van—if I felt his presence then that too was a strange manner of comfort.

Finally, late in the day, we reached Tewkesbury, where we could ford the River Severn, only to find that the Yorkist army that had hounded us had overtaken us. We were cornered. We had no choice but to fight. The stag must turn and face the hounds. I should have felt terror, but I think I was too exhausted to feel anything.

CHAPTER THIRTEEN

The Queen's household was accommodated at Gupshill Manor just south of the town, crowded together like rats in a basket before the terriers were set on them and wagers made. That night I daresay none of us slept. By daybreak I had risen—dressing was not difficult when I had taken off so few garments—and sought the silent solitude of the chapel, where I sank to my knees in despair before the serene figure of the Virgin.

"Blessed Virgin. For whom shall I pray?" How difficult it was. I named silently in my heart those I loved, praying for the Virgin's intercession. I offered prayers for my father's soul. As for the Prince . . . "How can I pray for his victory?" I whispered against my fingers.

The benignly smiling expression did not change; the blue folds of her robe fell in seemly array over her compassionately outstretched arms, and as if the direction of my thoughts had summoned his presence, the Prince's voice interrupted from the door arch.

"I have always known that I would win England back by the sword. Today I shall do it. Edward of York will be dead before the day is out. I want you to pray for me, for my victory." With a clatter of mailed feet, the Prince was looming over me. His eyes glowed with passionate fervor, fever-bright.

Why not be honest? Why not voice the fears of many Lancastrians?

"Edward!" Rising from my knees to face him—I would not be intimidated—I deliberately used his name. "How can you be so certain? You have no experience of battle. They have more guns. They can blow our army from the field."

"I shall bring them down. Nothing will stop me! God will not allow me to lose." He leaned close. "Are you sent to me by the devil, to undermine my confidence? Have you followed your sister in your mind to hope for my defeat?"

"No, Edward, I have not," I snapped. "If I had treason in mind, I would have found a way to escape during the march. I would be with Isabel even now." His convictions were overpowering and beyond my changing.

"When you see me again I shall hold the crown of England in my hands. Do you wish me well?"

"I would never wish you ill, my lord." It was the best I could do. "God keep you from harm, Edward."

Taking me by surprise, as I expect he intended, he leaned closer and brushed my cheek with his lips, a falsely affectionate gesture of farewell that set my nerves to jangling. I tried not to step back, but everything in me shrank from him, so I did. Nor could I keep my fear hidden from my eyes as I watched him, a vole beneath the talons of a hawk. And Edward, hawklike, pounced, raised his hand to curl around my throat, at first a light-fingered stroke but one that quickly firmed into a disconcerting pressure. In that moment he was all malice, eyes gleaming with the all-too-familiar bloodlust. I stiffened under his hands. The bruising on my cheek might fade as if it had never existed, but I would never forget the manner of its inflicting. What did he intend now?

"Gloucester is with the army," the Prince purred, the pads of his fingers increasing their pressure. "He commands the west wing. I suppose you know that. I shall enjoy killing him, you know. I shall bring his head back to lay at your feet."

"Why would you do that?" Disgust shook me, but I kept my eyes steady on his. *Don't show fear. Don't allow him any hold over you. He will feed on your weakness if he sees the panic in your face.*

"Because then I will have no rivals for your loyalties, my dearest wife." Palm hot on my throat and damp with excitement, fingers pressing harder, he brought his lips to within a mere breath away from mine. "Even your admiration will be for me alone. How should I not want a *Neville* to admire me? Perhaps you will even grow to love me."

"You will do as you must," I whispered, nauseated by his closeness, his implications.

As rigid as the statue of the Virgin, I tolerated the strengthening pressure. Not once did I allow my gaze to drop before his, forcing the contact to remain true. For a second his fingers tightened further against me, the edges of those finely pared nails digging in, then just as quickly they withdrew as he allowed them to trail down lightly, seductively, over my breast. A lover's gesture, yet in his eyes I saw a kind of loathing for me and all I stood for. Not a hawk at all, I thought inconsequentially. A cat tormenting a helpless mouse, still alive between its teeth.

I shivered in horror. I couldn't stop it.

"Treacherous whore!" he whispered against my hair, as if it were an endearment, and took my mouth with his. Brutally savage, his teeth nipped and scraped, his tongue possessed, even more vicious than on our abortive wedding night. He held me strongly when I struggled, pushing futilely with my hands against his chest. "Do you wish me well in this battle, virgin wife?" he muttered. "Do you wish me well when I hunt Gloucester down?"

Not requiring an answer—and before God I could not offer one—Edward thrust me away, hard enough so that I stumbled against the altar steps to keep my balance. I knew he hated me and would destroy me if he could.

"Do you send me to battle with a prayer for my victory?" he demanded.

How could I? "You will do what you will, Edward, but you'll not get my blessing if you've vengeance in mind."

"I shall be King with or without your blessing!" he snarled.

How unwise to strip my feelings so naked. I knew I would pay for my ill-considered reply, but wish him well? Never! As Edward strode from the chapel to lead his army against Edward of York, my heart was as heavy as stone.

A defeat! An utter rout!

The news came to us before the end of the day. There was blood on the messenger's clothes. The Queen insisted on every detail so that she would know the whole. We stood on either side of her as if we would protect her, but we could not shield her from the brutal facts. We shared the grief that stunned us all. The Lancastrian army put to flight with over two thousand men fallen. A complete rout. All the Queen's bright convictions destroyed on the battlefield.

The Prince, the glorious hope of Lancaster, was dead.

My husband was dead.

The disaster, the whole bloody detail of it, was laid out before us as the Queen demanded the repetition of the facts over and over again. She looked around as if she could not quite bring her surroundings to mind; then she crumbled before our eyes, almost senseless, sinking to the floor. Never had I seen Margaret of Anjou cast aside her innate dignity, but now she lay on the tiles, her skirts in the dust as harsh sobs racked her.

The messenger stepped back, the ladies surrounded her, hands and veils fluttering, panic building in the room as the Queen's authority drained away with her tears. I simply stood, hardly able to absorb what I had just heard, burying my emotions deep. Not so much the Prince's death—I could do nothing but admit to a wash of intense relief—but the manner of it appalled me. Its perpetrator, as described to us without sentiment at Margaret's insistence . . . I forced myself to concentrate purely on the immediate dangers, and discovered within me the ability to take charge when crisis loomed.

I dared do nothing else, fearing that I too would shatter.

"Your Majesty!" I went to her, pushing aside the ineffective women, knelt beside her, and simply held her as she rocked and moaned her loss, all but unconscious. I had not seen such terrible grief. How frail her slight frame felt, worn down through the months of strain, her skin stretched taut over her bones beneath the layers of her gown. She clung to me with clawlike fingers.

"All is lost. My son is dead. How I have been punished." Her tears soaked into my shoulder.

"We cannot stay here," I urged. "We must escape. . . . You must not be taken prisoner." At first my words failed to slice through her grief. "You must go from here, Your Majesty," I repeated, shaking her a little so that she would look at me.

"Where shall I go?" she asked in hopeless despair.

I had no idea. I turned my head, raised my brows at the messenger who still stood uncertainly beside the door.

"There's a family nearby, my lady." He spoke to me. "At Payne's Place. They'll hide you, at least for tonight. Until the worst is over . . ."

"No. No. I must remain. . . ." Margaret looked wildly around the room, pushing away my supporting hands. "I cannot leave here." As if her son were not truly dead but would return to her before night fell.

But I had taken the messenger's meaning. "The Yorkist blood is up, Your Majesty. They'll have no respect for your rank if you fall into their clutches." I grasped her hands to fix her wayward attention again. "It's not wise to stay."

The Queen frowned at me, still prepared to dissent.

"The lady speaks the truth, Your Majesty," the messenger confirmed, his anxiety showing. "A bloodbath out there, and will be worse before it's better."

The Queen closed her eyes for a long moment. "I hear you."

The messenger took us to Payne's Place, secreted in a little valley some few miles distant, where we put the Queen to bed. No more tears. No more words. When she lay rigidly between the linen sheets, eyes staring blindly up at the silk tester, she finally spoke, her words addressed to me.

"I don't want you with me. I don't want you near me."

I knew why. I could not blame her. We both knew from the messenger's telling who had killed the Prince, whose hand had wielded the dagger that pierced his heart.

Whether she slept I knew not. To my surprise, considering that my bed was a pallet on the floor in an unused and dusty chamber, I did. But I tumbled headfirst into a dream that was no dream.

I stood in Tewkesbury Abbey, beside one of the heavy pillars of the nave, a cloak falling straight from shoulder to floor, a deep hood hiding my face. At the center of the nave stood a small group of men. If I had stretched out my hand I could have touched any one of them, but they paid me no heed. All showed signs of the recent battle, still wearing some remnants of armor, still smeared with dust and sweat and blood. There was the reek of death about them. Of danger. They had come straight here from the battlefield.

There was Edward of York, King Edward. He had removed his helm with its gold circlet and dropped it against the rood screen. His tabard blazed with the Sun in Splendor despite the gloom that hemmed us in. With him was Clarence, sword still in hand. And Gloucester. My Richard. Feet firmly planted, legs braced, he made up the trio of royal brothers, no less impressive for the coating of muck and gore from a vicious fight. His eyes were hard, gleaming like obsidian, his face lined and weary. His hands where rings glinted were clasped on his sword belt.

He still wore my ring.

My eyes moved on. Surrounded by guards, there stood the Prince. He had suffered rough handling. Apparently unhurt but disheveled, hair awry, one sleeve all but rent from the body of his tunic, he looked less than princely. Mud was smeared from forehead to chin and the ostrich feathers barely showed through the filth on his breast. Face pale, he stood with guards restraining him, gripping his arms. I knew how he must have hated that.

"So you would fight against me." King Edward broke the silence.

"I would," the Prince snapped. "And I will, until there is no more breath in my body."

"See!" The King gestured. "A traitor by your own words. You have no right to the crown."

"More right than you! My birth is beyond question. You'll not deny me my birthright." Petulance blossomed. His fair skin flushed with anger, his sneer ugly. "Challenge me to single combat—if you dare! You know I would be the victor. I am the true King."

The King tilted his head, considering, lips pressed firm.

"A traitor condemned out of your own mouth. The penalty for such is death. After victory on the battlefield it is my right to deal out summary justice."

The threat lay heavy, thick in the air to fill my lungs so that breathing was well-nigh impossible, white-hot as a lightning strike. Red as blood. I was held in its grip. So I stood as witness to the final event.

"The penalty is death!" the King repeated.

"You cannot kill me. I claim the right of sanctuary."

"There is no sanctuary."

The Prince stared wildly around. "Usurper!" he spat with no lessening of aggression. "I will have my father's heritage. . . ."

The Prince leaped at the King. With what intent? Impossible to know, but I saw Richard slide a long-bladed dagger from his belt. My attention was gripped and held by that bright metal. I could not look away.

And Richard struck. He buried the long blade in the Prince's gut, a final vicious upward thrust to pierce his heart. There was a cry. The Prince gasped with shock, eyes wide and staring in pain, in astonishment, his hands clasped tight to the hilt as if he could undo the deed. He slid to the floor in a graceless heap as his blood and his life drained away.

Aghast, I looked at the body. Murder? Was this murder? Blood seeped through the fine linen of his tunic to stain the already mired feathers. It spread on the floor to creep toward me. When I looked down it lapped my shoes; my skirts were spattered by it. Beside the Prince the knife had fallen on the slabs of paving. I was transfixed by it, by the glint of metal through the blood.

I cried out in denial. But whose name I could not hear. Was it the Prince's or Richard's? No one heard. They turned away, the deed done. In my dream, I was alone with the body of my husband.

I crouched beside him.

Then I was alone no longer. There was the Queen in a sweep of black mourning, touching my shoulder, gripping it in frenzied fingers. "So you have seen my son done to death. Gloucester murdered my son. Does this please you? Your lover murdering your husband?"

"No. It does not please me."

"Now you are free. Free to go to him."

I woke abruptly with dry throat and staring eyes as the horrors of the dream stayed with me. This was not a battlefield killing in hot blood. It was revenge, deliberate blood-soaked murder by Richard's hand, just as the messenger had told the Queen. I lay still. If I could, I would have pulled the covers over my head and hidden from the world.

Who would choose, of their own free will, to return to a town the day after a battle? The day after a bloody massacre?

Not I! But that was what I did. Without permission, without any real plan of how I would go about my task. Duty and honor, respect, and all the splendid, glowing qualities instilled in me since birth told me that I should. For good or ill, Edward of Lancaster was my husband and now he was dead.

I took a cloak. I bribed with a handful of gold a reluctant groom, who answered when it suited him to the name of Sim, to saddle two horses, and prepared to make my escape. I did not fear the Queen. So sunk was she in melancholy that she would not notice my absence, and might thank God that I was gone when she did.

I was about to lead my mount from the stables when a shadow loomed at my shoulder. Beatrice! I had forgotten. The Queen might be out of her mind but her orders would still stand, and Beatrice was nothing if not dutiful.

"By the Virgin! You frightened me!" I glared at her as my heart thudded hard enough to choke me. "What are you doing?"

"What am *I* doing?" Her perfect brows rose elegantly, at odds with her disheveled appearance and stained gown. Even her veiling, usually immaculate, was the worse for wear. I dared not think what I looked like. "What are *you* doing with a horse and an escort?"

"Going to Tewkesbury." There was no point in lying about it.

"You cannot leave."

"I can. I will." I turned away and tightened the girth. But she grasped my arm, her fingers digging in.

"So you are fleeing. I should have known that you were spineless, deserting the Queen when she is most in need." Beatrice's sharp features tightened. Her disgust with me was patent, but so was the fear that we would be captured and would pay the price of all traitors. All of it was channeled into a virulent attack. "As treacherous as all Nevilles. It runs in the blood. There's nothing left for you here now, is there? Once out of here, what's to stop you from throwing yourself on York's mercy? You have your sister to stand for you, and Clarence will have the King's ear." Her accusations built, one on another. "And so, I wager, has the Duke of Gloucester. He'll see you as a godsend, a ripe plum dropping from the tree into his hand. A widow now—how fortunate!—and your mother's heiress. If your mother is attainted as a traitor, your inheritance might come to you quicker than you thought. And Gloucester will not believe his luck."

The poisonous words hung between us. My fingers stilled on the girth. I had not thought of it. If my mother, secure in Beaulieu, was attainted, then my position as heiress might become immediate. And as a widow I could wed again. . . . I had not thought of that either. Since

I had been wife only in name, being widowed had made no impression on me. My laugh, harsh in its cynicism, must have startled Beatrice, for she released my arm as if I were the bearer of the plague.

It seemed that I had become a valuable commodity again.

But now was not the time for such deep thoughts.

"I'm not planning to play the traitor, Beatrice. I'm going to find my husband's body, and when I do I'm going to see that it's treated in a seemly manner. Have you even considered that?" I had done nothing but consider it throughout the long night. "He is—was—Lancaster's heir, for all his faults. What has been done with the Prince's body? Displayed as a spectacle for the townsfolk of Tewkesbury, who would mock the naked and despoiled heir of Lancaster?" The Londoners had flocked to gorge their senses on my father's heartlessly displayed body. As far as I knew the Prince had been stripped and cast on a town dung heap. "Do you want the Prince to lie unburied, with no Masses said, no comfort for his soul? It is not fitting that he should be degraded in death."

I mounted. Action had roused my spirit so that I would brook no refusal. "Leave go of my rein, Beatrice. Come with me if you must, if your duty insists—or get out of my way."

I did not want her but I got her. And perhaps I was not disappointed. Pride would have prevented me from asking for her help, but it was a small comfort not to have to ride into blood-soaked Tewkesbury alone. A lurid vision of Richard, his knife buried to the hilt in Edward's breast, rose once more in my mind.

One day I would have to face it, but not today. I blocked it out.

I had never seen a town in the aftermath of battle, but I had heard tales often enough. Of soldiers running free with the fire of victory in their blood and an excess of ale swilled down their throats to strip away all humanity. But never could I have imagined such wanton destruction. Such careless violence against all who crossed their path. Bodies lay on all sides, limbs tumbled, clothes and possessions of any

value plundered, flesh disfigured with wounds. I turned my eyes from
those who were children. From the women who lay in obscene parody
of love. I did not need to look to know what had been done. The dead
here were not Lancastrian soldiers, caught in flight. These were helpless, unarmed, innocent townsfolk, trapped within the walls, in the
nightmare of a victorious army on the loose.

"Quiet!" Sim murmured as we picked our way through the streets.
"Don't draw attention. Don't speak to anyone. They won't ask your
name before they hack you to pieces, lady. Or worse . . ." It was some
consolation that he drew a long-bladed dagger from the side of his
boot. I loosened my own where it was tucked into my sleeve so that it
came readily to hand. "Where do you want to go, lady?"

Sim's voice dragged my attention from the sprawled figure of a
child, no more than five years, hair matted with blood and facedown
in the gutter. I forced myself to think. "To the marketplace. Perhaps
we need to ask. . . ."

Sim grunted disapproval. "I'll do the asking! Keep a still tongue,
lady!" He hauled on the bridle and rode on. We followed slowly, working our way through the gut-churning mess. Without warning, from
a narrow alley off to one side, men emerged to surround us. From
their leather jerkins they were soldiers, but if they had ever recognized authority, it was gone now. Hands grasped my bridle, snatched
at Beatrice's. My horse jibbed and tossed its head against the restraint.

"Look what we've got 'ere, lads. Fine horses. Finer clothes!"

"Let go of my reins!" I forgot Sim's warning.

"A tasty mouthful! Lively with it!" A filthy hand grasped my arm
to pull me from the saddle. "Young too. Now let's see what's under
the cloak. . . ."

I drove my heels into the horse's side so that it bucked and kicked.
My attacker swore. Now his hands grabbed my cloak to give him
more leverage. At my side, when I had time to notice, Beatrice was
suffering similar indignities.

"Take your hands off me!" I snarled.

"Better to talk sweetly, pretty girl. Unless you want to get hurt."

A sneaky hand curled around my ankle. "We deserve a reward. We've just won a battle for the King." He tugged, almost toppling me from my mount. "You're just the prize I want." His grin became feral. "My friends 'ere—you can be their prize too. Both of you." He leered at Beatrice, whose face had gone as pale as death.

I kicked out but to no avail. Then Sim's dagger appeared in his hand, flashed in the light. So did mine as I struck home. I didn't know where it found flesh but there was a howl, the splash and warmth of blood, and the hands dropped from my cloak.

"By Christ! You'll pay for that. . . ."

Sim was at my side. "Get back! If you harm these travelers you'll pay with blood. They're Yorkist—come here at the invitation of the King. So back off!"

It gave our attackers a moment's thought. We did not wait to see how long but spurred forward while their attention was lax, careering down the street without thought for those who lay dead or wounded in our path, beneath our hooves.

"My thanks, Sim," I said, gasping.

"We're not out of it yet. And there's trouble ahead."

At the end of the street we could see where it opened out into the marketplace. There was a commotion, with crowds milling, a rumble of voices. As we approached a roar of approval burst from a hundred or more throats. It had an animal satisfaction about it, chilling my already cold blood. Sim waved us to a halt. "Wait here. Use the knife if you have to."

He rode forward, bent to ask a question of a group of men on the edge of the crowd, listened, asked again, shook his head, then returned.

"Well?"

"Lancastrian leaders," he replied laconically, which gave me no warning. "Taken prisoner—lured from the sanctuary of the abbey with promises of a pardon but then condemned to execution as traitors and rebels. This is the punishment now. Beheaded in the marketplace—all of them."

It seemed to take forever to grasp what was happening, but another roar of approval jolted me into awareness.

"It's murder . . ." Beatrice muttered.

"Military justice, lady. Gloucester held a trial this morning. They raised arms against the King. It's treason." Sim's bland acceptance in some ways shocked me more than the deed itself. "Doesn't waste time, does he?"

No. Gloucester had wasted no time in ridding the King of his enemies. But nor could I waste time. I must find the Prince's body. Then I would allow myself to think about what I had learned of Richard of Gloucester in the last two days.

"Where now, lady?"

"The abbey. Take me to the abbey church." It was the only place I could think of.

An uneasy calm returned to me. Here I would find help. It was a family place, a sacred place of prayer where my mother's Despenser and Beauchamp family had come over the generations. So would I, the youngest and least experienced of their noble ranks.

Then we entered the churchyard. There could be no pretense that we were entering sacred ground. I came to an abrupt halt in the gateway to witness more evidence of brutal murder. Bodies covered the grass, were piled against weathered headstones. Townsfolk as well as soldiers had fled here for safety, but they had not been saved. My throat slammed shut; my mouth dried.

Sim lifted a careless chin toward the plundered bodies of two men of means, what was left of their clothes dark with dried blood. He hawked and spit on the grass. "God damn all Yorkists!" But I got the impression that he might have said the same of Lancastrians, depending on his company.

"I can't believe they would do this." By now Beatrice was glassily pale with shock.

"Believe it, lady." Sim sniffed.

We did, when we discovered the door of the Abbey locked against us. My blood beating in my throat seemed to me as loud in my ears as Sim hammering on the wood. It took a long time. Footsteps, slow, dragging, approached. They halted behind the door. A long pause followed, which caused Sim to beat again with his fist. A grille was finally opened and one of the monks peered out.

"Who is it?"

"Travelers seeking sanctuary," Sim replied. "Two women."

"No sanctuary here. I am bid by my lord abbot to refuse entry to anyone."

"Refuse entry to God's house?" I handed my reins to Beatrice and pushed my way past Sim to the grille. "Open the door, sir. I would see the abbot immediately."

"I dare not. . . ."

I put back my hood. He would not recognize me—how would he possibly recognize me in my bedraggled, bloodstained state as one of their noble patrons?—but I hoped that a show of authority would do the trick. "I am Lady Anne Neville."

"My lady!" He blinked, startled. "What are you doing here? It is not safe!"

My name was the key. The door was opened, barely, and we slipped inside, leaving Sim without to guard our horses.

"My lady!" The monk was all but wringing his hands in distress, his round face impressed with lines of fear and strain. "See what they have done. Despoiled, desecrated. There is no sanctuary."

If the graveyard was bad, this place was worse, because through the wanton destruction still shone the solid elegance and grandeur of the church, like a handsome woman scarred and disfigured by deliberate mistreatment, yet with the remnants of her beauty still evident. A mob had swept through, destructive as a tidal wave, looting and vandalizing, hacking down what they could not carry away. Any who stood in their path were savagely dispatched, their blood staining the floor.

Why was nothing done to prevent this? Why had the King allowed

such pollution of a holy place? Shivering, I stepped hurriedly back
when I realized that I was standing where a pool of blood had recently
spread across the stone paving, fighting to remember why I had come
and what I needed to do.

"I have come to find the Prince's body."

"Lady . . ." I saw fear in his eyes.

"Do you know where he is? Where he was taken?"

"Hush!" He looked over his shoulder as if he expected marauding
Yorkists to spring from the walls. "Come with me."

He beckoned and set off at surprising speed, considering his el-
derly frame. I followed him away to the left, Beatrice beside me. It
was dark and quiet there behind the main altar, unlit, the only sound
our own footsteps. The chapels were dark, unused. The monk hurried along, not even turning his head to see if I kept up with him. I
was tempted to demand once again to speak with the abbot, but then
ahead I saw the glimmer of candle flame. The monk halted and motioned me into the Lady Chapel, hidden from general view behind the
high altar.

"Here, my lady. We hid him from those who might steal him away
and despoil him."

There he was: my husband, Margaret's precious son, laid out on
a crude, unadorned trestle. His body had been washed, bloodstains
removed from face and hands. His tunic, in which they had reclothed
him, stiff and disfigured with blood, bore testimony to his wounds,
but the monks had chosen to leave him with the plumed feathers, black
on red, of his rank and inheritance. I could not fault them in that; he
deserved that much. His face drew my eyes: impossibly young, colorless, and almost translucent. A calmness wrapped him around such as
I had never seen in life. The candles at his head burned steadily so that
there was no shadow on his features. All the lines had been smoothed
from his face by death, leaving him beautiful, at last at peace. I might
have felt sorrow, except that in life the Prince had never sought peace,
only violent death for his enemies and glorious victory for himself. It
seemed that he merely slept, his hands crossed on his breast. They had

placed his sword at his side. Someone had combed his hair so that it gleamed with russet warmth. It was the only sign of life as it fluttered a little in the ever-present draft.

"The Prince was killed here?" I asked, my voice little more than a croak.

"Yes, my lady. In the nave."

"In King Edward's presence?"

"Yes. The King and his brothers. There was an argument."

So the messenger's tale had been true. I would ask, even though I did not want to hear the answer. "Was he killed by the Duke of Gloucester's hand?"

"Yes, my lady."

A rustle of noise sounded behind us in the transept. Beatrice gasped aloud.

"The birds. They get in too." The monk smiled wanly. "But you must not stay."

"No. I must return to the Queen." If nothing else, I must tell her what I had found, what I had done. From my sleeve I took the bag of gold I had brought for such an occasion, filched from Margaret's own coffers in the chaos and scramble of flight. I knew what must be done, and what better place? "Keep him safe until law has returned to the town," I instructed, pressing the leather bag into the monk's hand. "I want the Prince buried in the monks' choir, in the very center, so that all shall see it when they enter the church. As for a monument to his life . . ." I could not think. Not yet. Perhaps it would be best not to draw attention to his final resting place. "I will return and arrange that—when the future is clearer. And Masses for his soul. I want Mass said daily."

The birds fluttered again, making my heart trip uncomfortably against my ribs. I knew we must go. For one final time I touched the Prince's hand, as cold as the stone beneath my feet. So much wasted life, so much promise spoiled by driving ambition and his mother's careless nurturing. On impulse I leaned down and touched my lips to his forehead. Not in compassion, but as a token of an ending between us. It was the first time I had kissed Edward of Lancaster of my own volition since the chaste caress of my marriage day in Angers Cathedral.

"Take care of him."

"We will, my lady."

We left the Lady Chapel to retrace our steps, my thoughts inward and dreary. Now that I had fulfilled my immediate duty to the dead, I could see nothing of a future for me other than as a permanent fugitive: an exile at the French court or a prisoner of York. I had known the Tower of London in happier times, had enjoyed its hospitality, but I had no wish to live out my days incarcerated there in cushioned captivity. I had no wish to be a prisoner at all.

"Lady! Beware!" the monk hissed in my ear. There was a commotion at the main door. A blast of cold air. Footsteps, determined and confident, but leisurely enough. One man, alone, and not on the hunt. The panic that had immediately flared to life within me settled into a dull simmer.

"This way!" The monk pushed us into the magnificent chantry chapel of my Despenser grandmother, with its elegant pillars and fan vaulting, to the side of the high altar, where we could crouch out of sight of the nave. Then he left us to our fate.

"The King!" Beatrice breathed against my ear. "Will he see us?"

I shook my head. I dared not speak as, unaware of his audience, King Edward strode to the rail before the altar. Unbuckling his sword he knelt there, head bowed, the light from the solitary pair of candles highlighting his golden hair.

"Almighty God be praised for this victory." His voice, soft enough, carried easily in the empty space. "I swear this will be the last battle to tear Englishmen apart, to spill English blood on English soil. I will place my sword here as a symbol of my intent." He continued to kneel, eyes fixed on the cross as if he would determine the future there.

And I recalled another starkly different dedication, when the Prince, all for show, for personal aggrandizement, had sworn his enmity and desire for blood. This was a quiet moment, a personal dedication between King and God, for no man's consumption. Then, the Prince had used his vow to vilify his enemies—my father, who had given his life for him. I shook with useless anger, until there came the echo of the heavy latch on the outer door, more footsteps. Breathless, unmoving, we peered through the spaces in the carving, straining to see through the intricate stonework. But I knew who it was even before I saw his figure, his face. After all those months of separation, I sensed him.

Richard!

I think I felt shock more than any other emotion. I had not thought to see him here, could never have envisaged seeing him again in such a situation as this. He stole my breath at the same time that awareness raced through my blood. I could only take a distant impression of him as the brothers stood together in the chancel, but it was enough. They spoke, believing themselves to be alone. I would have recognized Richard's voice anywhere: assured, the hint of a sharp edge, used to issuing orders and being obeyed.

"Is it done?" the King asked.

"Yes. All executed."

Here was a man, not a boy, not a youth, as my memory prompted me—a man who carried himself with experience, confidence. Here was a soldier, hardened and bloodied in battle, transformed over the months of conflict and exile into a royal counselor who wore his power as comfortably as the embroidered gloves I had snatched from him.

"A nasty business, but necessary." Edward looked around him at the empty niches from which statues had been dragged and shattered in a frenzy of destruction, at the absence of silver and gold except for the cross on the high altar. "Now we'll see to restoring this place." He grimaced down at the floor beneath his feet. I could imagine what horrors might still lie there. "It needs to be cleaned, if nothing else. Get the bishop of Worcester here, Richard. Then we'll arrange the burial of the Lancastrian lords. Traitors they might be, misguided and weak, but they fought bravely. They deserve honorable burial."

Richard followed his brother's gaze. "Our troops behave like animals. They bring shame on us."

"Difficult to blame them." The King shrugged. "We use them; we supply them with ale until their courage will carry them against death and mutilation. We can't damn them for the consequences. There is a price to pay. Victorious armies expect some reward."

"Too much," Richard replied. "Enough is enough. The indiscriminate killing must stop. I've given orders to our commanders." He waited as Edward bowed his head before the altar for a final time. While my breath eased. Soon our danger would be over. "What now?" Richard asked as the King moved to walk with him.

"Margaret. I need to find her. She's too dangerous to leave at large."

I stiffened.

"She's fled the town," Richard advised.

"Then we find her. My scouts are out and she can't have gone far." Edward took Richard's arm in a companionable mood. Even at a distance I saw the King's face light with a glow of triumph and a sudden thought. "I was thinking." The smile became a little sly. "Margaret has Anne Neville with her."

I smothered a gasp behind rigid fingers.

"True," Richard agreed.

"Anne Neville is now unwed."

"Also true."

"And her mother's heiress. Have you an interest there?"

Richard tilted his head as if giving it some thought. Clearly, *Yes!* was not springing to his mind. The blood that had run so hot at my awareness of him now ran icily and sluggish to the tips of my fingers, to my toes. To be considered so cold-bloodedly by the man I had thought to love until death. By the man who I thought loved me.

"She would be a wealthy bride, Dickon," pursued Edward in the face of his brother's silence. "If her mother was attainted, she would come into her inheritance now. Do you want her? You could look higher, of course. Mary of Burgundy is still unbetrothed."

"Higher than a Neville?" Richard smiled sardonically. "Is it possible?" Suddenly he looked up, around.

"What?" Edward asked.

"Nothing. Just ghosts perhaps."

"Or roosting pigeons. So? Anne Neville? What about her?" Edward repeated. "If she falls into my hands I must find a husband for her somewhere, and you were willing enough to take her when Warwick was my man. In truth, she's too valuable to allow to fall into the *wrong* hands. Some would call her a traitor and deal with her as such. . . ."

Traitor? I waited, my breath held. I thought Richard would reply. Surely he would want me, argue my cause. Then more footsteps brought Clarence in haste to create the three-cornered unity of royal brothers.

"What's this?" he demanded, looking suspiciously from one to the other. "Some deep policy?"

"Nothing of importance. Just the disposition of Anne Neville." Richard cast the matter aside as if it were not worthy of his concern. "I'll think about it, Edward. When all this is over, perhaps."

Disposition of Anne Neville! He would *think* about it! When he had time! I was mortified, furious, emotions storming through me, almost pushing me to my feet to stand before him and demand an explanation. Only Beatrice's restraining grasp on my cloak stopped me. Was this the man who had promised me his undying love? How dared he discuss me so dispassionately. At the same time I longed to go to him, to risk everything. To put myself into his keeping. But his cold words kept me behind the clusters of stone-carved foliage as they moved off down the nave. *You are now free to go to Gloucester,* a vengeful Margaret had accused in my dream. If I did, I had no guarantee that I would be welcome.

"Gloucester has a presence," Beatrice murmured.

He had indeed! Not one I appreciated! I felt her eyes searching my face.

"Yes, I suppose he has. He is Constable of England, after all."

"He thinks of you as a future wife."

"Do you think? It seemed to me that he was quite undecided as to the suitability of my person for a Prince of the Blood!"

We were silent as, at a distance, we followed the royal trio to the west door.

"Will he execute the Queen?" Beatrice asked, since it was clear that I would not rise further to her comment. "As he has the rest of the Lancastrian commanders?"

"The King or Gloucester?" I asked through clenched teeth.

"Both. Either."

"Who knows? All *I* know is that there's treachery at the heart of the damned Yorkists."

And I was not speaking of the King. Or of politics!

We rode out of Tewkesbury, tension thick between us. Beatrice would have buried me in questions, but my few short answers shut her up so that she paced behind me in a silence as surly as Sim's. I didn't care. There was little I did care for on that silent journey. At last we rode through the gates, into the stable yard.

It was chillingly quiet.

"Where's the Queen?" I demanded when our host came out to meet us before we could dismount. I knew why before I saw the relief in his face.

"Gone. Yorkist scouts have been seen in the area. I sent her to the priory at Little Malvern. . . ."

By the Virgin! A longer journey was the last thing I wanted. Turning my weary horse, I acknowledged that this was to be our destiny, passed from hand to hand, from one fearful house to another. Even though my belly clutched at the unpalatable thought, I knew that we must get the Queen to the coast and back to France. On the turn of a coin we had become outcasts, as untouchable as a leper with his bell in the marketplace.

Why had I not stepped forward from the chantry to beg pardon

for the role I had been forced to play? Why had I not cast myself on
Richard's mercy, drawing on all that had once passed between us?

Do you not love him?

Yes. An easy question and an easier answer.

So do you suspect that he does not love you?

Here was the crux of it. I no longer knew. All was a muddle in my
head. So cold, so calculating as he was in his reply to Edward, with no
urgency or desire to reclaim me, even when I was offered. Would he
take me just because of my wealth? If he could find no one better? He
had actually mocked my Neville blood. Yet he had loved me once. . . .

It is possible for love to die. He may no longer have feelings for you.

But why would it die?

Because you are a traitor, daughter of a traitor.

I could not argue against it. If I threw myself at Richard's feet,
and if he would not forgive, I would be shut up in the Tower before I
could blink.

Or married off to tie a man—any man—to York's crown.

Edward's own careless words came back to me. I was too valuable
to be allowed to fall into the wrong hands.

*If Richard wed you, would you ever know his motivation? Wealth
and power—your mother's inheritance—are always more important
than love.*

No! And then an even nastier little worm ate through the apple. . . .

*Would you wish to ally yourself to such a man? He has blood on
his hands. The knife that killed the Prince was in Richard's hand. How
can you excuse that?*

"Well!" Beatrice eyed me askance as I swore aloud. "You've been
poor company."

I hitched a shoulder. I knew it. And I was no nearer to the truth.

I was exhausted by the time Little Malvern Priory came into view, a
poor foundation, the retreat of a handful of aging monks hidden away
in deep woods in a quiet valley beneath a range of hills. It would offer

little in the way of material comfort, but it would at least provide refuge until we could plan our escape.

My timing could not have been worse.

Hardly had I arrived, to be brought into the cold austerity of the parlor set aside for travelers; hardly had I braced myself to answer for my absence to the Queen, and been relieved that she had taken herself to bed, than there was a thunderous hammering at the door. It was dark now and the monk was reluctant to open the door again. With a sharp premonition I accompanied him, to stand at his side.

"Who is it who asks for hospitality?" His old voice quavered.

"Sir William Stanley. Here on royal business."

My heart sank to the region of my sodden shoes. I knew that name. A man of dubious loyalties who had, for the time, thrown in his lot with the Yorkists. I shook my head when the monk glanced at me.

"It is late, sir. The brothers have retired."

"Open in the name of King Edward. Open the doors!"

"We can offer no hospitality, sir."

But I knew the door must be opened. Our luck had run out.

"I have reason to believe that the Angevin woman is here. Open the doors, brother, and you will come to no harm." Sir William would not be put off.

I motioned for the monk to swing the door wide. Someone had betrayed us. As there had been no sanctuary for the Prince in the abbey, so there was none for us. So there we were. Prisoners at the mercy of the King, to be escorted across the country at his will.

We would soon discover whether such mercy existed at his hands.

CHAPTER FOURTEEN

King Edward had us brought all the way from Tewkesbury to Coventry, to the royal accommodations where the King's council often met. What a desperate little party we were, I decided, seeing us through Yorkist eyes as we arrived—weary, travel stained, one barely speaking to the other. How the King could consider us a threat to his safety or the security of his crown I could not imagine. Despite that, the guard about us was strong. The Queen traveled in a litter, curtains closed against the world.

I rode in a black cloud of gloom, at odds with the spring weather, the prospect of an ax over my neck as I dredged through my memories to piece together what sort of man the King was. Fair in his dealings, Edward had no reputation for bloodletting. If he could pardon Clarence, he could not be all bad. But my mind switched scenes. He had executed the Lancastrian officers without compunction. He had not saved Warwick at Barnet. He had not saved the Prince from being cut down in cold blood by Richard, Edward's own brother.

So how would he deal with me?

I had no one to stand for me and plead my cause. I had no confi-

dence in Clarence, and the whereabouts of Isabel I did not know. As
for Richard . . . who knew what was in his head? I would have to plead
my own case.

I shivered in the slight breeze.

Would you wilt and weep before Edward of York?

I straightened my spine as I rode. I would be honest and forthright. What had I to lose? I would disguise my fear and pray that the
King was of a mind to be kind to a traitor and the widow of his most
bitter enemy.

I was escorted by guards into Edward's presence, where I came to an
abrupt halt just within the door of a surprisingly intimate little parlor.

Thank God! Richard was not there. Clarence, yes, legs crossed,
arm negligently thrown along the back of a low settle. No one would
know how my knees trembled behind my skirts as I curtsied. Edward
was lounging, legs extended, ankles crossed, but he immediately leaped
to his feet and came forward to take my hand, to draw me to a seat beside the fireplace. He did not look hostile. I tensed my muscles against
sheer fright at the extent of this man's power over me.

"Lady Anne. Or should I address you as Princess? You have been
greatly elevated since we last met." Edward sketched a mock bow.
I searched his face to see if there was malice in it. I could see none,
and when he sensed my resistance, he nudged me to sit in his own
great chair, looking down at me, his hands clasped around his belt, his
stance easy and relaxed. "I suppose I have to decide what to do with
you. What do you think, Lady Anne?"

So, malice or mischief, he would cast the problem into my lap. I
sat and concentrated furiously on my survival. King Edward held my
life in his hands.

"Well, what do you suggest?" he repeated, as if we were discussing the direction to take in a hunt. "You are branded Lancastrian.
Your father and husband both bore arms against me and are dead,
your mother has walled herself in so that she need not face my justice,

and thus *you* are the only Neville traitor to fall into my hands. You are my enemy, little Princess. Now how should I deal with you?"

There was a decided twinkle in his eyes. They were warm and reassuring, the deep brown of ripe chestnuts. But I was wary. He might well be playing with me, lulling me to see if I had any knowledge of use to him. To allow me enough rope to hang myself. Or perhaps he simply considered me still too young to challenge him, the younger Neville daughter to be treated with condescension. Knowing that I dared not drop my guard, I decided that attack was the best defense. If he punished me, then so be it.

"I cannot answer you, for I don't know your intent, sire. If I were a man, I would already be dead at your hands."

"True." His mouth twisted as if he might be contemplating the possibility. Then his expression smoothed again into a friendly smile, so that I understood how his enemies could say that he was not to be trusted. "So I suppose I should execute you."

"But I have no value as a Lancastrian," I replied sternly. "The Prince is dead. The Earl, my father, and my Neville uncle also. The Countess is in sanctuary. I have no one to come to my aid. What value have I?"

"As you say, lady. A masterful summary."

He strolled to the table where flagon and cups had been set, poured, pushed one in the direction of the silent and watchful Clarence. When he returned to press the second goblet into my hands I had to grasp it firmly, lest the wine splash on my gown. I held tight and waited.

"You are potentially a very wealthy young woman."

"I know, sire. But that fact does not *necessarily* make me a threat to you."

Edward chuckled. "I see. And I think that you would bargain with me, lady, for your life."

"I did not choose to wed Edward of Lancaster, sire."

He tilted his head, assessing, inscrutable in inner debate, like a fox deciding whether the chicken in its path was worth the effort of

stalking it. Discomfited at his knowing stare, I dropped my gaze to
the dark wine in the cup. Beside him, Clarence took my attention as
he stretched his arms in indolent self-satisfaction, yawning as if he felt
the whole episode tiresome in the extreme. I despised him more than
ever. I would not look at him. Had not his defection caused the Earl's
death? Yet I discovered the strength to push aside my hatred that simmered and threatened to burst into flame. I could not allow myself to
be distracted. Other concerns would wait, even my own future, but
Edward could at least ease my heart of one of its burdens, the heaviest
of them. I took another sip of wine against the dryness in my throat.

"I have one request, sire."

"Only one?" Edward's mobile brows rose. "Ask it, then."

"That you would tell me of the manner of my father's death."

It obviously surprised him. "I thought we had agreed that your
head could be forfeit, lady. *That* should be your one request, should it
not? To beg for mercy?"

"Perhaps it should, sire. But this is a wound that will not heal."
On an impulse, knowing Edward's turn for the dramatic, I placed the
cup on the floor and pushed myself from the chair to fall to my knees
at his feet. "I wish to know of the Earl, sire." I raised my eyes to his
and held them, pleading, compelling.

"What a determined young woman you are," he remarked, not
unkindly. "It will only bring pain."

"Not as great as the not knowing. Not as great a pain as the version that was given to me, which I cannot believe."

"Very well." He nodded briskly. "But come, you mustn't kneel as
a petitioner for something that demands nothing of me." He urged me
to my feet, placed me back in the chair, the cup in my hands. "What
do you want to know?"

It poured out, the terrible shame I had lived with—of the Earl's
flawed leadership, his cowardice, his betrayal of his men. That at the
last he tried to bargain for his life when flight became impossible.

"Your informant lied." Edward spoke gently. "Or deliberately
misled you. So you want the truth? I'll not lie to you, so brave a Prin-

cess as you are." He hooked the toe of his boot around the leg of a stool to pull it forward, to sit close before me. Removing the cup again, he closed his hands around mine, a warm comfort. Without emotion, he told the tale.

"Listen, then, lady. This is how it happened. I attacked early, when a man at twenty paces was only a glimmer in the dawn. It took them by surprise." He glossed quickly over his own skills, I noticed. "It was all over—after three hours of hard combat. I saw the Earl in the thick of it, fighting bravely. To the end the Earl remained at his command, dismounting to fight on foot with his household knights until there was no hope of victory. His conduct was exemplary."

I nodded, feeling his hands tighten around mine. "That was not the action of a coward." I said it quietly, almost to myself.

"No. It was not. His conduct brought honor to the Neville name."

I sighed a little. The Queen's informants had given her the truth as she would wish to see it, a truth that was twisted and despoiled out of all recognition.

"Did you have to kill him, sire?"

Edward shifted on his stool. "I gave orders to spare his life—but Yorkist troops got there first and hacked him down. So no, I did not save him, and if that is to my blame, then you must place it squarely on my shoulders."

The honesty in that handsome face was uncomfortably disarming. I could not speak. His fingers were gentle now on my wrist and I thought there was no little grief in the lines of his face. But I shook my head, willfully refusing to be comforted.

"Then did you have to display him naked? Humiliate him so?" I choked a little over the words as the image leaped to life in my mind of that final humiliation.

"Yes." Now the King's lips narrowed and I saw the implacable will to protect his power. I had asked for the truth and I got it in all its raw realism. "Yes—and I would do it again tomorrow without a second thought. It would be a fatal mistake to allow Warwick to be resurrected as a figurehead for malcontents. Did you not know? There were already claims being circulated that he yet lived—within an hour of his death. That he would return to raise the banner of Lancaster once more. Warwick, dead and a spent force, had to be seen. It was necessary and I'll not excuse what I did. All I would say is that his body was not desecrated. He was taken to Bisham with all honor for burial." I nodded, knowing the Augustinian abbey there to be the resting place of past Nevilles. "I could have dismembered him as a traitor. Many advised me to do it, but in death I would not treat him with disrespect."

I blinked so that I would not weep for my loss. I believed him. What use in harboring resentments? Those who played the card of traitor, as the Earl had, risked all on its turn.

"Does that satisfy you?" he asked.

And I nodded at last. I hesitated. "May I make one more request?"

"Another?" His amusement had resurfaced through the sharp regret. "Ask, then."

"It is about my mother that I would speak, sire. I miss her. If you would pardon her so that we can be reunited . . ." The hands around mine suddenly clenched. I glanced up through my lashes, instantly warned by the tightening in his jaw, his abrupt release of my hands. I did not think he was angry but his reply was short.

"I haven't decided and will make no promises. The Countess can stay at Beaulieu for now, as it is her choice, guarded there by my own men." He pushed back the stool, stood when I would have spoken, looking down at me so that I had to look up. "She is powerful and wealthy, unless I decide to strip her of her money and lands under attainder. But don't fear. I'll not execute her." His smile was thin lipped. "I don't make war on women. And now, little Princess, if all your requests are at an end, what shall I do with *you*?"

"I'll answer that."

The intervention startled me. And Edward. For the first time Clarence spoke, thrusting himself to sit up and lean forward, elbows on the table. I thought his eyes gleamed in some sharp anticipation.

"If I can make a suggestion, brother? Why not give Anne into my keeping? I'd like nothing better than for her to live in my household, in the care of her sister. The Duchess is settled at Warwick. No doubt Lady Anne will enjoy a return to her old home. Certainly she can stay with us until you've decided on a more permanent settlement. I know that Isabel has missed her sorely and would be pleased to have her company again."

I could feel my brain dissecting his words, as smooth and innocent as new cream, but as suspect as a deep, dark pool where the bottom was unfathomable, dangerous for the unwary traveler. His words seemed harmless enough, although I could not imagine Isabel welcoming me with open arms in light of our recent disaffection. Nor did Clarence's claim to brotherly delight ring true. *A more permanent settlement.* That meant my marriage. Since I was to be allowed to live, as an important heiress I could not be allowed to remain unwed for long. Edward would find someone whose loyalty it was necessary to cultivate with a marriage to a Neville heiress. It would all be out of my hands, just as it had been in the past. After the strains of the morning I felt the energy drain from me, leaving me strangely hollow and unresponsive. The arrangements for my future suddenly did not interest me: They could do as they wished.

Edward beamed. "A family solution. Very neat." He thought for a moment, then stooped to take my arm and raise me to my feet. "It is decided, little Princess. You will live at Warwick and will be free to come and go under your sister's jurisdiction. She will be responsible for your security and safety. Life will not be intolerable for you, sister."

Intolerable? I did not want to be at the mercy of Clarence and Isabel, but it was the best I could hope for. "My thanks, Your Majesty. I am grateful for your pardon and your generosity."

My voice was colorless, my curtsy impeccably formal. The audience was clearly over and I would have turned to leave, when the door opened. . . .

Not now. Not this.

I was too weary and emotionally drained to deal with him now.

I think he did not at first see me, preoccupied with the bundle of scrolls he was carrying, complete with royal seals. There he was,

when I would rather not have had to face him until I had ordered
my thoughts, considered my response. Richard, Duke of Gloucester.
Constable of England.

When he saw me he froze on the spot.

He has a presence.

Beatrice's observation leaped starkly to mind. I had seen the
changes from a distance, when peeking through the carvings at
Tewkesbury. Now I experienced the maturity that had only been
hinted at in the abbey. And I was not pleased. His stare was deliberate, questioning, first of the King and Clarence. Then, after one single
glance that slid from the crown of my head to my shoes, doubtless dis-
approving of my dire appearance, he performed a somewhat sketchy
bow in my direction.

"My lady. You have traveled safely."

His words, his face, were blandly impersonal. He had obviously
mastered the art of dissimulation to perfection. It slashed bright color
across my cheeks.

"Yes, my lord. As you say." I could respond in kind. If we were to
play at wooden indifference, as if we had never met beyond a cursory
acquaintance, then I would be amazingly chilly.

It was very strange, the whole exhausting episode that unfolded.
Richard barely looked at me, only once in that first moment when his
eyes touched on mine, and then they were dark and flat. His mouth
showed no curve in greeting. Rather his whole body stiffened as if
he withstood a blow from a mace. I expected something from him.
Surely I had that right, even after a twelvemonth of separation. Of all
the emotions I had withstood since the invasion, nothing hurt me as
much as Gloucester's cold rejection.

Gloucester might not look at me, but I looked at him right enough.

He was definitely *Gloucester.* Not *Richard.* As had the King's, his
plate armor had been shed. His brigandine, although protective with
its strips of metal, was of velvet, the nap luxurious, the color deep blue
and jewel bright. Over it his collar of office glowed, the dark rubies
catching the light, bloodred. To my mind, as my eyes were drawn to

them, they gave him a dangerous glamour. The Richard I had known would not even consider his appearance, but was this man Gloucester the same? I did not know. He wore his authority easily, yet there was a brittleness about him, a sharp confidence. I did not think that his authority as Constable would be lightly questioned despite his lack of years. Somewhere along the line the Duke of Gloucester had acquired the knack of power and had developed it, deliberately or by chance. In physical appearance he was much as I remembered, but with subtle differences. The dark sweep of hair, tousled and untidy from restless fingers, his face thinner, more austere, the face of a scholar rather than a soldier, yet I knew from common gossip that he had fought with distinction in battle. At Tewkesbury his initiative and cool leadership had won many men to him to sing his praises.

But he has blood on his hands.

I allowed my inspection of the Constable of England to move down to his hands, long fingered, capable, juggling with the rolls and their seals. They could hold a knife to appalling effect.

And just what does he see in me?

I wondered. *I* saw a man of power, of influence, of authority. Of arrogance, even in the proud tilt of his head. But what did he see in me? My heart sank at the obvious answer. I doubted that I had grown with the same alluring attraction as he had, and my feminine vanity shuddered inwardly at my present appearance despite all my efforts to brush and repair. Three weeks on the move, in weary flight, on horseback across rivers and in the muck of spring roads, had destroyed my clothing beyond all acceptance. Did he see an untidy, weary young woman, gown once fine but now irreparably stained? A careworn widow whose nerves had had quite enough for today? I would not blame him. I despaired at what he must see.

"A family reunion?" He turned to stand at the center of the three of us, strangely dominating the event. He dropped the scrolls onto the table.

"Yes, of sorts," Edward replied with an appreciative glance in my direction. "We've been discussing what to do with Lady Anne."

"And?" Gloucester's gaze remained limpid, his voice soft. "What's your decision?"

"Clarence had offered to take her in," Edward remarked. "To live at Warwick under his protection. It will be good for her to be with Isabel."

I saw it because I knew him. Because I was watching him. Gloucester's reaction was remarkable in its control, but I saw the muscles in his shoulders tense; I saw the little grooves beside his mouth deepen infinitesimally. His eyes were icily hostile as they fixed on Clarence. Yet still his tone remained polite, courteous, merely interested.

"A generous offer, Clarence."

"No . . ." Clarence's smile was fat with complacency. "Merely the perfect solution."

"Altruistic, some would say. Who did not know the truth of it."

"What bug's got under your skin, Dickon?" Edward asked, alert to trouble. "It would solve the immediate problem."

I simply looked from one to the other, my senses reawakened, fully engaged. Something lay between them that went beyond the surface.

Gloucester swung around to the King. "No. I don't agree. It's the worst decision."

"Why?" Clarence leaned back, lifting his cup of wine in a flamboyant toast.

"I know your game, Clarence. It must not be."

"I have no game, little brother." His words conveyed the faintest hint of malice.

"Yes, you do. And it's a vicious and self-interested game. She should not go to Warwick."

"But the King agrees that she should. . . ."

They faced each other like dogs fighting and snarling over a bone. I feared that I was the bone, yet did not understand why I should be. Silky smooth, Clarence was enjoying himself, and I knew that the last place I wanted to be was under his dominion in Warwick Castle. Nor did I want to be *here* to be snapped and snarled over. I could tolerate this battle of wills over my future no longer.

"If you will excuse me, Your Majesty," I interrupted without compunction. "I am indisposed." I curtsied again to Edward.

"Of course." Immediately he led me to the door. "You can be at ease now. It has been a long journey for you, lady, but you are safe and come home at last."

Edward laid a large hand lightly on my shoulder. I felt the warmth of it through my shabby sleeve and, unlike Gloucester's greeting, I knew the King did not refer to the miles of my coming home. Sensing the first true compassion since I had set foot in England, I felt tears threatening. As quickly as I could, without looking in Gloucester's direction, I left the room. I could not bear to stay to be squabbled over—and to what purpose? I had no answer to it. I did not like it. Nor to being an "immediate problem" to be solved.

What had happened to Gloucester—*Gloucester*, not *Richard*? It was as if he had acquired an outer shell. Not smooth, as an egg might be—Richard would never be smooth—but all-encompassing, seamless. No vulnerability, no weakness was allowed to show. After this meeting I doubted he had any weakness, and the vulnerability of his early years at Middleham had gone forever. At Tewkesbury I had found him cold, perhaps the result of a preoccupation with the aftermath of victory. Here, there was no excuse for his detachment.

Except . . . I had seen it as he entered the room. He might no longer have an affection for me, but he still wore the ring, the little gold circle with the ruby stone, on the smallest finger of his right hand. What should I make of that, if anything? Or the fact that he had turned it, again and again with his left hand, when Clarence had issued his challenge and demanded my presence at Warwick Castle?

We left promptly the next day. Edward would make haste to London with Gloucester, taking Margaret with him. Meanwhile Clarence would escort me to Warwick.

And then, amidst all the noise and bustle and tumult of horses and wagons, of armed men and traveling litters, much like a military operation, there was Gloucester himself, leading his horse over to where I awaited my own orders. I stood stony faced and braced myself to keep my thoughts locked tight within me.

"Lady." He inclined his head.

"Gloucester." I mimicked his terrible and deliberate formality.

"You will be comfortable at Warwick." Would I? Unimportant words, yet I sensed that his cool disinterest of yesterday was not as secure, but was rather a banked heat. I considered an equally bland reply—and instantly rejected it.

"Yesterday you did not wish me to go! As I recall, you condemned it!"

To my vexation, I got another bland response in return. "The King would have his way."

"Then of course I must do as the King wishes." I looked away.

"Anne. Some advice . . ."

I turned my head slowly. "Advice? I've had a bellyful of advice of late."

"About your position in Clarence's household . . ."

"What advice can you give me? What do you care?" My resentment flashed into life. "You hardly greeted me yesterday, hardly had a word to say to me. Had I had a safe and comfortable journey? No, I had not! Is that all you could say after twelve months or more? You looked at me as if I were a useful counter in a particularly nasty board game. Why should I now listen to your advice?" I was not proud of my venom but it eased the pain a little to hurt him as he had hurt me. And I saw the result immediately. It was as if I had slapped him, his face white and stark, but I was not sorry. He had *hurt* me. "It's perfectly clear to me that any connection between us is at an end. Unless of course you have your mind solely on my inheritance." Remembering Tewkesbury, I drove the point home.

If anything, his face paled even further, bone white.

"Anne . . . I know what it looked like. But I dare not . . ."

"Dare not what? It seems to me that you dare put your hand to anything, if what they say is true."

"What?" His brows snapped together.

"Did you not cut down my husband, unarmed and helpless and a prisoner, in cold blood?" I faced him, the curl of a sneer on my mouth, daring him to deny it. Praying that he would.

To my horror he did not. The bloom of anger surged into his face again like battle flags. Before I could step back, before I could read his intent, his hand gripped my wrist fiercely to hold me still. "There's no time for this now. Too many ears, too many interests involved." His voice was little above a murmur but the urgency had returned in good measure. "All I can say is don't let them—" He rapidly cut off his words, dropped my wrist.

"Don't let them *what*? Don't let *who*?"

Clarence loomed at my shoulder. "We are ready, Lady Anne." He acknowledged Gloucester—stiffly, I thought. "I'll see you in London, Gloucester. Within the week."

"Don't waste time," Gloucester advised briefly. "We shall need you if the revolt in Kent is as widespread as rumors say."

There it was again. Some antagonism that had nothing to do with common rivalry between brothers. I looked from one to the other but could see only the shimmer of tension, like two full-grown stags on first sighting. Wary, watchful, but neither willing to take the first step toward outright aggression.

Then it was broken. Clarence mounted and Gloucester took my hand to help me into the litter.

"Thank you, my lord."

"Once, in an earlier life, you called me Richard," he murmured as he tucked a cushion under my arm. The quick brush of warmth almost destroyed me.

Almost. I snatched my hand away. "Once, I thought you loved me."

Which put an effective end to any further conversation.

I had expressed a preference to ride but I was given no choice, Clarence deeming it safer to escort an anonymous lady behind closed curtains rather than the Lancastrian widow for all to see. At least there was one advantage as I crossly pulled the drapes against the passing scenery: complete privacy. As soon as we were on the road I opened my clenched fist to reveal the screw of parchment that Richard had pressed into my palm. I smoothed it.

You are of age and cannot be forced into any act against your will. Don't let them persuade you to enter a convent.

No superscription. No signature. No evidence of who or why, in case it was found by an unfriendly observer. I frowned at the two lines. Why would Isabel—why would anyone—try to persuade me to enter a convent? The curtains were twitched back.

"Are you comfortable?" Smiling, Clarence bent from his horse.

"Certainly."

"We shall soon be at Warwick. You will be welcomed there, back with your family." His handsome face was all concern for my well-being, all anticipation of my homecoming.

What was he planning? There was *something* but it remained undefined, shadowy yet undeniably present, like the rich pattern on a damask partially obscured beneath a layer of gauze. Accepting the futility of trying to read Clarence's devious mind, I gave myself over to some hours of inactivity as I clenched my fist over the evidence. Once, I had treasured such a note for the closeness it brought me to its author. Now I was not so sure. As for its content, I needed no convincing and took a solemn vow on it. I would never enter a convent. On that I needed no advice or instructions from anyone. No one would persuade me to it. No one was ever likely to suggest it.

Why should they?

The towers of Warwick Castle, rising solidly above the protective stand of trees, glowed warm and welcoming in the evening light. For the first time on the journey I pulled back the curtain so that I might see the familiar walls, the sweep of the Avon, the wash of early summer foliage. Memories flooded back, happy ones. My childhood here, although the weeks were few in comparison with those at Middleham, had been in high summer, when the river ran low and the gardens were sultry in the still air. The swans with their fluffy offspring had dabbled in the shallows and my prospects had been entirely safe and predictable. How inviting to live here again, in familiarity, with old servants and comfortable affections. No spies, no lurking suspicion, no fear of imminent capture or death. No tensions or bitter jealousies, no deliberate ploys to hurt with sharp words. I could perhaps be happy here again.

Except for the one garish unknown, the random shape in the pretty mosaic I had created from memory and hope. Isabel. How would she receive me? Nor did I know how I would react to having her stand in authority over me. I felt the little flutter of fear as the litter lurched to a halt, curtains quickly looped back. Servants came forward, faces I recognized, with smiles for the Neville daughter. I was helped from the cushions, feeling like a child again, cosseted and welcomed.

"Anne! At last." The clear voice reached me across the courtyard. "We have been waiting an age." There Isabel stood, on the steps. I wondered fleetingly if she would wait for me to go to her, in the manner of petitioner and petitioned, but she did not. As she ran down the stairs, her face was alight with what could only be joy. "Thank God! You are safe."

I might have hesitated but the pull of reunion with its compassionate words was suddenly strong and I fell into her embrace. We hugged, arms tight, and all was well again, as if we had never been parted, never exchanged bitter words. She was my sister and she would care for me. In the depths of my misery I did not question the warmth of her greeting.

No doubt I was too ingenuous in my acceptance.

"Isabel. I am so glad to be home." I battled back the tears that pricked my eyelids, and the sudden guilt that I had ever doubted her. The past was gone. I was a widow in disgrace with no claim on anyone's throne to stir her resentments. There was nothing to spoil our affection now.

We stood for a moment, hands clasped. My sister looked well, the strains of the weeks in France smoothly erased. Life at Warwick with Clarence suited her, had restored her fair beauty and a more amenable nature. Perhaps there was the prospect of another babe to heal her grief. And there, on the staircase, Margery waited, beaming widely her affection for me, as she had done all my life. Once again I was swept up in warm arms, crushed to her comfortable bosom. If I felt tearful before, I could have wept for the delight of it, no longer alone and beleaguered. I laughed shakily at my emotional reaction, inelegantly wiping the tears away with my hands.

"Come. Come in; all is prepared for you," Isabel invited. "Your old rooms in the east wing are just as you will remember them. You'll live here with me for as long as you wish."

Or as long as Edward decrees.

There was the fly, dropped into the cup of ale to stir up endless circles. I was not free to dictate my own life. Deliberately I shook my head to dislodge the unpleasant thought. Tomorrow was soon enough for that.

"Are you hungry? Thirsty?"

I shook my head.

"You should be," Margery announced, fixing me with a gimlet stare. It was as if I were back in the nursery. "You're too pale. That disgraceful gown—just look at it." She raised her hands in horror. "It hangs on you. You're no better than a willow wand. We need to feed you up."

I laughed. "I expect you will. I would not push aside the cook's chicken pasties, if a little dish of them happened to appear at my elbow."

Margery's eyes twinkled. "Always your favorites! I'll see to it." She bustled off, giving Isabel and myself some space, as perhaps I had intended.

"Do you wish to sit for a little?" Isabel asked, solicitous of me as if I were a guest.

"I'd rather stand and walk for a while," I replied dryly. "I would not recommend traveling by litter to anyone. But Clarence insisted."

"He would think it best to preserve your privacy."

"And anonymity?"

"Yes. Of course. Until everything is settled. Your unfortunate Lancastrian connections will soon be smoothed over."

As were yours and Clarence's? Was it easy to smooth them away? Was the Earl's death part of the payment? It would be more than churlish to ask, so I did not. Life with Margaret had at least taught me to guard my tongue and not blurt out the first thought that came into my head. Meanwhile Isabel waved aside all difficulties as if they were a cloud of summer midges. "Come, then, and walk in the garden by the river. It will be warm there still."

So we did, arm in arm, while I continued to be taken aback. I had not expected this generosity. Isabel babbled on with comments and enthusiasms on her plans for her future and mine.

"You'll stay with me until the King decides." She confirmed my earlier thought but seemed to find no difficulty with it. "I expect he'll want to have you married again soon. You'll have to become resigned to being used to catch and hold a wayward supporter for Edward." She must have seen my grimace. "It needn't be so bad. Let's pray he chooses someone young and at least attractive. Until then we shall enjoy each other's company. We shall be settled in London for Christmas and Twelfth Night. . . ."

I let her ramble on, commenting and nodding as demanded, wondering all the time when she would touch on more personal subjects. They stood between us, insubstantial as ghosts, yet potent and tangible. They could not be blotted out forever, nor were they, but it was not until we sat in a walled corner where honeysuckle was coming into bloom, where some residual warmth lingered to tease the perfume from the lilies that grew in profusion, that anything was said. The sun had gone but the air was heavy, enticing the first bats to dart and swoop after invisible prey, when Isabel made her first allusion to the recent past.

"Anne . . . I'm sorry about the Prince. Whatever our differences, I would not have had it end like that."

"No." Now that she had opened the forbidden casket of pain and loss, I discovered that I did not know what to say to her. That I despised him and feared him in equal measure, that I was grateful beyond words to be freed from that unhappy household? I could not help thinking that Isabel was far more accommodating of my presence now that I was no longer a Princess, no longer a rival to her own bright visions of the future. With Edward's son still an infant in arms, Clarence's power in the realm would be prime. And so Isabel could afford to be generous with her consolations. Then I took myself to task for my ill will. Cynicism was not an attractive trait and I would not cultivate it.

"I can't talk about it yet," I managed gruffly. "The last weeks have been a time I wish to forget."

"Then we shall." In friendly agreement, she stood. "Let's go back in. It grows chill."

So she still would not touch on the matter close to my heart. Well, if she would not, I would. I remained seated as Isabel stood, looking up at her, marveling at her ability to close her mind to anything that threatened to stir her complacency. I might have accused her of being superficial—except that I thought she was not. My suspicion returned that her deliberate silence, her unnerving cheerfulness, were all part of a carefully constructed ploy to achieve some ends not yet disclosed to me.

"I have to talk about the Earl and Countess."

"As you wish." Unwillingly, she sank back to my side, her expression carefully guarded. "What is there to say?"

"I am told that our father is buried at Bisham."

"Yes."

No more, no less. There was a tightening of the muscles in Isabel's cheek. She did not want to talk about it; that much was plain. "Have you been there?"

"No. Not yet."

Not ever, I suspected. "Why not?"

"He died a traitor."

"He died bravely in battle!"

Isabel hitched a shoulder.

Clarence's defection was to blame for his death! My mind might spell it out but I could not say it, not unless I wished to destroy our newly patched relationship with one blow. I let it drop, picked up another thread. "The Countess is still at Beaulieu."

"I know." I sensed a trace of impatience.

"Why does Clarence not allow her to come here? Surely there would be no difficulty?"

Isabel hesitated. Out of the corner of my eye I saw her folded hands curl into the embroidered overhang of her sleeve. "Clarence thinks it is better that she stay where she is. She's safe and not in any discomfort out of the public eye."

"Do you expect her to stay in the abbey for the rest of her life because it hides her from public view? Why should she not live here, in seclusion if necessary? Is it Edward who resists? Can Clarence not persuade the King?" I could not work through the layers. Why should it matter where she lived? The Countess was hardly preparing to lead an army against Edward. "Why does she need to remain in sanctuary at Beaulieu, Isabel? Edward is hardly likely to execute her, is he?"

Isabel shrugged again, relenting only under my persistence. "No, he won't. And I think Clarence will try to bring her here, once the country is at peace again. It is just thought to be better that she remain there for now. As Warwick's widow she might stir passions again if she returned to Court."

"But we are Warwick's daughters!" There was no logic here.

"Anne . . ."

"What, Isabel?"

She sighed. "It is, after all, the Countess's choice to remain at Beaulieu."

"Have you heard from her?"

"A letter to me—to intercede for her. To persuade Edward not to confiscate the Beauchamp inheritance from her."

The inheritance. So was the inheritance the problem? I could not imagine why it should be. "But why should he? The Countess is not legally responsible for her husband's treachery. Why should her own personal inheritance be threatened?" I frowned.

"I don't know."

"The Beauchamp-Despenser inheritance should eventually come to us, as it was always intended, as joint heiresses. Is that not so?"

"Yes . . . no! I don't know!"

I watched my sister react to my questioning. Uncomfortable, on her guard against me, she veiled her eyes with her fair lashes. "Is there some difficulty, Isabel? Is Edward planning to disinherit the Countess?"

"It has been talked of," she replied carefully, eyes on tight-clasped fingers. "Edward has his own plans to which I am not privy." Then, apparently with effort, she looked up at me, a plea in every line of her face. "There is no problem, Anne. Clarence will always guard our best interests; you must believe that. Let us not talk politics. It will only ruin and divide us. I beg of you." Then with the return of a sharp edge I knew well, she added, "Why do you always have to be so suspicious and spoil things? There *is* no problem!"

I tried to read between the words she refused to speak. There was something here. Or then . . . perhaps I was mistaken and there was nothing. Perhaps just the aftermath of rebellion and division. I let it go—for now.

"Forgive me, Isabel. It comes of living with Queen Margaret for so long, where it was wise not to trust anyone. I think I've caught the habit. We'll talk of pleasanter things. . . ."

We stood, Isabel taking instant refuge in smiles and good humor. "Far more pleasant! We need to discuss your appearance." Arm around my waist, she tugged on my sleeve. "That garment, for one, can be consigned to the midden. You look like a camp follower! Do you have anything suitable to wear that does not carry the mud of every road in the west of England?"

I cast my mind over my meager possessions. How ridiculous to think that I, who had been a Princess, could now pack everything I owned into one small traveling coffer. "No. And far worse than mud! You don't want to know! Your kitchen servants are dressed better than I." I could not tell her of the torturous journeys, hour after hour on horseback, to evade Edward. The flight from battle. The horror of Tewkesbury in the aftermath, scenes that still haunted my dreams. I could not speak of any of that. Perhaps in time I would.

Oblivious, satisfied that the difficult subjects had been temporarily buried, Isabel steered me back along the paths toward the living quarters. "Then you must borrow some of mine until we can remedy your lack. If you are to appeal to a new husband . . ." There was the mention of marriage again. My attention was caught, held, considered, until Isabel dragged my thoughts back. ". . . and here is Margery, doubtless to summon you to a feast. Consider yourself a goose being fattened for Twelfth Night." My sister pinched my waist, an affectionate gesture. "She'll not be satisfied before you are plump and comely, and the seams on your new dresses strain!"

She hugged me close, laughed, so that I felt warm and enclosed in family love again. She was my sister and perhaps we could be happy together. As long as we did not touch on sensitive subjects.

CHAPTER FIFTEEN

My days at Warwick as Isabel's guest settled into the easy routine of summer. For me it was a confused, insubstantial time, a sort of healing, I suppose, when I confess I deliberately turned my mind from both past and future, from everything outside the safe walls of the castle. The fear and anguish of battle, of flight and death, receded into a vague existence that seemed to have nothing to do with me. The Prince was part of a different life, from which I distanced myself. I *would* not think of it. Nor would I allow myself to consider the next unknown chapter in my life. I would remain here in my family home. I would stroll and ride, read, stitch, and enjoy the balm of music. I would not admit to desperate boredom or the times when my thoughts escaped my will and strained toward London and what the Plantagenet brothers might be doing there. I convinced myself I no longer had an interest in politics and power; the government of the country would continue quite well without me. Nor was I moved by the death of old King Henry in the Tower, struck down by a fatal melancholy, so the official account proclaimed, on being told of his son's death. The unofficial rumors were far more interesting. *Assassination*, whispered some. *Richard of*

Gloucester, murmured those who claimed to be informed. The news was quick to reach us at Warwick.

Did Richard have a hand in it? Quite possibly, I thought, recalling his fearsome authority at Tewkesbury. Most likely, I acknowledged, since I no longer knew of what he was capable. I considered it, but briefly and dispassionately, then buried the whole matter, refusing to allow so monstrous an idea to worm its way through my deliberate distancing. I closed my emotions off from everything that might touch my heart.

Isabel mentioned my remarriage at regular intervals. I saw her plan. If she planted the seeds and nurtured them, I would grow accustomed to the idea. I was biddable and amazingly amenable to her gossipy suggestions. Even Margery raised her brows at my unnatural compliance, as if waiting for me to break out into habitual sharpness of tongue and observation. I did not. I was not sufficiently interested. Richard was never mentioned in Isabel's parade of suitable husbands. I did not even bother to consider why not, but remained sunk in lethargy, willfully rejecting all that might distress me or resurrect my pain. Until a conversation jolted me out of my introspection.

It developed as a result of one of Clarence's flying visits between the north and London, a matter of hours and mostly spent in private words between himself and Isabel. I thought nothing of it and kept to my room. It was not my concern.

"Well? What did he have to say?" I walked in on Isabel as he departed, without any real interest in the answer. Until I realized that she was doing her clumsy best to hide the tears that blotched her cheeks. "Isabel . . . what's wrong?" Immediately I was beside her, my arm around her shoulders as she scrubbed furiously with her palms.

"Nothing."

"Are you ill?"

"No."

"Was it something Clarence said?"

"No, no . . . Nothing like that." Her smile was heartbreaking, her pale skin blotched and red. "His news was good—we should join him in London soon. . . ."

I would not accept that. "Something has made you sad. . . ."

"It's nothing! Have I not said?" Suddenly our delicate friendship that had developed over the weeks fell away as she extricated herself from my embrace. "Just a matter between husband and wife."

"Forgive me. I did not mean to pry." Seeing the set of her lips I retreated.

Meanwhile Isabel picked up her stitching and a little silence descended on the sun-filled room. Respecting her mood, I turned the pages of a book of poetry but found the insipid theme of romance did not hold my attention. Nor did I think that her mind was on the choice of color for the overstitched leaves that would entwine artistically along the length of the embroidered belt. The comparative merit of red or gold was not a reason for the tight indentation at the corner of her lips.

"Anne . . ." Confirming this, she looked up from her stitches, with the impression that she had come to a decision. "Have you perhaps thought of marriage again . . . ?"

Not another attempt to entice me into wedlock. I did not try to hide a sigh. "No. I don't think of it. And certainly not without a husband in the near prospect."

"Do you wish to marry again?"

"Not today, for sure!" I tried for a little humor to dispel the unaccountable edginess in my sister. "Besides, will not Edward settle it? No point in worrying over it until he has."

"I just wondered if it was distasteful to you. . . ."

"Well, I am now of an age. And as a widow I can give my own consent or refusal if I find the man unpalatable. Don't worry." I smiled. "I'll not be pushed into some desperate misalliance. Unless he is young, handsome, and extremely wealthy, I shall say no."

"Yes, of course you will." Momentarily anxious, Isabel pasted an encouraging smile back in place. "It's just . . . well, there is another alternative. If you decide that marriage is not to your taste . . ."

"Hmm?" I was no longer really listening. I turned a page. Another paean to the delights of love for me to yawn over, until Isabel reached out to close her hand over mine. I looked up.

"I am considering establishing a convent. As our ancestors did with their patronage at Tewkesbury. I am of a mind to do the same."

"Oh?"

"If you rejected remarriage—*you* could enter the convent."

"What? A nun?" My brain was now engaged, book discarded.

"You could take the veil. It would keep you out of the affairs of men, if you did not choose to have a political marriage arranged for you by the King, and it would allow you considerable autonomy, with the prospect of becoming the prioress eventually. You might enjoy it."

"*Enjoy* it? I doubt it very much!"

Don't let them persuade you to go into a convent.

The written words leaped suddenly, strongly into my mind.

"Don't be hasty. Take a little time to think about it." The sweetness of Isabel's smile was an essay in persuasion.

My docility lessened by degrees. "I don't need time. I think I don't care for it. I think you must be out of your mind to suggest it."

"Consider your authority as the lady prioress, backed by Neville money and consequence."

"Consider me as a nun, Isabel! Have you lost your wits? Me taking an oath of obedience!" Knowing me as she had all her life, I could not believe that she would make such a suggestion. I had a sudden vision of myself in dark robes and wimple, my freedom curtailed, my life one of penance and prayer, with a need to guard my tongue and conform to the rules of the order. I stared at her, aghast.

"Would it be so very bad?"

"Yes!"

"What's this? The Lady Anne to take the veil?" Margery, entering the room with a pile of clean shifts over her arm, lost no time in giving her own opinion. "An unlikely prospect."

"Isabel thinks I would make an acceptable lady prioress," I remarked, brows raised in her direction. And that little beat of fear in my throat.

Don't let them persuade you. . . .

"Does she, now. I can't think of anyone less suitable." Margery clicked her tongue against her teeth and scowled at my sister. "A good husband is what she wants."

It seemed to me that it was on the tip of Isabel's tongue to snap a short, rude reply to Margery, but she quickly covered it with another empty smile, hands raised in surrender. "Perhaps you are right. There's no urgency or compulsion. I simply thought I would like a convent of my own founding, and for it to come under the guidance of my sister. Our own foundation, as the Despensers did at Tewkesbury. It seems a good idea."

"No. It doesn't." I left her in no doubt.

"Then it shall not be."

As she applied her needle once more, as if we had not had the conversation, I felt a need to stand, to escape the little room. "It's a fine day—too fine to remain indoors, and the poetry does not take my mind. I will ride out—through the water meadows."

Isabel immediately put aside her embroidery. "I'll go with you."

"There's no need." I spoke more sharply than I had intended.

"I shall enjoy it as much as you."

I was already marching toward the door. "If you wish."

As we set out on a pair of lively horses, with servants to escort us and a pair of armed guards at our backs, it came to me in one of those strange moments of recognition. How could I have been so blind? One way or another, since the morning I had stood before King Edward at Coventry, I was never allowed to be alone.

Edward's court was in a celebratory mood.

It had a purpose, of course—Edward was never without purpose: to impress the King's subjects as much as the interested foreign visitors with the sun of York's ascendancy. Openhanded to an astonishing degree, Edward had put on a show of sumptuous magnificence, heavy with gold plate, exuberant with masques, banquets, and dancing. By his side, her lovely face unlined in spite of her ordeals of past months, Queen Elizabeth presided over all with preening self-satisfaction.

"Her smugness irritates me beyond measure," Isabel whispered in my ear.

"I suppose she has cause." I had become more tolerant of late.

"Because she has carried a son at last?"

In the face of Isabel's ever-simmering resentment I kept silent. There was no sign of her falling for another child, since the death of the infant off Calais. Any grief she still suffered was tightly controlled and she would not confide in me, but it was no surprise to me that she despised the fertile Queen, with her three daughters and now a healthy son.

The little Prince and heir, the infant Edward, made his first formal appearance in a carved oak cradle hung with gold tassels and crimson satin, from which the Queen lifted him in her arms to show him off, so that the same long-limbed, golden beauty as his father could be noted and admired.

"He's beautiful, a worthy heir," I murmured tactlessly.

"Do you think so?"

Here was another source of her bitterness—that this babe had ousted Clarence from his position as heir to his brother. "Clarence will never wear the crown, Isabel. You must accept it." Was I unfeeling? I was honest. Others might have watched their words.

"There's no need to sound so thoroughly *satisfied*!"

My sympathies dissipated further. "I'm not. Why should it matter to me how many sons the King might have? Or to you? Clarence is powerful in his own right. What more do you want, Isabel? He now has half our father's Neville land. Isn't that enough for you and for him?" I found it difficult to believe that my sister would be so grasping. After the Earl's death the King had divided the Neville lands between Clarence and Gloucester, and Clarence as the elder had seized the major portion.

Regardless of our surroundings, Isabel turned a furious look on me. "Clarence deserves more! He deserves to . . ." Then quickly she drew a breath on what he might deserve. "It doesn't matter. Now is not the time to talk of it."

There would never be a good time, in my opinion. A bright flush stained Isabel's skin from the neckline of her gown to the roots of her hair, and I was relieved to let it go, turning back to the happy scene before me where the Queen beamed her delight. The baby fussed and waved his tiny fists whilst Edward chuckled and smoothed his large hand over the child's wispy hair before signaling to the musicians to strike up for a round dance. With such energy behind it, the festivity was quite as lively and exciting as I recalled from past days. I might have viewed it all through jaundiced eyes, but it was difficult when the King was in the mood for high-spirited dancing and foolish games.

I admit to enjoying myself.

Except that the Duke of Gloucester was at court, and was keeping his distance. It was as if we existed in separate circles. They might brush together or fleetingly overlap, but nothing invited intimacy. We did not exchange more than two dozen words and the customary cool acknowledgment when it was necessary for good manners. He would bow over my hand, as precise and graceful as ever. And as responsive to my presence as an oak plank. For my part I would curtsy with a profound elegance that even Margaret of Anjou would fail to find fault with. I had learned some lessons to perfection at her court.

"Welcome to court, Lady Anne. I see you are restored to good health."

"I am." Good health indeed! No longer looking thin and worn as I had when last he set eyes on me? Was that a deliberate slight on my appearance? Vanity caused me to clench my teeth. And if he was not prepared to make any further effort, then I was certainly not going to demand his attention. Not that I wanted it, I reminded myself when my heart sank and my mood became less than festive. If he had cast me adrift, it was his choice and I wished him well of his future bride, whoever she might be. If it was necessary to discipline myself against allowing my gaze to slide across the room to where he was invariably the center of attraction, it was, of course, to be expected. He was much in demand. Royal brother, royal counselor, Constable of England. Unmarried and personable. What unmarried woman in the room did not have an eye to him? I didn't! By the Virgin, I wouldn't! I would not give him a moment's thought!

I broke my vow on only one occasion and that was at the King's playfully malicious intervention. I saw the mischief in his face as he ordered the minstrels to strike up for a ceremonial progression and tugged on the Queen's hand to lead her into the formal steps. By chance I had been standing with her, engaged in some stilted conversation, but on her husband's invitation, the Queen willingly agreed to dance.

"I might regret this," she murmured to me, acknowledging Edward's enthusiastic style, her delicately arched brows raised in self-mockery, but she allowed herself to be persuaded. Edward's smile flashed into a grin as he saw the opportunity.

"Gloucester!" He hailed his brother. "Here's Her Highness the Princess, without either a husband or a partner to keep her company. Come to her rescue. Dance with her."

The nerves in my belly beat like the wings of trapped butterflies. I would not dance with him. I would make some excuse. . . .

"No need, brother. I was about to offer myself as Lady Anne's partner." Clarence amazingly appeared at my elbow, all smiles. To my astonishment, he took possession of my hand as if it were his right, as if it were decided without any response from me.

"Dance with your own wife, Clarence," the King intervened. "Gloucester can do the honors here. He dances better than you."

The compliment to Richard's abilities to tread the measures I did not believe for one moment. Nor did Edward, judging from the glint in his eye. I stood, as mute as a statue. What was happening here?

"If you wish it, sire." Clarence bowed, but his grasp on my fingers tightened.

A little silence followed, the outcome still up for debate, until

Gloucester smoothly filled it. "It will be an honor for me to dance with Lady Anne."

I narrowed my eyes at him. Was this irony? But he promptly held out his hand, indicating that I should transfer mine from Clarence's to his, all the time his eyes pinning Clarence, daring him to refuse. Fascinated, Edward stayed to watch the storm of ripples that he had created by throwing this particular stone into the pond. Which left Clarence with no choice but to back off. But there it was again. The strange triangle, Richard, Clarence, and myself, the vibrations between us strong enough to taint the air. Why had Edward pushed the issue; why had he involved himself at all? What did it matter to him if I partnered Clarence or Gloucester? The devil leered in the grin he cast in my direction as he obeyed his wife's promptings and joined the dancers.

"My lady." Gloucester led me into the gathering of couples who were already joining hands in the round dance. "Since everyone is so keen on it, let us dance. We must make sure to give every appearance of pleasure to those who have an interest in it. Or then again"—his smile became wry—"perhaps it would be better if we didn't."

A strange thing to say. And almost as if speaking his thoughts to himself. I looked up at his stern face. "I'm sorry you were forced into something you did not wish to do."

He looked down, clearly brought back to the immediate. "Forgive me. That was unpardonable. I was merely thinking aloud. A bad habit and a rude one, as I am sure you would tell me. And I am not reluctant. I enjoy dancing."

And what should I make of that? Dancing, yes. But not the company. But there had also been the touch of humor, of past intimacy. By the Virgin! It was like floundering in a choppy sea without map or compass.

It was never easy for even the friendliest of partners to exchange words in a round dance, but we didn't even try. That did not mean that I was not aware of every soft brush of his body against mine, of the cool pressure from his fingers on mine as we stepped and turned.

No words were exchanged, except once, when we came close in the dance and the progression was almost at an end. Gloucester leaned, almost unobserved, so that he could whisper in my ear.

"I see, from your magnificence tonight, that you have not taken the veil."

I stepped away, then back, and arched my brows at the sharp appreciation in his glance as he took in the glory of my red brocade, the rubies set in gold, the hennin with its gold-edged drifting gauze. "No, I have not."

The dance moved us apart.

"Thank God!" he added as we came together again.

And that was it. When he kissed my hand at the end, his lips were cool, yet they burned. Surely Richard would feel my blood hammering through to my fingertips in response.

"There, my lady, we have pleased everyone except brother Clarence."

He had that right enough. Clarence positively glowered.

"Thank you, Your Grace," I replied with all maidenly modesty, when it was in my mind to demand, *Why? What is between you? What is my role in it?*

"It was entirely my pleasure."

He bowed as he prepared to leave me. I thought it had not been a pleasure for him, despite his words. There were dangerous undercurrents encompassing the Plantagenet brothers that also threatened to drag me under.

At the last vanity prompted me. Not that I cared, of course, but I would know how he saw me after so long apart, even though I might not enjoy the answer. Would he still see me as the immature girl he had kissed in the chapel at Warwick? Or as a fashionable woman in a steeple hennin?

"Richard . . ."

He turned his head.

"When you saw me for the first time—at Coventry. What did you think?"

"I thought . . ." The line was dug deep between his brows. "I thought, 'Here is a lovely woman, grown into her beauty. A woman who is strong and courageous.'" I must have looked taken aback, as I was. "You seem surprised, but you are beautiful. You are a woman any man of sense would—" Delivered in a brusque tone, the words were quickly cut off at Isabel's approach. Richard turned on his heel.

All of which cast me even deeper into a quagmire of uncertainty. There was one certainty. Without doubt, Richard's elegance in dancing had improved beyond recognition. I did not care to speculate on the fair partner—probably in Burgundy—with whom he had practiced.

Once the idea had become lodged in my mind at Warwick, it would not go away. It was impressed on me at every turn that I was being softly but thoroughly guarded. It was almost as bad as my days at Margaret's court, but with more subtlety. I went nowhere unless with Isabel or Clarence, or with a substantial escort of soldiers and servants from Clarence's household. Whether it be an audience or a feast, Isabel was invariably at my shoulder. If the hedonistic pleasures of shopping enticed us, an armed guard accompanied us, far removed from the usual pair of servants to carry any cumbersome parcels. An uncomfortable sensation of being free and an honored guest, yet at the same time a discreetly guarded prisoner, grew stronger until it squawked loudly in my consciousness.

My strange lethargy, in which I tolerated every situation, finally snapped into burning resentment when, rising early one morning, I found one of Clarence's servants stationed in the corridor outside my room. He followed me to the chapel. And then back to my room. Discreetly, I must admit, but still I felt this presence, his eyes on my every move. After weeks of slumbering, my temper rose.

"I'll not have it!"

"Thought it wouldn't last long," Margery observed as I drew her aside later in the day.

"What wouldn't?" I eyed her suspiciously.

"Not a thing, my lady." Her smile was a positive smirk. "But it's about time!"

"What is?"

"That you showed your teeth, lady!"

I did. In a tight snarl. "Put on a cloak, Margery, and come with me."

"Where are we going, lady?"

"I think, if my judgment is correct, that we shall not be going anywhere!" I would test it for myself. With only Margery in attendance, when I had made the excuse of resting in my room, I took myself, unobtrusively, to the stables, where I sought out Clarence's chief groom.

"Two horses, if you please, Master Whittaker."

"Ah . . ." He left off grooming Isabel's favorite mare, and his narrowed scrutiny slid from me to Margery, then back. "Will you be going far, mistress?"

"To Westminster."

"His Grace of Clarence has left no such instructions, my lady."

"His Grace of Clarence does not know. I am not answerable to His Grace of Clarence for my movements," I snapped with an impressive show of authority. I knew he would find it difficult to refuse me. Yet he did.

"Forgive me, lady. It's not possible. His Grace says there's a disturbance in the city. No one must go out without an escort. I don't have enough men to send with you. I dare not let you go."

"Not even for the Queen's audience?"

"No, my lady. I dare not." A weak excuse, his unease evident when the groom would not meet my eye, but I did not push it. It had proved my point.

"What do you know of this, Margery?" I asked as we retraced our steps.

"Nothing, lady. Except that you are to be kept close." Margery sniffed. "I'm not in Her Grace's confidence."

"So Isabel knows. Of course she does." I considered as we mounted the stairs. "Do they mean me harm?"

"I don't know, my lady. I don't see that they can."

Neither did I. But it did nothing to dissipate my mounting suspicions.

My docile acceptance finally came to an end on the occasion of a banquet at Westminster from which Isabel had for once cried off. The musicians had barely packed away their instruments when Clarence informed me peremptorily to make ready, as he was busy but would escort me home to Cold Harbour, his town house. No, we could not stay longer; he had other demands on his time.

That's it, I decided. Enough was enough. I would not be ordered about like some lowborn retainer, at the convenience of others. As soon as I got back to Cold Harbour, I would ask my sister outright and refuse to be put off. Did they suspect me of being part of some nefarious scheme to overthrow the King? Unlikely, but whatever it was, something was amiss.

We saddled up in the courtyard. Clarence helped me to mount, hampered as I was by the heavy skirts of court dress. The escort—substantial as ever—fell in behind. We were moving toward the gateway when a young squire approached at a run.

"Your Grace . . . Wait, if it please you!"

We reined in. The lad slid to a halt, breathing heavily, removing his hat to bow. I did not know him but he wore royal livery.

"What is it?" Clarence asked, impatient to be off.

"His Majesty requests your presence, Your Grace. There's news. From Burgundy. His Majesty asks that you will stay."

Clarence, not entirely pleased, dismounted. With a cynical smile I watched him stripping off his gloves. He would seize any opportunity to be in Edward's confidence. "Inform His Majesty I shall be with him immediately." Turning to the sergeant at arms, he made to dismiss the escort.

"Do I have to stay as well?" I asked. I did not see that I should.

"It would be best."

"Surely I am well enough guarded to reach Cold Harbour without mishap!"

"I think—"

"I think it would be ridiculous to dismiss the whole troop when I could be home within a half hour." I put temper in my voice. "Do I have to sit and wait for you in some antechamber? Who knows how long the King will keep you!" I could see him weighing the sense of my suggestion. I raised my chin as if I would give him an argument. "I would go home. Now."

It swayed him. His handsome features tightened into a frown, but he obviously did not relish a lively difference of opinion in public with the escort straining to hear. Without another word to me he engaged in some rapid orders to the sergeant and then we were off.

"Take care. Stop for no one!" were Clarence's final orders.

It was late enough that the city was quiet apart from the clatter of our horses' hooves in the narrow streets. We made an impressive little force. Some of the men carried torches to illuminate dark corners where thieves could lurk, and I heard the metal slide of swords being loosened in scabbards. I was conscious of no real danger and rode, comfortably surrounded, lost in my plan to interrogate Isabel. Until a roar of laughter and coarse shouting erupted from a rabble who staggered from the open door of the Golden Lion at the far end of the street. Now they lurched along the road in our direction in the manner of the very drunk, oblivious to the body of armed men riding down on them. The sergeant shouted a warning, which they ignored, intent on raucous singing. The sergeant swore and ordered our party to draw rein. No point in riding them down. He drew his sword.

"Get them out of the way," he ordered two of his men with a grunt. "Don't kill them unless you have to."

"Out of the way, lads." The soldiers pushed forward.

Coarse laughter swelled. "Come'n join us, friends." A small barrel was held precariously aloft. "We've wine enough for all."

Then all changed. The drunken revelers threw off their mummery, magically transformed into a troop of disciplined, well-armed men. More emerged from a dark lane to our left, these on horseback, as well as others from the rear. Light glinted along blades, drawn and ready for use. We were surrounded, outnumbered, and overpowered. After a token resistance in the enclosed space, my escort was disarmed before my own bridle was seized and I was dragged, clumsily, helplessly, from the horse. It was all too quick for fear. A heavy cloak was bundled around me to pinion my arms and legs and silence me when I would have cried out. A deep hood was pulled smartly up over my head. Strong arms lifted me, passed me on like an ungainly package to the arms of another on the back of an animal that set off carrying both of us at a smart canter. I fought, kicking, struggling as much as I might.

"Keep still. You'll not be harmed."

It was a soft voice, no ruffian for sure, that hissed in my ear. My thoughts whirled as I was held tighter. Revenge? Ransom? Who would kidnap me? Only someone who had a desire to be revenged on Lancaster. But why not kill me on the spot? Was it robbery? If they coveted my jewels, why not simply snatch them? I struggled more.

"Quiet, lady."

The voice again. I had the strongest of impressions that my abductor knew who I was. This was no indiscriminate felony. Well, I would not be compliant. I twisted my head and, through the folds of the hood, I bit the hand that held me close.

The hand was snatched away on an oath. "Damn you! You were always a vixen." And there was the ghost of a laugh.

He definitely knew me. I was grasped even more tightly as we picked up speed with the sharp strike of hooves on cobbles. Then came the sound of a challenge of guards ahead. Guards . . . ? From the muffled echo I knew that we passed under an archway, and then the horses stopped. My captor dismounted and I was hauled down from its back. No sooner had my feet touched the ground than I was swept up again. Carried inside some building and up a flight of stairs. A deep hush fell, the footfalls changed from stone to wood. Through a door that someone opened. Muttered words reached me but I could make nothing of them through the wrappings. As the door closed behind us, I was promptly dropped to my feet and released. The cloak was unwrapped and fell around my feet. I emerged—disheveled, ruffled, undoubtedly afraid, and in no good temper.

"By the Virgin!" My veil had become detached. I snatched it off as I took in my surroundings, a richly paneled room hung with valuable tapestries. Lighted sconces warmed the polished wood, highlighted the rich scenes in deep reds and blues. There was a standing table, stools. A court cupboard with silver cups and a flagon. Logs hissed comfortingly in the hearth. This was not the dwelling of a poor man. Suspicions instantly crowded in. "Where am I? How dare you . . . !"

And as I turned on my abductor, my jaw dropped.

"Francis . . . Francis Lovell! What are you doing?" There was his handsome, smiling face and tawny hair, his eyes alight with conspiracy, just as I had last seen him on his visit to Warwick well over a year ago. I might feel a lessening of tension in my chest, but my thoughts remained in chaos.

He grinned. Made me an elegant but mocking bow. "Kidnapping you, my vixen. What does it look like?"

"And why would you need to do that?"

"Following orders." He picked up the cloak and folded it over the nearest stool. He rubbed his hand. "You bit me!"

"I'd have bitten harder if I'd known it was you. You frightened me! Whose orders?" I frowned at him as my suspicions grew stronger. "Where am I?"

"At Westminster."

"I only left Westminster a half hour ago! Why kidnap me? What in God's name am I doing here?" The thought came to me, swift as an arrow. "It's not your conspiracy, is it, Francis? Just who told you to bring me here?"

"I did."

In my righteous fury I had not heard anyone enter the room, my attention wholly on Francis Lovell. But I recognized the voice, would have known it anywhere. I swung around in disbelief.

"You are here because I ordered it," the Duke of Gloucester explained in the mildest of voices.

"You! You kidnapped me!"

Richard closed the door at his back and advanced into the room,
soft footed, a calculating look in his eye. I thought it might hide a
circumspection, except that I did not think the Richard I was coming
to know would have a need to be circumspect.

"Kidnapped? Yes. I suppose I did."

"Why would it be necessary to do something so outrageous?"
Anger sparked as I recalled the fear that he had stirred up. "I was terrified. If you wished to speak with me, I have been here all evening. As
far as I am aware, you made every effort to avoid me."

Richard, still dressed as I was for a court occasion, in shimmering satin with the chain of office winking on his chest as he moved,
ignored my observations on his unorthodox method of setting up a
conversation. "I want to speak with you now," he replied simply.

"But do I wish to speak with you?" I would not be pacified. "Am I
to do your bidding when and where you choose? You waylay my escort
and frighten me half to death. Not to mention using Francis here as
your disreputable second. You didn't even have the courage to abduct
me yourself."

"It would have been . . . unwise."

"Exactly!"

"Nothing disreputable about me, lady!" Francis laughed, obviously fascinated by the exchange. "I can't say the same for His Grace
of Clarence."

But Richard had stilled beneath my attack. I thought it might be
anger that imprinted his face as he raised his hand, a quick glance of
warning to Francis. "I am no coward, as you should know, lady. Your
abduction was . . . Let us say that it was necessary."

"It was beyond belief! I want to go home—now." I turned to Francis. "I don't want to be here. Take me back to Cold Harbour. Since
you left my escort lying in the road, *you* can escort me."

"Ah . . ." Francis slid a glance toward his coconspirator, leaving it to Richard to answer.

"No. You will remain here until I decide that you will leave."

A little frisson of—of what?—shivered along my skin, like the draft of cool evening air after a long, hot day. Not fear. Perhaps of anticipation, a desire to measure what was in truth between us. Richard's face was as implacable as his will. Edward might cloak his determination with charm and a winning smile. Richard did not bother. I thought I would test that will, as I was wont to do at Middleham, to see if I could break it. I put all the disdain I could into my voice.

"You will simply follow his orders?" I demanded of Francis.

"By God, I will. I'll leave you two to sort out your differences." And with a rueful smile, and a swift movement to press an encouraging kiss to my cheek, Francis was gone, leaving me to face Richard.

I steeled myself to show no trace of any emotion. I was every inch the Princess. "Perhaps you will do me the courtesy to explain."

Richard waited until the door was closed at Francis's back. "You want an explanation. Well, I will tell you. I want you to wed me."

"*Wed* you?" It was the last thing I expected to hear.

"Yes. And soon."

"That's . . . that's ridiculous. . . ."

"You don't believe me."

"No."

"I cannot make it any plainer." There it was, the flash of temper I remembered when his will was thwarted. It came to me that since he had become Constable of England very few people dared to question the will of Richard of Gloucester. He did not take kindly to it. But in my present mood, I would defy him. It would give me the greatest pleasure.

I thought carefully and planned my response. "You are very plain," I admitted. "Perhaps I don't question your intent—although I can hardly believe it—but I certainly question your motive. I think it has something to do with Clarence. I don't know what lies between you and your brother, but I will not be a part of it. I didn't understand Francis's reference, but if my marriage is part of some scheme between you, I won't have it."

"Ah . . . Francis was indiscreet. You always were quick of understanding."

"It wasn't difficult!"

Richard frowned at me, hardly loverlike. "My motives, as you put it, are of the best. My sentiments have not changed, Anne."

"Have they not?"

"I remember when I parted from you in the chapel of Warwick Castle, telling you that you had my love for all time. Have you forgotten? The words were not spoken lightly." The obsidian eyes glittered with frustration, but I was not of a mind to be gentle.

"I have not forgotten. I believed you. But we are no longer children, driven by childish emotions." It was like throwing a gauntlet at his feet, and I enjoyed seeing his eyes narrow. "We both know—who should know better?—that personal desires and politics do not always play out well together. That love can languish under the demands of honor and duty." I lifted my chin, a gesture guaranteed to stoke his anger higher. "*I* remember hearing that *you* would wed Mary of Burgundy."

"A marriage that never came to fruition. But *you* wed Edward of Lancaster." The implied criticism was harsh, his eyes dark with what I might in happier times have read as jealousy. Now I thought it was fury.

"I did. It was not of my choosing."

"And I suppose any feelings you had for me died a sudden death when the future crown of England hovered over your pretty brow," he added bitterly.

I shook my head, horrified that he should so condemn me without a hearing. As a log fell in the hearth with a shower of sparks, I found my voice. "I have been at court well nigh a month. If marriage is in your mind, why have you made no effort to engage my attention or my affections? I think I should tell you that it hurt me."

Richard exhaled in a sigh, but still held my accusatory gaze. "I know. I knew that it must. I'm guilty as charged, without excuse. But if you think it was easy for me to see you hurt. . . ." His words faltered. "Before we get into that . . . Since you still doubt me, let me prove the honesty of my actions. Come with me."

"Where?"

"Don't argue. I see you still argue about everything. Did you argue with the Prince?"

I flushed. I would not tell him that often it had been too danger-ous to argue with the Prince.

"I see that you did." Richard opened the door and with a flourish waved me through before him. When I still hesitated he waited. His eyes caught mine, held them with their dark fire, daring me to refuse. If I did, I thought he might just grab my wrist and drag me with him. So with head high I walked through.

"Where are we going?" I tried again.

"Wait and see."

I gave up, knowing it was all I was going to get. It was proving to be an evening of surprises.

CHAPTER SIXTEEN

I walked with him along corridors and through reception rooms that I knew well, and then into those I did not. Quiet rooms, softly lit, with none of the usual bustle of courtiers and squires or self-important clerks with their documents and matters of business. Family rooms. We did not speak until Richard touched my arm by a closed door, where he gave a light tap, opened it on the invitation from within, and motioned for me to enter before him. I walked in, not knowing what to expect. If he thought he could persuade me by some subtle seduction in his own chambers, he was far from the truth of it. . . . Startled, I halted, made a rapid curtsy. I had not expected to be shown into the private chamber of the King.

The Queen, Elizabeth, was with him. It was an unexpected sight to touch the heart and the senses, since they were spending a few precious hours together, alone. Edward lounged in a high-backed chair before the fire, a sumptuous robe cast open over shirt and hose. A cup of wine was at his hand; a hound sighed in the warmth, its head resting on his crossed ankles. Elizabeth curled at his knee, leaning against his leg, her hair, all the lovely silver gilt of it unbound and free, drifting onto her shoulders and across his thigh. A cozy domestic scene, entirely private, of man and wife enjoying the quiet at the end of a day, with more than a little hint of sexual satisfaction in the way the King's hand stroked that silken hair. Uncomfortable as an interloper in this intimate moment, I found myself taking a step, then another in retreat, until Richard's hands clasped firmly on my shoulders, holding me in place.

It was the profoundest sensation. How could I be standing here in the presence of the King and Queen, yet all my attention be drawn to the man behind me? How could I be conscious of nothing but the warmth and support of his hands? I felt the strength of his clasp and of his body at my back, the whisper of his breath against my neck. Then it was over. His hands slid away and I stood alone.

"Do we disturb you, Edward?" Richard asked.

"Yes!" Edward turned his head with a lazy smile. "But now that you are here you'd better come in. . . . An unexpected visit—but a pleasure. Come and sit." Dislodging the hound, he pushed a stool toward me with a casual toe.

Still guilty at encroaching on their privacy, and ridiculously moved, I was suddenly transported back to just such intimate moments at Middleham with the Earl and Countess. But now my family could never be reunited. Destroyed, blighted with treachery . . . Shocked, I found myself struggling against tears of self-pity, fighting to resurrect my previous anger with Richard, with Edward, with the world at large.

"Do sit," Elizabeth invited with a soft laugh edged with mockery. "You look tired, Anne. And, if I might say, a little the worse for wear. What happened?"

I realized I still clutched the creased remnants of my veiling. I could not imagine what sort of picture I presented. "It's a long story!" I sighed, suddenly very weary.

"Then tell us," Edward requested.

Silently, I raised my brows at Richard.

"I see!" Edward laughed. "What's afoot, Dickon?"

I sat, leaving Richard to prowl restlessly and tell the tale. Typically, he lost no time in coming to the point. "I want to wed her."

Edward immediately glanced at me, then fixed his stare as he sensed my hostility. "Ah! But does the lady wish to wed you?"

"She is . . . reluctant. She doubts my sincerity."

"I'm not surprised," Elizabeth remarked. "You've hardly played the role of interested suitor these past days. No lady cares to be ignored as if she did not exist."

I felt like some strange creature, newly discovered under a stone, with three pairs of eyes picking at my thoughts. And I felt the heat glow in my cheeks. Richard hitched a shoulder, the nearest he came to admitting his fault, but I saw the tinge of equally disconcerting color mirror mine. It delighted me that he was as embarrassed as I.

"There were reasons . . ." he stated. "But now I need to convince her. Do you have any objection to the match, Edward?"

Reasons? What possible reason could there be? But Edward was answering.

"None in essence. An excellent match, despite everything." His smiling eyes became sly. "But I know one who will object from here to the gates of hell and back!"

"Since when do I need to take Clarence's ambitions into consideration? And particularly in the matter of whom I marry?"

Clarence? It reminded me. Without thinking of the company, spurred by earlier events of the evening, I interrupted. "Where's Clarence now?"

"I don't know. Should I?" Edward looked from me to Richard and back.

"He was summoned urgently by a squire in royal livery, to attend on the King," I explained. "Which, I now presume, was a ruse."

Richard's careful composure immediately cracked into a smile that lit his whole countenance. "My brother is, I trust, engaged in a lengthy and entirely tedious discussion on some trivial point of trade with Burgundy. I hope it will last at least another hour."

"You set it up!" I glared at him.

"I did. I got Clarence out of the way," he explained to Edward, "with a royal summons."

"And then he got Francis Lovell to set a trap with drunken riff-raff from the Golden Lion to abduct me!" I added, still ruffled by the abduction.

A roar of laughter filled the room. "Did he now!" Then Edward became serious again, his mind focused. "So, as we were saying, if Lady Anne agrees—but we are still not certain of that, are we?"

I opened my mouth to reply, furious when Richard answered for me. "Yes, she will. She must."

"I have not said so!"

"But you will!"

"I dislike . . ." *I dislike your masterful arrogance!*

Edward intervened. "Enough! Let's presume that you can persuade her and win her compliance, Dickon, though I wouldn't wager on it. You'll need a dispensation. You're too closely tied as cousins to wed without."

"I don't see a difficulty there. Warwick got his papal dispensation for Clarence and Isabel. Where there's enough gold . . ." Disturbingly Richard was staring at me, weighing up some internal debate, before he turned back to his brother. "That's not the problem. But I have to ask . . . will there be difficulties with her inheritance?"

"Difficulties?" Edward pushed himself to his feet to stand face-to-face with his brother . . . or was it *against* him? For a moment I was unsure and there was no longer humor in his reply. The atmosphere in the little room had switched instantly, acquiring a bite. "Too gentle a word by half. It's a good match, as I said. I can see strong advantages in it, for you and for the security of the realm, to have Warwick's daughter closely tied, but there'll be an explosion over it. You know it as well as I. We'll just have to juggle the consequences and contain the damage. But hear me, Richard: I'll do whatever it takes to stop a return to war and conflict in England. Even if it displeases you in the process."

I could not follow the drift of this. I could feel apprehension building tight in my chest as Richard's grim expression and reply matched his brother's. "And you hear me, Edward, King or no. I'll fight Clarence every inch of the way. Whatever the cost."

"I know you will," Edward retorted, temper now showing its teeth. "And you don't give a damn over the dangerous position it could put me in!"

"No, I don't. I want her and I won't let him stop me." Edward's quick spark of anger was again reflected in Richard, fierce as wolves claiming their prey. Until Richard's aggression dissipated with equal speed. "No, Edward . . . That's not true. I don't wish danger on you or to the hard-won peace. Too much blood has already soaked the land. But I'll not allow Clarence to dictate the terms on this. Anne will not be robbed of what is rightfully her claim to the Countess's possessions. And I want her as my wife."

"And as I said, I'll support you as much as I can," Edward agreed.

While I was left on the periphery to try to untangle the issues. My inheritance. My status, with my sister, as my mother's heiress. I looked across at Elizabeth. Her expression was beautifully guarded, but she too knew the implications here. Why was my inheritance such a crucial matter of debate?

I stood because I was too anxious to sit. I took a step toward Richard, forcing him to look at me, away from the King.

"You say you want me as your wife, Richard. And then you talk about inheritance. Is that all there is between us from the past? The wealth and land that will come to me at my mother's death? Do you, after all, wish to wed me only for the value it will bring you?"

Perhaps I was naive to ask it. Was I wrong to expect more at Richard's hands? Had I not been led to believe that there was more between us in those heady days before our exile? Foolishly I had expected, longed for, love from Richard because he held my heart in his hands. Now it seemed to me that he had dug a grave and buried that love, covering it over with a common lust for a wealthy and wellborn wife. Hearing the plea, the tremor of despair in my voice, I flushed with ripe embarrassment but pursued the point. "Are you so insistent on my compliance because of the Beauchamp inheritance that will come to me?"

I had not realized what mud I was stirring up.

There was no compassion in Richard's answer, only a stark realism that struck home, as it was intended. His explanation was brutal.

"You speak of the Beauchamp inheritance that will be yours." His voice was raw but without hesitation. "Don't misunderstand me, Anne. Without me as your husband, to fight as your champion before the law, you are unlikely to get an inheritance of any description! You will be a pauper, destitute, dependent on whoever might be prepared to offer charity until the day you die. Or forced into an unpalatable marriage with some hanger-on of Clarence's, who, for a considerable bribe, might be prepared to take on a penniless daughter of a dead traitor. Without me as your husband, that will be your future. A cold and bitter one."

I felt the hot blood drain, to leave me white and shivering with cold.

"I don't believe you. . . ."

"Forgive me. It was cruel of me to beat you with the truth." Richard's brows became a black bar, his eyes dark with anger.

"She doesn't know?" Edward asked. "Well, I suppose there's no reason why she should. Clarence will hardly have broadcast his plans, and I doubt Isabel would speak out of turn. That lady will see where her best interests lie—to have it all arranged and the knots tied tight. And if *you* haven't broached the subject, Dickon . . ."

"*What* don't I know?" I could feel my temper flare again, fueled by sick fear. "I wish someone would be plain with me! Ever since I joined Clarence's household I have felt an undercurrent of *something*. Isabel suggests and persuades and speaks in riddles. And now you do the same." I forgot that I spoke with the King and the Constable of England. Or I deliberately ignored it. They were just two infuriating men who discussed the matter over my head as if I were witless, a woman to be maneuvered around and managed for her own good.

"Tell her," Edward stated simply.

So Richard spelled out my family's treachery. "Clarence has ambitions. He wants the whole Beauchamp-Despenser inheritance of the Countess for himself. He wants the titles, the lands and income—

everything. He can't have the whole Neville inheritance because I hold
the northern estates as a gift from Edward. But the Countess's lands,
the Despenser inheritance, for which you are joint heiress . . . Clarence
intends to claim the whole in Isabel's name as Warwick's elder daughter, thus disinheriting you." His eyes held mine as if he willed me to accept this terrible truth. Willed me not to disintegrate beneath the blow.

"But that cannot be. It's my right. . . . My mother's inheritance
will be divided equally between us. I have always known it. . . ." How
could this be true? "No! Isabel wouldn't!" I rejected the thought. "I
don't believe my sister would be so callous."

It would make me nothing but a destitute widow. I had nothing
from my brief and fatal marriage to the Prince. So if Isabel took everything, what would become of me? It was suddenly clear as day. If
I consented to become lady prioress in Isabel's planned foundation, it
would be the ideal solution for everyone. I would be shut away from
the world, robbed of a voice and power to object, while Isabel's conscience would be absolved from guilt, in that she had provided for me.
If she had a conscience at all.

"Don't fall under any illusions! You will find that she would,"
Richard urged. "Think, Anne. Use your good sense. Think of what
you know of her. Isabel will not stand with you against Clarence, and
you know it." His words were harsh, provocative, refusing to allow
me to fall into dismay.

"But if it is the law—it surely can't be done."

"By law, the inheritance is undoubtedly yours," Richard admitted. "But Clarence plays a clever card. He'll argue before the courts if
necessary that as the widow of the Prince of Lancaster, your property
is forfeit. You are as much a traitor as Warwick and the Countess, so
the whole of your inheritance should go, in total, to Isabel, who has
proved herself a loyal subject of the King. And thus into Clarence's
hands. Who changed sides from traitor to loyal subject at the most
apposite moment."

"But my marriage was not of my making."

"Clarence can make the argument and many would listen." Now

there was the shadow of compassion in Richard's eyes that wrung my heart. "You are a woman with unfortunate connections, and power-less in comparison with the influence of the Duke of Clarence."

"No . . . ! I am a Neville!"

"What will that matter if he persuades—or forces—you to enter a convent? Or if he arranges for you to wed some self-seeking lord who will do exactly as he is told by Clarence in return for a Neville bride? With no one to stand for you, what chance do you have? Only *I* have the authority to stand for you and thwart Clarence. I am the only man who can defeat him for you."

I was beyond speech. This was not arrogance in Richard's claims but blatant truth. Then my mind began to race. I turned on Edward, casting all caution and respect to the winds.

"Why can *you* not rule in my favor? If it is wrong, a trick, a ma-nipulation of the law by Clarence, why can you not stand for me be-fore the courts? Surely *you* could demand that Clarence acknowledge what is mine by the laws of inheritance."

"It sounds a simple matter, but it isn't." Edward's voice might be soft with understanding, but his words were as cold as the grate of a key in the lock of a prison door. "It's important for all manner of reasons that I leave the decision to the letter of the law. Because if I judged against him, it would drive Clarence to become my sworn enemy again. He's fickle, self-interested, and untrustworthy. I know it. But I need him with me, not against me. His followers turned the tide for me against Warwick at Barnet. He's popular and powerful and I cannot have him taking up arms against me. I won't push the country into open warfare again. Not even for you, my dear. It's unfortunate, some would say despicable on my part, but that's as it stands. I'll not be responsible for the spilling of more English blood."

"But you are the King. . . ."

"And as King I must abide by the law in such matters. I will listen to the arguments over your rights and I will make a judgment, but I will not willingly drive Clarence into opposition."

I stood, head bent as I absorbed Edward's damning explanation.

Until my thoughts returned to the most painful wound of all. "And Isabel knows of this. She would go along with Clarence's plan."

"Yes," Edward acknowledged.

Of course she would. Isabel had been the one to introduce the thought of retiring to a convent, with the prospect of power and influence for me as lady prioress. If I had suddenly discovered myself to be surrounded by enemies, it was Isabel's betrayal that hurt most.

"She would shut me in a convent," I repeated.

"Yes."

"It is unjust!" I covered my face with my hands, struggling to hold back the tears that blocked my throat and threatened to spill. I would not weep! But the pain of it threatened to overcome my willpower.

"Anne . . ." Richard was there at my side, but I drew back, resisted him.

"No!" I would accept no comfort from him. I did not even know that he would offer it. He wanted my land more than me. "I shall not faint or weep. I am not so weak. I am so angry!" I muttered behind my fingers, even more furious that I could barely restrain the tears.

To my surprise it was the Queen who rescued me. A silent, critical observer so far, and still seated on the floor, Elizabeth leaned to tug on the hem of my gown to draw me to sit in the King's chair at her side. "Sit here. It is not necessary for you to distress yourself." As I sat, because my knees threatened to give way, she waved a hand at the King and Gloucester and I heard her sharp tone: "I will deal with this. Go and talk of how to really draw blood. You have done a good job here between you."

"She needed to know," Edward retaliated.

"Yes, so she did. But now she needs some advice."

So they withdrew to the window embrasure, and I sat beside Elizabeth. The revelations of the past hour sank in and became plain, but the hurt did not lessen, and with my fingers I wiped away the tears I could not control. Until, to some extent composed, I looked up and found her pale eyes fixed on me. Speculative. A hard diamond edge. Certainly no compassion.

"What makes you so indecisive?" she asked, as if she could not imagine such a state.

"Richard says he wants to marry me."

"And so?

"It's all so complicated. . . ."

"I see no complication."

"I thought he loved me," I tried in the face of her palpable disdain. "But I think he loves my inheritance more. Perhaps he always did."

I felt her eyes narrow on my face. "That need not be a bar to marriage."

"It would make for a cold future together."

"I presume you love him." I thought her lip curled a little.

I did not answer directly. Instead I spoke the one thought that came directly into my mind. "I think he killed Prince Edward."

"Perhaps he did."

"Does that not matter?" Her icy self-possession, her brutal acceptance, shocked me.

"To kill can be a political necessity." She gave a cold shrug. "Have you asked him?"

"No. We have barely exchanged any conversation before tonight. I could hardly ask him if he murdered my husband in the middle of a round dance, could I?"

"Perhaps not." She gripped my clasped hands with one of hers and I felt the power in her. "Listen to me, girl. I'll give you some valuable advice. Better than any from the King or Gloucester." She leaned close so that her words would not carry. "Unless you wish to be a cipher, it is necessary to fight for what you want in this life. If you don't, you will be pushed and manipulated to suit the interests of the men who surround you. And sometimes—to get what you want—you must be prepared to accept the apparently unacceptable."

I found myself drawn into her gaze, fascinated. Here was a lethal ambition that would stop at nothing. I knew why Richard hated her, and in that moment I knew I must never trust her. They said that she had drawn Edward into an enchantment to ensure her place in his bed and at his side. I could well believe it. I might have thought she was being kind to me in her advice, but she was not. She was only tolerant of me because I was no threat to her.

"I can see your thoughts," she mocked, the direct stare gleaming, causing me to flush. "You have to make a decision, Anne. Forget love. Do you want him?"

"Yes." I could be nothing less than honest.

"Do you wish to marry him?"

That was the sticking point.

"Of course you do. All that matters in this life is power. If you wed Gloucester, the knight who will stand for you and fight for you, you will get your precious inheritance. If you reject him, you will get nothing. Do you want that? Do you want to live out your days as a nun? If you reject him you have less wit than I would have expected from a Neville—and I'm wasting my time here."

There it was. I might stiffen against her criticism. Her advice might be delivered without any compassion for my situation, but I could not deny its truth.

"Take him. You'll be a fool if you don't! And you'll deserve to take the veil!"

She raised her hand to attract Edward's attention. I watched them approach, reading nothing in Richard's face other than impatience. Presumably with me. This time I stifled the sigh.

"So," Edward said hopefully. "Will you take my brother? You have the right to refuse. You are under no man's authority in this."

"Not even Clarence's?"

"No. He is not your guardian. I merely put you into his care. You are your own mistress here."

I looked at Richard, my chin a little tilted, a little raised. "Well?" I asked. I would not make it easy for him and he recognized it, the faint lines at the corners of his eyes, the glint of light there betraying his awareness of my challenge. Even so he remained dispassionately aloof, and his request was not in the words of a lover.

"This is not how I thought of wooing you, lady. Rushed and dangerous with an unfortunate need for secrecy. I hope you are not blind to my feelings for you. I would be honored if you would become my wife."

Cold, efficient, it smacked of a business transaction. He had not even touched me, much less declared his undying affection! Resentment still bound me. Unsurprisingly I retaliated in similar vein.

"Nor is this how I would wish to be wooed." Still I balked. "I am unsure of your feelings toward me. The best I can say is that I will consider your request, sir."

"That's settled then." Relief swept Edward's face, as if I had given my consent. I saw nothing in Richard's as the brothers looked at each other. This plan had, it seemed, already been in the making, with or without my agreement. "I shall put in hand the matter of the dispensation," Edward stated. "You, Anne, will return to Cold Harbour under a royal escort—with some explanation of attack by footpads from which you were rescued. Not difficult." He swept the little problem aside. "You will continue your life there under Clarence's protection until all is arranged. This meeting never happened. The matters discussed here and agreed on will not be spoken of."

Had I agreed?

I had said no such thing. I had given Richard nothing beyond notice of my dislike of his dealings, a cool promise to think about it. As a well-mannered daughter of Warwick I had to crush the scream of vexation that bubbled to my lips. The King, I had been led to understand, had decided with or without my consent.

"Will you be here at Westminster?" I asked Richard in a deserted audience chamber, the briefest of moments before an escort was arranged for me.

"No. Edward sends me north. I shall return before the dispensation."

I suppressed the intense regret that I should not see him. *I have not yet said I will wed you!* So much remained unspoken between us.

Tell me you love me! Now, before I must go. If it is so, then tell me! I didn't say the words. I couldn't. Nor could I speak of my love for him.

Then the echo of Edward's footsteps could be heard and we must of necessity part. It would not do for Richard to be seen with me in the public rooms of Westminster or in the outer courts. No one must see or hear anything that placed us together, that could be reported back to Clarence.

"Adieu, my dear girl," Richard said gravely. He lifted one hand to smooth my unveiled and untidy hair from my forehead. "God be with you and keep you safe until I can come for you."

The blessing touched my senses, and all my previous resentments softened. For the briefest moment I caught his hand, enfolding it within my own, savoring the warmth of his palm, before I lifted it to press it against my cheek, all the while trying desperately to hold at bay my anxiety at my growing isolation. Returning to Cold Harbour was like being thrown back into the lion's den. "Don't forget me," I murmured.

"How could I ever? It would not be possible this side of the grave."

I breathed out softly, my lips turned against his palm. It was not much of an avowal of love perhaps, but enough to light a little flame that would warm me through the following days. There would be no time for more between us, as I could hear Edward's voice approaching, summoning me. Instinctively my grasp on Richard's hand tightened. At the same time he pulled me off balance against him. The next moment I was in his arms and they were banded tight around me, his mouth hard on mine. My whole world became encompassed by the strength and nearness of his body, as the flame between us, a mere flicker no longer, leaped to a scorching heat. Stunned into awareness, with no comparison to make between this and the sweet kisses of our young courtship, I could do nothing but cling to him, allowing him the hot possession. I had dreamed of this for so long but with no understanding of the magnificent reality. I was breathless from the power of it.

Then he released me as suddenly as he had swooped. My inexperience, I realized, was glaring, as I was abandoned in a little space to look at him in wordless amazement. Was this how a man kissed a woman he loved? What drove Richard to this? The look on his face was more one of pain than delight before it was smoothed over. I had no familiarity with such emotions at Prince Edward's hands to deduce it for myself. For sure, it seemed to give Richard no pleasure, rather a fury of need.

"By God, I want you, Anne, and I will have you yet." He spoke his intent as if it were a sacred oath. "No one, not even the King, will stand between us." But no, I realized. It was no sacred oath after all. More the determination of a predatory male to own the object of his desire. Richard Plantagenet desired me and would possess me, letting no one stand in his way.

The ruthlessness might shock me but not the sentiment. For if I had ever questioned my love for him, I could no longer. Whatever he had or had not done, whatever blood had been spilled by his hands, that one kiss had stirred my emotions into blazing life. And I, with my heart bounding in my chest, my lips tender, could find not one word to say to him.

Then Edward was at the door.

"Anne . . ." Richard said.

"Yes?"

He shook his head. "Nothing. Be safe."

I went with Edward, too shaken to speak, but turned at the last to look back. Richard still stood where I had left him. His solemn regard touched mine, and held. He bowed formally before he walked away.

I found myself escorted back to Cold Harbour. On that short journey I buried the disturbing remnants of that embrace in the deep recesses of my heart. Instead I took to turning over in my mind the one subject that had not been touched on in the whole discussion. Deliberately so, I was certain. The Countess, my mother, shut away under guard in Beaulieu Abbey. The lands and titles under such intense discussion were hers. But they were not free to be inherited. Nor would they be until she was dead. She was barely more than forty years old.

Suddenly I had another fear to squeeze my heart.

*   *   *

"You seem very calm. Surely you were frightened," Isabel observed.

"I am calm now. I was terrified then. But I am safe, as you see."

The explanation of the attack on me and my escort, and thus my late return under royal protection, caused no undue comment at Cold Harbour. These things happened. How fortunate I was to escape the ale-soaked thieves who prowled the streets after dark, with nothing more than a ruined veiling and a fistful of bruises to show for my adventure. I played my role to perfection.

"You'll not leave these gates without a stronger escort in future," Clarence decreed, scowling heavily at no one in particular.

Magnificently guileless, I agreed. "Obviously, it's not safe."

"And Francis Lovell came by chance to rescue you," Isabel marveled.

"Yes. Wasn't that fortunate."

Beneath the surface my blood simmered, but I would keep my temper with Isabel, however much I was provoked, however much the devious plotting hidden behind her smooth face and friendly smiles disgusted me. I must exercise every last ounce of will to preserve an innocent and compliant demeanor. If she suspected any attachment, any suggestion of marriage, I would be parceled off to a convent quicker than an arrow could leave the bowstring of a Welsh archer. My sister had learned her lessons well from her grasping husband. It astonished me that I could pretend an apparent indifference to Isabel's constant closeness and well-disguised deceit, but I polished my skills of benign geniality as outrage swam just below the surface. The only blessing was that Clarence was much occupied at court. I could not have borne to sit across from him every morning over ale and bread while I kept my fury within bounds.

Richard went north to Middleham. How I wished that I too could be at Middleham. Cold and gray at this time of year, with rain squalls and biting winds, it could be drear and dismal beyond bearing. I would have given anything to be there with him.

CHAPTER SEVENTEEN

In the end, I lost my nerve. Because I was alone, without counsel, without anyone I could trust. Was it weakness of spirit? I think not. For six long months I had been in Clarence's keeping. Who could control every thought, every word, for so long? If I had had a confidante I think I should have held firm, but I could not even unburden myself to Margery. She was kind and loving, but she was in Isabel's employ, so where would her ultimate loyalties lie? I did not distrust her but I could not tell her of my deepest fears. And I was so weary of guarding myself with Isabel and Clarence, watching every word I uttered. Isabel stuck to my side like an apothecary's leech.

I was alone. I did not appreciate until that moment how very lonely I was.

And so I panicked.

Isabel began to talk of an immediate return to Warwick. It seemed an agreeable scheme that raised no suspicions until she suggested that we visit Tewkesbury on the way. Would that not be the most suitable place to endow a convent, the magnificent abbey already extended and embellished with Beauchamp-Despenser money? What better place to establish a convent for daughters and widows of wealthy families who chose to serve God before the lure of the flesh?

In an instant of recognition I saw myself enclosed there. By the time Richard returned from the north I could find myself spirited away and enclosed behind the abbey doors at Tewkesbury, condemned to holy captivity even if I had not made any vows. Neither Richard nor the King would be able to rescue me.

I would be locked away until the day of my death.

Panic flared. My nerve broke. Risking interception, I wrote. The letter took no writing. There was little I needed to say to make my fears known and I took no care over the content.

> *To the Duke of Gloucester*
>   *Circumstances have changed. We are to return to Warwick before the end of the month. I fear that my own destination is to be Tewkesbury, where I shall be kept close in sanctuary, much as my mother is at Beaulieu, until I can take the veil. I think I can expect no overt help from the King, so I must look to you for rescue.*
>   *I beg that you will come and remove me from this house.*
>   *I fear you may be too late.*
>
>   *Your faithful cousin,*
>   *Anne Neville*

Who to take it for me? I dared trust no one of Clarence's. I had to take the risk.

"Margery . . . do you have any acquaintance in London, any family?"

"A cousin. A glove maker in Cheapside. He's married with a growing family."

"Anyone of an age who would take a letter for me at all speed?"

"Why?" Her casual interest deepened. "Where do you need to send a letter, lady?"

"It doesn't matter where. But I am in need."

"I don't see—"

I grabbed her arm. "Do you wish to see me become a nun, Margery?"

There were no more questions from her, which convinced me my fears were truly justified. The letter was sent. All I had to do was wait and restrain myself from hurling accusations of treachery along with a mug of ale at Isabel's head.

Disaster struck, prompted by the King's own hand, although even he, with his intimate knowledge of Clarence's capacity for deception, could not have foreseen the outcome. The whole affair was so cunningly managed, so outrageously clever and, above all, willingly connived at by my own sister, who had proved herself to be cold and vindictive beyond belief.

We heard the peremptory strike of hooves on cobbles as Clarence galloped his horse into the courtyard at Cold Harbour. The firm slap of his boots as he strode up the steps, until he burst through the door of the parlor, where Isabel and I were passing an hour over a game of chess. He was short of breath; his chest heaved. His face was drawn with anger; his eyes blazed with it.

"Out!" he snarled at Margery and Isabel's ladies. They scurried to obey.

My blood froze in apprehension. With the passing of days I had begun to dream that Richard would arrive at our door in time to rescue me. My breathing shallow, I waited to hear what had caused this outburst. Clarence rounded on me before the door had barely closed.

"What trickery is this, madam?"

"I know of no trickery." I rose carefully to my feet, abandoning an attack on Isabel's queen from my bishop. I would not answer such an accusation sitting down, but my legs were weak with fear.

"My lord?" Isabel came quickly to Clarence's side, to touch his arm in what I considered ingratiating concern, but he shook her off and advanced on me, fists clenched. I stood my ground, even though I knew he would like nothing better than to strike me, to vent his anger, but his control was better than that.

"Your sister is not as innocent as she looks." His words were for Isabel; the smile that touched his fine features was thin, feral. "That sweetly compliant exterior, so much out of character, as you yourself have remarked. Sweet words, gentle acceptance. 'Yes, Isabel. No, Isabel. Any bloody suggestion you make, Isabel!' She fooled us well and truly. She has not changed at all! Behind our backs she has been following her own plans, aided and abetted by my brother."

"Helped by the King?" Isabel's expression was one of disbelief.

"Gloucester! Who else!" Clarence did not take his eyes from me as he circled me. I could feel them as they bored into my very soul with the well-honed sharpness of a dagger. "I am informed, this very morning, by Edward himself that there is an agreement already made—that your sister will wed Gloucester." Now he was facing me again. "I won't ask you if it is true. I know it is."

With magnificent hauteur I refused to confirm it.

"And Edward also informs me"—now his tone was silky-smooth—"that there is already an agent in Rome with the ear of the Pope, seeking a dispensation."

"What of it? It is my right to make such an agreement." I must brazen it out, even though I had agreed only to consider the offer. I kept my eyes on those furious blue ones, horrified by the hot revulsion I saw there. How had he kept it hidden for so long, pretending to be my caring brother whose sole aim was to smooth my future path? He would have me clapped in a nunnery within the hour if he could.

"Gloucester is on his way back to London," he continued. "I expect you know that already. And when he gets here, his intention is to take you from my house. And the King orders me—orders me!—to hand you over into his keeping." He spat out the final words.

So Richard had sent ahead to warn Edward of our planned journey. And Edward, in his attempt to prevent my abduction to Tewkesbury, had instead cast the spark to light this conflagration. God's blood! I cursed silently. How could Edward not have seen the repercussions? How could he trust Clarence so blindly with my safety? But I allowed none of my terror to surface.

"I will go with Richard when he comes for me," I replied calmly, despite the galloping thud of my heart.

"You will not, Madame Anne!" Clarence snarled in my ear as he circled me again. "As I informed the King, *I* am your legal guardian. You were put in my charge, and that of your sister, by Edward himself. You will do as I say. Any court in the land will uphold my legal rights over you. *I* will make the arrangements for you, not Gloucester! The last thing I will allow is for you to marry him, however compliant Edward might be."

"You have no such legal jurisdiction over me or my actions." Still I held tight to my courage. "I am of age and as a widow have every right to determine my own future. I can give myself in marriage where and when I will. I will wed your brother if I so wish. He has asked me, in the King's presence, who saw no objection. What right have you to question it? You cannot stand in my way."

"The King . . . ? Ah! Of course!" Clarence fisted his hands again as the realization struck. "So that was the reason for the playacting— the neat little charade of the attack by the drunken louts from the Golden Lion. I suppose Gloucester arranged it for you to return to court. And I suppose my own abortive discussion over some damned penny-pinching aspect of Burgundian trade was part of the whole. I should have known, if Francis Lovell was involved. He and Gloucester were always thick as thieves."

I remained silent but did not bend one inch.

"What do we do now?" Isabel chewed nervously at her lips.

"Whatever Edward agreed, she'll not become Gloucester's wife."

"So what will I do?" I could no longer hide my disdain. "Take the veil?"

"Exactly! You'll go to Tewkesbury, for your own good."

"No. For yours, not mine. I know what you intend, *brother*! Did you think I was ignorant of your deception? You would disinherit me, rob me of my rights." I turned to face my sister as my sense of ill usage blossomed into fury as strong as Clarence's. "How could you do this, Isabel? How could you pretend to be my concerned sister, to have my best interests in your heart; how could you smile and talk of meaningless nothings and all the time be in league with him against me? Does blood mean nothing to you? Does family loyalty mean nothing? I have to accept that money and power mean more to you than family ties."

White as the costly lace at her neck, Isabel sought helplessly for a reply. Nor would she look at me, turning from the accusation in my face. The influence had been her husband's, but still I could not forgive her.

"I know why you would send me to a convent. All that talk of following in the tradition of our ancestors, dispensing patronage for those who wish to become brides of Christ. By the Virgin! Did you think to fool me? Any convent would do, anywhere so that Richard can't marry me." I renewed my attack on Clarence. "Because he is the only man in the land who can challenge you, a royal duke, and hope to be heard and listened to. I'm amazed that you did not wed me to some poor cipher of a husband who could not stand for me against a mouse! But Richard would stand for me. And he will, when he comes to claim me, and your plans will be as ashes beneath your feet."

"Gloucester's no knight in shining armor. He wants your inheritance as much as I."

"But he would give me the status of his wife. Not rob me of everything I have and imprison me in a nun's cell for the rest of my days!"

For the first time I saw beneath the anger the slightest flicker of fear in Clarence's face, but he would not retreat. It spurred him on into sheer madness.

"I shall win. You'll not defeat me in this and nor will Gloucester. Do you think I am unaware of my own worth to the King? Edward will never decide against me. He dare not make me an enemy." He advanced, driven by enormous energies, to stand a mere arm's length before me, to cow me into submission as he continued his attack. "Once I had hopes of a crown—until your father rejected me in favor of Lancaster, forcing me to bow and scrape and accept it with the

empty promise of some distant throne if the Lancastrian line came
to an end. Do you know what it took for my pride to accept that? It
made me sick to my stomach, but I had to stand there and acknowledge Edward of Lancaster as my sovereign lord. No wonder I turned
my coat and came to terms with Edward. But he now has a son to rule
after him. Do I not deserve recompense for that? I deserve recognition for the victory I brought to Edward at Barnet when I gave my
troops to the King's use." His voice rose on every statement until he
all but shouted. "What better than to take *all* the Neville inheritance
for my own?"

"You'll not get it!" It pleased me to say it, to see his disgust.

"No. I know full well. Gloucester has the northern Neville lands,
with Edward's blessing. But that will not stop me from taking *yours*,
dear sister. *I* will be the heir to the Countess of Warwick's lands and
titles. All of them. And only me."

"Is that justice?" It was no more than I already knew.

"Don't talk about justice, Princess." I felt his hatred like a slap to
the face. "Who would blame me for taking the property of the woman
who wed the Lancastrian heir? Which loyal Yorkist magnate in England would listen to your demands when you would have worn the
crown at the side of your Lancastrian husband?"

The argument was not new to me. I was forced to accept the truth
of it, but I held on and snapped my defiance at him. "I will go with
Richard when he comes for me. Then we shall see who will listen to
my demands for justice when his voice is raised on my behalf."

"No, you will not." Suddenly Clarence's stance had softened, as
had his voice. His smile held an uncomfortable humor, as if he enjoyed a joke at my expense. It made me shiver as his rage and bluster-
ing had not. What was he planning for me?

"Will you bar the door? Refuse Richard entry with swords and
longbows? Cannon even?" I asked in as neutral a tone as I could
manage.

"Nothing so obvious. I shall entertain my brother right well." His
smile broadened so that I saw once again the handsome man who had

captivated Isabel and even now held her in thrall. "He will simply not find you here when he comes."

"Then do we go to Warwick now, immediately?" Isabel asked.

I had sudden visions of us fleeing across the country, hell-for-leather, with Richard in hot pursuit.

"No, my dear. No time for that. He would overtake us, I have no doubt. I have no wish for a confrontation on the open road. I have a far better plan."

I could not guess. I hid my shaking knees and waited. Who could have guessed that Edward's efforts to preempt Richard's return and save me had cast me into even greater danger?

I was escorted to my room by my stiff-backed sister. Although I sensed from the set of her shoulders that she was not entirely at ease with this plot, whatever it was, equally I knew she would not defy Clarence. Always she had believed the best of him, however uncaring his treatment of her. If she could follow him from York to Lancaster and back again without a qualm, she would not disobey him now.

Still I tried. "Isabel!" I quickened my step to keep pace with her, trying to pull her to a halt, to listen to me. "Wait! You can't let him do this!"

She shook me off, standing back to all but push me into my bedchamber, and I saw that she had a key in her hand. Would I then be locked in here? But it could not be forever, I assured myself as I stalked past her. Only until Richard's threatened visit was past, or until Clarence could arrange my removal to Warwick or Tewkesbury without any risk of my being discovered. Once I was allowed out of Cold Harbour again, there would surely be some opportunity for flight. This was not like Angers—someone would come to my aid.

"You will stay there."

She left me, locking the door after her to ensure my obedience, knowing that it would at least cross my mind to attempt an escape. But short of running through the streets of London to cast myself on the mercy of the King, I did not know what to do. Then, before I could order my thoughts into some sensible plan, she was back. In her arms was a bundle of clothes, a pair of stout leather shoes neatly balanced on the top.

"Here!" She tossed them onto the bed. "Put these on. Quickly." Her lips were folded hard. She did not once meet my eye.

"What . . . ?" I could see enough of the garments to think she had run mad. "Isabel . . ." Surely I could appeal to her. She was my *sister*!

"Don't argue!"

"I won't do it!" I folded my arms, attempting to stare her down, mutinous to the last. And I continued to face her even when my belly lurched at the lack of compassion I read in her face. It was almost as if she had absorbed Clarence's hatred into her own soul, and her next words tightened the knot in my chest further.

"You do it yourself, Anne, or I summon a servant to dress you. Do you want that? It will be far more degrading."

"Don't you dare speak to me of degradation!" But because she left me no choice, and I had no wish to be manhandled into the garments, I did as I was bidden. "What in God's name do you intend . . . ?" Viciously, with the worst of ill grace, I pulled off my overgown, not caring whether I tore the delicate braiding, turning my back brusquely so that she could unlace the rich silk below.

"You'll find out soon enough."

Her fingers were as rough as mine, yanking the laces apart, so that soon the fashionable undergown with its embroidered panels also fell to the floor. I pushed it aside with my foot.

Isabel was not satisfied. "Everything!"

So I stripped off my stockings and fine linen shift, then began to don Isabel's choice of garments. The new Anne Neville, I thought in disgust, as I pulled on the coarse woolen material. Lady Anne, or Princess Anne, had never worn cloth such as this, a coarse weaving that snagged her skin and lay roughly on neck and wrist. Lady Anne Neville had never tied her hair into a swath of such poorly woven material, would never have considered anything so unfashionable or unflattering.

A thin shift that barely reached my knees, a skirt made for another so that it hung loosely on my small frame to drag on the floor, a wide tunic to cover all and be cinched with a cord belt. I could imagine myself in the muddy brown and dark green of my new ensemble. Lady Anne with her dark hair and pale skin would never have chosen such colors.

What was Lady Anne to do with this new creature? Not a thing. This was a servant, dull and anonymous, to blend in with the other servants in the house. Was this to be my disguise, my future? Did Isabel intend to work me like a servant in her own house? Never far away in recent days, panic lurched again beneath my heart.

Isabel cast an eye over me. As if to answer my question she pursed her lips and issued more orders. "Tuck up the skirts, sister. They're too long. Fold up the sleeves as well, to your elbow. There'll be no leisure for you for a little while." She pointed to the floor. "Put on those shoes."

"I can't believe this, Isabel." It was all I could think to say.

"You will," she snapped.

While I tugged on the rough leather, Isabel began to gather my possessions together in a heap on the bed. My gowns and shifts from the presses. My Book of Hours from the nightstand. A jewel chest. Soon everything I owned was tumbled together on the coverlet, even my own rosary that I had hung on the prie-dieu, and the room was stripped of any evidence that I had ever been there. If anyone came to search for me they would find no trace of me here. If Richard came to find me he would believe that I had gone from London. I stood and watched my sister busily stacking my shoes beside the rest. She ignored me and my baleful look until the door opened, and Margery, after struggling with the latch, stood there, a bowl and ewer in her arms. She halted, clutching them to her bosom as with suddenly narrowed eyes she took note of the room. And then of me standing in the midst.

"Lady Anne . . . ?" She turned to Isabel. "My lady!"

"Close the door," Isabel ordered. "I should have locked it, but no matter. You would have to know sometime."

Obeying, depositing her burden, Margery turned, her broad face an essay in disapproval. "What have you done? Why have—"

"Nothing that is your concern," Isabel interrupted briskly. "And not one word about this. If one word of gossip over the whereabouts of my sister reaches me, you will be dismissed from my service."

"Isabel Neville!" Resorting to her role of nurse to a naughty child, Margery puffed out her chest. "How dare you treat your sister so, to bring dishonor to your name! I don't know what you intend but—"

"No. I am not Isabel Neville, a child to be scolded and disciplined. I am the Duchess of Clarence. I don't care how long you have been in our household, or that you were my mother's nurse before mine. You have no power over me and my wishes. I can reduce you to earning a living in the gutters of London if you condemn my actions." And having brought Margery to a state of appalled silence, she turned to me. "Are you ready?"

"Ready to be a servant?" I laughed at the enormity of it. "Have you let Clarence influence you to the extent of betraying your own sister?"

She did not reply, other than to snap out an order. "Come with me. You don't speak to anyone, look at anyone. You walk behind me in silence, as any servant might. Unless you wish to be locked in a cellar." To an astounded Margery, she added, "Finish packing these into a traveling chest. When Gloucester comes, my sister is already at Tewkesbury. She left last week, having felt the need to embrace a contemplative life. Do you understand?"

Aghast, Margery simply looked at me, lost for words. I shook my head and managed a wry twist of my mouth. "There you have it, Margery, from my sister's own lips. Who would have believed that she would go to such lengths to get our mother's money and land? The Countess under guard in Beaulieu and me locked away in Tewkesbury. Or, it seems, put to work as a kitchen slut." I could no longer keep the bitterness from spilling out to flood the room. "Who would have thought the noble and beautiful Duchess of Clarence capable of such a magnificent revenge against her own sister, for daring to be joint heiress of their mother's fortune?"

"My lady!" Hands clasped together, Margery tried a final appeal. "You can't do this. What will people say?"

"Who will know? This is how it will be."

"Yes, Your Grace." And in that moment I saw the gleam of tears on Margery's lined cheek. "I understand only too well."

"Good. And keep a still tongue in your head."

Isabel opened the door and walked through, not even questioning that I would follow, and I did because there was no alternative.

But not before my eye had been caught by the shine of mother-of-pearl and dark, well-polished wood beneath the folds of a velvet damask cloak. That was one thing I would never allow Isabel to dispose of. She could take my clothes and my jewels, even my Book of Hours, but not that. I snatched the little inlaid wooden box that had been with me since my childhood and enclosed my most cherished possessions. I pushed it urgently into Margery's hands.

"Keep it for me. Hide it."

I followed my sister.

I had never before been in the kitchens at Cold Harbour. Not that they were any surprise to me when I stood there at my sister's shoulder. These rooms set aside in one wing near the river were smaller, compact, as befitted a town house, but still uncomfortably reminiscent of Middleham. The cavernous fireplaces belched soot and smoke. Grease coated the surfaces and the permanent smell of roast meats choked the air, as did the stench of the nearby midden.

I was to become closely acquainted with this world within a world.

Isabel dealt with the delicate situation forthrightly, embroidering a total fabrication, arrogantly ignoring the looks of disbelief on all sides. Not Clarence, of course. He wouldn't do it, I sneered silently. The Duke of Clarence standing in the middle of his own kitchen, where his fine clothes might be soiled with grease or made rancid with smoke? Never. So it was Isabel who addressed herself to the steward.

"Here is a new servant come from Warwick, Master Pritchard. Her name is Mary Fletcher." I had to be impressed. Isabel did not even hesitate, simply adopting the name of a dairy girl at Warwick. Nor did her eyes flicker, not once, unlike those of the cook and steward, who froze into rigid amazement, not knowing where to look. How could they not know the identity of their newest kitchen wench? Isabel continued in an imperiously cold voice, her stare pinning the unfortunate steward. Her words painted a vivid picture of what my life was to be like from now on.

"Put her to work here in the kitchen. Watch her closely. There must be no communication between her and any who are not servants in my household. She does not go into the audience or family rooms. Keep her *here*. She will sleep with the other kitchen maids on a pallet in the room off the scullery. You will on no account allow her out of your sight, or that of one of your trusted officers. I put this burden on you, personally, Master Pritchard."

"Yes, Your Grace," he managed. I saw a quick glance slide from Master Pritchard to the cook. "Ah . . . and how long, Your Grace?" Master Pritchard inquired with barely a quaver in his voice.

"Until I decide otherwise."

"Of course, Your Grace."

"You will treat her like any servant. I rely on your loyalty to myself and my husband in this. Any failure on your part will result in instant dismissal. Do you take my meaning?"

"Yes, Your Grace. Of course, Your Grace."

Without another word, Isabel turned on her heel and swept past me, to leave me standing in the shocked silence. What did I think of this? Indeed, I could not think at all. I would have been embarrassed to see the length to which my sister would go to get her hands on the Beauchamp inheritance—or to please Clarence—if I had not been so thoroughly outraged. To work as a servant in Clarence's kitchens, from Princess to kitchen wench, within a year, all my rank and dignity stripped from me. It was monstrous! I might have laughed, but there was no humor here. And how would Richard ever find me? Who would come to my aid? No one would ever look for Anne Neville in her sister's kitchens.

Which is exactly, I told myself as I was put to work scouring a fire-blackened pot, *what Clarence has planned.*

*   *   *

"Use this. It helps."

Master Hough, the cook, shoved a pot of grease across the table toward me. He was busy dismembering a coney, stripping off the skin with callous unconcern. I did not think he had noticed my hiss of pain as I picked up—and dropped—a hot pan from the fire grate. The clatter of metal on stone must have alerted him. It was the first sign of overt sympathy I had been shown, and meant more to me than a thousand words of comfort. I wrinkled my nose at the heavy ointment, but there was also the whiff of herbs. Rosemary, I thought. I rubbed it onto my burned fingers, and onto a recent scald on my wrist for good measure. I sighed as it soothed.

"You are very kind, sir." It was all I could say.

"This will not be forever, my lady," he whispered before giving his attention back to the unfortunate rabbit.

But it seemed like it. Because there was nothing else they could do, Master Pritchard and Master Hough put me to work. I became Mary Fletcher. It was a different world, a different life, and I did not have the skills for much of it. All I had were stamina and a burning determination to survive and one day be revenged. They carried me through long days of hard work and a succession of sleepless nights on an even harder pallet in a scullery, where the stench of the midden became even keener. Until finally I slept from sheer exhaustion. If I learned anything in those miserable days, it was the lack of respect the servants felt toward their royal master. They saw beneath the gilded wealth and handsome exterior to the selfish arrogance. They had no love for him, or for my sister. They obeyed the Duke and Duchess of Clarence from fear of dismissal, and nothing more.

I was not given the worst of the tasks. I have to give some credit to Master Hough, who shielded me as much as he could without drawing attention to it, but my life as Lady Anne Neville had not prepared me for such an existence. I washed and scoured, cut, chopped, and scraped. I carried and swept. My back ached and my muscles strained with the unaccustomed work. I was never allowed out of the kitchens, not even to fetch and carry from other parts of the house. My nights, as ordered by my sister, were spent on a straw pallet in the room with two kitchen girls who had to be up before dawn to coax the fires back into life before the rest of the household woke. In my blacker moments I also thought I shared it with any number of lice, fleas, and rats.

I was not ill treated; I received no blows or harsh reprimands, as was customary for those around me who were too slow or too clumsy. I think they did not know how to treat me. But it was a lonely existence. No one spoke to me beyond the next instruction. *There will be no communication*, Isabel had ordered, and so that was how it was. Eyes avoided mine. Gossip or friendly chatter stopped immediately when I entered one of the sculleries. The kitchen maids kept their distance, not through any dislike of me but for fear of getting too close and the repercussion for them if they did.

So my life became a series of burns and blisters and aching limbs. I found that I was not quick or handy enough to dodge the burning cinder or juggle the hot dish. I tried. I did not complain. Whom would I complain to? It was not their fault that I was foisted on them. I suppose they tolerated my clumsiness well enough. No tears were shed by me, even in the dark of the night, when I might have buried the sound in my pillow. No one must be allowed to pity me. I clung to my pride as a drowning man would hold fast to a floating spar of wood, and through it all I was buttressed by my determination to foil Clarence's plan to separate me from Richard and secure my mother's wealth.

This will not be forever.

Master Hough had thought that he could see an end, but I was not convinced. How long would I stay here? Until Richard had paid his promised visit, decided that I had left London of my own free will, and given up, to chase after me to Tewkesbury or Warwick or on whatever goose chase Clarence sent him? How could I be sure that Clarence would release me, even then, from this drudgery? Was this to be my life forever?

Did no one miss me *now* enough to come and find me?

No one would recognize me; of that I was certain. No one would see anything other than an ill-dressed, grubby kitchen girl, rank and unwashed, with soot on her face and scars on her hands. Margery did not come near. She would not dare.

Three nights after I was hidden away, as I sank with a groan onto my pallet, I felt the hard edges immediately beneath me. Under cover of darkness, I turned back the thin cover. My box. Margery must have sent it to remind me that I was not alone. Absurdly, upon opening it, it renewed my flagging hopes as I saw in the dim light that she had also rescued my Book of Hours and tucked it inside. I did not look further beneath the book, fearing that the contents would remind me too strongly of past happiness and would weaken my resolve. A metal bird that I could not bear to be parted from. A pair of stolen embroidered gauntlets. Items of such little intrinsic value but immeasurably comforting to me. That night I lay awake with the box in my arms. Would Richard come to find me? When would he come? If he did, would there be any hope of his discovering me? The questions were endless and unanswerable. Except that, as the days passed, I feared the final answer was no.

The warning came from an unexpected source.

"Gloucester's here," Master Hough murmured one morning after the household had broken its fast, hardly moving his lips as he stirred a dish of pea pottage. "He's with my noble lord of Clarence, God rot him!"

My fingers gripped hard on the edge of the pewter platter I carried. At last! But to what avail? Richard might be here, but there was nothing I could do about it. Within the hour he would ride away with no intimation that I was hidden under his nose. I glanced toward the kitchen door. If I ran now, could I make it up the stairs and into the private rooms before anyone could lay hands on me?

"Don't even think about it," Master Hough muttered. "His Grace of Clarence has guards stationed. You'd not get within a stone's throw."

Inwardly I groaned. No, there was nothing I could do.

Or was there? I had only this one chance to take my fate into my own hands, shake it, and determine its direction. How could I not even try? I cast about for some action I might take.

Under my pallet. Of course. The wooden box still lay hidden, and within it, under the Book of Hours, was what I needed. If ever there was a time to toss the dice in a dangerous gamble, it was now. I must do it now! Abandoning the platter, I fled the kitchen with an excuse of visiting the privy. When I returned, Richard's magnificent gloves were tucked into the filthy bodice of my tunic.

"Master Hough." I stepped close under pretext of recovering the platter. "Would you give something to His Grace of Gloucester for me? If I asked it of you?"

His eyes were bright with curiosity. I saw no denial there.

"Would you see that His Grace gets these?"

I revealed the gloves, risking all. If he refused, God help me . . . Chin tilted, he looked at me, then took them with a brusque nod, pushing them into his belt as Master Pritchard bustled through the door. For the rest of the morning he went about his tasks as if nothing had passed between us, leaving me to hang precariously on my last spider's thread of hope. At some point, the gloves disappeared from Master Hough's belt.

Surely Richard would recognize them, the sumptuous embroidered emblems. How could he not recall my petulant confiscation of them in the chapel at Warwick? He would know and he would find me.

The day slid, hot and grimy, toward evening.

My ruse failed. No one came to rescue me.

Gloucester presumably left Cold Harbour, accepting Clarence's lies. The gloves either did not find their way into his hands or he had no recollection of them, of the circumstances of their loss. That smallest speck of hope dwindled to nothing. Weary to my bones, I went to my bed and wept in despair, caring nothing for my pride nor who heard me.

CHAPTER EIGHTEEN

Running feet sounded, pounding on the stair, echoing in the corridor. A stumble and slide were followed by a sharp curse. One of the serving lads, Jem, hurtled through the door in search of some source of authority with terror on his face.

"We're under attack, Master Hough." He gasped, lungs heaving. "Soldiers broken in!"

I had awoken heavy eyed and dull, slow to get into the daily routine. It took a moment for my brain to pick apart the words. I simply rejected them. Master Hough was also unmoved, hardly looking up from the dough he was shaping into round breads. "Nonsense, boy! We're at peace, or so the King says. Who'd attack this house?"

"They're in; I swear it. Through the gates. Courtyard's full of 'em."

"Lancastrians, were they? The Queen of Anjou herself, come to break her fast with His Grace of Clarence?"

"Didn't stop to see, master." Jem was oblivious to the heavy irony and the smirks around him. "But no women. Horses and weapons.

And soldiers. Dozens of 'em." His eyes gleamed, either in fear or excitement.

"Well, I daresay that'll put His Grace's nose out of joint, so early in the day." Master Hough hefted a pallet of loaves and headed for the oven.

"Do I bar the door, Master Hough?"

"Don't be foolish, lad. Too late for that, if they're through the gates. Just pray they're out for the blood of the nobility, not the loyal citizens of London like you and me. Get back there, Jem. Let's know only if my kitchens are to be overrun by a rabble of military." He rubbed flour from his hands with the resignation of a man who had seen it all over the years. "If we're to be taken prisoner, I'll not bother to start to roast the pig."

Despite the general disbelief, we stood about, unable to concentrate on any task. I read fear on the faces around me. War had brought siege to other noble households in London, ending in capture and execution of master and servants. Yet who would lead Lancaster with both old King Henry and the Prince dead? Jem returned at a run.

"You won't believe it! By God, you won't! It's Gloucester!"

"Ha! Then I suppose we'd better start roasting the pig after all. An invasion, forsooth! Just the Constable come to pay a courtesy call on his brother. You been drinking too much ale, Jem?"

But Jem was afire with news—and I, no longer heavy and unresponsive but light-headed with the possibility of escape, fell on every word of it, my fingers holding on to the edge of the table as if my life depended on it. "Not a *visit*, Master Hough! They've got weapons drawn. And you should hear the shouting from Clarence's rooms— enough to wake the devil himself. Don't know what's going on, but they're at each other's throats. There'll be blood spilled between them before this day's out. You'll see!"

Blood drained from my face, from my hands, until I felt icy cold in the heat of the kitchens. A darkness clouded my vision so that I held tight.

He'd come. At last—my captivity would be over. How could I have doubted him? *Breathe!* I instructed myself. *All you have to do is wait.* The noise began to reach us now, a distant hum and rumble of men on the move. The thud of booted feet, a mass of voices, occasional shouted orders.

"Sounds like they're searching the house." The cook tilted his head, listening, then shrugged his inability to prevent whatever occurred. But Steward Pritchard pushed his way into the room, thrusting aside Jem, who still hovered in the doorway.

"Master Hough . . ." Flustered as I had never seen him, flushed of face, Master Pritchard surveyed the room in a distracted manner, finally focusing on me. Without a word he swooped, took my arm in an ungentle grip, and would have dragged me from the room, again shouldering aside any who stood in his way.

"No . . . !" With my rescue at hand, the days of my role as a biddable servant were over.

I thought the steward hesitated, but only for a moment. "His Grace's orders are that you come with me."

"No. I won't." I would not be hidden away. My only chance of rescue was to remain where I was, in full view. If they were searching the house they would surely come here. I would not be locked away behind some solid door where I would never be found, where I might die and my body never be discovered until I was a moldering skeleton. In the fear of such a happening my imagination leaped to the extreme, lending force to my resistance. Master Pritchard was far larger and stronger than I, but I planted my feet and tore at his grip with my hands.

"Help me here!" Pritchard ordered.

No one did. They simply looked at us with a kind of awakening horror at the eruption of violence in their midst. The steward tried to grab my other arm but I used my fists against his chest.

"I won't be locked away. How dare you. Take your hands off me." All dignity was gone, all sense of exerting the authority of my name, replaced with a mindless terror. Now that freedom was so close, I would fight like a vixen in a hunter's trap. I used my foot against the steward's shin, my nails against his hands, encouraged by his grunt of pain, but I could not break his hold. I was being dragged toward the door.

"His Grace's orders must be followed," Master Pritchard muttered through clenched teeth.

"What's this, then?"

A sergeant at arms, sword drawn, blocked the doorway, men at his back. All eyes were drawn to him and the gleam of the metal blade. We had been so busy in the melee that we had not taken notice of the approach.

"What's going on?" he repeated, advancing farther as the knot of servants fell back.

A spiked silence fell, with more than one set of eyes sliding toward me.

"What do you want here in my kitchen, Sergeant?" Wiping his hands on a rag at his waist, Master Hough looked as if he would rather be anyplace but here.

"We're instructed by my lord of Gloucester to search for Lady Anne Neville. We're led to believe she's somewhere in the house." The officer looked around the kitchen, boredom writ clear, over the cook and steward, the maidservants. His glance swept over me, as smooth as butter. I doubt he saw Pritchard's fingers dig into the flesh of my upper arm. He certainly did not see the King's cousin and sister-in-law in the kitchen wench being taken to task for some misdemeanor.

The steward drew himself to his full pompous height. "I doubt you're likely to find a highborn lady such as the Lady Anne here." His fingers dug deeper yet. "She has already gone to Tewkesbury, as I'm sure His Grace of Clarence has made plain."

"Not true!" No amount of pain would keep me quiet. I stood straight and fixed my eyes on the sergeant, praying that he would see below the surface grime. "I am Anne Neville."

The guffaw was not unexpected, I suppose. I might try for confident dignity, but it could not offset my servile appearance. What a marvelous disguise Clarence had chosen. I doubt that at that moment even my mother would have recognized me. The sergeant laughed at my presumption. "Are you, now, mistress? And very haughty you are too. And I'm the King of France. Good day to you." He made a mock bow.

"No! You must listen. . . ."

With a hand lifted in apology to Master Hough, the sergeant would have turned on his heel, not even bothering to make a search. They were leaving. My hopes of rescue promptly disintegrated. "Sergeant. It is not as it seems. . . ." I heard the plea in my voice, but he didn't.

Then, when I could have wept from frustration, they fell back against the wall to allow passage along the corridor. I heard the fall of soft boots, and Gloucester stood in the kitchens, the sergeant snapping to attention.

"Nothing here, Your Grace."

"I think there is, if my information is correct. . . ."

Cloaked in velvet, jewels bright on his breast and in his hat, his magnificence incongruous in this setting, Gloucester stared around in uncompromising fashion. One hand clenched white fingered on the hilt of his sword in its scabbard: I thought it would not take much to push him to draw and use it. Grim faced, unsmiling, he swept a hard stare over the occupants of the kitchen much as the sergeant had done, lingering on the cook and steward, moving over me, then on . . .

His eyes snapped back, instantly arrested, certainly astonished, with a quickly hidden glint of amusement at what had been done. Doubtless at seeing the Neville heiress, cross and filthy, glaring at him when he failed to recognize her. But any humor was rapidly replaced with sheer anger as he acknowledged what he saw: me under restraint, Master Pritchard's hands heavy on my arms. He took a step forward, dangerous, menacing.

"So you are entertaining the Princess in the kitchens. An unusual circumstance, even for Clarence's household."

"Your Grace, I can explain. . . ."

"I doubt it. Take your hand from her arm." The hands dropped away. No one would defy Gloucester in this mood. "You will answer for this if the lady is harmed, Master Steward."

But his attention was now all for me, the grim lines of his face softening in what might almost have been a smile, as he removed his hat and bowed low before me.

"Your Highness. I would not have expected to find you here. I have come to pay my respects."

And the weight was suddenly, miraculously lifted from my heart. Richard was here; he had found me. His amusement at my expense lifted the horror of it all, relief flowed through me from head to foot, and I picked up my disgusting skirts with soot-smeared hands and swept a curtsy worthy of the Princess he had called me.

"And not before time, Your Grace. I had hoped to see you some days ago." Levity swirled in me, an instantaneous joy, tempting me to laugh aloud.

"So I think."

I saw the anger return, tightening the muscles in his jaw, but he kept it close as he held out his hand. I placed mine there as if we were at some royal audience. Again I felt the urge to laugh. How ridiculous, the royal Duke and the kitchen wench. He raised my hand to his lips in a grand gesture, but not before his fingers had smoothed over the roughness there. As he lifted his head, his stare bright with fury holding mine, I knew that, even without words, he sensed what I had suffered.

His tacit acknowledgment soothed all my pain.

"You should not have been subjected to this." His lips barely brushed my fingers, but they were more a balm than any potion of Master Hough's, on my hand and on my heart.

"How did you know?" I asked.

"You sent the gloves."

"But that I was *here*."

"Margery told me. She wept at my feet."

Keeping hold of me, he stepped back to lead me out as if I were the greatest of ladies in silks and precious stones. I stopped in the doorway to look back, grasped his hand hard, and remembered his words of retribution to Pritchard, the grim expression in his face. So I smiled at Master Hough.

"You were kind to me. I thank you for it." Looking up at Richard, I assured him, "I was treated well. They followed orders because they were threatened with dismissal, but I was not mistreated."

"You have my gratitude." Richard inclined his head gravely, drawing me after him. By now his impatience was a palpable thing, even as I took the time to recover my precious box. As we walked along the corridor, he stripped off his cloak to wrap it around me, pulling up the hood to shield me from any interested gaze with a thoughtfulness that almost undermined my control. Then we were out, into the light and fresh air of the courtyard.

Freedom.

Unless Clarence chose to bar the way.

It was a shock to step out into the world again. With the light bright, the winter sun surprisingly warm on my face, I felt that I had been incarcerated for far longer than the weeks it had been. The noise and bustle of the troops in the courtyard startled me, a considerable force still returning from their search of the property and milling in noisy disarray, all bearing the white boar livery. Directing his escort to mount, Richard led me across to where his squire held his horse. Where he would take me, I did not know, but neither did I care, only that I should never set foot in Cold Harbour again. Soon, very soon, I would ride through those gates to freedom.

It was not to be, as I must have known. Not without a confrontation.

Clarence was waiting for us. Not Isabel, as I saw immediately. She had made herself scarce, probably watching even now, spying on us through one of the windows that glinted like so many eyes around the courtyard. I was not unhappy that I did not have to face her. What would I say to a sister who had plotted and conspired to reduce me to nothing so that she could take all? But there was His Grace of Clarence, standing on the top step, surveying his courtyard as if in command of a victorious army. How I detested him, his arrogant assurance, his certainty that he could still prevent me from leaving. I despised him to the depth of my heart.

Richard barely acknowledged him beyond a curt inclination of his head. I supposed they had said all that was to be said. But in a sense it gave me satisfaction to see Clarence's anger at what had transpired.

"Gloucester! She'll not leave without my permission! And I don't give it!"

Beyond care, beyond watching his words, he addressed us as if we were alone and private, not distressingly public with the whole force at our back, with ears and eyes straining to enjoy the airing of the dirty linen of the nobility. Hot emotion coated him from head to foot, a determination to be obeyed. He could barely stand still, an uncomfortable comparison with his brother, who remained impervious through it all. Gloucester's anger had turned to ice, and was the deadlier for it. I felt it all but vibrate through him as he kept his hand on mine. Only a muscle flexed along his jaw—the only sign of temper. I could face Clarence without fear, knowing that nothing would persuade Richard to let me go now, even when Clarence strode from his position and seized Richard's bridle from the squire.

"You'll not leave with her," he repeated, teeth clenched.

"You'll not stop me. We leave together."

Hackles raised, they were two fighting cocks squaring off. Brothers by birth, yet so dissimilar in looks and temperament, their hostility charged the air between them with a dangerous tension.

"I am her guardian, God damn you! I say where she will live, whom she will wed."

"You are not her guardian. She is of age. And what guardian would consign his ward—and a Neville, by God!—to work in the kitchens as a drudge? You'll pay for this, Clarence. I swear you will."

"And who will exact the price, little brother? You?" The sneer was ugly; venom filled the courtyard. Suddenly Clarence had a sword in his hand. I suppressed a whimper, a sure symptom of my nervous state, as he raised the point to rest against Richard's breastbone. But if Richard was unnerved, it was not apparent. With a careless hand he pushed the blade away, never taking his eyes, dark and stony, from Clarence. His laugh was hard and humorless.

"Will you run me through, unarmed and unprovoked, before so many witnesses? That's not your style! Look around you, brother. It may be your house, but all I see are my men with enough force and weapons to call you to account. You'll not live out the minute if you harm me or mine."

When Clarence's eyes flickered at the threat I knew him for a coward. The point of his blade wavered, yet still he would not retreat from verbal attack. "She's not yours. She'll never be yours. God damn you to hell!"

"Not for rescuing the lady from a situation that was humiliating and degrading."

By now I was beyond weary. I tightened my fingers on Richard's sleeve, clutched his cloak around me to bolster my dignity, and, whatever the wisdom of it, I stepped between them in an attempt to bring an end to the increasingly tense confrontation.

"It is my wish to leave this place." Inwardly I marveled at the steadiness of my voice when tears of exhaustion and relief were not far away. Still, I was able to raise my head, firm my shoulders. "I will go with Gloucester. It is my choice. Put up your sword."

"You hear her." I was drawn gently back into the protection of Richard's arm. "The game's over. You are undone, brother."

The sword was slammed back into its scabbard. "I'll not forget this!" Clarence's parting shot was an empty husk.

"Neither shall I. I should thrash you for it. She did not deserve such outrageous treatment."

The chasm yawned at our feet. I was not the cause, yet I felt the guilt. This rift between them would never be mended, nor the one between myself and Isabel. I was sorry for it, but the healing was beyond me, just as the creation of the divide was not of my doing. Ambition and greed had destroyed my family and now seemed likely to do the same with Richard's. For now there was nothing more to be done. Richard signaled to his men to mount up, then turned to me, the lines about his mouth softened despite his lingering temper.

"Will you come with me?"

It was a quaintly polite request given the circumstances, allowing me the opportunity to change my mind if I so wished, but he knew the answer.

"I will." And I meant more than just the journey out through the gates. As had he.

So Richard swung up onto his horse, holding the animal in check as the sergeant lifted me, so that I might ride pillion behind him, my box stowed safely away.

"Hold tight. Hold on to me."

And I did, Clarence scowling after us, as I left Cold Harbour forever.

The journey was astonishingly short and entirely uneventful. I had thought it might be to Westminster, or even to the Tower of London, where accommodation could be found for me. Any closetlike room in any one of the towers would be preferable. Not Warwick Inn, my father's London house, where it would be a simple matter for Clarence to take me into custody again. Perhaps Baynard's Inn then, Richard's family home in the city. But Richard had other ideas, and led his force rapidly through the streets of the city. We rode in silence, with an urgency I could feel through the palms of my hands pressed against his waist. Conscious of my appearance, I kept the hood pulled up, the folds of the cloak close wrapped, not wishing to be seen and recognized and gossiped over. On the other hand, everyone must know the royal Duke. There were calls of support when the white boar was glimpsed, causing him to raise his hand in acknowledgment.

Meanwhile, as his stallion checked and sidled at the noise and bustle around us, I held tight as I had been instructed, my cheek turned against the chilly velvet of his doublet. It was no hardship to do so, not so difficult to enjoy the firmness of his soldier's frame. It crossed my mind that he must be cold in the sharp wind without his cloak, but it had been a grand gesture. I snuggled into the soft folds without compunction. Then we were riding along Newgate and I knew where he would take me. It was the obvious place for a lady whose freedom was under any form of threat. So it was no surprise when we turned into the mellow stone buildings of St. Martin le Grand and its welcome sanctuary. The gates were opened as we approached so that I could only presume we were expected. The peace of the sanctuary fell about me.

It was a seamless arrival and I played my part as if in a dream, with words of gratitude, only now realizing how physically spent I was. I barely listened to the low-voiced conversation between Richard and the priest who came forward to receive us. Nor did I respond when the silent priest led me into the warren of corridors, apparently unmoved by my sudden and unusual arrival. Rooms suitable to my rank had been made ready, I noted, well furnished and comfortable enough. There was a quietness here, a calm distancing from the world as the noise of the city seemed far off beyond the closed windows. A fire had been lit to welcome me. The impression of thoughtful care was suddenly overwhelming.

Yet I felt that Richard was in a hurry, with no thought to stay. He stood just within the door as the cleric bowed himself out. "You'll be safe here. I've spoken with your uncle, who's only too willing to ensure your sanctuary. Clarence cannot harm you here."

"Thank you." I knew my uncle well. My father's brother George Neville, Archbishop of York, would allow no man to dictate to him. I would be safe under his fierce protection. Now that Richard and I were alone together embarrassment took hold of me. Unsure of what to do next, I took off the cloak and folded it over the settle. Then as the warm air surrounded me, I sniffed. The combined reek of smoke and tallow and fat, of unwashed clothes and my own unwashed body, rose to my nostrils in pungent waves.

"You might want to burn this." Stroking the soft nap, I regarded him quizzically. "I don't think I should return it to you in this state!" I tried to smile my apology but seemed drained of all feeling. All was still so uncertain, because although I was free of Clarence I could see no clear way before me. Nor could I see the way for myself and Richard. Then I caught his eye. It held a speculative gleam.

"What?" Even I could hear the edge in my voice.

"I don't know whether I should laugh at your amazing appearance, Princess, or return to Cold Harbour and run Clarence through with his own sword."

"By the Virgin, don't you dare laugh!"

To do him justice, he did not. I think he read me well enough to sense that it might just push me over the edge into a cataclysm of either tears or temper. Instead he looked me over from head to foot and I cringed at what I knew he must see. I was Mary, a kitchen maid, from the coarse linen veil covering my greasy hair to the skirt of my overdress, looped up in my belt to keep it from the ashes. From my grease-spattered bodice and grubby sleeves to my ill-made shoes I was not a picture to delight the eye of any man. And I was woman enough to despair at what he must see. I dropped my gaze to the level of his own luxurious boots. I could not bear to see disgust or distaste in his face. I resisted the desire to scratch as I waited for him to leave.

To my horror, Richard advanced.

"Don't come near me!" I raised my hands, palms out, eyes now lifting to his. "Don't tell me what I look like!"

But still he came on, and reached out to take my hands, until I thrust them behind me to hide the evidence of my work in my sister's kitchens. Undeterred he took my arms, drawing me forward, persisting until my hands lay within his. I stared in dismay at the contrast. True, his were the hands of a soldier, with calluses from sword and rein, but they were still well tended. Jewels flashed on his fingers; his nails were well pared. They were the hands of a courtier. Whereas mine, even in the short time I had mistreated them . . .

I hissed in a breath as I contemplated the ruin. "The remnants of poor Mary Fletcher."

"Who?"

I shook my head, ridiculously shamed that he should see me like this, as if it were my own fault. I could not speak, watching him, needing to see the truth. If it was disgust, then I must know it. But his face took on a grim, unreadable cast as he smoothed his fingers over my roughened knuckles, gray with ingrained grime. What he thought of my nails, ragged and torn with black edges, I could not imagine. Then there were the burns and rough patches, a red weal across my wrist that my sleeve could not hide. When I drew in a breath in discomfort at the pressure of his hands, he released me.

Perhaps he was disgusted after all.

"I must leave you, Anne. I have business with the King."

"Of course." My disappointment was intense, but I would not show it.

"You are alone here, but you are entirely safe."

"Yes."

With a little smile, and despite my stiffening, he rubbed his knuckles gently along my cheek before bending to replace them with his lips, as soft as a breath. It was the most unexpected of salutes, and considering my unwashed state it was an act of true chivalry. Then he was on his way, opening the door. Well, of course he would have other things to do. But at the door Richard looked back and his smile widened at sight of my scowl.

"Do I look so very bad?" I asked.

"Yes. But you'll be beautiful again. I'll send someone with hot water."

I returned the smile. "By the Virgin, I shall be grateful."

And laughed aloud when I realized that he had left the cloak behind.

A lengthy moment of sheer and utter bliss.

I sank up to my chin in the liquid heat. True to his word, Richard had given the order, resulting in a procession of servants bringing to my rooms a wooden tub and buckets of hot water. My knees under my chin, it was a tight fit even for my small frame, but the heat and the scattering of herbs lulled me until I found myself drifting into sleep, until I shook myself awake, the sharp perfume of rosemary restoring me to clear thought as its oils soothed my hurts.

What now?

The room was quiet around me. After so many days, weeks, when my every movement was watched, both in England and in France, it was a moment to be savored. One of the young maids, Meggie, had offered to stay and see to my needs but had left to find a suitable robe and a shift and hopefully a pair of shoes that would come close to fitting. Nothing would persuade me to don my filthy servant's garb again. So, absorbing the stillness, I brought my mind to bear on the future.

Marriage to Richard, when His Holiness the Pope saw fit to grant his dispensation. Delight touched me from head to foot, soft and luxurious, as comforting as the scented herbs, coupled with a disturbing fire between my thighs that owed nothing to the heat of the bath. It licked and bloomed at the thought of belonging to Richard at last, driving bright color to my hairline.

Enough! I rubbed my hands over my face, directing my thoughts elsewhere, to the matter of my inheritance. Richard would support me, fight for what was mine. I could put that to one side until the marriage documents were signed and sealed. Another worry raised its head to take its place, causing me to sit up, muscles tight. What of my mother, who seemed destined to live out her days in Beaulieu with no one to fight for her cause, while her inherited wealth was discussed and squabbled over as if she were already in her grave?

But *I* would fight for her, I promised myself. I would never allow Clarence to grab what was not rightfully Isabel's. As soon as I was Duchess of Gloucester I would insist on the Countess's release. Richard would get it for me.

Promising to write to her, to reassure her of my intentions on her behalf, I sank back beneath the water to the tip of my nose.

The maid returned and bustled around me. She soaped and washed my long hair, rinsing it again and again until it squeaked through her fingers and I sighed with sheer pleasure. Clucking much as Margery would have done, she proceeded to rub a salve into my hands. It would take longer to put those to rights. Dressed in a shift and a loose robe, both of which swamped me and trailed on the floor, my hair combed out over my shoulders to dry, I was left alone again to sit at the window, idly watching the comings and goings in the street below. Sliding my feet out of the overlarge shoes, I tucked them under me and set myself the task of taking stock.

I should have been full of happiness. But the sharp darts of worry returned, a flurry of accurate arrows to pierce and annoy, with Richard at their center. The specter of Edward of Lancaster's death continued to hover over me, my mind following that tortuous path again and again to dim my previous delight. Nor could I rest as my mind covered the same old ground, that an ambitious man would wed an heiress even if he hated her worse than the devil! No, Richard did not hate me. But did he want to wed me for my wealth, claiming my inheritance much as Clarence was claiming Isabel's? Was that why he had put himself at such odds with his brother to rescue me? If that was so, there was little to choose between the two brothers, Clarence or Gloucester.

No. I would never believe that.

In sudden, honest recollection, I pressed my fingers against my lips, savoring the reminiscent clench in my belly. Richard had come to me, rescued me. Richard had not kissed me as if his only interest were my wealth. I remembered the stark lines on his face, the brilliance of his eyes as he stared at me. The heat, the force, the *fierceness* of it. Was that the kiss of a lover? I had no experience to guide me except that it had turned my knees to water, my heart to the sweetness of honey. I would gladly repeat it if Richard were of a mind. . . .

I hoped he would return, and soon.

But he did not.

*   *   *

I remained in my room. Dinner at eleven o'clock was heralded by Meggie with a mug of ale and a platter of bread and hard cheese before she was gone, leaving me to fill the long hours of the afternoon, so that when there was a knock on the door of my parlor, I leaped to my feet to open it.

"Margery!"

Flushed, her veil ruffled as if she had come in a rush, she stood on the threshold, as stout and stolid as ever, with a beaming smile and the shine of moisture in her eyes. Before I could say more than her name in astonishment, she had enfolded me in her arms, crushing me there as her whole body heaved with emotion.

"My lady! My little Anne! Thank God!"

Squirming to be released, I pulled her into the room but did not leave go of her hands.

"You can't imagine how glad I am to see you, Margery. How have you come here?"

She wiped her eyes on her sleeve and sniffed. "Gloucester's doing. He came back—I told him I won't serve your sister longer. I've left Cold Harbour and brought your belongings with me. All packed up ready, if you remember." She gave a watery chuckle. "I'll serve you. You're all that's left. . . . Your father dead, your poor dear mother shut away, and Isabel in league with the devil. What *that man* has done to her. I would never have believed her capable of such cruel selfishness! So I've come to serve you, as your mother would wish. I'll not let him lay hands on you again. I swear it in the name of the Blessed Virgin." Once more she hugged me tight and we shed tears as women will, until Margery stepped back with a deep sigh and mopped her eyes.

And then there was a commotion on the threshold, a cursing Francis Lovell and two soldiers struggling with a large chest between them that they placed just inside the door.

"There! Your clothes and possessions, as I said." Back in her element, Margery moved to throw back the lid and inspect the contents, clucking her tongue over the layers of gowns and underskirts, bodices and shifts. "The Duchess tried to keep them but I was having none of that. They're yours and she's no right to them. . . ." She took the time to scowl at my strange attire and bare feet. "I'll unpack them for you. You need some suitable clothes if you're to receive guests." Her scowl was turned on Francis, who merely grinned back. "I think we might be here some time until all this mess is sorted out. And I won't answer for my actions if His Grace of Clarence tries to set even one foot into these rooms." She looked around with pursed lips. "Could be worse, I suppose. . . ." I heard her grumbling mildly as she bustled about and into the adjoining bedchamber.

"Francis! How can I thank you? You don't know what it means to have Margery with me. I admit I was beginning to feel melancholy."

He shook his head, denying his role with typical self-deprecation. "That won't do. It was Gloucester's decision. He didn't like to leave you alone here."

"I was feeling abandoned." I paused. "I thought he might return."

"Urgent matters of state. But he thought you were sad and very alone and that Margery would do the trick. She was more than willing to come, as you'll be aware." His eyes might twinkle but I thought he was stepping warily around the "urgent matters."

"I suppose Richard is very busy."

"Yes. He holds the reins. The King's traveled west to the Marches."

"Francis . . . I know he wants the marriage . . ." I stated carefully. "But do you think he cares for me?"

"Do you think he doesn't?" Francis's brows rose in quizzical disbelief.

"I don't know."

"Then you don't know him very well. If you'd had to live with him, as I had, since you went missing, you wouldn't doubt it."

"No?" I pounced immediately. "Then tell me, Francis." Here was a chance to discover what lay behind the enigmatic exterior that Richard had cultivated with such success.

"Nothing much to tell, except that he was beside himself with worry. He didn't spell it out but he knew what Clarence was capable of. If Clarence could accuse his own mother of prostituting herself, and his brother of bastardy, to strengthen his own claim to the throne . . . If he could do that . . . Richard feared the worst. And when he got your letter—we were at Middleham in the throes of a land dispute—he swept aside the two protagonists who were squabbling over a strip of woodland without a word beyond that he would be back—sometime—and rode with barely a stop and the horses all but foundering. And then when he couldn't find you there . . . I thought he would ride immediately for Tewkesbury, staying for nothing but a snatched meal and a fresh mount. But Isabel told him you had changed your mind about the marriage and chosen to take the veil and so all was cast into disorder."

"Did he believe her?"

"No. Not for a minute. He blamed Clarence."

So, I thought, Francis's summing up had put me firmly in my place. I might doubt Richard, but he had never doubted me. I felt my cheeks flush uncomfortably, a justifiable twinge of shame.

"And then he was given the gloves," Francis continued, obviously unaware of my discomfort. "A servant stopped us just as we had ridden out through the gates. I thought he would turn about immediately and demand to search Cold Harbour from cellar to turret. But good sense prevailed. And me whispering in his ear." He chuckled reminiscently. "It would have given satisfaction to ruffle His Grace of bloody Clarence's fine feathers, but far better to do it when we were better prepared. So we came back this morning with a proper force and did the job well. Richard spent last night prowling his rooms like old King Henry's caged lion at the Tower. And with a temper to match. I left him to it in the end."

"So he cared."

"Yes, foolish girl," he replied as he would when I was a child, not adult and a Princess. "He cared." Francis hesitated with his hand on the latch. "He says to look in the chest. Then *you* will see what *he* can see. He says it will put your mind at rest—unless you're determined to be churlish!"

*   *   *

I rummaged impatiently in the chest.

"What are you looking for?" Margery huffed impatiently at my side as I got under her feet.

"I don't know. Something from Richard . . ."

Then I found it, wrapped in its covering of linen. It had slid down the side, and I knew what it was as soon as I put my hand to it. A mirror, a polished silver disk, as I discovered when I unwrapped it, its handle engraved with curls of leaves and vines. I purred with pleasure. Where had he acquired such a lovely thing? I held it before me. It did not reflect a true image, but was good enough for its purpose.

He said I would see what he saw.

I realized that it was a long time since I had last looked in a mirror. At Middleham, when Richard had kissed Maude and I had been heartbroken at what I saw, at my lack of attraction, I had studied my reflection with displeasure. What a child I had been then. But not now. Carrying the mirror to the light from the window, I looked. And was astonished. I had changed through these recent months of exile and marriage, of battle and sorrow and guarded freedom. Always dark and sallow skinned and slight of stature, because those would never change, I had to admit to an improvement. Maturity had laid its kind hand on me at last. I pursed my lips in sharp appraisal. My hair shone after Meggie's ministrations. My cheekbones were high and almost elegant beneath smooth skin. Broad brow, straight nose, firm lips. I touched them, outlined them. My eyes, I thought, were my best feature, of darkest blue and offset by dark lashes, even if at times they were uncomfortably forthright and direct. Perhaps I had grown into my looks, whereas I swear Isabel's had been evident from the day of her birth. Beautiful? I would not have said so. But not so bad . . . If a man had a taste for slim, dark-haired, dark-eyed women.

Perhaps what Richard saw pleased him after all.

"He sees the spirit. The courage." Margery smiled as she read my thoughts with uncanny accuracy. "It makes you glow, lady."

I allowed myself to enjoy the moment with a warm complacence.

By the time Richard returned—and not so many hours later, if truth be told, however inclined I was to be scathing of his absence—I was well scrubbed, sweet-smelling. Clad in my own garments, cosseted by Margery, I felt my confidence restored and my sour mood lightened by Francis's visit, yet I was circumspect. I might long to see Richard, to have plain speaking between us at last, imagining that he could smooth out the golden path to future happiness, but I was not so naive as to believe that he could do so. Francis had painted a clearer picture of matters at court by what he said and even more by what he did *not* say. It was not as simple as whether Richard might or might not love me. All manner of separate strands existed to complicate our relationship, strands of power and politics and double-dealing woven into the whole, not least the rift between him and Clarence.

So I waited for him with some apprehension, although my smile of welcome was heartfelt and I prayed that it masked my doubts. For her part, Margery all but fell at his feet in gratitude. She was a lost cause, I realized, her loyalty completely won over. I would never get a balanced view of Gloucester's faults and failings from her.

Richard took Margery's hands when she curtsied and lifted her bulk to her short height, kissing her knuckles with a gleam of humor. "Do you approve of your new quarters, then?" He was of a mind for jesting, I decided, so I would go along with it.

"No, Your Grace. I don't." Margery was never one to hold back, although her face flushed with pleasure at his concern. "They're not suitable for the Lady Anne. But in the circumstances . . . When I think of her in that kitchen, it's enough to make my blood boil."

"It won't be for long. The sanctuary is the best I can do, and Archbishop Neville's name is enough to deter most men."

"So I should think, Your Grace. But where we can go for the lady to make a permanent home, I don't know." Her grumbles would continue forever. "It's not suitable that—"

"Margery! Enough!" With a laugh I waved her to silence before she could get into full flow as Richard turned his considering gaze on me.

"You look rested, lady."

"I am." His stare encompassed me as if he would detect any weakness in me. I straightened my shoulders against any such intrusion.

"And you have survived your ordeal well."

"Undeniably. I can gut a pike and pluck and stuff a capon with great skill."

"I'm relieved to hear it." The gleam in his eyes intensified. "If ever I fall on hard times I can rest assured my wife will rise to the occasion."

His *wife*! I swallowed hard but clung to the light banter. Better than the dangerous waters to come. "Master Hough praised my lack of squeamishness when the capon escaped its basket and ran around the kitchen and I had to take an ax to the creature's neck."

"And who might Master Hough be?"

"Clarence's cook, of course. A most skilled man whose praise was in scant supply. He wouldn't let me near the venison!"

"I'm sure you managed admirably, with or without the venison."

I could no longer control my smile. "Yes, I did. I thought of Clarence with every chop of the capon's neck!" And I brought the edge of my hand down with relish.

"Ah! Bloodthirsty too."

But we were deliberately skirting around a mess of problems here. I knew it, as did he. Margery left us at a sign from me, not unwillingly but with a stern glance in my direction. It said quite plainly, *Watch your words; remember your manners.* She would always have a care for me and I would trust her to my grave, but I needed no chaperone for what I would say. As soon as the door closed behind her, all the wit and good humor fell away, as quick as a snuffed candle.

"What is it?" he asked softly, cautiously. He came to me, took my hands.

So I had failed to hide my fear. "It's just that . . ." I closed my eyes, took a breath; Richard waited with such patience as I untangled my worries. There were so many questions, so many barriers still seemingly between us. Francis had told me Richard cared. But there was that other, monstrous obstacle that I had refused to face for too long. I could do so no longer.

"What troubles you, Anne? I can resolve it, whatever it is."

He was so confident. His belief that he could erase my fears and my grief brought me to the edge of tears. But I must not. I stripped my terrible fear bare, without finesse.

"Did you kill the Prince, Richard? Did you kill Prince Edward?"

"Yes."

"Oh!" It took my breath away completely. I had been hoping that he would deny it, make some excuse. That my dream had been only a vicious twisting of the truth or that the priest at Tewkesbury had mistaken the dreadful event. Perhaps it had been King Edward all along who dispatched his intemperate enemy. But Richard had claimed the deed without hesitation. "Oh . . . !" My mind seemed frozen with the horror of it, unable to move from that scene of Richard with the bloody blade in his hand.

"It's no secret. I don't . . ." And I saw the exact moment, when his eyes snapped to mine and searched my face, that understanding dawned on him. Brows drawing together, he let his hands fall from me as if the touch scorched him. "You thought I murdered him in cold blood. Is that it?"

"I don't know. But I think you might."

"That I would murder him?"

"It is what I was told."

"Then hear the truth. It was no murder. I'll swear it if you wish, but I'll make no easy justification for my actions." His eyes, bright with furious conviction, fixed on mine. "I killed him when he was brought before us in Tewkesbury Abbey. Even as a prisoner, defeated and disarmed, with nothing between him and death but Edward's mercy, he remained intransigent. 'By what right,' he dared ask the King, 'do you take what is mine? I am King of England, not you.'" Richard gave a bark of laughter. "I don't know whether it was courage or rash stupidity. It was certainly outrageously foolhardy." Although his gaze remained on my face, I thought he did not see me. As if he were focused on that memory of more than six months ago. "I remember Clarence approached Lancaster with soft words, to quiet his temper. If anything, he saw it as a further betrayal and it lit the flame. Even though he was surrounded, hemmed in with guards, Lancaster tried to snatch Clarence's dagger from his belt. He got it too—I admit to being careless with the King's person. I had no thought that Lancaster would go to such lengths. Next thing we knew, before we could restrain him, he was lunging toward the King."

It was so like my dream. Same actions, same outcome, but how different was the interpretation. And it was so much in character that I could imagine the Prince wagering all on that final throw of the dice, a foolish and hopeless attempt to cut down his enemy with Clarence's dagger, even when surrounded by men who would have no compunction in killing him if provoked. The Prince would never accept defeat. Never this side of the grave.

I sighed, a slow acceptance. Yes, that was undoubtedly what would have happened. "Richard . . ."

"For that reason I killed him," Richard continued as if I had not spoken. "As Constable of England, the personal security of the King and of the realm is given into my keeping. Would you have me stand back and allow Lancaster to stab Edward to the heart?"

"No. I would not." I knew it for the truth.

"Anne . . . did you care for him?" In one stride Richard stood close before me, had reclaimed my hands, forcefully now, and I saw the lines of anger in his face. I knew I had hurt him, questioning his integrity. His eyes were all darkness on mine so that a flutter of trepidation, not unpleasant, caught in my throat. "Did he have a place in your heart?" he demanded harshly. "You were with him, wed to him for nigh on six months. Did he kiss you like this?" His lips were hard and sure on mine, leaving me breathless. "Did he touch you like this?" His hands swept down from shoulder to hip, a deliberate, almost insolent act of possession that set up a tremor in my limbs.

"No. Nothing like that." Startled by this sudden slip of control in a man who governed every emotion, every action, I was even more shocked by my own delight that I could move him to such emotion. Yet I could not tell him the truth, not all of it. Shame held me silent, as if the blame were mine.

"You were mine before you were ever his." Desire, rich and ripe, flowed over me from his words.

"I always was. But you had left me. . . ."

"Not of my own volition." Then, with difficulty and a bid for softness: "Did you love him, Anne?"

So that was it. I had not realized the depths of his jealousy. It might be difficult for Richard to ask it, but there was no hesitation in my answering. My assurance came directly, fiercely even. "No. I did not love him. I pitied him—at first. As I grew to know him—I feared him. Even hated him." I would not explain how he had struck me when he had found Richard's letter, how he had exulted in my humiliation when my father was dead. How he had made vicious accusation, without foundation, of my supposed intimacy with Richard. I could not tell him that. It was too shaming for me. I said what I could, and what was in my heart. "I did not love the Prince. And without doubt he despised me, unless he needed someone to impress with his skills and his glorious ambition."

"He was handsome enough." Richard still was not convinced. "He had the measure of me there."

I laughed softly. So my love was as susceptible to vanity as I. "He was handsome. But there was a darkness in him that repelled me." In a strange reversal, I felt in that moment unutterably sad for the Prince, slain for his intemperate ambitions, for the grief and humiliation he had willfully heaped on me, for all of us caught up in this conflict.

When I blinked and tried to focus on the jewels in Richard's collar my eyes blurred with tears.

"Look up," Richard murmured, gentle in response to my grief, hands now loosely around my wrists. "I would not distress you. Then there are no secrets between us?"

"No. There are none."

Yet I saw the shine of doubt in his eyes. He hesitated, as if the thoughts were difficult to express for a man who leaned toward reticence. Then he plunged. "You raised the matter and I answered. I need to know that you accept what I did. Oh, I admit readily to jealousy. I hated that he should have you when I could not. But that had no part in Lancaster's death. My killing of the Prince was an act of sheer necessity. If you cannot accept what I did, Anne, it will always lie between us. In its shadow there can be no trust. Sometimes duty and the needs of the hour demand a course of action. I am not always proud of what I have done, but I have never acted in cruelty or self-interest. You should know me well enough to know that I would not." He hesitated the length of a heartbeat. "I know you never gave your consent to this marriage—even though Edward presumed that you would. You said only that you would consider it. I need you to consider it now. Can you accept me as I am, blemishes and all? Sins and all? If you take the good parts you have to take the less than good. Can you accept that? Otherwise I see no happiness between us."

I let his words, this amazing stripping of his soul, lie on my heart as I searched his face, seeking the thoughts behind the stern set of his features. When had he become so difficult to read? When had he decided that it was better to hide his emotions from everyone as if they did not exist? Life at court, I supposed, where enemies masqueraded as friends, where it was necessary to guard one's political back from the assassin's knife. Once I would have pried and poked until I cracked the smooth face of the surface, regardless of his feelings. I could no longer do that, unless he allowed it.

"Will you wed me? With Edward of Lancaster's blood on my

hands?" he asked again when I still hesitated, suspended in my own indecision.

Richard needed honesty from me at this time more than ever before. So I would give it. "I said I would consider marriage and I will. I would like this night to do so. Give me until tomorrow, Richard, and I will give you my answer."

It tore my heart to do it, to see the flicker, the faintest flicker of doubt that I had sown in his mind. But I would weigh his words and make my decision. And in the way of a woman who had been made to feel insecure, unwanted, unloved—and had still not heard the man who would wed her actually speak the words that his love was hers!—I would keep him waiting just a little while.

Richard stepped back, bowed formally.

"Until tomorrow, lady."

How difficult it was to balance one side against the other. I had long acknowledged that the boy I had known had gone for good. Now I was faced with the man. Could I love him, respect him? Put all the past behind me with the guilt and recriminations? If I couldn't, as Richard had intimated, there was no comfortable path forward for us.

One thing was clear: This was not the simple continuation of our childhood relationship but a different and complicated leap into a world of power and political scheming. How strange it was. We had so many shared memories, such intimate knowledge of each other, and yet . . . It was as if the foundations were the same but the walls were different. Different construction, different perspectives. I saw in this man a wielder of power, a man who would enjoy its rewards. I thought he might be ruthless in getting his own way. He was certainly more reserved, more taciturn than he had ever been, more unapproachable. Could I truly love him?

"Is it possible for a woman to love a man who has blood on his hands?" I asked Margery as she braided my hair.

"Depends whose blood, and why it lies there, my lady." She attacked a knot with vigor.

"Because the man who was killed was a danger to others, and to the kingdom."

"If you mean my lord of Gloucester's dispatching of the Prince of Lancaster . . . good riddance, I say!"

I sighed. I would get no fair balancing of judgment here.

How much blood had my mother been forced to accept on my father's hands? Too much, many would say, and not all in battle. Yet she had remained true to him, loyal until the day of his death. Had she ever questioned, ever cast recrimination as I was now doing? Of course she had. She would not be the woman she was if she had accepted all without judgment.

"Ask yourself this, lady." Margery prepared to leave me to my solitary contemplations. "If the Prince could have killed Gloucester, would he have given it more than a passing thought? Even if it was stabbing him in the back?"

"No."

"Why, then, do you need to worry your sleep?"

I presumed that Richard had spent as troubled a night as I, since he was at my door barely after dawn. He launched into his obviously prepared speech before I had pushed aside my cup and platter. Gone was the cold composure, the careful distancing. Here was the boy I had loved, full of tense energy. For the first time I felt that the outcome between us mattered to Richard on a purely personal level.

"Before you give me your decision—let me say this, Anne. Whatever the outcome . . . you have my love, my regard. There will be no compulsion. . . ."

All my intentions of graciously soft and smooth words fled. "No compulsion? You'll hound me unmercifully until you get your own way! We both know it, so don't tell me that you'll allow me to retire unwed, or accept the hand of another."

"Am I so obstinate?" I saw the flare of temper in his eyes. "Not as obstinate as you . . ."

I stopped him with a hand on his arm. "Hear my decision first. Then tell me I'm obstinate. I accept what you did. I acknowledge the need. I'll not allow the Prince of Lancaster to stand between us in death as he did in life. He will not be allowed to be a restless ghost to divide us."

Richard flexed his shoulders as if a weight had been lifted. I could see the storm of relief move through him. So I would leap the second barrier. "Now I need to know this—do you love me, Richard?"

"You know that I do."

"No, I don't! When we were together at court, when we were young, then I knew, or I thought I did. Even when we were at Warwick and all was so difficult . . . But so much has happened since then. Treachery and exile for both of us. I am not so ingenuous, believing that love will overcome all. We are so taken up with power and inheritance, the demands of Clarence, the threat of renewed warfare. You have barely exchanged a handful of words with me since my return to court. You were driven to abduct me, but even then it was all dealing and negotiation. How do I know that you love me? You have not said so." I could feel my anxieties rising again as the words poured out. "I will wed you but my fears have not been laid to rest. For all I still know, you want my inheritance more than you want me."

"We've been over this before, Anne. I thought . . ." He looked beleaguered.

"Richard . . . I understand what you say, but I've spent an unconscionable length of time as a kitchen maid because of it. I am carried along like a twig, helplessly into every ripple and eddy of a stream in full flood, and I don't like it. Do you love me, Richard? We were children when we last spoke of this. If your heart has changed . . . I would rather know the truth. I will marry you because it is in the best interests of both of us. I can accept that. But do you *love* me? Because my heart aches for you." I could not make it plainer. I never thought I would lay myself open to such possibility of hurt, but I had done just that.

"Yes. I do."

"Is that it?"

"I love you with every bone in my body."

I thought he was smiling at me. I would not have it. "You have been distant and silent, Richard, keeping me from your confidence. Deliberately so, to my mind. And don't smile at me! I am no longer a child to be patronized!"

The smile vanished. "This seems to be the day for truth. Your intuition is as strong as ever." Amusement glimmered again before solemnity set in. "I stand accused and am guilty, but in my own defense I would say this: My purpose, first and last, was always to protect *you*. Clarence would stop at nothing to block our marriage. I could not put myself weakly into his hands by singling you out. It was better that he think I was uninterested or looked elsewhere for a wife. So I remained cold and distant, as you rightly say. I did not seek you out. I did not ask you to dance. Look at what happened when he discovered my interest! He would parcel you off to Tewkesbury, and when time ran out he put you into his kitchens! I had to safeguard you until I could marry you and protect you myself. I couldn't rely on Edward, so all I could do was lure Clarence into thinking that all had ended between us, that he could plot to take your inheritance without fear of redress."

"You kept your distance to protect me." I could feel the first knots begin to untie, the fist of ice to melt.

"Yes."

"I wish I'd known. Why didn't you tell me?"

"And have you reveal it to Isabel?"

"I would never have done such a thing! I am not indiscreet!"

"In all honesty, I was uncertain how close your sister was in Clarence's plans, or how matters stood between the two of you. I dared not risk it."

Which reasoning I might accept. But: "You never said you loved me," I challenged, returning to my primary grievance.

"I kissed you!"

"A chaste salute when you brought me here and I reeked of tallow. Unless you count the . . . the *assault* on my person at Westminster."

"Assault? Which assault?" His brows rose expressively, annoyingly.

"So it seemed to me. I was swept up, all but smothered, and dropped back on my feet with an avowal that you would have me against all odds. I don't know if that was love. Your kiss was no wooing, I swear! I don't even know if you enjoyed it!"

Richard laughed outright as light dawned. "Anne, my love, my heart! I enjoyed it. My only excuse—that my control was not at its best. All I wanted at that moment was to keep you with me, safely behind locked doors, never to let you out of my sight." He cocked his head as I remembered him doing as a child. "Did you enjoy it?"

"Yes . . . No. That doesn't matter!" I glared, horribly flustered.

"Then I see that I must put things right, so that they do matter." Richard advanced. "That is . . . if you wish it, lady."

I did. Oh, I did. After all that had separated us I had no intention of holding back with a simper and virginal modesty. So it was not Richard who covered the distance between us in the end. I took the step; I lifted my arms to slip around his neck and pull him close; I lifted my face to encourage his kisses. But it was Richard who spoke the words. For both of us.

"I love you." He sighed them against my mouth. "You are the half of me that makes me whole. My other self."

"And I love you."

There was no distance between there and the bed, for two lovers of a consenting mind.

"I should go . . ." Richard murmured reluctantly, continuing to press his mouth all along the line of my jaw to the soft skin below my ear.

I held on, fingers burrowed into his tunic. "You will notice, dear Richard, that I have no chaperone."

"Where is she?" His mouth moved deliciously to where the blood beat at the base of my throat.

"Gone to visit her family." I gasped as his lips burned. "She'll not be back for hours. . . ."

"I should go. . . ."

"Stay with me," I whispered against his lips. Nothing would separate us now, even though the sun illuminated the room with its sharp brilliance, hardly setting the mood for a subtle seduction. Chastity was a fine commodity for a righteous woman, but desire was in my mind. Nothing would separate us—except for the one omission that leaped starkly before my eyes. The omission that I could sidestep no longer.

"There's something you should know," I warned him tentatively, pulling on Richard's shoulder.

"It can wait," he murmured against the soft angle where neck met shoulder, applying himself, quite expertly, to ribbons and laces. "Everything can wait."

"It can't!"

He would discover anyway, but I would rather he knew before the event. So I told him, fighting to ward off that illogical sense of shame. Sitting on my bed, I told him the how and where and why of it, forcing myself to watch the reaction on his face. Did I tell him of the terrifying closeness between Margaret and her son that curdled my stomach? No, I did not. Some things were beyond me to talk about. I kept them locked tight in my heart, like a damaged jewel at the bottom of a casket. I did not tell Richard that, but as I told him the rest the tears that had never fallen then dripped silently down my cheeks into the lace of my collar. The first and only tears I had shed over the Prince since that dreadful night. Then I found that I could no longer speak, for on a shattering sob I could not stop the tears, as if I wept at last for myself, for my father's death, for the loss of my mother and my sister. Even more ashamed, I covered my face with my hands and turned away. But Richard would not allow me to grieve alone. He held me silently within the shelter of his arms until I could cry no more.

The storm passed. Richard mopped prosaically at my wet cheeks. "I must look terrible." I sniffed, horrified by the prospect of red and swollen eyelids.

"Never to me," he stated bluntly, making me look up at him, at the raw pain in his face. "I didn't know, Anne."

"The whole Angevin court did." The old mortification swept over me. "I felt dishonored beyond bearing."

"He never touched you."

"Not without six layers of clothing between us." My voice caught on the wretched attempt at humor.

There was no answering gleam in Richard's eyes. Rather they had a flat and hard glitter, as did his reply. "I despise him for it. I would kill him again, today, tomorrow, and thank God as I spilled his blood, for inflicting that on you." The low pronouncement was far deadlier than any blaze of fury.

"It was not entirely Edward's own doing." I felt driven to excuse him.

"Ha! God's blood!" His hands tightened about mine. "Would I degrade you publicly at the insistence of my mother?"

No, he would not. I knew beyond doubt that Richard would never put me through such degradation. "I just thought I should tell you."

"Well, now you have. So there's an end to it." Such a casual dismissal, I might be piqued by it, except that I knew his motive. There was nothing casual about Richard of Gloucester. He would draw my thoughts away from the horrors of the past, any inclination I might have to dwell on them. I could feel by the tension in his shoulders that his own anger had not dissipated to any degree.

"Thank you." I kissed him. "An end to it. A beginning for us." And I saw at last the hot temper begin to lose its grip and his mouth curved into the hint of a smile.

"Your courage astounds me," he said. "And now I'll do all in my power to make you forget. It has no part in our life together." His smile widened. "I find that I am not sorry that you are a virgin widow, after all. My kisses were an assault, did you say?"

"I did."

"Let me make amends."

As the bars of sun spread across the quilt, making of it a strangely gilded prison, Richard proceeded to teach me, his virgin widow, step by amazing step, all the things the Prince had callously retreated from. I gloried in it, Neville pride subsumed beneath Plantagenet possession. Who possessed whom? I swear Richard's control was not what he thought it to be when he showed me how passion could make a woman forget the worst of experiences. I was astonished at what I did not know, eager to learn, delighted with my new knowledge. He made love to me as I would have expected, with a thorough intensity, a consideration, as if I were the center of his world.

He was, for sure, the center of mine. And if an assault was what it was, I welcomed it. Glowed in response to the onslaught of mouth and hands. Curled my fingers into his dark hair as he wound mine into a living shackle around his wrist. Shivered beneath the power of a fluidly muscled body.

I cried out when Richard made me his. A glorious victory.

At last I lay beside him as my breathing settled, as did his, as sleep stole up on us. Richard was rarely at rest, I mused, as I simply lay and watched him, the lines about his mouth relaxed, the firmly determined mouth a little soft. There was the hint of vulnerability again when he was unguarded. So much energy to stir and drive him. Where would it take him, and where would it take me as his wife?

I too fell asleep.

"What happens to me now?" I asked, allowing the nails of my right hand to track across the hollow of his back, splaying my fingers against the sleek muscles of his hip. Richard shivered. One of my new skills, happily practiced, to undermine his control.

Richard grunted in pleasure, words muffled with his face buried in the pillow. "You must stay here."

"Indefinitely?"

At last he turned his head. "Impatient as ever!" But his hand on my cheek, the lips that followed, were infinitely loving.

"I am. Can I talk to you about my mother?" And silently I cursed myself as immediately I saw the warmth and openness of the past hours drain away. We might pretend that all was put to rights between us, but there were still shadows that disturbed him and left me uncomfortably aware of the dark corners of my ignorance.

"I know it brings you grief, Anne, but not now. Not yet. I've not forgotten her and I know you want a settlement for her."

"And her release," I persisted. "I won't have her kept in Beaulieu for the rest of her life."

"There are difficulties there. . . ."

"I don't understand why. . . ."

"Later. I will do what I can; I promise it. When the time is right. Does that satisfy you?"

"No!"

"Why did I think it would?" He gave a wry twist of his lips. "But I swear on my honor that I will not forget. Allow me a little space in which to maneuver."

"And exactly how would you plan to maneuver now . . . ?" My fingers stroked, lured.

"I'll show you. . . ."

And he did.

I had to be content. I had so much else to make me happy. It shamed me, but my own joy filled my heart to the exclusion of all else.

Edward was back, leaving the nobility of the Welsh Marches simmering in discontented peace. Richard was summoned to report. Now perhaps my own future would be settled.

"What does the King say about me?" I asked Richard as soon as he crossed the threshold. The peace, the seclusion of my sanctuary were beginning to pall.

"Nothing that pleases me."

I had wanted plain speaking, had I not? I got it and didn't like what I heard. "He won't support us against Clarence?" My brows rose at the perfidy of it. "He was fulsome enough in his praise for me as a prospective wife when you first asked his permission."

"Nothing quite so definite. But you know how Edward is. He dislikes to commit himself to anything without some escape route if he becomes hard-pressed." Richard bared his teeth at the memory of some edgy conversation with his brother. "The King's moved to play fast and loose with any promises he's made in the past. With the Welsh threat on his mind he wants Clarence with him, not against him. We knew that was so, but I'd hoped he would not be so easily swayed. And Clarence—God damn him!—is breathing fire and damnation over this whole business."

"So, does the King want us to marry or not?"

"He's considering it again."

"Do we have a dispensation?" I demanded, my annoyance building.

"No."

"Would the King actually work against it? Advise the Pope against it?"

Stretched out in the one chair the room boasted, Richard studied his feet, crossed at the ankle, as if he had never seen the soft boots before, while he thought. I could see it was a matter that had worried his mind. "I don't know. He might. I know why he's doing it and can't damn him for it. He'll protect England from further bloodshed, as I would if I were King, by any means he can, and if that means keeping Clarence at least marginally satisfied . . ."

"So it's hopeless." I stared accusingly. "Do I stay here, unwed, until I die?"

"Well . . ." Ignoring my crossness, suddenly Richard lifted his gaze from his footwear and smiled fully at me with a quizzical gleam. He pushed to his feet, took my hand, and drew me with him to the window to look out over the street, his fingers tapping restlessly on the ledge. "There's one remedy to all of this," he announced, turning his head to look at me.

"What?"

"I've an idea. But you must trust me. Do you trust me, after all that has happened?" He studied my face as if trying to read my thoughts, with just a hint of mischief, as if he might dare me to take a risk. Like leaping the stones across the river at Middleham without falling in. Then—at eight years old—I had risen to the challenge, retaining my pride even at the cost of soaked shoes and skirts and the sharp edge of Margery's tongue. But now . . . After my recent experiences, it struck me that I might be wise not to trust any man.

"Is there danger?"

"Danger? No." His lips curved. "I didn't take you for a coward, Anne Neville!"

"I'm not! But . . ."

"Do you trust me?"

I frowned at him. "Yes . . ." Because Richard, I decided, was not just any man.

"Prove it!" His hands, moving slowly down the length of my back, arousing shivers and bringing me close against him, left me with no real choice.

Richard's scheme, whatever it might be and for which he demanded my trust, had perforce to be shelved, since the recalcitrant Welsh, launching another uprising, demanded Richard's renewed absence. His leave-taking was brief, his squire waiting below with horse and weapons, a tidy force already on the march to the west.

"I'll be back when I can." A fast kiss, a pressure on my hands within his, palm-to-palm.

"I shall miss you."

He cast an eye around the empty room. "Shall I buy you some creature to keep you company?"

"Not finches!" I announced, more than abruptly, before I could think.

"I was thinking of a lapdog to sit at your feet and yap to give warning of visitors!" he remarked dryly, startled. "I won't force one on you!" He must have seen the distress in my face. His brows arrowed together. "Why not birds? My mother has a popinjay I wouldn't wish on the devil, but singing birds in a cage . . . Surely . . . ?"

"No!" I shook my head furiously.

"Ah . . ." He rubbed his thumb contemplatively along the line of my jaw. "Perhaps you'll tell me sometime." And he let me be.

"Yes. Keep safe, Richard."

So he was gone. And I cannot admit to being too disappointed in his absence, for in those weeks of lonely vigil I seemed to spend much of the morning hours vomiting painfully. It was a situation guaranteed to engage my mind from missing him.

"Death could be easier." I gasped as nausea shook me once again when Margery placed a bowl of some noxious substance before me— hot milk laced with mint, I thought with a grimace—with instructions to drink.

Margery surveyed me, hands on hips, uncertain whether to frown at me in holy disapproval or rejoice. "You should have felt more sympathy for Lady Isabel. You'll soon come around, when the first weeks have passed." Then rejoicing won. "I warrant His Grace will be pleased. Who'd have thought you'd have been caught so fast?"

"I wish I hadn't!"

Unlike my mother's early difficulties, I had fallen for a child almost immediately. Despite my denials, I did not know what I felt about this unlooked-for complication, even when the sickness stopped abruptly, leaving me full of energy and rude good health. I could not imagine Richard being delighted at the prospect, while I was battered by a crowd of difficulties. Unwed. No prospect of marriage within the near future. No dispensation on the horizon. No one to give me advice or a word of comfort, certainly not Isabel, and I firmly slammed the door against any thought of the Countess, whom I found I needed more than ever. *Trust me.* I doubted Richard had this in mind when he had assured me of his competence to manage all things.

"Let's hope my lord of Gloucester is still of a mind to wed you!" Margery returned to her mode of righteous censure. I could almost see fornication written in her mind. Richard might do no wrong. It was I who had been at fault.

"Let's hope indeed."

I would not choose to have my child born out of wedlock with the condemnation of the Church and the tongues of the gossips lashing against me. Women were expected to be chaste, the tolerance offered to men not extended to me. And who had lured whom? I remembered with contrition my own willfulness and in a lowering of spirits wished it all undone. . . .

Except for this complication that was not complicated at all, this promised child brought Richard close. At night I folded my hands over my belly and dreamed of an unattainable future where there was nothing to disturb me beyond the wealth of the next harvest or the state of the honeycombs in the beehives at Middleham. I would relinquish everything for that.

"Come home, Richard," I whispered into the soft down of the pillow. What would he say when I told him? I would have to trust him, even as I awaited his return with less than unalloyed pleasure.

They weren't quite the first words I uttered on our reunion, but not far off. I knew he was back in London, knew I must wait on the convenience of the King, who demanded a thorough dissection of the Welsh situation. Knowing I would never be first in Richard's priorities, I had come to accept it. Even so I paced impatiently, peered through the window every time the clip of hooves signaled an approach.

And then he was with me. I thought he looked tired, as if he had ridden long and hard. Nor had he stayed to change his garments, one of those little details that lit a flame beneath my heart. At least only the King took precedence. Without words he held me tight in a cloud of dust and horse and sweat. I reveled in it, in the scrape of his jaw, rough with dark stubble, against my cheek as his hands fisted in my unbound hair, for I kept no state.

"I have missed you beyond measure." Such simple words, so few, against my throat to calm all my nerves.

At length Richard sat with a sigh while I poured him ale and he drank gratefully. "It was a long, dry journey. The Welsh—"

"Richard—I have fallen for a child."

"Ah . . ." The rim of the pewter mug paused at his lips. He put it down carefully, his gaze following his hand, lingering there as if he could see something I could not.

"A child. A Plantagenet and Neville heir," I repeated, watching his face. By the Virgin! Why could I not tell what he was thinking? Even when he raised his eyes to mine, I saw a calculation in them.

"Well?" I demanded.

"A child? You are certain?"

"Yes."

As I watched, a gradual warming, a growing light, ousted the habitual severity from his face, and I realized for the first time what this might mean for him. For Richard was as isolated as I, his family as disparate and divided as mine. We both knew what it was to be alone, unsure of family trust and loyalties. We both knew when to guard our tongue, veil our thoughts, hide our emotions. But here was the promise of our child, our own family, a priceless blessing. And then Richard was on his feet and he was laughing. An outpouring of sheer delight that left me in no doubt of his reception of the inconvenient news, and made me smile in return.

"Anne, my love, my joy. Why could you not wait, for once in your life!"

"It was not my choice!"

"No. I don't suppose it was." I found myself swept off my feet, pulled close beside him on the settle. "It complicates matters, but I can't regret it."

"Complicates! I don't want this child to be born unrecognized, without the sanctity of marriage." I muttered the worst of my fears into his shoulder, fears I had never been able to voice to Margery. Within my own family I knew the arrangements for the inconvenience of children born out of wedlock. The Earl had a daughter, Margaret, a product of his youthful hot blood. Care had been taken with her upbringing, and marriage arranged to a man of standing, but I did not want that for a child of mine.

"That will not happen."

"No dispensation, no marriage!" I retorted with prickly temper.

"No faith, my cynical one!"

His mouth smiled against mine as he kissed me, silenced me, and his hands seduced my thoughts as he found a need to celebrate by repeating the crucial deed all over again, despite the dust of travel. I was reduced to breathless pleasure. Nor was I in any way unwilling, discovering that the rough scrape of his unshaven chin held its own charm. And although I would never have wagered on it, the aroma of horse and honest sweat was far preferable to the costly perfume of frankincense and civet.

But how could Richard have such conviction in his ability to direct the future to his own needs?

CHAPTER NINETEEN

A hammering thundered against the outer door of my rooms, breaking the silence of St. Martin's sanctuary. I awoke, eyes wide, senses alert.

"Margery!" I whispered to the hunched mound on her bed by the window. "Margery!"

It stirred and she sat up, her movements indicating that she was as fraught as I. Not even daylight, I registered, on a cold, gray February morning. My heart began to hammer just as heavily as the fist at the door as my mind cleared from sleep. Perhaps Archbishop Neville's name was not as powerful as we had thought. Was it Clarence, come at last to drag me back to Cold Harbour? There was no one to stop him if he were so determined as to come at this hour with a force at his back, if he would break the holy protection of sanctuary. Well, I would not go quietly! Grabbing a robe, I climbed from the bed. Then Margery was at my side, taking charge, any fears masked behind brisk efficiency. She opened the door into the outer chamber.

"Bar the door until I return. Use the bench against it if you must," she ordered, and then vanished, leaving me to decide not to manhandle the heavy settle. If Clarence had come for me I doubted a bench against my bedchamber door would save me.

I pressed my ear to the door. Surely Margery would not exchange words with any one of Clarence's men who had come to take me into custody. More likely to use a fire iron against his skull. With common sense returning, my heart rate settled, only to spike again when Margery returned, rapid steps moving her considerable bulk along.

"Make haste!" She was already issuing orders, all the while pouring water into the bowl, opening my chests, searching out my comb. "We've no time to waste."

"For what? Tell me! Tell me—or I don't move from this spot!" I folded my arms. "Who was it?"

She did not even glance in my direction but unfolded a favorite red damask overskirt from the clothespress. "Lord Francis. He waits without. Gloucester sent him."

"Francis? What does he want?"

"He'll doubtless tell you when he sees you."

"Did you know about this?" I suddenly thought she seemed less than surprised.

Ignoring my furious question, Margery thrust a shift into my hands. "Get dressed, lady."

Will you trust me? If you will trust me we can accomplish anything we desire. Richard's words, whispered intimately against my lips in a moment of passion, might have a fine ring about them, but what exactly did Gloucester, in this high-handed manner, have in mind?

I struggled into whatever petticoat and overgown Margery handed me. She laced me in with little thought to my comfort and all for speed, whilst I braided my hair and covered it with a simple veil and fillet. We were ready within the quarter hour, with Francis striding to and fro impatiently beyond the door. With barely a greeting between us we were riding through the streets, a thin mist rising from the river to shroud us and dampen our garments. Some hardy souls were about, but most had still to brave the bitter cold of the east wind. No one registered our passing.

Francis led us in the direction of Westminster.

"Where are we going?" I asked breathlessly as we hurried our mounts along.

"Here!" he announced, and directed me to dismount in a small, deserted courtyard. Horses were already there, blowing in the cold air, steam rising from their rapid journey. I recognized Richard's stallion amongst them, although he was not in sight. Without any greeting I was helped down by a waiting squire, who disappeared into the darkness of the nearest archway to carry the news of my arrival. I was too overwhelmed to worry about where I was or what I was doing. Richard had left me no time for second thoughts.

As Margery fussed over my appearance and attempted to pull my veil into seemly folds, Richard came out, a priest nervously attempting to keep up with him. It was only then that I looked around, determining where we were in the shrouding mist. This was St. Stephen's, and Richard came to a halt under the archway to the porch, enveloped in a heavy cloak. Instantly I joined him.

"What are we doing here?" I demanded, conscious of the furtive glance of the priest in my direction.

"Welcome, my dear love," Richard murmured softly for my ears, drawing me apart a little. "I knew you'd come quickly." Although the groove had dug itself between his brows as it did when he was thinking, planning, he grasped my hands in his before turning one up to kiss my palm. He even took the time to smile at me. "Not what I would choose but the best I could do. Times are chancy. You'll not find much ceremony in the proceedings today, lady. A poor affair, but necessary." He indicated the liveried men of his private force, the gleam of the white boar on their breast, keeping a discreet watch. "I asked if you would trust me and you said yes. Now I must ask you to prove it. Are you ready to take that step?"

I knew immediately. And felt the urgency of it. "To marry now? Today?" I clung to his hands, sharply anxious. "We can't, Richard." My scrambled thoughts clicked over the days of the calendar. "It's Lent. Church law does not permit us to wed in Lent."

"Yet we will do it."

It felt as though I were being rushed along in a storm, a stray autumn leaf in a winter gale. "Do you have a dispensation?"

"No."

"Then it isn't legal."

"We'll worry about that later."

"Richard, we can't. . . ."

His hands around mine closed tight. "I'll get the dispensation, I promise you. But I want you and I need to protect you. I can't do that effectively against Clarence unless you are my wife. Even now he'll be with the King, arguing his case. Edward is a reed in a stiff wind and will bend for his best interests. I might have waited but now I cannot. Not when you carry my child. My heir." How typical of him to presume that the child would be a son, I thought inconsequentially. His eyes glinted in the grayness, implacable, refusing to allow me to look away as insecurity gnawed at my nerves. "This is the final time for you to make a choice, for you to accept or refuse. Will you wed me? Now? Today?" His lips, cold in the icy wind, brushed my fingers. "I think you love me enough to risk all. You'll not refuse me."

I tried to read his face, the secretive depths of his eyes. And now I could feel the tension in his hands, his fingers, through the fine kid of his gloves digging into my wrists, the driving insistence within him that would persuade me but would never force me against my will. Within me I felt a softening, a smoothing out. I had reached the eye of the storm. The still, quiet center, where all I wanted in the world was here, a priceless gift, being offered to me in his hands, still clasped around mine.

Never had I handed my will so readily to another. "It shall be as you wish. If you say yes, Richard, then I say yes. If no, then I say no."

First there was astonishment at my capitulation. Then satisfaction, an ebbing of tension. "I say yes."

"Then that is what I want." I stretched on my toes to kiss his cheek.

"Come then. All is prepared." He led me in.

*   *   *

I became his wife. A marriage that Richard carried off with such organized efficiency, such arrogance, in the sure and certain belief that no one would question him. It might have been a secretive, crack-of-dawn affair, but his assurance, his authority through it all demanded my admiration. As if there were nothing untoward in a royal marriage held without guests or any extravagance whatsoever in Lent, when penitence and denial were the order of the day. A priest raised from his bed at dawn, a fraudulent official document presented to him that wasn't a dispensation despite its weight of seals and gilt lettering, the exchange of gold to the benefit of St. Stephen's and its reluctant but compliant cleric. And two private individuals, Richard and I, entering into matrimony before two witnesses. Margery supported me with stolid loyalty. Francis stood guard, hand on sword hilt. But no one appeared at the door to denounce us for any real or imagined impediments.

We exchanged our vows simply, the arched and pillared space around us cold and silent. How different from the triumphant festivity of my first marriage. Then my new husband had more concern for his own achievement in taking one more step toward his invasion of England. More concern for the elegant fall of his own cloak than for the happiness of his bride. This morning in St. Stephen's could not have been more stark in comparison, and I thanked God for it.

For Richard pressed his lips to my finger where he had pushed on his overlarge ring. And then to my lips as if to sanctify before the altar the commitment we had already made. His eyes spoke of adoration, and his child's heart beat below mine. This morning my heart was engaged and I knew it would remain so until my death. I would love Richard forever, secure in the knowledge that I too would be loved, that I would never be abandoned or humiliated.

*   *   *

"Do we make a run for it to Middleham, or do we brave the wolf in his den and tell him what we've done?" I tried for a lightness I did not feel. My heart was full of joy, but fear lurked and snapped its teeth.

"My heart says Middleham, my dear wife." Richard fleetingly kissed my temple, his thoughts running ahead. Something I realized I must grow to accept. "But my gut says Westminster."

"Who wins?"

"Gut. We'll not stir the fire more than we need. Edward in a temper could scorch us all."

So that was where we went. It was still early, the brutally bare ceremony over in the blink of an eye, but the King had a reputation for being at work as soon as there was light in the sky to read by, breaking his fast and hearing Mass before the seventh hour, so there was no surprise to find him occupied with documents to hand in the paneled room he used for such business. Nor was it a surprise to find Clarence with him and the King looking burdened.

At the door, with no servant to announce us, Richard drew me closer against him with one arm, anchoring me to his side. It drove home the reality for me far more than the rapidly muttered Latin in St. Stephen's. I need fear no longer. Here was my protection, his heart beating strongly against my spread palms as I turned momentarily toward him for courage. I would never be unprotected again. The wonder of it, the sheer comfort of it, enveloped me as he pressed my lips with commanding fingers to silence me.

"We may not have quite won the war yet," he murmured, "but we've won this battle. Let's announce our victory." He drew me forward beside him, pushing back the door.

Hard-pressed, Edward sat behind a table, face imprinted with a mix of boredom and frustration, two documents under his hands. Clarence leaned on the table before him in full spate. I picked up the general flow. *Inheritance* figured. So did *Lady Anne.* I did not hear *convent* or *my ward, my decision* but could guess at it. The King appeared to be listening with half an ear but looked up with a warm smile, glad of a reprieve, as we entered.

"Richard! And Lady Anne . . . ?"

I saw the question, the sharp awareness, come into his face as he saw me, as his mind grasped just what I might be doing at Westminster at so early an hour. And why Richard might be holding me firmly by the hand. A bubble of suspense grew in my belly. I was not beyond enjoying the anticipation of Richard's announcement that my future was out of their equally unscrupulous hands.

"No, sire." Richard, ridiculously formal, superlatively solemn, because he too was enjoying the moment, drew me forward. "Allow me to introduce to you—to both of you—no longer the Lady Anne Neville, nor yet Princess of Wales. But my Duchess. Anne, Duchess of Gloucester."

For a long moment the words dropped into a silence.

"What?" It was hardly more than a whisper. Clarence pushed himself upright, sleek and dangerous as a hunting cat. "God's wounds! I don't believe that you, even you, Gloucester, would do this. . . ."

The King was more circumspect. "Well, Richard. This is more than a surprise. . . ." He stood slowly, abandoning the business at hand, and walked around the end of the table, where he came to stand before us in a familiar stance, hands loosely clasped on his belt. I saw disquiet in his braced spine, in his frowning eyes, even though he smiled at me. And then his gaze fixed on Richard, a whiplash. "And the matter of a dispensation?"

Richard snapped his fingers while I marveled at his defiance. "So much for a dispensation. It is done."

"It's not legal!" Clarence snarled, the sleeping cat come to life.

"It has all the legality I need for now." The reply might be for Clarence, but Richard's focus was all on the King. "We were wed by a priest at St. Stephen's an hour ago, in the sight of God and before witnesses. It's as legal and binding as it needs to be." He produced the written document from the breast of his doublet, handing it to Edward, who spread it and read the priest's authority.

"It will not stand before the law," Clarence challenged.

"And will you question it before the law, brother?" Now Richard accepted the challenge and returned it. "I will fight you every inch of the way to prove my marriage to Anne Neville valid."

"I will deny that validity without my permission, by God!"

"We've been over this old ground before. Anne is of age and her own mistress to make her own choice. . . ."

"She was given into my keeping. . . ."

"And you chose to put her to work in your kitchens. . . ."

"So that *you* could not abduct her and thwart my authority. . . ."

All the old arguments rolled on around me, and since I knew them by heart I allowed my thoughts to turn inward, to experience again the event that had turned my life onto its head. Fast and bleak it had undoubtedly been, but I relived the moment I made my vows as if it had carried all the splendor and authority of a royal celebration. I became lost in that heady moment until . . . the tone of the exchange around me became more acrimonious, beating its path into my wayward thoughts, and I looked up to see Edward raise his hand to silence Clarence. But Clarence had no intention of being silenced.

"You think you have won, brother." No smack of compromise here, the warning to Richard harsh and unrepentant. "But I warn you: Don't celebrate too soon. You may have Anne, but you'll not get her inheritance. And the Countess of Warwick, traitor that she is, will stay in Beaulieu under guard until the day she dies. I swear it on the blood of Christ."

"She will not!" I reacted, unable to remain silent, astonished at the venom of my attack on Clarence. "She deserves no such imprisonment. The Countess has no sin other than by association. The treachery"—it hurt me to admit it, but I did—"was the Earl's alone." Then I could not resist: "And yours too, as I recall, Your Grace! You were quick enough to clasp hands with the Earl before your ultimate betrayal of him!"

Clarence, also surprised, paled with cold fury. "Vixen! You would speak for an attainted traitor. . . ."

But Richard intervened. "Enough, Clarence. Curb your temper. You'll show my wife the respect due to her. Nor will you deny her what is hers by the law of the land." Richard's grip was warm and strong, crushing my fingers, impossible to ignore. *Leave it to me*, it transmitted. *Let me shoulder this burden.*

"The law, by God!" Clarence continued. "I'll show you the power of the law! You'll not get a single rose noble from that inheritance. Not one acre of land, not one castle! They'll all pass to my heirs; I swear it."

"Your heirs are destined to be disappointed," Richard snapped back.

He has not mentioned it. That I carry his child. Why has he not said?

"I'll fight you for it if I have to. . . ." I watched as Clarence's eyes glittered at the prospect of such a conflict. Richard took a step and I felt his hand move to the hilt of his sword, but at last, Edward stepped between them.

"Quiet now. Hardly the time for bloodletting. The inheritance is a matter yet to be decided, and I'll do so, but this is not the time. We neglect the bride." Claiming my hand from Richard, he placed me at his side, a cunning little maneuver to produce a formidable barrier between the two warring brothers. "Little sister, let me salute you." He kissed my fingers in royal style, and then my cheeks. "This is a moment for rejoicing, not bitter words. I think we should search out the Queen, who will rejoice with me. It's early, but why not? We'll celebrate your union in good style with a toast of my finest Bordeaux. A better way to spend a cold morning than letters from Burgundy detailing the perfidy of King Louis."

Thus my wedding feast.

Richard remained solidly protective, ever watchful. Clarence turned broodingly silent, bad-temperedly glowering. He wasn't a hunting cat at all, I decided, watching him toss back yet another cup of wine, disillusion permanently etched on his features. He was as sleek and grossly unpleasant as an eel for all his beauty. I never did like eels, even when stewed to perfection with milk and saffron. And then there was Edward, hearty, enthusiastic, but falsely so, I thought. He laughed too loudly and too long, drinking the rich red wine as if it were small beer. The Queen managed to be caustically welcoming despite her astonishment at being summoned to preside over an uneasy celebration within her own rooms. She managed to rise to the occasion, even if her hair was still unbound and her gown an informal bedchamber robe, yet she could not resist a spiked aside that it had taken me long enough to act on her advice. But better late than never, and now I must be sure to hold tight to my royal bridegroom and make the most of my victory. I made a suitably equivocal answer, sensing that her own distaste for Clarence and a desire to see his defeat were far weightier with her than any goodwill toward me. All it needed, I decided as the cups of wine were raised, was a wretched Isabel to complete the family reunion.

And the Countess, of course. Her absence and Clarence's callous condemnation lingered in the air as I smiled and answered the toasts in good heart.

"A rare welcome into the dubious embrace of your new family. I think we should leave," Richard finally whispered in my ear as he guided me toward the door to escort me to his own rooms in the palace, with a skill honed in extracting himself from tedious diplomatic receptions.

"Why is Clarence so vindictive against my mother?" I whispered back.

"Hers is the inheritance," Richard explained simply. "And he wants it."

"I fear the King leans far toward Clarence." Looking back over my shoulder, I saw Edward raise his cup to his brother, the subject of the toast unknown but creating a crow of laughter between the pair of them.

"Yes, he does." Richard followed the direction of my eyes. "But not too far, I think, and only at this juncture. The rebellion amongst the Welsh lords has turned his mind to war again, and so to Clarence's vacillating loyalties. We must simply encourage Edward to lean in our direction."

Our escape was foiled.

"A moment, Gloucester, before you leave us." As if reading our intention, the King raised his voice to bring us to a halt on the threshold. "And you too, Clarence!" Did Richard note the formality in the request, the snap of command? Edward was smiling no longer. I certainly noticed and shivered in the warm room at this sudden change in temperature.

"I've had my belly full of the ill will between the pair of you." The King's stare moved from Gloucester to Clarence and back again, a critical appraisal showing no favoritism to either. "I will make a judgment on the Beauchamp-Despenser inheritance." Suddenly a slyness was there to coat the smooth words. "I have decided. You are both requested to appear before my council next month. You will each summon your arguments and put them before myself and the worthy councilors. And you will do so personally." The glance flicked toward Clarence was a warning that a man of law's clever words and slick delivery would not be acceptable. "I will listen to you both. Then I will decide. My decision will be final. Do you accept that?"

"I don't see why—" Clarence whined.

"Nor do you have to," the King stated with biting authority. "It is my will."

Worse for the heavy wine, Clarence crumbled under the weight of royal displeasure. "Very well. If I must."

"Gloucester?"

"I agree and will abide by your decision," Richard replied promptly.

"So be it." Satisfied, the King returned to the wine and his good humor.

I could barely wait until the door had closed behind us. "You said you would abide by his decision. What if it goes against us?"

"I must be sure that mine is the stronger argument, mustn't I?"

I looked up at his mildly thoughtful expression. For the hundredth time I wished I knew what was behind it. "You didn't tell him—that I was carrying your child."

"No, I didn't, did I?"

*　　*　　*

I would have my wedding night at last, in the privacy of Richard's cramped accommodations at Westminster. I could not imagine any better place as I stepped into his arms. No ceremony. No bawdy jokes. No priest to bless the bed. Nor was I a shivering virgin bride. The touch of Richard's hands, his mouth, his body, his knowledge of all my secrets, were a source of wonder and pleasure. In this room, this damask-hung bed, we could pretend to be two private individuals with no one to answer to but ourselves and the demands of our own bodies.

Velvet brushed and caught against velvet, silk against silk. Heated flesh slid against heated flesh. Richard possessed me, filled me, made me his own, while I surrounded him, tormented him, so that for a little while he could lay aside his ambitions, that masterful control of his emotions that I had recognized and challenged all those years ago at Middleham. It pleased me that Richard could forget himself in what I could give him.

But he never forgot me. Richard had a way with words, even under extreme provocation from my lips and fingertips. I was his treasure, his jeweled prize.

A sweetness engulfed me that obliterated all my doubts.

I received a letter from my mother.

It was the first—at least the first to reach me—since my capture at Tewkesbury. I knew that the Countess had spent much time in writing letters of petition to anyone who might have influence with the King—to Clarence, to Queen Elizabeth, to Edward's mother and sister, to anyone who could persuade the King to look kindly on her present situation. I had read some of them penned by a clerk in my mother's name to Isabel. But she had not written to me, knee-deep as I was in Lancastrian treachery, even though by circumstance rather than by inclination, presuming that I would have no influence with King Edward. But times had changed. If she knew of my marriage, the Countess would see the opening of an opportunity.

The letter was in her own hand, her own words. This was no

formal request in the dry words of a clerk at Beaulieu and it tore at my emotions.

> *My dearest Anne,*
>
> *The news of your good fortune brings me some measure of peace. My heart is glad for you. Perhaps it was meant that you should wed Richard Plantagenet. He always had a care and affection for you. Happiness in marriage can be a great solace, as I know. I miss your father more than I can express. Warwick's death was—and is—a great loss to me. I cannot write it.*
>
> *Gloucester has the King's ear and so I would cast myself on your mercy. If you have any influence over your husband in these first days of marriage, I would beg you to use it. I yearn for release from this place that was once my sanctuary from imprisonment and death and now has become my prison.*
>
> *Am I to remain here forever? Are my possessions and property to be stripped from me? I am forgotten, discounted, locked away from the world, when all must know that I am entitled to the jointure settled on me at the time of my marriage. Is not every widow entitled to at least that?*
>
> *Your sister, Isabel, continues to be under the hand of Clarence, who has no thought to my comfort. She has done nothing for me. I beg of you to use your influence with Gloucester, and thus with the King. I am no threat to Edward's crown. Edward saw fit to pardon you. Why should he cavil at pardoning me? All I ask is the freedom to travel unmolested to London, a safe conduct, to plead my case before the King.*
>
> *I beg of you, I exhort you to use your skills of persuasion on my behalf. Time hangs heavy on my hands and I have no consolation but prayer.*
>
> > *Your loving mother,*
> > *Anne, Countess of Warwick*

It hurt me to read this sad letter, a physical pain that gripped and would not let me rest. The pride was there, the determination to demand what was hers by legal right, but what depths of grief and loneliness were contained in the few short lines. The Countess might hold fast to her inner strength. I could sense it in the reluctance with which she begged for my intervention. Yet, alone and friendless, she must be worn down. I wept over the document until the words were blotched and difficult to read. The utter hopelessness there, the cruel understanding of what was to be her fate . . .

Heavyhearted, reluctant, I began to make my reply.

My dear mother,

It pleases me to hear from you, although your low spirits cause me sorrow. I am in good health and Margery cares for me as you would wish her to. It might bring you some consolation to know that I carry Gloucester's child.

Nothing is yet decided over the inheritance or of your future. Edward is still in debate but I—and Gloucester—will do what we can. . . .

I came to a halt to read over the lines. Stilted, disjointed, what a terrible letter it was, when I loved her so much and would wish to give her hope. I could give her none at all.

"What should I tell her?" I asked Richard when I showed him the Countess's letter.

"The truth isn't palatable."

"No."

"If she is free," Richard added, confirming my thoughts, "she has power." Pulling up a stool, he sat beside me, taking the quill from my hand and rubbing at the ink that marked my fingers as it invariably did when I wrote, grunting as the stains transferred to his own fingers. "And the Countess could well marry again. She is by no means beyond the age of remarriage. There are any number of men at court who would consider her and her inheritance a prize worth winning."

True. I watched him as he picked up my poor attempt at a reply. My mother had little more than forty years. Richard raised his brows at my scratchy efforts; then he put the letter down before me.

"Shut away behind the walls of a convent," he continued, "the Countess is faceless and voiceless, conveniently forgotten by the world, with no one to speak for her."

"Whereas if she were free and at liberty to return to court and to marry again, her fortunate husband would fight for her rights." I sighed at the brutal truth of it.

"As I will fight for yours."

"So my mother's freedom is the last thing Clarence wants." I gripped Richard's sleeve to hold him still, as he would have risen to his feet. "And you, Richard? What do you want?" He sank back, hitched a shoulder, a little uneasy, but I would not release him. "Tell me the truth. Do you want her to remain in the convent? Is it not in your interests too that the Countess remain there?"

He did not like the question. I saw it in the clenching of his right hand around the mistreated quill. But I knew he would not lie to me, however disturbing it might be. "Yes, it is."

"So, like Clarence, you would condemn her? Is that what you want?"

Richard turned the ring I had once given him on his little finger as he thought to soften the words. Even so, the truth was hard, difficult. "If you press me . . . I want a settlement to the benefit of all, I suppose."

"At the expense of my mother?"

"No, not at her expense. But neither can I stand idly by and let Clarence strip the whole parcel of her land and power for himself in the name of your sister. Nor would you want that."

"No, I wouldn't. But to demean the Countess in such a manner is an affront to love and affection." So calm and reasoned his argument, but calm reasoning had no part in this vicious campaign against my mother. Sensing emotions building inside me, I clenched my fingers harder into the flesh of his forearm, even when he winced.

"They would take all she has, everything, until she is destitute, with no thought for her pride. Shall I be a party to it also? How can I condemn Isabel for her part in it if I seek my own portion at the Countess's expense?" The thought appalled me, that I should be guilty of the same greed as my sister. "Chivalry, in truth, is dead," I added bitterly.

"Yet see this, Anne." Richard would not allow me to lose my sense of the whole. "If we do not engage in this war you will forfeit all. Both you and the Countess. I will fight for your rights, but . . ." He hesitated, then added carefully, choosing his words: "It may be that the Countess is the one to pay the heavy cost. It may be the only way." Now he stood, drawing me with him. "Most of all I want you not to be troubled. Your health is very precious to me."

"And that of the child!" My reply might be sharp, but his arms were strong and I held tight. His love enfolded me when all around seemed stark with hatred and malice.

"That, too." His lips were soft against the hollow at my temple, his breath warm against my cheek.

"My health, as far as I am aware, is not a problem, Richard!" I would not quite give him the victory. Or allow him to distract me. "My mother is the problem!"

"I know." He was smiling down at me, appreciative of my tactics. "And I can't yet give you an answer, however much you become a nagging wife."

"I am no nagging wife!" But I let it go with a huff of breath. He had gone as far as he would to reassure me. His kisses did more.

"So what do I tell her?" I asked when I was once more seated, inky quill in hand, and my heart settled into its normal rhythm.

"The truth, as you have. That it is in Edward's hands. I think that she sees the future without your spelling it out."

Am I to remain here forever? Yes. She saw her future clearly.

So I took Richard's advice. When I was alone in my chamber I fought against the inclination to weep. It was a life sentence that Clarence connived at, and at that moment I felt the loss of my mother's presence far more than I feared for land or property. All I could do was to leave the burden of it with Richard, that somehow he would foil Clarence's plans. And that somehow my mother would not have to pay the heaviest cost.

"I don't suppose I can come and listen."

"No."

Well, that was plain enough!

Edward would hold the meeting of the King's council in the formality of the great paneled and tapestried audience chamber at Westminster. Sitting in bed, frowning heavily as Richard readied himself for the occasion, I sniffed my derision. The magnificence of the setting would be suitably fitting to decide who would get his hands on my mother's vast wealth, but my mood was sour. Whatever the outcome, the Countess would not come out of it with her prayers answered.

I pouted as Richard sat on the edge of the bed to thrust his feet into soft leather boots. So he must put his case for his claim on my mother's inheritance, must plead *my* claim, without my presence. It sat ill with me.

"I have as much right to be there as the councilors."

"You have no right, dear heart." Leaning his forearms on his thighs, hands loosely clasped, he smiled at my fractious insistence, knowing its root cause was fear. He knew me too well. "You're not a councilor. Besides, you know the arguments—you've heard them all. Isabel is older and therefore the heiress. Clarence is eminently fit to administer the property and has a call on Edward's gratitude. While you"—he rose, walked around the bed to collect a businesslike sheaf of documents, raising a hand to smooth my tumbled hair in passing—"*you*, my petulant love, were wed to the Lancastrian traitor. *You* deserve nothing! Why would you wish to sit through the same accusations again, with the ranks of the council picking them apart with their grubby fingers?"

"Mmm! Not an attractive picture!" But *he* was, I thought, as he shrugged into the close-fitting dark blue tunic and applied a comb to his disordered hair before hunting out a smart beaver hat. Clasping my arms around my knees, I watched as he proceeded to add the finishing touches: the impressive chain of office, the ring-brooch fastened into the soft fur of the beaver. "But I want to listen to you. And ill-wish Clarence, of course."

"You can ill-wish him from a distance." His sharp glance was a warning. He buckled on his sword belt, squared his shoulders against the weight of the chain so that the rubies gleamed balefully, as red as blood, and came to stand before me.

"Well?"

Jeweled, fur trimmed, dark hose and tunic molded to his figure, he was magnificent. He might not have the golden beauty or the stature of his two brothers, but he took my eye. I hid a smile. I would not add to his consequence.

"Good enough," I managed.

"Unfortunately"—the curl of his mouth was wry—"Clarence has an impressive appearance."

"Clarence is an arrogant, unprincipled bastard!"

"Arrogant and unprincipled, certainly. I can't vouch for my lady mother's constancy. Now, kiss me before I go."

I did. His hands were warm on my shoulders, his lips a strong promise on mine. "Pray God that my words are persuasive."

"I will. Soft, persistent as summer rain, to drench Edward to the skin before he realizes it. Better than a winter deluge."

"More subtle, certainly. Edward likes subtlety." Drawn by my hands in his, Richard sat again for a brief moment on the side of the bed and brushed my hair away from my face. "What will you do?"

"I can't stay here on my own or I'll sink into despair. I'll go to the Queen, I think. There'll be conversation and spiced gossip if nothing else to occupy my mind."

"If you must." I noted the lack of enthusiasm. His hostility to the Woodville Queen remained as strong as ever. "As long as you give no weight to anything she says. The Queen has deep ambitions. What are you thinking?" he asked, chin cocked.

That she had already given me advice—of a questionable nature—that I had acted upon. But I would not tell him that. "Only that I love you." Which was not untrue.

"Which I shall keep by me as a talisman to my good fortune." His smile was confident, the quick pressure of his mouth on mine firm. "I shall come and find you."

"God keep you, dear Richard. God give you victory."

Were those not the words the Prince had demanded from me before Tewkesbury? And knowing that he intended to hunt Richard down, to destroy him in a fit of blind, vengeful hatred, I had refused to give them. There had been no victory for the Prince that day, only an all-encompassing defeat. Left alone, I simply sat and stared blindly at the gleaming linen-fold paneling as I prayed with mounting anxiety that Richard would not suffer similar ill fortune.

CHAPTER TWENTY

I was not destined to reach the Queen's private rooms. As I stepped into the antechamber, chance brought Isabel on the same errand: to hear the outcome as soon as it was known. This was our first meeting since I had been released by Richard from Cold Harbour. I had not sought out my sister since my return to court, nor had she found a need to visit me. What could we possibly have said to each other that wasn't full of denunciation and blame?

Her face was suddenly cold and still, as a winter pool is held motionless with the beginnings of ice. But that was not what took my notice. Beneath the shuttered withdrawal, Isabel was ill and unhappy, her features drawn from too many disturbed nights and too little nourishment. There was a crow's-foot of lines beside her eyes of which I had no memory. Isabel, always the beautiful daughter, looked far older than the five years that separated us.

Clearly the tight knot of resentment that existed in my breast also afflicted Isabel, who drew back from me as if she would not wish to contaminate her skirts.

"I suppose I shouldn't be surprised to find you here, Your Grace!"

Her face was pale and bleak, any vestige of animation draining away. "Come to whisper in the Queen's ear, have you? To buy her support against Clarence?"

"Isabel! I came to see if there was news," I retaliated.

Isabel's reply was as sharp as the furrows on her forehead, her eyes raking me from head to foot. "Did you? You seem confident enough of the outcome, Your Grace. I expect you'll be delighted if Gloucester's victory is at my expense."

"I am not confident of anything!" Would she not even acknowledge me as her sister, call me by my given name? Her present hostility was as painful as her past treatment of me. "I have no liking for any of this. . . ."

"I think I will not stay. . . ."

"Because I am here?" I accused. "I am the injured party here, Isabel. *You* would disinherit *me*!"

She ran her tongue over dry lips and would not look at me. "You have no rights. It is not fit that you should take any of our mother's lands. . . ."

"Neither of us should have our mother's lands! She is not dead!" Anger at her cruelty stirred me into accusations that I had not intended to make. "The Countess wrote to you because she thought you would be a loving daughter and would bring some influence to bear! You did not reply. You did nothing to give her hope." I couldn't stop the words even though Isabel's eyes swam with tears. "She thinks you have rejected her. As you have."

"Yes. I have."

How infinitely merciless she was. It was beyond my understanding. "How could you do that, Isabel? She loved you and nurtured you since the day you were born. She saved your life when you could have died on that accursed ship off Calais. She is your mother. She loves you."

"No! She damned me. She let my child die. She is the cause of all my sorrows." Isabel covered her face with her hands.

Such a shattering accusation. It dropped into the atmosphere like a stone, uttered with such grief that my furious denial was stopped on a sharp intake of breath. When had she thought this? Had she always thought it, that the dead babe was caused by some oversight in our mother's care? That the Countess could by some miraculous power have changed that tragic outcome as our ship rode the storm in the reaches off Calais? In all the years that had passed since that tragic event, I had never held the slightest suspicion that such a thought had taken root in her mind.

"Isabel! It is not so! I was there and I know it. The Countess did all she could and more. . . . Margery too."

"My child died. I lost Clarence's heir. I should have the inheritance in recompense. Clarence says . . ."

Her words were lost in a hiccupping sob, but I did not need to hear what Clarence had said. It all clicked together in my mind, as neat and complete as a ring in a horse's bridle. Reunited with Clarence for almost a year, she had still not quickened to carry the heir that her husband desired. And Clarence was already blaming her for her failure. It wrung my heart, so that I cast aside my anger and moved to block her retreat, to attempt some sort of reconciliation, despite everything. Still, she shrank from me as if she could not bear my closeness.

"Isabel. Don't do this."

"Don't do what?" She snatched her hand away from my tentative touch. "Who would blame me if I refused to take the hand of a traitor, my own sister, who would deny me my place as my mother's heir? Who would attack me for mourning the death of my child? Don't touch me!" Her control wavered as hysteria rose in her voice, her eyes wide with inexplicable hatred. "My child should never have died. I will never carry another; I know it. Clarence will never have his heir and I must carry the blame. At least if he wins the Beauchamp lands . . ."

All I could do was stand and watch as Isabel disintegrated into helpless sobbing. Isabel's miseries, her motives, were written as clear as black ink on a sheet of finest vellum. Afraid of Clarence, of his criticism, his biting tongue, she hoped he would love her again if he could get his grasping hands on the vast entirety of the Countess's inheritance. And Isabel, misguided, vulnerable Isabel, would support him in it, even if it meant learning to hate her sister and her mother.

For nothing was clearer to me: Here was Clarence's work, destroying all Isabel's fine judgment, all that bound us together in the past. It must be Clarence. How could Isabel not remember those critical hours in that hot and airless cabin when she had wept and cried in her agony, the Countess turning back her sleeves, tucking up her skirts, and working through those terrible conditions to bring her daughter and the child to safety? None of the ultimate tragedy had been her fault.

Oh, Isabel. How wrongly you have read it. How unhappy you must be. And I can do nothing to comfort you.

As helpless tears pricked behind my eyelids, I made a decision. I would not tell Isabel of my pregnancy. I dared not, not today. One day she must know, but not yet. The pain for her would be beyond bearing. And what hope now of smoothing over this rift between us?

None that I could see.

"Isabel is the elder." Clarence's increasingly strident tone preceded him to the door of the Queen's antechamber, where Isabel and I were still trapped in an agony of raw emotion. "Who is more fit to administer the property than I? And you owe me, Edward. Whichever way you argue it, my wife's loyalties are beyond question. . . ."

Unlike her sister's!

Not again! I made no effort to hide my exasperation as they entered, immediately crowding and dominating the wood-paneled room. Clarence did not even take the time to acknowledge Isabel. Richard, bringing up the rear and to whom my eyes were automatically drawn, grimaced silently in my direction with raised brows.

So nothing had been settled, nothing at all. Nor ever would be, as far as I could see. The air reeked with the stench of hostility and a heat of temper. Why have a public debate if Edward was still of a mood to prevaricate? I listened crossly as Clarence persisted in battering our ears with the same force of his argument. I was so weary of it. *I* would have taken every acre, every gold coin from Clarence for his impertinence in overlooking me, and given it all to Richard, but Edward could not, of course. Nor would it be right to rob Isabel, however much I might once have contemplated revenge. Her sorrow and the intimate nature of it had drawn the bitterness from me. As for Edward, frustration dragged at his broad features as Clarence grasped his arm to make the point. To alienate Clarence now, as Edward well knew, would be to dig a bottomless trench into which we all might fall. The King, whatever else, was awake to every danger, although at present annoyance had the upper hand.

"You already have all the Neville estates to which your wife is entitled."

"She is entitled to the Countess's estates as well."

"Your wife is entitled to half. You cannot unravel the Neville settlements for the two girls."

"Why not? You can *unravel*, as you put it, whatever needs to be unraveled. It is what *I* want."

"And what *I* want is for *you* to be more amenable, brother. The spirit of compromise would be a blessing in this dispute. . . ."

"*Amenable?* I think this is no time to be amenable—"

So far Richard had stood on the edge of the exchange. "Sire," he broke in, his voice at its quietest, cutting through the fury. "There is one argument strongly in my wife's favor that I chose not to use in the council chamber."

"*Another* argument? By God, Gloucester! I thought we'd wrung every last farthing out of it. I hoped we had!" Querulous, irritable, the King's reply did not augur well. But my interest was caught. I thought I knew all Richard's ploys.

"No. A private matter, and still early days. I would not wish to announce it publicly." Deliberately Richard turned his head to look at me, over his shoulder, a sort of warning. I knew immediately what he would say. And oh! How I wished he would not. As he faced the exasperated Edward again to add the final persuasion, my own eyes focused on Isabel, who listened halfheartedly if at all, her mind, it seemed, centered on her own tightly clasped fingers.

"Richard . . . !" I whispered. *Don't do it!*

Of course, it was not worth the saying. How could I have explained? And so I must allow Richard to speak as he wished. Although such an announcement should have been an occasion for joy, I tightened my lips and listened as my heart sank.

"Anne carries my child. My heir."

Ill humor forgotten in an instant, Edward guffawed, drowning a whimper from Isabel at my side. "You haven't wasted time, Dickon!"

In no manner distracted, Richard laid his case, stone upon stone, to build a formidable bulwark. "Not only is it legal that my wife have a claim on the Countess's inheritance, as was always intended, but equally the child, my heir, should have a claim on the lands of his grandmother. The child will not be born with this matter still in dispute simply because Clarence is intransigent. My wife is no more a traitor than he is. We all know Clarence took an oath of loyalty to Edward of Lancaster and he did it of his own free will, whereas my wife's marriage to the Prince was at the instigation of her father. It was not her decision nor to her liking; she suffered at his hands and saw his ultimate death as a blessed relief. Now she carries my child, the next generation to buttress the house of York for the future."

Clever, clever. Clearly and forcefully put. Brutal, yes, but effective, cunningly damning Clarence, subtly reminding Edward that as yet he had only one male heir of his own marriage, and at the same time enhancing my status as mother of a Plantagenet Prince. I could not but be impressed by this piece of devious plotting at Clarence's expense.

How meticulous Richard had been. I should have burned in admiration. Instead, I awaited the inevitable cataclysm.

It was as if Isabel had been shot with an arrow to the heart. A sharp cry escaped that she attempted to muffle as she pressed her hands over her mouth. Her eyes turned to mine, drowning in horror and despair, speaking the words *how could you!* as if she actually uttered them. And I wished I had told her before. I wished it with all my heart. Her sense of betrayal would be even more agonizing now.

Unwittingly, unaware of the tragic drama that was being played out, Richard drove the blade home with terrible ruthlessness. "Since Clarence as yet has no heir, I think it gives me a claim that can't be dismissed by clever rhetoric."

When Isabel's face crumpled in sheer misery, I went to her immediately, to grip her hands even as she made every effort to snatch them away. "Isabel. I never meant for you to hear like this. . . ."

"How could you!"

"I would never hurt you so cruelly."

"Yes, you would!" Her voice hitched and broke. "You have always wished me ill. You always had the ambition to stand in my way."

"No! Not true. That was never true." Holding her wrists, I shook her, so that she must look at me to read the truth in my face as well as in my denial. "We have not always been close; I admit it. Yes, we argued as children. Yes, circumstances drove us apart, but would you think me capable of this? It was you who put me to work in your kitchen! How can you now accuse me of such heartlessness?"

But Isabel shook me off. "I hate you, Anne! I hate you!"

The bitter, vicious words slammed home and I could not blame her, for suddenly fate had decreed that I should have at my fingertips everything she lacked. And not least my husband's love, whereas she, if I read her aright, was trapped in a loveless marriage. Oblivious to her distress, or more like indifferent, Clarence did not even turn his head at his wife's torment.

Isabel continued to weep out her grief, but my attention was elsewhere.

"Also, sire," I heard Richard offer, a postscript to his shattering announcement, "unlike my brother I am willing to compromise. I am willing to forgo my office of Great Chamberlain in my brother's favor."

Which made my ears prick immediately. My father's office, given to Richard by the King himself as a public show of gratitude for Richard's service. In God's name! Why would he, without any external pressure, give it up to Clarence?

"You would?" Edward, also surprised, took Richard's arm to lead him toward the Queen's rooms. No doubt to escape the raw female emotion in the room, Isabel choking on sobs, and I frantically failing to console her. I could hardly blame him.

"Yes. I would. I will forgo the office of Great Chamberlain . . ." Richard restated, with the briefest of rueful glances at me as he walked beside the King. "But I expect some recompense. . . ."

"I thought so!" Edward returned. "And what would that be?"

The voices faded from the antechamber as they entered the Queen's rooms and the door closed behind them. Like Edward, I had no idea what the recompense would be, nor did I greatly care as Isabel's tears continued to tear at my heart.

"Well? What did he say?" Richard and I were finally reunited. Isabel, still wretched and tearful, had returned to Cold Harbour in the care of a royal escort. Nothing I could do or say to her could console her, so I abandoned the attempt. The pronounced lines beside Richard's mouth indicated that the occasion had not been without stress for him, so that I felt our faces must mirror each other. A touch of weariness, of sorrow. The strain of waging a difficult battle. But with a determination to look forward to the future and a deep satisfaction that we were together to give love and comfort. My hand crept into his to find solace in his clasp that closed firmly around me. "What did he say?" I repeated in some dread.

"Which of the two? They were both equally intransigent!"

With a humorless little laugh, he struck a pose, hands fisted on hips and chin raised in arrogant pride, looking down his nose at me in remarkable imitation of Clarence at his most obnoxious. "Gloucester can have Anne Neville, but not her land." Then resorting to his own dry comment: "In so many words, even after all Edward's persuasions, Clarence swore to fight me through every court in the land to keep it. Then he damned me to the everlasting fires of hell for my presumption."

The child, of course. That was why Clarence had damned him. The imminent heir. Clarence would never forgive Richard for that. And now Isabel would suffer even more for her failure.

"And Edward? What did he say in his royal wisdom?" I did not bother to hide my weary disdain.

"He would think about it. He would give the matter his full attention."

"He's been thinking about it and giving it his full attention—or not!—for the last year." My disdain was transformed into waspish displeasure.

"I'd rather you did not say that to him." Richard directed a measured glance in my direction.

"Why not?" And I just might if he caught me in my present mood.

"Because sometimes it is necessary to employ a veneer of tact and respect to get what you want. A battering ram is not the only means of getting into a beleaguered castle."

"A cannon?"

"That's even worse. Force will not pay here."

There was the difference between us. Richard had far more tolerance than I, and a fistful of guile. He would smile and give soft words, yet still hold firm to the rightness of his cause. I would leap in and ruffle the feathers of all concerned. With an arm around my shoulders, Richard pulled me to sit against him on a cushioned settle. We remained like that for some time. The day had cast long shadows.

"And my mother?" I asked finally.

"The Countess is to remain where she is."

"I see." Not only long shadows. The day had brought no good news on any front.

"By the by." Richard turned his head. "What was wrong with Isabel?"

I sighed, a little groan. "I'll tell you later."

A mess of bitter recrimination, of suspicion, greed, and grief that could never be disentangled. None of us came out of it well, I decided.

CHAPTER TWENTY-ONE

I
f I travel to Middleham, will you come with me?"

"Do you want me with you?" I asked with a good show of ingenuous innocence.

Richard grinned over the bread and meat on the platter between us. "I have no intention of leaving you here alone. I was merely being courteous—and giving you the chance to refuse."

"Were you, now!" I pushed the platter away after inspecting the beef. Not even Richard's insistence that I take care of myself could persuade me to eat roast meat at the beginning of the day. His smile softened even as he watched with an eagle eye as I ate a wizened pippin from last year's harvest, and my heart fluttered. Richard's love for me, not always spoken but discernible in his eyes, his face, the slide of his fingers against mine, was as light and sumptuously enfolding as a sable cloak.

"We'll not be parted now." Richard's face settled in sterner lines. "I recall how often your mother remained alone when Warwick went traveling on the King's business. Sometimes I thought she was more widow than wife even in those days. I'll not have it so for us."

It was an unfortunate reminder of affairs still undecided. "Will you go without knowing Edward's decision?" I asked. It was four weeks since the council had met, a long month in which Edward had remained exasperatingly perverse. The Countess remained incarcerated at Beaulieu, and in spite of all my efforts, Isabel refused to see me.

"He won't make it any the quicker for my presence at his elbow." Richard cut into the beef with enthusiasm even as I shuddered. "I've made all the gestures I can, all the arguments I can. He'll decide for himself, as and when he chooses. He is the King," Richard stated, as was always the answer. "He can take all the time he likes."

Which effectively ended the discussion, and by tacit agreement we did not speak again of what could not be mended. Apart from one final barbed shot from me to Richard's back as he left me to arrange the transport.

"You should not have resigned the office of Great Chamberlain in Clarence's favor, Richard." I could not resist, the memory too clear. "That was my father's office and the King saw fit to give it to *you*. Edward has already agreed that Clarence should have the titles of Warwick and Salisbury from my father. What more does he want? And don't tell me 'everything'!" I pounced, as I read his obvious reply. "I say you were too willing to compromise. *I* wouldn't have done so. I would have wished him to the devil first!"

It was impossible to forgive Clarence's smug triumph when Richard made his offer to help smooth the diplomatic path. Nor was he slow in accepting it, and with not one ounce of gratitude as far as I could see. How could Richard tolerate it?

Richard looked back, as if contemplating the wisdom of a response when I was in my present mood, then shook his head.

"I did it, and it is done."

Not united over the matter, but accepting a comfortable truce, we put it aside.

My pregnancy was not so far advanced as to make travel uncomfortable or dangerous. Richard saw to my care with an insistence that would have wearied me if his presence had not filled me with joy. Some days when the heat pressed down, I rode in a magnificently appointed traveling litter, but more often I joined him on horseback and we rode as we once had over the moors above Middleham when we were very young. He had acquired for me a little mare with a deceptively gentle demeanor but a mind of her own—much like me, he announced after a tussle of willpower with the wily creature, except that I rarely even looked gentle.

We traveled slowly and with intent, making it a sort of pilgrimage, at my request. Peace lay softly on the land, unless one looked below the surface, hence our formidable escort, the banners and pennons of Gloucester unfurled. Beneath my own placid exterior too lurked distressing concerns that refused to be completely banished. I knew Richard had done all he could. So much praise I had heard for his eloquence and the force of his words at the council, yet Clarence too had impressed. Even now Edward would be balancing the weight of one brother against the other. I shut the thoughts away, respecting Richard's determined silence, only to find them lurching toward my continued estrangement from Isabel. Unreconciled, I could see no way forward with my unhappy sister.

Westward from London to Bisham Priory we journeyed, where I stood before the tombs of my Neville grandparents: Richard Neville, Earl of Salisbury, and Alice Montagu. Their effigies looked up at the carved canopy, serene in their belief that the Nevilles would hold fast to their power and land for all time. No more! The Nevilles had been destroyed as a political force, my father's Neville lands made forfeit.

Beside them, beneath a simple slab, was where my father lay. *Richard Neville, Earl of Warwick.*

I would make him a worthy memorial. I imagined it in finest alabaster, carved by the most skilled stonemasons. He would wear the armor fashioned for him in Italy, his great sword and poignard, his head on the magnificent battle helm.

"He deserves a memorial." Richard had accompanied me and stood at my side in silent support, uncannily percipient to my thoughts. "I remember him as a great leader of men but also as a cousin of

humor and great charm, with time for a young boy. I admired him and
strove to be like him. He was too young to die."

We did not speak of the treachery that killed him, hacked down
on the battlefield, or of the fatal desire for power and supremacy that
drove him to the ultimate destruction and dismantling of Neville
power.

And then we continued westward again. This was not an easy
journey for me, but I was compelled to make it. If I was silent and
withdrawn, Richard allowed it to be so, understanding my pain.
Since our marriage I had told him of much of my life with Edward
of Lancaster—even about the finches—although not all of it, with its
cruelties and humiliations, of being used so blatantly. I think Richard
knew that there was much unsaid and so tolerated my silence. At night
he held me in his arms until I fell asleep.

Tewkesbury repelled me. Only duty drove me to walk through
the churchyard and seek entry at the abbey as I had once before. The
monks had put all to rights and wildflowers bloomed innocently in the
grass where blood had seeped. This time Richard left me at the door,
and I was glad of it. What did he think of the moment here when he
slew the Prince? I did not ask him but I knew in my heart that he would
do the same today and tomorrow if the King's life were in danger.

I did not have to knock and demand entrance. The latch on the
door opened to my hand and I walked slowly up the nave alone. The
abbey had been cleansed, all trace of desecration removed except for
the defaced carvings that showed the scars of sword and mace. And
there it was. The simple unmarked brass over the tomb in the center
of the choir, as I had instructed.

What should be written there as a memorial for Edward of Lancaster? The metal gleamed coldly, drawing the eye with its blankness.

What to write to mark his passing?

Here lies Edward of Lancaster, Prince of Wales.
The sole light of thy mother,
the last hope of thy race.

I doubted Margaret, still Edward's prisoner, would ever recover from his loss. Of a certainty, the Lancastrian cause never would. Of the rest, I could not think. Not now, not yet. I abandoned the struggle.

I left a purse of gold with the monks.

Leaning against the church wall as evening fell, in desultory conversation with his squire, Richard waited for me. I touched his arm. "Thank you."

"For what?"

"For bringing me here."

"You had a ghost to lay, I think." With his thumb he rubbed at a groove that he must have seen dug deep between my brows.

"Yes."

"And have you?"

"I have."

"Then it was a journey worth making." Richard lifted my cloak from where it lay over his saddle and wrapped it around my shoulders. "Come—it's too cold to be standing here. The monks will give us accommodation." He covered my hand with his, drawing it through his arm, and I felt the protection of it. Richard said no more and I pushed the past away where it belonged. It had no part in my life now and I would look forward.

Middleham. My heart soared at the prospect; my spirits lifted with every mile. It drew me, a moth to a candle, except that this glowing beacon would bring no searing pain. I anticipated the warmth and the welcome there.

"There! There it is." Tightening my hands on the reins, I pulled the mare to a halt on a little rise on our final descent from the range of hills. The weather was closing in from the west, promising rain with heavy clouds swirling around us. A little wind had begun to tease with malevolent warning, but below us the massive towers and walls loomed out of the murk, dominant and impressive in the valley. The protective moat was cast about like a glittering sleeve of gray

metal. The stone might be cold and forbidding, overpoweringly grim
in the overcast light, but nothing could dampen my pleasure. It spread
through me, throbbing at neck and wrist, so that I could barely contain it. "Whatever happens, we shall have this."

Hooves on the road from York in the valley below us, off to our
right, took our attention, caused us to halt and our escort to form a
defense, but the newcomers were insufficient to suggest an attack, a
little party riding fast to intercept us. As we rode forward down the
slope to meet them, they came abreast and reined in, with at least one
familiar face.

"Your Grace." In acknowledgment of Richard, breathless, Chester Herald removed his hat and beat at the dust in his tabard, where
the bright red and blue and the golden lions of England were overlaid
and dimmed.

"What is it?" Richard pushed his horse forward, instantly alert.

"I've been following you—or not, it seems, Your Grace. The devil's own journey. We thought you'd gone straight to York." The Herald grimaced as he unlatched and took a document from his satchel.
"From His Majesty, to be delivered to you with all speed." He wiped
his mouth with the back of his hand and grinned. "I trust you'll invite
us all on to Middleham, Your Grace. We wouldn't refuse ale before
the return journey."

"Of course." But Richard was preoccupied, backing his horse into
a little space, where I instantly followed. He removed his gauntlets,
opened the sealed letter. I watched as he read it.

"Well? Is it important? Shall I die of suspense?"

"It would take more than that to bring you low!" I sat and glared
until he took pity on me. "It's Edward's decision."

"And?"

When he would have pushed the document into my hands, the
promised squall hit us with devastating force. The heavens opened,
drenching us in seconds.

"Tell me," I insisted as I pulled the deep hood over my face and veil, tucking my cloak beneath my legs to protect my garments. The sleeves of Richard's brigandine were already darkening with the wet.

"Not here, Anne. You're already soaked to the skin." He slipped the document into the breast of the jacket, then raised his hand to signal to the escort to proceed, but I would not move. Not the most sensible of decisions perhaps, but I needed to know *now*, when all had been in dispute for so many months.

"What does the King say?"

"Come on!" Leaning across, he would have grasped my reins and dragged me forward if I had not edged the mare sideways and around to face him.

"Richard! The longer you procrastinate, the wetter we shall get."

Since the deluge chose to abate as quickly as it had arrived, Richard yielded, but not without a struggle. "You're as stubborn as the animal you are sitting on! Well, then . . . of all your mother's lands, which would you choose to have for your own?"

Lifting my eyes to look around me, it took me no time at all to decide. I knew little of the southern lands—they held no memories for me. The castle at Warwick would provide a splendid home, but . . . As for Tewkesbury . . . The little shiver that roughened my skin had nothing to do with my clammy skirts. I would have no regrets if I never set foot there again. Isabel—and Clarence—could have Tewkesbury with my blessing, as long as I could have . . .

"I would have this country," I announced, with a sweep of my arm to encompass the mist-shrouded hills. "It's what I love more than any other. The country that my mother loved."

"Then you've got what you wanted." Now I allowed Richard to take my rein to pull me back in the direction of our impatient escort. But there was no triumph in him, merely a direct gaze that held mine, a little thoughtful. "The Countess's inheritance is partitioned. Clarence, in Isabel's name, is to get all the lands in the midlands and the south. He will get Warwick Castle. Do you mind?"

"No. And I? What do I get?"

"You, my love, all the lands in the north, and the Marcher lord-
ships in Wales."

I let the news seep into my consciousness, accepting the relief of
it. I was no longer a penniless woman, lacking any form of livelihood,
dependent on others for charity into my distant old age. Richard had
restored me to a woman of wealth and consequence, and not merely
by taking me in marriage. I could not find it in my heart to begrudge
Isabel's share of the land. I had Middleham.

"It is as it should be," I stated at last. "Edward has done right by
us after all. But by the Virgin! I thought Clarence would get it. I truly
did."

"So did I," Richard admitted candidly but with a hint of smugness.

"Do you think the child swung the balance?" I pressed my hand
to my belly, again feeling the pain at Isabel's lack and the distance
between us that was not merely one of miles.

"It may be so."

We turned our horses' heads in the direction of the castle and
rode together, until I could remain silent no longer.

"Are *you* satisfied, Richard? Did you hope for more?"

"Satisfied?" My lord frowned over his thoughts. I doubted he
would ever be satisfied as long as he had breath in his body. I had come
to accept that he was as ambitious as any man I had ever met, from a
family that could rival the Nevilles in a lust for land and power. But
his words were not uncomfortable for me. "My duties for Edward are
in the north. And I too have a fondness for Middleham. The King has
been fair and chosen well."

I opened my mouth, closed it again.

What is to become of the Countess?

It was an unfinished thread of the tapestry, but I dared not ask.
Since Richard had not spoken of it I presumed that she remained incarcerated. I willed myself not to dwell on it yet. I would not let it
spoil the occasion.

"It's by far the best I could ever have hoped for," I acknowledged.
"I owe it all to you."

"Yes, you do." Richard's quick smile, lighting his somber features, rekindled the happiness within me. We spurred our mounts forward, outstripping Chester Herald, so we approached the barbican alone at a smart canter. "And Clarence will detest it," Richard added, his eyes alight with unholy mirth as the guard shouted orders to those within.

"Now, why should that please me?" I could not stop myself laughing aloud, even as the rain beat down again, cold on any unprotected flesh.

"It is my pleasure to amuse you, lady. I shall expect payment later for all services rendered." The gleam in Richard's eye was full of promise.

Then for my homecoming there was only the final distance, a matter of yards, for the horses to cover. I recalled briefly, sharply, wanting to escape from Middleham when my heart was broken by what I saw as Richard's betrayal. Now it was a refuge. Just as I had anticipated, Master Hampton, our old steward, was there to lift me down as soon as we had entered the courtyard, receptive smiles from my people there to welcome me home. My damp and clinging skirts were no longer a burden to me, nor the veil that dripped chillingly against my neck. Rather there was a joy, a lightness that I had not known for so long. Middleham belonged to Richard, and the lands that surrounded us belonged to me for our child to inherit. I was surrounded by an affection and loyalty that took my breath away. Here there was no talk of treachery and deceit, no suspicions of betrayal and lies. Blotting tears with my sleeves, I took Master Hampton's hands and thanked him for his good wishes.

Now was not the time for empty longings.

A knight of Richard's household pushed through the crowd to accost him and murmur in his ear. Taken up with my own battle against sentimental foolishness, I barely noticed, except that I knew from the tilt of Richard's head that the news pleased him.

Suddenly all was turned about. Richard was beside me and, grasping my shoulders, he spun me around, so that he held me to face across the space of the courtyard, with its milling horses and scurrying servants, toward the massive keep, to the main entrance on the first floor with its flight of steep steps.

"What?" I squirmed against his tight clasp.

"Look."

"At what?" I glanced warily up at him, where he stood behind me.

"At the door arch. The steps! Look, Anne!" His fingers tightened as he shook me lightly, his eyes bright with understanding.

So I did.

Heavy skirts lifting in the damp breeze. Her hand raised a little tentatively, I thought, to secure her veil against her neck. I could not see her face clearly, but I imagined the tears in her eyes, if they were like mine. Then she was not tentative at all, stepping forward and raising her hands in greeting. The Countess had returned to Middleham. How long since I had seen her; how long since I had all but given up hope of our ever being reunited? Now she was here at Middleham, which she had always loved. My fingers tightened over Richard's where they still held me. Emotion rushed to block my throat.

"How did you do it?" I managed at last.

"The spirit of compromise, dear heart, as Edward advised, although the outcome was in doubt to the last minute. . . ."

And I laughed softly, tilting my cheek to rub it against his hand. "I know how you did it!" Richard would not have told me. He never would. It was not in his nature to boast of this little victory that meant so much to me. "I know what your 'spirit of compromise' entailed! You gave up Great Chamberlain so that Clarence would be indebted to you."

For the briefest of moments he angled his head so that his cheek rested against my veil. "I hoped Clarence wouldn't be able to resist it. Cheap enough to allow Clarence his titles and the pleasure of being Great Chamberlain. In return, I had the Countess brought here—she arrived two days ago. I think the Earl would have approved."

"Oh, Richard! He would!" Then a sudden doubt. "Can she stay?"

"Yes. She's under my protection now. With some circumspection on our part, there'll be no more talk of imprisonment."

"You did not tell me."

"How could you doubt me, faithless one? As for telling you—I was not sure, and I would not raise your hopes only to have them dashed—but so it is. Go to her. She is a proud lady, but she will be lost and a little sad, I think."

I did not need him to tell me that. But still I hesitated. Richard's hands loosed their grip to free me, but I turned in his arms, holding on. My lips found his, despite our very public situation, in a quick but impassioned kiss. "Thank you. For everything."

No doubt surprised by my spontaneity, he eyed my damp lashes cautiously. "Don't weep. I meant to make you happy!"

"You have. You'll never know how much."

Then Richard nudged me forward. I walked, slowly at first as a strange shyness took me, across the courtyard. And then I began to run, while my mother, the Countess, stood with open arms to receive me.

EPILOGUE

LATE AUTUMN 1472

Middleham Castle, North Yorkshire

Yesterday I gave birth to my son. An easy birth, so Margery said with callous heartiness, although I denied her opinion at the time. As I shrieked against the pain, Margery assured me that I bore it all with a fierce courage, as a Neville daughter should. I expect she was right. She's seen enough Neville births over the years, my own included.

I would have called the child Richard, for my father, the Earl. But Richard, *my* Richard, insisted that it was politic to honor the King, his brother. Honor the King? I was not in the mood for it and said as much, but I could see by the set to my lord's mouth that there was no arguing with him. So after a bout of sharp disagreement, I went into dignified retreat and the baby is Edward. Edward, Lord of Middleham. It has a fine ring to it, for a day-old infant.

I find it difficult to take my eyes from him. The child has such a shock of black hair. Dark blue eyes. He will mirror my own coloring, unless his eyes change, as they often do, to become even darker. Then he will truly be Richard's son. So small and helpless he seems, overwhelmed by the carved cradle that held both me and my sister, Isabel. But he grips Richard's finger with a will to live. Neville tenacity, Richard says, determination to have his own way, like his mother. But Richard smiles when he says it.

My mother the Countess remains with me here at Middleham. I still hold that as a miracle wrought by Richard. Quieter than before, sadder and with despair in her face when she thinks no one watches, yet still she has the same dignity she always had as the sought-after Beauchamp heiress and Countess of Warwick. I think she will never recover from the loss of the Earl, and refuses to lay any blame at his feet for the destruction of our fortunes. She is more tolerant than I. I have abandoned any attempt to force on her acceptance of the destructive ambition of the Earl, because she will not listen and becomes distressed. Because I love her, I let it go, and leave her with her memories of the magnificent Earl of Warwick, who loved her and whose power once determined the wearer of the crown of England. For her strength of will she has my admiration. The same old authority braces my mother's shoulders against the injustice of the world. When Richard is absent on royal business, she forgets and takes the reins back into her own hands as she was always used to do at Middleham. And I allow it, until memory returns to her and she steps back, acknowledging my preeminence.

Isabel is absent and intransigent. I have not seen my unhappy sister for well nigh six months, since that day of naked emotion outside Queen Elizabeth's parlor. The rift is as deep as ever, and will continue to be so, as things stand. I don't know what to say to her to heal her wounds. And so I say nothing. Perhaps it is not kind, but what point in pursuing the hunt when the fox has gone to ground? As long as she remains under the influence of vile Clarence, there is no softening in her. She has made no attempt to heal the wounds with the Countess, another sin to hold against her in my mind.

As for Queen Margaret . . . She can no longer have any pretensions to that title. I try not to think about her but occasionally she slips below my guard. How could she not when her influence on my life was paramount during those difficult months in France? She helped bring us all to ruin. God forgive her, because I cannot.

King Edward took her to London, where vicious abuse was hurled at her along with mud and stones and filth from the gutters as she was exhibited through the streets on her way to being incarcerated in the Tower. Was she forced to inhabit the same rooms that had enclosed old, mad Henry in his final years? I doubt she found any solace in them. She would be there now except that Elizabeth Woodville—for what devious means I cannot guess, since Elizabeth is never moved by interests other than her own—pleaded for her. So Margaret waits out her days in softer captivity at Wallingford Castle.

Of what does she dream, now that her son is dead?

My heart does not overflow with compassion for her.

And then there is Richard, who is the light of my life. And I of his, so he says. I believe him, for there are no shadows between us, unless it is the legality of my marriage and the legitimacy of our son. But no one questions it. No one challenges Richard of Gloucester, not even King Edward, who allows him the ultimate authority to preserve the peace of the realm as Constable of England. Sometimes I cannot believe the turnaround in my fortune from the depths of degradation to this miracle of happiness. Sometimes, when Richard is gone from me, I fear for the future. When he returns, when he sees the sleeplessness in my face, he chides me, kisses away my fears, heals me with the strength of his arms and the demands of his body. Yet still it lingers, a shade to tread on the hem of my gown when I least expect it.

Margery clucks over the infant, who is awake and fussing, snatching at the air with tiny hands. When he is old enough, Richard will give him a wooden sword and teach him how to use it, as his father taught him. There will be battles to fight still in this war-torn land. But I will give my son a far more precious gift: a little metal bird, well traveled now, with dents and scratches on its metal feathers. When he learns to blow across the tail it will still warble with its shrill voice.

He will treasure it, our dear, much-loved son. As I did. I pray to God that he will not need its silly foolishness to keep the hurt and humiliation at bay, as once it comforted me. But for now, as the babe cries in furious hunger, Margery says that since my son has inherited my temper he would surely survive Noah's flood without any help from a battered peddler's trinket that should have been thrown out on the midden years ago.

Richard smiles at me. His eyes are dark with pride and love.

Anne O'Brien taught history in the East Riding of Yorkshire, England, before deciding to fulfill an ambition to write historical fiction. She now lives in an eighteenth-century timbered cottage with her husband in the Welsh Marches in Herefordshire, a wild, remote area that provides much inspiration for people and events in medieval times. Web site: www.anneobrien.co.uk

THE VIRGIN WIDOW

ANNE O'BRIEN

A CONVERSATION WITH ANNE O'BRIEN

Q. What inspired you to write The Virgin Widow?

A. It was to answer the question: Who was Anne Neville? Her name, even for lovers of historical fiction, does not spring readily to mind. She was Queen of England, wife to one of the most infamous kings, Richard III, and daughter of the ambitious Kingmaker, but Anne herself is a shadowy figure without form or depth. Other than the date of her birth and death and a minimum record of the significant events in her life, we know nothing of her preferences, her opinions, or her personal reaction to the influences that shaped her. None of her emotions, none of her intimate thoughts have filtered down to us: There are no personal reminiscences or letters, nor are there any accurate contemporary portraits except for stylized sketches such as from the Salisbury Roll. She was described as gracious and fair, but that was the ideal of womanhood, and would have been said of any newly created royal Princess. It has to be said that, on first glance, Anne lived for only twenty-nine years and left little imprint on history.

Anne makes a fleeting appearance in Shakespeare's *Richard III*, where Richard, complete with Shakespearean hump and limp, woos her over the corpse of King Henry VI, the most recent of Richard's victims.

Anne's words to Richard:

O, cursed be the hand that made these holes!
Cursed the heart that had the heart to do it!
Cursed the blood that let this blood from hence!

And Richard's reply, suitably unloving:

Was ever woman in this humor wooed?
Was ever woman in this humor won?
I'll have her, but I will not keep her long.

Not the obvious subject for a romance.

Despite this lack of evidence—or perhaps because of it—I saw such possibilities in this relationship. It seemed to me that, surrounded as she was by strong characters, Anne Neville too might have been a young woman of considerable spirit. I could not believe that, coming from the Neville household, she would be a nonentity. Without doubt, Anne was used as a pawn in the unscrupulous political dealings of the Wars of the Roses, as would any young girl of birth and fortune. But what if she had inherited all the self-will and pride of her Neville and Beauchamp ancestors . . . ?

I considered this "blank sheet" of Anne's personality to be a gift to a historical novelist. How could I resist putting words into Anne Neville's mouth and encouraging this young woman of the fifteenth century to emerge as a living entity? So I was inspired to re-create her.

Q. Was this the first time you wrote about major characters who were historical figures? What challenges did you encounter along the way, and how did you go about doing the research?

A. *The Virgin Widow* was my first novel about major historical characters. I found it fascinating, and it was certainly not without its challenges.

Primarily there was the essential decision of what to include and what to cut. With so much information it became a matter of balance, to preserve the historical accuracy of the period but at the same time to keep the pace and the dramatic interest of the story intact. I had to remind myself frequently that I was writing a novel, not a history book. Some facts and events, although interesting in themselves, had to be omitted.

Then there was the clash of opinion among historians over aspects of Anne Neville's life. Such as the completion of Anne's marriage to Edward. Or the actual date of the birth of Anne and Richard's son, so was conception before or after marriage? In such matters I make no apology and compromised, as a novelist must. When the evidence is unclear, when knowledge is limited and the dates of significant events not recorded, when historians are in debate, the door is open for a novelist to choose the most dramatic possibility.

The one major decision for me to make was: Is there any evidence of personal affection between Anne and Richard? Although there is no evidence of an attraction between them during their upbringing at Middleham or afterward, when their marriage was mooted, equally there is no evidence that it did *not* exist. It was my choice to make it more than a dynastic marriage and to write *The Virgin Widow* as a romance.

As for research: I am a book person rather than an Internet browser, although of course I use both. Living very close to Hay-on-Wye, the Town of Books, I find it a gold mine for sources. Since so little has been written about Anne specifically, it was a matter of piecing her life together from a range of sources on the Yorkist and Lancastrian kings and the final years of the Wars of the Roses.

Q. *Shakespeare's portrayal of Richard of Gloucester is perhaps the best known, and is quite different from your interpretation. Why did you choose to take this new approach, and how close is it to the actual historical record?*

A. It was my intent to write *The Virgin Widow* as a romance. If this was to be realistic, I knew that there must be sufficient evidence that Richard, playing the major role of lover of Anne Neville, was not Dick Crookback, Shakespeare's villain. Opinions on Richard are polarized from hero to bloody murderer, and Shakespeare, writing in the Tudor era, certainly had his own agenda.

I tried to steer a middle course. By concentrating on Richard's life before he became King, I could sidestep the enormous problem of the deaths of the Princes in the Tower and who was to blame. Even though I avoided this, however, I have not argued against Richard's political assassination of Edward of Lancaster, nor his possible involvement in the death of Henry VI. Instead I have given Richard's own justification for the first, and left the second ambiguous. It was a bloody age to live in, and security of the crown was a prime objective. Richard is not without blood on his hands: His justification must stand on its own merit.

As for the rest, I have adopted the widely expressed historical opinions that Richard was intelligent, precociously gifted in administration and on the battlefield, and loyal to his brother the King. That's not to say that he was not ambitious, determined to secure what was due to him, and capable of devious scheming.

I hope I have made him sufficiently enigmatic to create a realistic character who is neither black nor white, but capable of being both challenged and admired.

Q. What happened to Anne and Richard after the events of The Virgin Widow?

A. Unfortunately it is not the stuff of romance. Their son, Edward of Middleham, a baby at the end of the novel, died in March 1483, when still a child. Both Anne and Richard are on record as having been stricken with grief. They had no more children. Anne herself died in 1485 after less than two years as Queen. She had been ill for some months, possibly from cancer, although the cause is not certain. She was no more than twenty-nine years old.

Richard of Gloucester's life as Richard III is well documented in history and in fiction. He became King of England in 1483, after the murder of his two nephews, the Princes in the Tower, their murder being placed at Richard's door. Richard himself died on the battlefield at Bosworth Field, August 1485, the crown passing to Henry Tudor, who became Henry VII, the first of the Tudor monarchs.

Q. What impressed you most about the characters involved in The Virgin Widow?

A. I think it must be the power of youth. Anne Neville, Richard of Gloucester, and Prince Edward were all very young, and yet they acted with authority and spoke with adult voices. Raised in precociously power-hungry households, in a world of treachery, double-dealing, and political infighting, they were not children.

When Anne married Edward at the age of fourteen, her opinions would have been well established under the influence of the Earl and Countess of Warwick. Richard, experiencing the chancy life of a powerless fugitive as well as that of an indulged royal Prince, was considered sufficiently mature to be created Constable of England and lead an army into battle when he was a mere eighteen years old. At the age of seventeen, Prince Edward expected to lead an army into battle.

King Edward IV was a mere twenty-nine years old at the battle of Tewkesbury in 1471 and had already ruled the country for eleven years. The Earl of Warwick was only forty-three when he met his death at Barnet.

All of them so young and so capable. An interesting thought.

Q. The second half of the fifteenth century seems to have been a particularly volatile period in English history. What do you think accounts for that?

A. The root of the problem lay ironically in the successful reign of King Edward III. He had five sons, all of whom grew to manhood, married English heiresses, and produced their own families. King Edward ensured their future status by endowing them with wealth, land, and titles—and so the first dukedoms were created. Edward III was enormously successful—but created a handful of very powerful magnates, all claiming royal blood and thus with a possible future claim to the English throne.

And then a twist of fate. These overpowerful lords might never have caused conflict if King Edward's heir, the Black Prince, had not died prematurely, leaving his claim to his young son as Richard II. Richard proved to be an immature and disastrously incompetent ruler, and the situation was compromised by his failure to produce any children—which opened the way to family conflict over who should rule.

The resulting wars, known as the Wars of the Roses (and in the United States as simply the War of the Roses), were fought between these great royal magnates, and they had the means to do it. With their wealth increasing, and the wars in France having ended, they had time and resources to look nearer to home. Furthermore, they had the money to spend on building up their own private armies of tenants and retainers, all wearing the magnate's personal livery.

It was a situation destined to cause unrest.

Q. *Anne's father, the Earl of Warwick, seems driven by overwhelming ambition, to the extent of putting his family and his own life in jeopardy. Can you explain the attitudes, held especially by highborn people, that contributed to this ambition and sense of entitlement?*

A. The attitude of entitlement and ambition is connected with the previous answer. With so many of the great magnates of the realm having royal blood and a direct connection with the crown, when thwarted to any degree in their ambitions they immediately began to exert their own power. Warwick's own descent was through John of Gaunt—King Edward III's third son and the most powerful man in England in his day. Even though this Beaufort line was originally illegitimate until recognized before the law, and Warwick never claimed the throne for himself, he still saw his rank as worthy of respect and authority in the highest reaches of government. The fact that he helped the young Edward IV take the crown meant that Warwick expected to be at the new King's right hand by right. The Woodvilles, who commandeered royal patronage for themselves once Elizabeth was Queen, were upstarts and commoners in comparison with the Nevilles.

The Nevilles were nothing if not proud. As the wealthiest of the magnates, Warwick had the money to pursue his ambitions.

Q. *Can you explain what legal rights women had during this period? Did marrying strengthen or weaken their power under the law?*

A. In general a woman, whatever her rank, stepped from the authority of her father to the authority of her husband, and her property and possessions became her husband's. Anne, as a daughter of one of the most powerful families in the land, would have known from her childhood that her life would be dictated by the will of others. Her marriage would be a matter of power politics and she would have no choice.

Widows had more independence, with a dower from their marriage that could be considerable. If they were of an age to make decisions, they could choose not to remarry by taking a vow to live as a *femme sole*, remaining in society but under a vow of chastity. In practice, considerable pressure could be used to persuade a widow, particularly a young, well-connected one, to remarry and bestow her wealth and her connections on a new husband. A woman of Anne's political importance could not be allowed by King Edward to remain unwed or free to be snapped up by a Lancastrian.

When all else failed for a determined woman, there was always the dubious escape route of the convent. Physical attraction aside, Anne would have seen marriage to Richard as the only acceptable path to take.

Bottom line: Men held power; women had to be very clever to subvert it.

Q. Can you describe attitudes toward the limits of royal power, and separation of Church and state during this time? For example, how big a breach was it if Edward and his brothers did, indeed, murder King Henry in the Tower of London? How blasphemous was it that they killed Edward of Lancaster in a church sanctuary? In both cases, were they setting a new precedent or simply following examples that came before them?

A. Royal birth aside, I think it is true to say that the one governing factor over who ruled England was the Machiavellian principle of "Might is right." A weak king who failed to control his magnates, or gave power to those who were considered unsuitable, risked rebellion, and there were precedents for it before Henry VI's instability made his hold on the crown untenable. So Edward of York and his brothers were following a pattern. Edward II had been done to death at his wife's instigation in Berkeley Castle, and Richard II was murdered in Pontefract Castle, both because they had failed to satisfy their great magnates. So this was not a new venture—but it had its dangers, as Edward and Richard were to discover. The removal of the head of the house of Lancaster merely brought a new claimant into the picture and spurred the remaining Lancastrians to raise arms against the Yorkists. The culmination was the victory of Henry of Richmond at the Battle of Bosworth Field and the establishment of the Tudor dynasty.

The death of Edward of Lancaster is one of the gray areas of historical fact. Contemporaries, including Clarence, reported that he fell on the battlefield, killed in "plain battle." It was not until the Tudors were established that chroniclers claimed that the defeated Lancastrian Prince was brought before King Edward IV in Tewkesbury Abbey to answer for his crimes, and was assassinated there at Richard's hand. In either case the chroniclers would have had their own interests in either whitewashing King Edward and his brothers, or defaming them. There is no clear evidence. I chose the Tudor version of murder in Tewkesbury Abbey for its dramatic possibilities. The fact that Edward of Lancaster was killed in a church sanctuary seems not to have been an issue in itself.

Q. Would you share some of your own life story, especially what led to your becoming a writer?

A. I have always been a reader and I have always enjoyed history, gaining a BA honors degree in history at Manchester University, and then going on to teach history. During these years I found it impossible to even consider writing a full-length novel—where would I find the ideas; how would I find the time to sit and hammer out 140,000 words? What would I write about? As a stopgap measure, I tried my hand at short-story writing, spurred on by some success in local competitions.

Leaving teaching—now with the time, an office, a computer, and no excuses—pushed me to come to grips with a full-length novel, and because history still grabbed my imagination, I wrote my first historical romance, a Regency, which was published by Harlequin Mills and Boon in 2005.

This gave me all the opportunity and confidence I needed. I was delighted—and quickly became hooked on writing. To date I have nine historical novels and a novella, ranging from medieval, through the Civil War and Restoration, and back to Regency, published in the United Kingdom, North America, and Australia, as well as in translation throughout Europe and in Japan.

Part of my inspiration for writing has come from moving to an eighteenth-century timber-framed cottage in the depths of the Welsh Marches in Herefordshire. It is a wild, beautiful place on the border between England and Wales, renowned for its black-and-white timbered houses, ruined castles and priories, and magnificent churches. It is steeped in history, famous people, and bloody deeds, as well as ghosts and folklore, all of which fired my enthusiasm for writing, particularly stories set in medieval times.

The next step in my writing was to take on a historical character, which was always my ambition—Anne Neville in *The Virgin Widow*. And that's where I am today.

As an interesting sideline I have signed up for a course in writing for the stage at my local theater and arts center. Stage writing intrigues me—developing characters and ideas purely through dialogue. I am actually given homework and have to meet deadlines—always good for the soul. I seem to have less and less time for anything other than writing. . . .

Q. Who are your favorite heroes and heroines in fiction? In real life?

A. In real life? Apart from Nelson Mandela, who must be on

everyone's list, I admire the famous student "Tank Man" of Tiananmen Square, who faced down the tanks in the 1989 riots. I think that was one of the bravest actions I have ever seen. For my heroine, the Burmese opposition leader Aung San Suu Kyi, who has suffered a decade of house arrest for her political stance. They will both be remembered in history.

My historical heroine has to be Eleanor of Aquitaine, since I have discovered so much more about her. She was a woman of true spirit.

Historical hero: I have always admired Charles II, a man who survived and left the crown stronger than he inherited it by double-dealing, sleight of hand, clandestine agreements, and pure charm. I don't think I would appreciate any of this in a modern politician, but Charles has an attraction of his own.

My fictional heroine—and a new one to me—is Ariana Franklin's character Adelia Aguilar in *Mistress in the Art of Death* and subsequent novels. A splendid character in this series of historical crime.

If I want a hero with all the mystery and high drama of romance, it must be Lymond in the series by Dorothy Dunnett.

Q. If you could meet any person who lived during the time of the Wars of the Roses, whom would it be and what would you talk about?

A. I think it would be Elizabeth Woodville, Edward's infamous wife, who makes a brief appearance in *The Virgin Widow*. An interesting character in her own right, undeniably ambitious and unscrupulous, she would have had her finger on the pulse of court issues. With so many enemies against her and the promotion of her family, it would be in her interests to keep well-informed, and so she would have been the perfect woman to give her version of events. What woman would not enjoy gossiping? I am sure Elizabeth Woodville did.

I would particularly like her views on the Edward/Richard/
Clarence dispute over Anne's inheritance. Was it really as bitter as
it seemed? I am sure Elizabeth would have had a view on Anne's
incarceration in the Clarence kitchens. The murder of Henry VI
would also be a topic for discussion. Where did the blame really lie?

In general terms I would value her insight into and comment
on the role of women during this period. Were they as mild and
accepting as they sometimes seem—or did they resist and secretly
subvert their husbands' power when they could?

And finally—was Elizabeth's mother Jacquetta, Duchess of
Bedford, really guilty of witchcraft to enslave King Edward and
bring him to her daughter's bed?

Q. Would you share a bit about what you're working on now?

A. I am now working on the early life of Eleanor of Aquitaine.
What an amazing woman she was. Living in the twelfth century, she was bound by so many restrictions as a woman and yet
managed to live such an adventurous life, defying every stricture
placed on her by social, political, and sexual mores.

Duchess of Aquitaine in her own right, she was much sought after
as a young bride, becoming the wife of King Louis VII of France at
the age of fifteen. It was not a happy union. Strong willed as ever,
Eleanor forced Louis to give her a divorce and within two months
she wed the one man in Europe with the strength and ambition to
protect her and her lands. This was Henry of Anjou, who would become King of England, thereby bringing Eleanor her second crown.
He was to prove a much worthier mate for the feisty Duchess.

Vibrant and opinionated, educated and cultured, elegantly
beautiful, above all with a determination to pursue her destiny,
Eleanor is a spirited heroine.

Q. *Did you travel extensively while researching the book? Readers might be interested in learning more about places you mention that still exist, and are open to the public, and those that were later destroyed or have been so changed that they bear no resemblance to what Anne and Richard would have experienced.*

A. There are some splendid sites to add to a reader's enjoyment of Anne and Richard. Although Middleham Castle is ruined, it is in a beautiful place and has all the atmosphere you could need. Tewkesbury Abbey and battlefield—the closest to where I live—definitely drew a cold finger down my spine. It was a very cold, dreary day when I went there, and I could imagine the bloodshed and destruction in the town. The Church of St. Mary in Warwick does not appear in the novel, but the Warwick tombs are so magnificent that they are a must on a sightseeing tour.

Any reader interested in discovering more about Anne Neville and Richard of Gloucester would enjoy visiting the following:

Middleham Castle: North Yorkshire
Where Anne spent much of her childhood, and Richard was raised in Warwick's household. Today it is an impressive ruined castle with an atmosphere all its own, well worth a visit.
www.middlehamonline.com

Warwick Castle
Anne and Isabel would have known this well as their home. It is in an excellent state of preservation, a magnificent example of a medieval castle in beautiful surroundings on the banks of the River Avon.
www.warwick-castle.co.uk/

Church of St. Mary, Warwick

Where the Beauchamp mausoleum is situated, containing one of the finest chantry chapels of medieval England, that of Anne's grandfather, Richard Beauchamp.

www.stmaryswarwick.org.uk/

Tewkesbury Abbey, Gloucestershire

Containing the mausoleum of Anne's de Clare and Despenser ancestors. Her grandmother Isabel Despenser has a superbly carved tomb and chantry chapel beside the main altar. Isabel and George of Clarence are also buried here. In the chancel floor is a modern plaque commemorating the death of Edward of Lancaster, Prince of Wales.

www.tewkesburyabbey.org.uk/welcome/planning-a-visit

Battle of Tewkesbury

The battlefield spreads over the water meadows south of the town and can be followed in a signposted walk. I found it very atmospheric.

www.tewkesbury.org.uk/battlefield/

www.battlefieldstrust.com/resource-centre/warsoftheroses/

Cerne Abbey, in Cerne Abbas, Dorset

Where Anne and the Lancastrians landed in the ill-fated invasion and Anne learned of Warwick's death at the Battle of Barnet.

www.sacred-destinations.com/England/cerne-abbas.htm

Battle of Barnet, Hertfordshire

A Yorkist victory for King Edward IV and Richard of Gloucester. The Earl of Warwick died on the battlefield.

www.battlefieldstrust.com/resource-centre/warsoftheroses/

Other royal palaces that Anne and Richard would have known:

The Tower of London

Although the Tower has a sinister reputation as a place of imprisonment, torture, and execution, in Anne and Richard's day it was very much a royal residence because of the security it provided. It was a favorite dwelling of both Edward IV and Richard III, although the royal apartments they would have enjoyed no longer exist. They were demolished in the reign of Charles II. The Tower itself must head the list of places to visit in London.

Windsor Castle

Another favorite royal haunt of the royal family, with the added pleasure of hunting in Windsor Park.

Untraceable or Unrecognizable

Anne Neville is buried in Westminster Abbey, although there is no memorial to her and the position is in dispute. She was interred either in the presbytery in front of the high altar or by the south door that leads into St. Edward's chapel.

There is no trace of the tombs of Warwick and Richard III. They were both destroyed in the Dissolution of the Monasteries in the reign of Henry VIII. Warwick was buried in the Neville mausoleum at Bisham Priory in Buckinghamshire. Richard was buried in the chapel of the Greyfriars in Leicester after his ill-fated stand at the Battle of Bosworth Field. At the Dissolution his bones were said to have been thrown into the River Soar.

Edward of Middleham, son of Anne and Richard, has a tomb in the church in Sheriff Hutton in North Yorkshire, where he died.

Cold Harbour, near Dowgate

The London home of George, Duke of Clarence, and Anne's sister, Isabel, and where Anne experienced life in the Clarence kitchens, no longer exists, buried under much recent rebuilding.

RECOMMENDED READING

The most recent and detailed historical biography of Anne Neville is:

Anne Neville: Queen to Richard III by Michael Hicks (Gloucestershire, England: Tempus Publishing Limited, 2006).

Also interesting and valuable sources, equally good for general reading:

Warwick the Kingmaker by Michael Hicks (Oxford, England: Blackwell Publishers Ltd., 2002).

The Princes in the Tower by Alison Weir (New York: Vintage, 2008).

The Life and Times of Richard III by Anthony Cheetham (New York: Weidenfeld and Nicolson, 1972).

An excellent general book on the Wars of the Roses:

Lancaster and York: The Wars of the Roses by Alison Weir (Pimlico, 1998).

QUESTIONS FOR DISCUSSION

1. Did you find Anne Neville to be an admirable heroine? What did you especially like and not like about her?

2. What does the Countess of Neville consider her proper role as a mother? When is she able to protect Anne, and when is she powerless to help? How does her mothering differ from parenting today?

3. Anne and Isabel have a contentious relationship for most of the book. Discuss the conflicts that alienate them and the motives that drive them.

4. Discuss the ways in which Anne matures over the course of the novel. How does she compare to girls her age in contemporary society?

5. Does Anne O'Brien convince you that Anne and Richard really love each other? How does she do that? What's your favorite scene between them?

6. Once he attains power under his brother King Edward's rule, Richard acts decisively, even ruthlessly and violently, to reach his goals. Discuss Anne's reaction to this aspect of Richard, and the accommodation she makes that allows her to love him despite her revulsion toward his violence.

7. Anne lived during a volatile time, when her fortunes shifted from the prospect of becoming Queen of England to facing incarceration in the Tower of London, and even possible execution. Have you or someone you know ever faced such a reversal of fortune? How did you deal with it?

8. A wife was regarded as little more than a possession of her husband. To what extent do the lives of Anne Neville and her family support this view of marriage in the fifteenth century?

9. How were the roles and lives of women in fifteenth-century England different from today? To what extent was this a good time to be a woman? Did Anne have a better life than many women of her time?

10. Why was King Edward not willing to uphold the law with regard to Anne's inheritance? Was he justified in taking this stand because of the circumstances?

11. Eventually Anne was driven to put much of the blame for her family's sufferings at the door of her father, the Earl of Warwick. Do you think she was right to do so? Were Warwick's actions justified?

12. What do we learn about Richard's character in his stance over the imprisonment of the Countess of Warwick and her eventual release? Does it make him a more or less likable character?

13. Anne's relationship with King Edward and Queen Elizabeth is uneasy. What do we learn about their characters and motivations?

14. This is a period of unscrupulous treachery and bloody warfare. Is there any proof that the ends justify the means in bringing peace and stability to a country? Were such ethics in the fifteenth century any different from today in our attitude toward modern conflict?